PRAISE FOR *ALTERED ESTATES*

"*Altered Estates* is a complex science fiction adventure—a fun ride through a sometimes familiar, often inventive augmented reality scenario."

—*Foreword* Clarion review

"Mathison favors traditional one-thing-after-another storytelling and scene-craft, with the always-odd events, conversations, pageantry, and moments of puzzle-solving related in crisp, engaging language . . . an epic puzzle-box novel bursting with riddles, mysteries, and surprise."

—*Publishers Weekly* BookLife review

"Occasionally confusing, always entertaining, and undeniably fun, Mathison's yarn is a truly unique reading experience. A trippy tale packed with high-tech inventions and old-school mystery that feels like a wildly captivating video game."

—*Kirkus* Indie review

"This unique blend of an English manor mystery and psychedelic adventure will leave readers both entertained and intellectually stimulated. Mathison's narrative is confident, smooth, and witty, always making readers feel as though they're in safe hands no matter where the plot takes them. The scenes and cleverly hidden references make it a delightful read for those interested in unconventional narratives and futuristic technology, and also those who want their mystery concepts a little harder to dig for and, therefore, much more satisfying to achieve."

—Readers' Favorite, 5-star review

ALTERED ESTATES

CHRIS MATHISON

GREENLEAF
BOOK GROUP PRESS

This book is a work of fiction. Names, characters, businesses, organizations, places, events, and incidents are either a product of the author's imagination or are used fictitiously. Any resemblance to actual persons, living or dead, events, or locales is entirely coincidental.

Published by Greenleaf Book Group Press
Austin, Texas
www.gbgpress.com

Distributed by Greenleaf Book Group

For ordering information or special discounts for bulk purchases, please contact Greenleaf Book Group at PO Box 91869, Austin, TX 78709, 512.891.6100.

Design and composition by Greenleaf Book Group
Cover design by Greenleaf Book Group
Cover Images: ©iStockphoto/MediaProduction and ©iStockphoto/designer29
Interior Images: ©iStockphoto/duncan1890, ©iStockphoto/VIKTORIIA KOTOVA, and ©iStockphoto/ Nastasic

Publisher's Cataloging-in-Publication data is available.

Print ISBN: 979-8-88645-123-8

eBook ISBN: 979-8-88645-124-5

To offset the number of trees consumed in the printing of our books, Greenleaf donates a portion of the proceeds from each printing to the Arbor Day Foundation. Greenleaf Book Group has replaced over 50,000 trees since 2007.

Printed in the United States of America on acid-free paper

24 25 26 27 28 29 30 10 9 8 7 6 5 4 3 2 1

First Edition

PROLOGUE

Kris Robinson, exhausted after yet another grueling day of getting into character, stands and stretches. How it got so late, he hardly knows. He calls out, "Elevate screen," to his smart desk, yawning as the embedded screen rises from beneath. He reckons he's watched this upcoming clip at least fifty times. He pauses to look around his temporary quarters one last time, knowing if all goes according to plan, he won't be back.

The apartment is dimly lit, except for overhead lights that hit posters of several Pixar and Disney films, as well as a photo of the original Tame Impala Project from two decades ago. A selection of their early neo-psych tunes plays softly in the background. An open laptop displays a 3D holographic version of the classic computer game *Myst*, with the island and the rocket ship in miniature floating above. On a nearby shelf sit several hardbacks. Their spines display works by Carl Jung, Julian Jaynes, Stephen Hawking, and others, on topics like synchronicity, bicameralism, plant intelligence, AI gaming, and chronesthesia. Kris marvels at how those fringe ideas from his younger days are now front and center in pop culture. Damn, he muses to himself, they're all practically mainstream now—who knew?

Kris puts on a headset with an attached microphone. "You say this is the last one and this is the last time I have to watch it. Promise?" He listens for a moment, then asks, "So, just to make sure, it happens first thing in the morning, just after I arrive at the office, right?" Again, he listens, then replies, "Yes, I've taken them all except the last one, which is right here."

Kris places a palm on his head, furrows his brow, and listens intently.

"Okay, thanks. I understand," he says. "I'm not worried about getting or being there. Just hope I can return with no problem. That's always the tricky part. Wish me luck."

He removes the headset and presses the PLAY button. On-screen, Kris sees himself—fortyish, toned, handsome—inside a cubicle, staring at computer code. The sound of a woman clearing her throat causes the on-screen Kris to swivel around. "Hey, Andrea," he greets warmly. "My, but you're in early this morning."

"Oh, Kris," says Andrea, a tall thirty-something brunette wearing formal business attire and a pained expression. "I wish it was a happier occasion." Her eyes well up as she hands him a sealed envelope. "I am so sorry."

Kris watches himself intently as, on-screen, he opens the envelope and skims its contents. "Let go?" he asks. Andrea's silence confirms his assumption. "Tell me why."

"Not just you, Kris," Andrea replies, sweeping her hand in the general direction of other cubicles, "the entire division."

"You too?"

She nods slowly. "Yeah. Me too. The acquisition team says we are redundant. The buyers have all our roles covered with their own people."

The clip ends. Kris removes his headset, switches off the monitor, and slowly exhales.

Kris believes he's viewed this clip and other recent "life events" more than enough times. Ready to call it a night, he regards that lone remaining vial he must consume. Shaking his head in resignation, Kris raises the vial high and toasts, "Cheers!" He gulps down the liquid. Smiling, he calls out to the empty room, "Hey, isn't anybody going to say, 'Break a leg'?"

Unexpectedly, just as he's about to stand up and leave the room, Kris hears a male voice from just outside his right ear. ***Break a leg!***

Kris's head snaps in the direction of the voice. He's stunned to see a three-dimensional miniature countenance of an elderly bearded man floating in the air above him.

Then the apparition chimes in jovially, as a toastmaster might, ***Imagine—a sip, a swallow, and voilà! A tabula rasa!***

Kris's body tenses as he calls out, "Who are you? Where are you?" ***Do not fear us. We are your Storytellers.***

With that reply, the old man disappears. Kris blinks hard and claps the side of his head. He steps back, exclaiming, "I really don't understand!" His pulse quickens, and his hands tremble. "I should see a doctor for this, right? A shrink perhaps?" he asks plaintively.

No one appears, but a voice echoes: ***You don't need to see anyone.***

At this, Kris feels as if he's received some sort of Jedi mind trick or hypnotic command. It calms him down a little. He now believes he doesn't need to see anyone—everything is probably fine.

Finally, he asks, "What story?" ***Yours.*** "You mean," Kris supposes, "whatever's going to happen to me as a result of all this preparation, all the hypnosis, all these drugs I took over the past three days?" ***Correct.***

Kris hears but doesn't see anyone now. He touches his forehead, then continues, "Only now I can't even remember what the drugs were, why I took them, or what's supposed to happen."

Yes, but it's already happened. Kris stands straight up and squints, trying hard to recall whatever it was that happened. He draws a complete blank. "But . . . I have no memory of it," he calls out. ***That's why we're here. To retell what happened.*** "And then I'll *remember*? If that's even the right word to use?" ***Depends on your mindset. And location in Time.***

Kris wonders silently what "mindset" and "location in time" mean. His thought receives an immediate reply: ***For example, your present location in Time is—***

"Whoa, it also reads my thoughts," Kris blurts out. From above, the old man's face reappears and breaks into a warm smile as he speaks to Kris in a fatherly way. ***Think to us. Or speak to us, good friend. Doesn't matter. Congratulations. Your mind is becoming bicameral.***

Kris tries to think of what to say or project next. Maybe something about his future? Finally, he asks aloud, "Will I get my job back or find another one soon? I'm nearly broke and really worried."

The old man is dismissive. ***Forget your job. Far greater things await.***

"Like what? Tell me," Kris implores. An elderly woman now appears overhead, and Kris stumbles a step back. ***No spoilers, dearie!*** she admonishes in a British accent. ***You'll find out when your story comes to them.***

"So there's more than one of you here?" ***An infinite number, actually. But don't worry. We won't all talk at once.***

Kris laughs and notices he's starting to relax a little. "Who are you really? Where do you come from?"

The original bearded gentleman speaks: ***You've just ingested cerebral blockers, correct?***

"Yeah, I think so," Kris stammers. "Maybe. Did I? Wait. Now I'm not sure. I can't remember. Now I can't even think straight about any of this. Nobody told me about you people. What are 'blockers' anyway?"

Doesn't matter. Think of our presence as a rather unforeseen consequence of taking those drugs you no longer recall.

Yet another Storyteller, a middle-aged male, appears, looking puzzled. ***To tell the truth, we're every bit as confounded as you are.*** Kris turns to the new apparition on his right, steps back, and asks, "Why do you say that?"

This Storyteller looks and sounds American. ***It's been years, thousands, actually, since we've spoken to a living soul. And we've never been able to communicate with a conscious one before now.***

"So who did you talk to way back then?" ***Unconscious souls. Primitives who didn't know who they were. All we could do was tell them where to go, what to do. They thought we were God speaking, commanding them.***

"So I'm the quote-unquote conscious one? Okay. Whatever . . . Jeez, what's next?"

Your story. Your wondrous story! the voices call in unison.

PART ONE

THE JOURNEY

CHAPTER ONE

Twice upon a Time,* murmurs a voice, *your story begins anew. Listen well and relive fully.

A knock at the door. You have no idea how long you were out as you slowly rise from the couch, gazing at the smiling face with the flowing white beard floating above, and stumble to open the door.

Standing there is a courier asking you to sign for a packet. What in the world? The packet has come from "Allensby, Bixby, Crosby & Sons & Daughters, Barristers and Solicitors" from a town in England you've never heard of. There are several items inside, the largest of which is a beautifully handwritten letter on stationery emblazoned with a coat of arms. You're not sure, but the script seems to momentarily flash before your eyes.

My beloved child,

My name is Arthur Hanover, and what I am about to tell you may come as rather a shock: I am your uncle, a relative you never knew existed and about whom no one has ever spoken. I have chosen this moment to reveal my existence because I am the last of my line and am growing old. More importantly, you will be named in my will as the inheritor of my title and estate. This includes my ancestral home, Hanover Manor.

In order to secure your inheritance, however, there are some documents that must be presented by you to the local probate court. This will require that you come to England.

To that end, I have enclosed an assortment of vouchers good for first-class travel to London and onwards to my estate. In addition, there is a cheque for £40,000, an amount I trust will be sufficient to cover your expenses during your journey.

You may, of course, choose to ignore this invitation and simply cash the enclosed cheque. The world is in such a state these days that I would not be surprised if you did. However, if I've assessed your character correctly, you are neither faint of heart nor lacking a sense of adventure. If you do make the journey, what awaits you besides wealth, property, and title is this: a complete explanation of your relationship to me. Curiosity, I am certain, is what propels gifted people like yourself through life.

But for reasons I cannot disclose, I must urgently request that you tell no one of this letter or your plans. It is for your own good, my child. After the court receives the documents, you may say and do as you please.

Finally, as a reassurance that I am who I say, I've included a copy of my entry in Burton's Peerage.

Affectionately,
Arthur Hanover
Hanover Manor

You double-check the addressee, but it's you and only you. Smiling, you suppose that this might be an elaborate prank and try to guess who among your friends may have engineered it. Or maybe it's simply the most elaborate junk mailing you've ever received. You look for a sweepstakes offer, the come-on, the fine print—there isn't any.

The packet contains an unsealed envelope stamped with the British Airways logo. Inside is an authentic-looking "Gift of Travel" voucher with instructions on how to redeem it. The tickets will be round trip, first class, open-ended, and good for one year. Also inside is a voucher from a British limousine service, Browns Chauffeur Hire, which states you'll be met at either Heathrow or Gatwick, depending on your flight. A Bentley limousine has been reserved and will transport you to and from a destination listed as "Hanover Manor." Behind the vouchers is a sealed envelope from Barclays Bank containing a draft made out to you for the amount stipulated in the letter—if this is a hoax, boy, someone has gone to a lot of trouble.

Another item is a reprint from the latest edition of *Burton's Peerage and Baronetage*. It's a capsule biography of one Arthur Reynold Hanover, with myriad references to his ancestors, who from medieval times have progressed from barons to viscounts to marquises. None of the names belong to anybody related to you—or at least not that you know of. Finally, there is a small blue envelope affixed with a red wax seal and bearing a handwritten message on the outside:

> *Open this only if you remain truly undecided whether to come. Otherwise, it's best that you discard it unread. A.H.*

Your phone vibrates. UK area code. A video call. An older man appears, partly in shadow. The alleged Arthur Hanover begins reciting the letter in the rich, cultured voice of a trained Shakespearean actor.

"Are you serious?" you shout.

Hanover pauses and looks at you. "I am very serious."

"You can't possibly be my uncle!"

"But I am." Hanover is unmoved, his tone grave. "Please pay attention. You have a limited time to act, especially should I meet my demise."

Stunned and now vaguely concerned, you walk around the room, waving your arms. "Am I on hidden camera?"

Lord Hanover shakes his head no, then speaks slowly with a measured tone. "Forgive me, but we both know you've lost your employment. You should seriously consider your next steps."

This hits like a gut punch, and your voice shakes with emotion. "I just got my notice this morning. Haven't told a soul. How could you possibly know?"

Hanover doesn't answer directly, only saying, "Reread my letter. Deposit the check. Come home to England." The call ends.

You reread the letter while replaying the call, now certain this is no frivolous joke or advertising ploy. But how in the world did he know you just got the ax? You're tempted to call someone. *Anyone*, really. Maybe to confirm you aren't crazy, or maybe just to talk some sense into you. But something keeps you from calling.

The reprint doesn't tell you much, but Arthur Hanover sounds highly accomplished: a member of Britain's Academy of Science and on the boards of several genealogical societies. You know that the British Isles is a region that takes bloodlines very seriously.

Then it hits you. Really hits. You sit down to catch your breath. One of your parents has a half brother, about whom they themselves may or may not know anything. Or maybe it's a secret from you. Did one of your own dear grandmothers once give birth to a child no one in the family knows about? Or was it one of your grandfathers who sired this Hanover character? Okay, so what if there's really some uncle out there you never knew you had? You could adjust to that.

But hold on. A family secret withheld from you alone until now, at the request of Arthur Hanover? To protect *his* reputation, or that of *your* grandparents—maybe as a condition of being named in his will? So now the end is near, and at long last it's time to inform you. That fits.

After traveling around in circles, your mind lands on another looming question, one you probably should have asked first: Why you? Why not leave everything to your mother or father? Then there's that salutation: *My beloved child.* God, you can hardly bear to think it—what if he's actually your father, and "uncle" is just a cover story designed to protect you and your parents, regardless of whether they're privy to these latest developments? Unfortunately, that fits, too. But it's too painful, so you shove that possibility aside.

If this Arthur Hanover really is some fabulously wealthy British lord, a scientist, an expert in genealogical matters, then he should be all over the Internet, right? Of course.

Your search results in a slew of links to sites and X feeds solely concerned with the doings of the British nobility. There are numerous photos. Your "uncle" looks like the elderly man he is, but still solidly built. His face is noble and wise. In some pictures, his hair is long and curly—like that of an aging rocker. In others, it's closely cropped as he sports a mustache and a goatee. Often, he's pictured with another British noble, a Lord Dennis

Rollinsby, a rotund, jolly-looking experimental physicist who is apparently his close friend.

You see nothing of yourself in Hanover's face and features. What you do see, gazing down beside you, is that small, disturbing envelope whose seal, for some reason, prevents you from breaking it just yet.

"Open only if you're truly undecided."

Clicking down the rabbit hole of Arthur Hanover leads you to a site entirely devoted to the Hanover residence. In a catalog of images, you find one spectacular, breathtaking room after another—a blaze of gold, silver, brass, marble, wood, exquisite fabrics and tapestries, wood carvings and furniture, antiques, and artwork.

It's an ancient mansion, but to you, everything looks brand-new. One of the images links back to a BBC documentary that was aired just last year. From the beginning of the program, which you find on YouTube, it's obvious that your "uncle" enjoys his lord-of-the-manor role to the fullest. The on-camera narrator, a tall, winsome man who looks to be fifty-something, begins, "Lord Hanover has retained the full-time services of a concierge, one Adrienne Van Scoy, to arrange dinner parties and balls, drama festivals, and the amateur golf tournaments the marquis is fond of hosting."

You press the 3DHolo button and watch as the scene enlarges and envelops the room. The camera briefly shows the concierge addressing a visiting group in Italian, then the shot returns to the narrator. "Van Scoy, a Dutch-English dual citizen, is fluent in seven languages and curates the manor's periodic art exhibitions." You're highly impressed and immediately attracted to this statuesque brunette. You walk into the scene to stand beside her. Meeting you, Adrienne—that alone could be worth the trip.

Now the camera pans outside. "Eighteen months ago," the narrator states, "Lord Hanover personally oversaw the complete renovation of the exteriors and interiors of Manor House proper, the auxiliary buildings, and grounds."

He turns, sweeping his hand before numerous period buildings. "The end result of this mammoth undertaking is, as you can see, a stunning collection representing architectural styles—from medieval and Perpendicular to Tudor, from Stuart to Hanoverian and Victorian. But, regardless of epoch, they're all newly built and in pristine condition, like an English town in a theme park or one of those re-created historical villages one often finds."

Asked why he was attempting to pay homage to seven centuries of classic British architectural tradition, Lord Hanover steps into the scene and unapologetically states, "I once attended Disneyland, where I saw three centuries of American civilization rolled into a single park, a place that is not even half the size of this estate. I came away inspired." You chuckle at that, wondering what it would be like, long-lost uncle or not, to actually meet this guy in person.

Now the scene switches to the kitchen, where several cooks are preparing pastries. "My recipe uses raisins, not currants," a chef boasts to the camera. He glances over at a rotisserie, in which a giant slab of beef is rotating. *"Eh, ça va, la vache?"*

The narrator snickers, explaining that Chef Noël Elle Léon is enamored of palindromes and has called out to an assistant, "Hey, how's the cow?"

It appears this newly hired French chef replaced a Hungarian who was dismissed in a hurry. The narrator, his account punctuated by chuckles, explains, "It seems a group of distinguished guests had suffered hallucinations after sampling a dish that included wild mushrooms from the manor grounds while sipping a mysterious pinkish tea that tasted anything but English. It was reported that numbers of the titled nobility were either collapsing in hysterical fits on the grass or frolicking indecently in the bushes."

The program introduces another servant notable in his own right—Reginald McCabe, the doorman, a short, stocky, powerfully built Scot. McCabe, says the narrator, has worked at top hotels on every continent and owns the world's largest collection of doorman uniforms. As the camera pans to the uniforms in close-up, you walk over to examine them more closely; they look like nothing so much as a huge multicolored fan. "McCabe," the narrator says brightly, "is considered by many hoteliers around the globe to be the world's greatest doorman!"

The tour next moves to a wine cellar, and you learn of Hanover Manor's estate-labeled wines and how they commission a French vineyard to grow the grapes and bottle the wine. A servant named Thomas Sutherland, an excessively handsome twenty-something, explains that the winery corks and labels the Hanover vintages only on the last day of February in leap years.

"We will bottle no wine before its time . . . which is leap day," the young man adds with a facetiously prideful smile.

"So, if we were to uncork the one you're holding," the narrator asks, "roughly how much are we talking about?"

"This being a midseventies *Bourgogne*," Sutherland replies, "my guess would be in the neighborhood of sixty thousand pounds."

Says the narrator, "A thousand quid per sip. Impressive."

You hit the PAUSE button, and the holographic panorama collapses; you've seen enough for now.

Well, one way to shed some quick light on the situation is to call British Airways. The reservations operator asks for the code numbers on your voucher, then says, "Would you like to reserve your flight?"

"May I inquire as to who purchased these tickets?" you ask. "They were a gift."

"I've no idea, since no credit card was used."

"Bitcoin, then?"

"Sorry, no idea."

"Is the ticket transferable?"

"The voucher is nontransferable," she says. "But you can exchange your tickets for those of equivalent value to another destination."

"How about a cash refund?"

"If you turn in your voucher," she replies, "the corporate office will mail you a check."

Good to know. You'll get back to them. For now, you make a quick trip to your bank and show the Barclays draft to the teller, who takes it over to her manager. The teller returns and informs you that the check is good and it can be deposited and credited immediately. She checks the exchange rate for you before you endorse and deposit it, which is irrelevant, really, since to you it's simply free money either way.

Back home, you place an international call to Browns Chauffeur Hire and get the same story as you did from British Airways: you may use the voucher or cancel and apply for a refund. Oh yes, the clerk well remembers the young lady who came in last week and made the arrangements. The woman herself was a chauffeur, or so she said. "As if I could forget her, Ms. Savannah Reddy! Sashayed in she did, tight leather pants, removed her helmet, and all that blonde hair fell down. Well, that was a sight the drivers went on about. Then tore off raucously on her motorcycle. Humph! Chauffeur indeed. And from the manor."

"Where is this Hanover Manor?" you ask.

"In the North. The Lake District, I'm told." She says the driving directions are in a sealed envelope on her desk.

This sparks a bright idea. As an inveterate "early adopter," you'd recently jumped on your satellite provider's new international package, which brings in thousands of local channels from all over the world. If ever there was a time to try this gizmo out, it's now. You check the township on the packet from the law firm and use Google Maps to locate it and other nearby villages—Loonton, Nuttey, and Witless. You grab your remote and tap in the numbers for a station—oddly named TVTV—that appears to cover the tri-county area surrounding Hanover Manor.

You're startled to hear the opening bars from the old TV series *The X-Files* playing. But this is not an episode. It's the morning news.

Remember those musical notes. It sounds like one of those voices again—but why does it want you to remember a theme song for a TV show from over thirty years ago? "Storyteller?" you shout, casting about for the source of the voice.

But no one's floating overhead or answering invisibly. You wonder if maybe your smart speaker is uttering random stuff. It happens occasionally. On-screen, you see two smiling anchors, one male and one female. In the upper right corner, a semitransparent revolving logo reading "TVTV" is superimposed. The caption at the bottom reads:

CROP CIRCLE MYSTERY SOLVED BUT UFO-ERS, X-FILERS UNCONVINCED

You press the button, wondering if the 3DHolo feature works on these overseas stations. You're jazzed to see that it does. The entire newscast is projected into the room. You walk into the scene and stand behind the news desk.

The female anchor is speaking: "And now for a story that has gripped the entire region and beyond. The Village TV has a guest correspondent on the scene. Raemond Starr, from *The Hollywood Reporter*, has journeyed here from Tinsel Town due to the sensation this story caused among film producers. Rae, we're told a local farm has been besieged with visitors from near and far. What on earth—or *off* it—is going on?"

The window enlarges, filling the screen. Rae, a slender man in his thirties, is standing beside a tall cowman dressed in overalls. "That's right, Meredith. Last Monday, Loonton cowman Donald McFarquarson discovered his one hundred fifty cattle in a fractious state at three a.m."

Rae extends his microphone to McFarquarson, who says, "I found the lot of 'em trembling and lowing their great silly heads off. I'd no idea what they were on about then, but it took me hours to settle everything down."

The window shrinks as Meredith continues: "Only later, in the morning light and from a nearby hill, did Mr. McFarquarson glimpse the reason for the commotion. His distraught charges had been huddled inside one of several enormous crop circles—an occasional phenomenon much fancied by UFO followers. Michael, you have more on that, right?"

The camera swings over to the male anchor seated behind the news desk. "Yes, Meredith, we do. Now, a more prosaic explanation has emerged. According to police inquiries, McFarquarson's neighbor, Colin Fyfe-Bibchester, hijacked an experimental all-terrain hovercraft on display at a nearby army base, then drove it onto McFarquarson's property. Once there, he circled the latter's cattle several times before eventually fleeing and abandoning the vehicle."

A backdrop of stills shows the hovercraft and the circles described. You wonder if you'll soon be rich enough to purchase one to pilot over the manor grounds. You sure hope so. Early adoption is a big part of your "thing."

"According to Fyfe-Bibchester," Michael explains, "he carried out the act for insults McFarquarson had directed at his sheep during a local livestock show."

The broadcast briefly inserts a prerecorded interview with the sheep rancher, who is short and speaks with a thick Scottish brogue. "The man was making fun of my flock. Calling them fuzzy, bleating wimps, as if his lot were some sort of bovine superheroes, which I definitely proved they were not."

The camera swings back to Meredith, who says, "Meanwhile, following widespread reports of the incident, McFarquarson's farm has been besieged by UFO researchers from throughout the British Isles and Europe, and by *X-Files* show producers from America, who say they want to use the circles and the cattle in a pilot to hopefully spark a third reboot of the series. Rae, what does McFarquarson have to say about all this hullabaloo on his ranch?"

The scene changes to McFarquarson's ranch again filling the shot.

A slow pan reveals several groups walking around with Geiger counters, recording devices, and other scientific measuring equipment. You decide to join them. Some are kneeling down, examining with magnifying glasses the hoofprints and other markings. Still others are inside the circles measuring circumferences and the like.

Rae turns back to the rancher, asking what he thinks.

"They're quite an excitable lot," McFarquarson replies, gesturing at the throng, "jumping about all goggled-eyed, measuring things, and babbling at each other. I've told them what really happened, but they don't seem to believe me. They say the truth is still out there."

"It may well be," Michael says with a sly smile as an illuminated "The Village News at 7" graphic spins into view, settling just below the news desk.

Meredith nods at her coanchor and smiles before turning directly to the camera. "That concludes our early morning broadcast. We do hope to see you back here right at eleven, when we shall be joined in studio by renowned experimental physicist Lord Dennis Rollinsby, who will tell us what he believes is really going on at Donald McFarquarson's dairy farm."

A photo of the jovial noble fills the backdrop as Meredith adopts a playful smile, saying, "And it's *not* what you're thinking."

Apparently for fun, the production crew decides to play more measures from the *X-Files* theme and run more footage of UFO sleuths roaming the property in an extended program close.

Remember those first four notes.

Now you're certain you hadn't imagined it, or that Google mistakenly voiced it, a moment ago. You look up and spot several smiling faces.

Right . . . Those measures are distinctive. Of course you'll remember them—have for decades. Used to have it as your cell's ringtone. Okay now, you decide, to get back to deciding.

For the umpteenth time, you glance at the as-yet-unopened letter, then at the travel vouchers and your deposit slip. They amount to well over fifty thousand dollars. You might need to find out about the legalities, any taxes involved, et cetera. But still, there should be a substantial sum remaining, right? And you've done nothing wrong, right?

So, do I go or not go? ***Dude, just go, why don't'cha?*** a bubbly teenage girl, one you hadn't seen before, calls out. It looks like these Storytellers come in all shapes and sizes—and ages!

"But why should I?" you ask. "I've now got more than enough money to get me through this." But the girl is insistent: ***Look! Listen!***

An incredible life-sized, three-dimensional scene shimmers into view. Your jaw drops. You see yourself seated at a long table facing a cast of costumed characters from *Alice in Wonderland*—a riotous collection of human actors and CGI creations. One of them glances up and says, "I daresay you've never even spoke to Time."

The scene dissolves into Lord Hanover's face that then morphs into a painted portrait of a nobleman, followed by your alleged uncle's appearance in a steamy bathroom mirror. The image cuts to a swimming pool in which he's floating face up, then to yet another breathtaking image, one that projects his enormous visage high in a moonlit sky as clouds rush by. In each tableau, his lips are moving, but you can't hear any speech.

Then comes a staggering sight you can scarcely believe. Your heart skips several beats. Again, you see yourself, this time seated at the judges table on a glittering TV set reminiscent of *American Idol*. On your left sits Raemond Starr, the reporter you just saw on the news. On your right, Lord Hanover *himself*. Now, your mouth is agape—because Starr and Hanover look maybe ten or fifteen years younger. But shock! In the vision, you look the same. Not the least bit younger yourself.

Onstage stand three Asian girls, apparently contestants, who somehow seem familiar. After a moment or two, the assemblage collapses into a colorful blur, then slowly melts away.

You look up at the ceiling and, hoping one or more will appear, call out, "Hey, Storyteller, were those scenes from my future?" After a moment, a middle-aged professorial-sounding one does.

Depends on your location in Time. From one vantage point, it's already happened. From another, it's yet to occur. "And when . . . it's actually happening?" ***Then you're inside Time.*** "Like now?" ***Yes, like now. Inside,***

there is only now. Outside, there is only then and soon. "So, were those actual scenes if, say, I go?" ***Yes, but they've already happened.*** "You mean I've already been?" ***It depends***. "Confusing . . . So am I now 'speaking to Time'—whatever the heck that means?"

The Storyteller breaks into a wide smile. ***Actually, Time has been speaking to you.***

You wander into your bedroom, undress, and lie down, certain that this was just about the weirdest experience you've ever had. Yet it was amazing, amusing, and only a little scary in the beginning. And those voices—sometimes responding to your thoughts; and other times, to your spoken words. And all so effortlessly.

But if they are Storytellers, again you wonder, what is the story?

A lovely female face appears and answers: ***This one, the one we're retelling as you're reliving. Twice upon a Time!***

CHAPTER TWO

You can't believe it.

Or rather, you can't believe *yourself*. You've lived with this inheritance thing for almost twenty-four hours now, and you not only haven't told anybody but haven't opened that second letter, either.

This morning you're hyperfocused on your alleged uncle saying, regardless of how you decide—to go or to not go—it would be "best" if his other letter were never opened. Does that mean whatever's inside could be disturbing, could make you less likely to go? Or more likely? And how long do you have to "remain undecided," anyway, in order to be officially undecided? In which case, Lord Hanover *wants* you to open the letter. Damn, now you know why they have words like *conundrum*.

So, suppose you don't go and apply for the refunds on the vouchers. Or cash in only the Browns voucher and take a vacation on British Airways someplace else. Get away. Relax. Plan your next life adventure. But would that be the end of it? If you decide on this course, you'd prefer not to hear from old Hanover or his lawyers again. Unless, of course, they insist on sending more money and free tickets with no strings attached. Ha ha.

It's been in the back of your mind all morning, and now the impulse rushes forward: just call him. A freckled face appears overhead and winks at you. ***What have you got to lose?*** Right. Your uncle requested that you not discuss this or open the second letter unless it was necessary. But he never said you couldn't try to contact him. Since he has sent the astonishing invitation and funds, even addressed you as his beloved, how could he possibly object to your calling to clear matters up?

You glance at your phone's recent call list and tap the number. "Good evening, Hanover Manor, Penelope Stratton speaking," intones a lovely voice that carries a trace of sadness. "To whom may I direct your call?"

You start to identify yourself, but an odd and scary thing happens: your mind goes blank—you can't remember your own name! "Hello," you stammer, "I'm—I'm calling for Lord Hanover. Is he—"

You are immediately placed on hold. A recording of light classical music plays underneath another clipped British female voice. "The butler has asked me to announce that he has completed his inspection of the premises and finds everything to his satisfaction at present. The day staff is therefore dismissed and may retire to quarters. In fifteen more minutes, the main gate of Hanover Manor will shut. Until then, the butler offers us this musical interlude of new selections by the young American composer Raemond Starr."

It seems like the phones and the manor PA are somehow integrated. But did she just say Raemond Starr? From the news? The song contest vision? This guy's popping up everywhere! The music comes up a bit in volume. The melody is incredibly lovely, longing, remorseful—until a crisp voice interrupts.

"James Farnsworth, head butler and administrator, speaking."

"Hello, I'm—"

"I know who you are," he interrupts coldly.

"Well, I would like to speak with Arthur Hanover." A lengthy silence follows, broken only by the clearing of a throat.

Finally, Farnsworth says in a lower, softer tone, "I regret to inform you that Lord Hanover passed away in Switzerland three weeks ago. We only learned of this . . . and other estate matters today."

"But that's impossible," you tell him. "I just talked to him yesterday."

Farnsworth reverts to his earlier icy persona, saying, "I don't know who you talked to, but it wasn't His Lordship." You're speechless. "You'll no doubt be coming." Farnsworth's tone is sinister. You are still unable to speak. "Well, good night, then." He abruptly disconnects.

You're momentarily overcome by this news and place your head in your hands. *Dead for three weeks? Then who called me that night?* A young male Storyteller immediately appears. ***Lord Hanover called you.*** *From the grave?* ***Hardly.***

You collect your wits and google for news about Arthur Hanover's passing and receive confirmation at several sites—but it's so odd that you missed this yesterday.

Gosh, a long-lost uncle you never knew you had—now he's dead and gone. Long-lost and newly lost. You turn on TVTV, wondering if they are already reporting on a mysterious heir to Lord Hanover's title and estate. Which would be you. Are you soon to be all over the tabloids? God, you hope not. But happily, none of the stories on the evening newscast, again anchored by Michael Jansen and Meredith Lane, are about Lord Hanover himself, but one airing now concerns the manor estate. The screen caption reads:

ROAD WRECKERS WREAK HAVOC
ON MOTHER NATURE AND MANOR

Your interest piqued, you press 3DHolo to immerse yourself in the scene. Meredith, dressed in a stylish yellow suit, introduces the segment: "Mother Nature is in dire straits. The metal monsters are everywhere. So says Mildred Simmons, head housekeeper at Hanover Manor, who is crusading to preserve the natural beauty and tranquility of the tri-county area. According to Simmons, widow of legendary estate gardener and environmentalist George Simmons, country lanes in Nuttey, Witless, and Loonton are being savaged by sharply increasing numbers of cars and lorries. We now go live to the manor to speak with Mrs. Simmons and her comrade in arms, American chauffeur Savannah Reddy."

Meredith's image collapses into a window as the main screen shows the housekeeper—rosy complexion, kind face, intelligent eyes, attractive, fifties—standing beside her teenage grandson Christopher Robin—bright-eyed and well put together—who you remember seeing pictured with Lord Hanover online, and Reddy—sassy, sexy, blonde—who you'd likely not soon forget. They are standing in a beautiful rose garden with large ivy- and flower-wrapped trellises throughout. You walk into the garden and stand behind them.

"Good afternoon, Mrs. Simmons," says Meredith from her window. "We understand you and fellow environmentalists are quite distraught over the marked increase in local traffic."

"Oh, Meredith, they're ruining absolutely everything. These great rolling beasts and their snotty drivers are smashing our beautiful roads and utterly destroying the peace. The birds are going deaf and starting to sing off-key, and there are mashed insects everywhere. It's simply horrible."

Michael replaces his coanchor in the window. The backdrop consists of photos of structures typical of Stonehenge, only smaller and fewer in number. A chyron labels it "Mini-Henge" as the newscaster picks up the story: "Simmons and her group cited the recently unearthed miniature Stonehenge near Hanover Manor as the major cause of the crush of visitors and caterers invading the area. Its presence has led to an increase in rubbish, unapproved druidic rites, and packs of wild ravening dogs, reportedly led by a particularly ill-humored, three-legged rottie named Crunch who wears a black patch over one eye. Mrs. Simmons, please tell us what effect this unearthing has had on the manor environs."

"Definitely, mini-Stonehenge has brought in the lot of them. Every type of cultist imaginable. Just yesterday, Savannah here had a *dreadful* encounter."

The camera brings the drop-dead gorgeous chauffeur into close-up, causing you to walk around to face her. "It's true," she says. "The rock worshippers, the butterfly charmers, the self-proclaimed village idiots riding backward atop donkeys—they all came. Seemed like an amped-up Renaissance faire for crazies. One of them tried to swipe my bike." Savannah's expression turns resolute as she says, "If something's not done, and soon, we may be forced to take matters into our own hands." Simmons nods in strong agreement.

Michael replies, "And what should be inferred from your threat, Ms. Reddy?"

To everyone's surprise, young Christopher steps forward to answer. "Lorry drivers who thrash our roads may one day find the roads themselves raging in reply," he states with cool, calm matter-of-factness.

Adds Mildred, "Whereupon suddenly and mysteriously the roads are strewn with nails, screws, and other jagged objects. We're serious. The lorries must stop taking these illegal rat runs through our manor environs. Or else."

You pump a clenched fist in solidarity—no one messes with your manor! Michael looks quite taken aback by Mildred Simmons's ferocity.

Meredith reappears in the window. "Good afternoon, Master Christopher. We understand it was you, in fact, who first alerted your elders that the birds and the bees were in acute distress. Can you please tell us how you learnt of it?"

"Ma'am, some plants told me what the birds and the bees told them," says the boy.

There is a protracted silence. Both anchors are clearly stunned. Mildred smiles pridefully and pats her grandson on the back.

"That's extraordinary! You *listen* to plants?" Meredith is flummoxed.

"Yes, ma'am. But I'm just learning how," Christopher replies.

This causes Meredith to stammer, "How did—? Sorry, I'm simply at a loss for words here."

The housekeeper speaks up, "When George was alive, he conversed with a broad variety of plants nearly every day. He'd begun instructing the lad just before he left us."

Adds Christopher, "Grampy loved all plants earnestly. And they loved him—and shared their talents to the extent possible in each species. Some are brighter than others, as in the animal kingdom, as with us."

"Well said, lad, well said indeed," Michael interjects.

Christopher nods in shy appreciation, then continues, stating it wasn't just the plants who cherished the association. "Bees buzzed around him excitedly whilst he toiled in the gardens. Often, numerous birds gathered to sing."

"Yes, we know," says Meredith as she turns to directly face the camera. "Many of our viewers will certainly recall a most extraordinary sight captured at George Simmons's funeral procession last year." A video insert shows a flock of birds overhead as Simmons's coffin is carried toward a funeral tent blackened by a swarm of immobile bees. "Not only the tent," Meredith narrates, "but the coffin itself was likewise covered with the insects. As were myriad floral, mushroom, and cacti displays. Yet none of the mourners, inside or out, were disturbed. A most extraordinary sight!"

The scene switches back to the manor. "Young man, we've now got to go to advert," Meredith says, wrapping up the segment. "But we certainly want you back to delve into this fascinating topic in much greater detail. Will you promise to return very soon?"

"Yes, ma'am."

As the newscast goes to commercial break, another middle-aged Storyteller appears. ***The boy listens to plants. Soon, you might be hearing them too. Sadly, we cannot.*** *Well, if they tell me something, can I tell you?* ***Yes! You can serve as interpreter.***

There's a lot to absorb here—mini-Henge, village idiots, raging roads, talking plants, mournful insects—but you can barely keep your eyes open.

You awaken still undecided but calm, rested, and clear in your thoughts. For the first time since receiving this momentous news, you eat a decent meal, and you think about your brief exchange with the butler. Naturally, the news of Lord Hanover's recent death must have been shocking, but why was Farnsworth so rude—downright hostile, actually?

Of course—Farnsworth said he knew who you were, but likely he's just found out, as you have, and is probably appalled to learn about a heretofore unknown heir, and a blood relation to boot. Then there's your family. Do any of them know about the demise of Arthur Hanover, somebody's son, somebody's brother? Does anybody know you've been contacted? You wonder if a relative or designated family friend will call or come by. You reread his letter one last time and finally decide that you are "truly undecided" enough.

You rub your thumb over the contours of the burgundy wax seal impressed with Arthur Hanover's signet ring, carefully break open the small blue envelope without tearing the paper, then momentarily close the flap, noting how the two halves almost perfectly realign themselves. You take a deep breath, reopen the envelope, and pull out several folded sheets of matching stationery. The first shock comes from seeing a typed sentence slowly materialize across the top of the first page: *This sentence will appear only if the envelope's seal has been broken.* Slowly, you read from the beginning:

> ***My beloved child,***
>
> ***Throughout your life, I've had people observe you—your personality, your relationships, your deeds good and not so. There were also periodic background checks. I even saw you several times myself, though always at a distance. I remember well the time when . . .***

You frown as you read the succeeding paragraphs. Each summarizes, in a concise, dispassionate way, several of your accomplishments and failings and some details of your romantic relationships. Arthur Hanover concludes his letter with:

> ***For these various invasions of privacy, I most sincerely and deeply apologise. But since I intended to leave substantial wealth, property, and a title to you, I felt it imperative that you possess a certain degree of intelligence and creativity, character and fortitude. And as I've mentioned in previous correspondence, you impressed me greatly. I've grown to know and love you as if you were my very own child. I beg you, begin preparations for your journey as soon as you have read this.***

You put the letter aside feeling mildly resentful but somewhat amused. You think about that opening sentence, recalling an article online that made mention of new ink technologies and of microchips embedded in paper documents as being among the various patents Lord Hanover holds. Maybe that's why his letters always flash at first, but for what purpose? "Any idea, Storyteller?" ***For your eyes only, perhaps?***

Looking up, you spy a dignified-looking elderly male. You laugh it off, walk across the room, pick up your phonc, and call British Airways.

Not having to deal with work makes taking off on a moment's notice much easier. You make sure your passport's current, reserve all your flights, and notify Browns of your late-afternoon arrival. With plenty of expense money, you splurge on new luggage and clothes, mainly tailored and formal items, considering the place you'll be walking into.

To casual acquaintances, you say this is a vacation you'd been planning. To family and close friends, you give assurance that everything is fine—you just feel like getting away. You smile, enjoying how this air of mystery may have caused you to go up a notch or two in the estimation of those who know you best. You feel no need to tell anyone that you've lost your job. One small flourish you've added to your travel plans is to fly to New York City a day early, shop and sightsee in Manhattan, and stay overnight at a fancy hotel.

Soon, you'll be jetting off to a new life, albeit a secret one. You congratulate yourself for acting completely normal, for not letting on to a single misgiving. Actually, you're amazed at how everything fell into place. The inner journey, though, has been slightly difficult. It's taken some time to get over the self-consciousness you feel whenever you recall your uncle's revelations. Sometimes you wish you'd never read that second letter.

Gradually you realize, though, that you already miss the guy. You could use someone wise and caring to talk this over with. Someone like Lord Arthur Reynold Hanover, your devoted uncle who knew you all your life. Tonight, an old standard hums softly inside your head: "Someone to Watch Over Me," which causes several singsong voices to say in unison, ***Indeed, we are the someones.***

CHAPTER THREE

The day finally comes—and off you go.

You've brought along some reading material for the flights—genealogy primers with titles like *The Status of Feudal Titles*, *The Five Peerages of the British Isles*, and *Errors to Beware of in "Burton's Peerage."* As you wait in the boarding area, you check your phone and see an email from a kindly university professor you visited yesterday profusely thanking you for your interest. You smile, recalling how thrilled he was to have a nonstudent stop by to inquire about his arcane specialty of blazonry. "Absolutely unprecedented," he marveled when you showed him the Hanover coat of arms. "My stars! A dove of peace in the center!"

"Don't you think," you asked him, "that some of these other etchings look like miniature napkins, silverware, teacups, and saucers?" Before he could answer, a young Asian female speaking accented English had interjected: ***Oops, my bad. I thought Manor House meant M-a-n-n-e-r House.*** Your head jerked, and you wondered if the professor heard the voice, but there was no reaction from him.

Apparently, these mystical beings are seen and heard only by you. But this time you hadn't caught sight of anyone above. It seems at times they are visible when speaking while at others you only hear them—like just then.

"Indeed," the professor muttered to himself while squinting at his magnifier. "Now what would those be doing on an ancient herald?" Then he looked up and said hopefully, "I assume you're off to England in search of your ancestors."

"Yes, in a manner of speaking," you told him.

"Wonderful!" he exclaimed, clasping your shoulders. "Well, you should be very honored indeed if you discover you are in some distant way related to a member of one of the great houses." His email promises a full interpretation of the emblem by the time you return—clearly you'd made his day, maybe his next scholarly article as well.

On the flight to New York, there's plenty of room in first class to spread your materials out. You make notes in a diary you've brought to chronicle your adventure. It's interesting to read how *Burton's Peerage* used to be called on to authenticate the genuineness of titles. Evidently impostors were in excellent supply. Nowadays, disputes over identity are resolved by DNA matching.

Will my sample need to be taken? ***Already has, my lord.*** The female Storyteller smiling above looks pert and youthful.

Burton's Peerage, you learn, suffers from numerous errors that have persisted from earlier editions. You're astounded when you read this entry:

> Whenever James Burton, and afterwards his son William, deemed a noble family's history not to be interesting or romantic or spectacular enough, as founders and authors of *Burton's Peerage*, they simply invented an entirely new one—a revised entry that sometimes chronicled marriages and births that never occurred, battles that were never fought in, much less died in. They frequently detailed inventions and discoveries the peer never made, art and music never created, prose and poetry never written—all fabricated in order to present noble deeds by individuals, some of whom never existed. As a result, even as recently as the 2023 edition, no scholar examining *Burton's Peerage* could, with absolute certainty, attest to which of the historical personages therein actually lived and died, and what, if anything, they or their "descendants" accomplished in life—outside of magical and astonishing deeds in the realm of fairy tales. Yet much of the history of the British Isles is based on this lore.

To get into the swing of things, you take a private airport limousine into Midtown Manhattan. There's a small stir while checking in at your hotel when you happen to mention Hanover Manor as your destination tomorrow. A desk clerk summons a manager, who rushes over and says, "Welcome. We are deeply saddened for everyone's loss. Lord Hanover often stayed with us, you know. Considered us as part of his family." He waves away your credit card. "Please, please allow us to host for tonight"—it's obvious the manager assumes you must be a relative or a close family friend—"if you are traveling there at such a time."

You merely nod vaguely, not disclosing that you are in fact Lord Arthur Reynold Hanover's sole heir while chuckling inwardly about how you'd likely be branded an impostor, and have the hospitality rescinded, had you uttered that phrase.

But wait. You made this reservation yourself—and on the spur of the moment.

Hey, Storyteller, what prompted me to choose my uncle's favorite hotel out of the hundreds here? ***We directed your choice.*** *Aha! You commanded me just like in the olden days?* ***Very good. You've been reading up on us.*** *But why?* ***So you could meet people who knew your uncle.***

You stroll around Manhattan for a few hours and chance upon a delightful trio of young Japanese women who call themselves Megumi, Reiko, and Namiko, dressed in full kimono on Fifth Avenue and passing out samples of a product called "Fountain of Youth Mushroom Skin-Care Serum." For a while, you chat amiably. You're curious about the kimonos, the makeup, the bun hairdos, and the floral decorations attached to them. "Gosh, how long does it take to get all dressed up like that?" you ask.

Reiko answers, "About two hours."

"Per person?"

"Hai so desu!" Megumi says, slipping in to Japanese while beaming and clapping her hands.

"We've been up since three a.m.," says Namiko, "dressing each other and doing each other's hair, nails, and makeup."

Adds Megumi, "With our gooey goo for sure!" You can already tell Megumi's the live wire of the bunch.

"You mean there's mushroom makeup in addition to all this?" you ask, pointing to the large skin-care display behind them.

"Yes!" Megumi replies emphatically. "Our mushrooms are magic. They make you look so many years younger."

You smile, thinking how refreshing these young ladies are as each now steps forward holding their business cards, bowing stiffly and presenting them in the formal Japanese manner. Somehow, this small ritual seems familiar, but you don't know why. You bow stiffly and respectfully in return and bid them adieu. It was a charming interlude, the highlight of your excursion.

Storyteller, those three were so, so . . . cute and charming, and they seemed somehow familiar, but I can't place them. Do I know them? **Kawaii aesthetic *is the term, I believe, you were reaching for***, replies a young man with an Asian accent who then quickly disappears without answering your question.

You sample some yummy casual café fare, then return to your hotel. On the way back, you suddenly stop and snap your fingers, realizing where you'd seen those three young ladies before—in that vision a Storyteller presented on the night the letter came. They were the teenage contestants in some crazy-looking song contest. But this afternoon they looked all grown-up. *What to make of this, Storyteller?* ***What you will.***

Before turning in, two hotel doormen surprise you by dropping by to pay their respects. It turns out your hotel was Reggie McCabe's last posting before he took the manor job. They say Lord Hanover himself recruited their former colleague here. "I've heard he's worked at some of the world's finest hotels," you tell them.

"It's true," says the younger of the two. "Whenever he leaves a place, usually after one or two years, he tries to purchase from the hotel one of the uniforms he'd been wearing throughout his employ. But they all regard Reggie so highly they almost always give him one as a parting gift."

"Ol' Reg's got the world's greatest collection of 'em," the older one states proudly.

"I know; I saw them on the BBC," you tell them. "The coats are exquisite. I was very impressed—the narrator said he's the world's greatest doorman!"

"He is!" the younger one shouts and claps his hands.

After promising to convey their regards, you bid them farewell.

On the flight—when not marveling at the cabin, the service, or your estimated transit time of only two hours—you try to figure out James Farnsworth. If Lord Hanover sired no heirs and left an ordinary will, might the butler have stood to benefit under normal circumstances? Mulling this over, you punch up a copy of *Highlife*. On the contents page, you tap a feature entitled "Mind Your Manners—Getting Properly Trained at London's British Butler Institute" and see James Farnsworth staring back at you from the intro featuring him as one of the school's most illustrious graduates. *Farnsworth! Another coincidence? **No such thing as.*** This Storyteller looks and sounds like an adolescent boy, like the Christopher Robin teen you saw on the news.

The profile confirms what you'd already suspected: Farnsworth grew up in the manor household and has been a butler all his life. "He's a well-educated, well-bred Englishman, noble in every way except his official peerage" is the writer's impression of him. You read that Farnsworth runs a tight ship at Hanover Manor, frequently running mandatory staff seminars on various aspects of manners and service, sessions so obsessive that the writer couldn't resist needling Farnsworth by reporting what the staff has nicknamed him—"Mr. Knives and Forks." You put the article aside and peruse your in-flight entertainment choices.

Interestingly, there's a BBC documentary about butlerdom through the ages. It soon seems downright spooky, though, because it relates so directly to your situation. "Most of today's nobility are descended from servants, and vice versa," says the narrator. "Faithful servants have been known to inherit immense wealth and property from their deceased masters, particularly in cases where there were no living heirs. Sometimes only one relative stands between them and a fortune—that's one basis for 'the butler did it' cliché in murder mysteries."

You shake your head at the grisly stills of butlers murdering superiors while the narrator describes numerous famous cases. This is followed by a historical reenactment of a butler smothering an aristocrat to which he bears a family resemblance!

The narrator concludes with, "At the same time, hereditary peers have been known to fall on hard times, sell off their titles, and then end up working as servants—anything to remain affiliated with a noble house. The nobility inhabits a dynamic world, always have, with occasional wholesale reversals of fortunes and roles."

Now it's all starting to seem a little unnerving. You're not sure what you'll discover at Hanover Manor. But there's one thing of which you're now fairly certain—James Lowell Farnsworth spells trouble.

CHAPTER FOUR

You get off the plane, pass through immigration, claim your baggage, and clear customs without incident. Wheeling your sleek new luggage, you enter the arrival lounge. Standing there is a smartly attired chauffeur, smiling warmly and holding a placard with BROWNS CHAUFFEUR HIRE printed on it.

"Mark Stephen at your service," he greets you, followed by a bow. "Trust your flight was satisfactory." He hands you his elegant name card. You walk through sliding-glass doors to observe one of the most imposing limousines you've ever seen—a gleaming black Bentley. A few waiting passengers throw curious glances your way. You half expect a tabloid reporter to rush over, hoping to find out about a new aristocrat or C-list celebrity on the scene.

Stephen is what your driver says everyone calls him. He's rotund and amiable, with gray muttonchop sideburns and a thick handlebar mustache. He seems familiar, like someone you've seen before but cannot place now. You sink into the richly appointed interior. Stephen opens the intervening glass window and says, "Up for a bit of London sightseeing this evening before we head out?"

"Sure, if you don't mind," you reply. "I've always wanted to see Piccadilly Circus. Is it nearby?"

"A little less than an hour. Lots to see on the way, m'lord." It feels strange to be addressed like that, but you figure you're going to have to get used to it.

You start to say, "Oh, Stephen, please call me—" but oddly enough, you've again drawn a blank. Must be the jet lag or something. Who knows?

Arriving at Piccadilly and inching through the traffic, you soon rub your eyes in utter disbelief. For out there on the sidewalk, again in full kimono, stand Namiko, Reiko, and Megumi passing out their samples. "Stephen, please stop and let me out," you request. "Sounds crazy, but I just saw some people I know. Do you mind circling around? This won't take long."

"Of course, m'lord." Your driver seems not the least bit surprised as he slows to a stop.

Departing the limo, you rush over to the trio. "Hello, hello again. I don't get it. Why are you . . . I mean, how in the world did you get here?" None of the ladies reply nor show any sign of recognition. Instead, they step forward shyly, bowing and extending product samples.

"Excuse me," you falter, "but didn't we all meet in New York just yesterday?"

"Gomen nasai, eigo-wa zenzen wakarimasen."

She's saying they don't understand English. *Are they really here or am I just imagining it?* ***Hard to say. But we don't think they're*** **really** ***there unless you think so.***

You have no idea what he means, but this is just too weird, so you simply wave goodbye and head up to the intersection where your driver will be coming back around. Soon you spot him. Once you're back inside, Stephen says, "Quite coincidental seeing old acquaintances on your first trip to Piccadilly, eh?"

A British-accented voice observes, ***There are no coincidences, but he may not know that. Most people don't.***

Thoroughly confused and not even sure what just happened, you decide to change the subject. "Stephen, how long will it take to reach the manor?"

"Oh, my guess is four and a quarter hours if traffic is normal."

"Any reason it might not be?"

"No, don't think conditions of the road will be a problem, m'lord. Bit of a nasty weather forecast out that way, but I could drive you there blindfolded. M'boy used to work at the Hanover. Often drove out to see him at weekends." He taps his clipboard. "That's why Browns assigned me this job. Doubtless I'll be collecting and carrying you back as well."

"What did your son do out there?" you ask.

"Colin was headwaiter," Stephen replies. "That is, until the concierge, Miss Van Scoy, for no good reason, mind you, gave him the boot."

"Oh. Sorry."

Stephen laughs, assuring you Colin's much better off in his new employment at the London Savoy. Relieved, you mention that you just read an article on the plane about James Farnsworth. "I would have assumed that the butler is in charge of domestic staff."

"Oh, I'm certain Farnsworth was behind it," Stephen replies. "But I shouldn't be the one to gossip." Stephen laughs, his merriment reflected in the rearview mirror.

Next you ask, "Have you ever dined at the manor, sampled its famous dishes?"

"In Noël's restaurant? Are you kidding?" Stephen replies, shaking his head. "First of all, help and help's families are not welcome in the grand dining hall. And I much prefer the steak-and-kidney pie and the stout with the company upstairs." He pauses to check his side mirror. "The Falstaff's where Lord Hanover always ate when he was in residence, you know."

You didn't know. "I'd have imagined he always dined royally."

Stephen chuckles, saying, "Oh yes, His Lordship confided to Colin last year. 'Had my lifetime allotment of béarnaise and hollandaise sauces but have yet to sing my share of ballads and folk songs' was how he put it."

You decide to be a bit more forthcoming. "Seriously, Stephen, tell me more about the manor chef. Is he trustworthy in your opinion?"

Stephen laughs again. "Oh, I doubt if he poisons the food, if that's what you mean. But everybody knows that Noël is Farnsworth's and Van Scoy's chief spy and henchman."

In that case, you tell him, maybe you'll opt for pub fare instead.

"Oh, upstairs?" he replies enthusiastically. "Bruce Sherlock's the landlord up there. The right sort, all right. Everybody loves the bloke. Especially since he added those 'Karaoke Nights' to the establishment's offerings."

"So Hanover Manor is open to the public? Really?" That's not how you pictured a stately English residence.

"Sure, always has been, on His Lordship's orders," Stephen replies. "What's more, when the Australian first set up that machine and locals started turning up, he had a serious run-in with Farnsworth over his quote-unquote unauthorized installation. Guess what the barkeep did?"

"No idea. Tell me." You already like this Bruce Sherlock guy.

Your driver cannot contain his glee. "Sherlock roared like a bull and permanently barred him from the establishment, he did!"

"Whoa, what happened?"

"They took it to His Lordship. The old man heard both sides and then backed Sherlock all the way, permanently authorizing karaoke. Issued a written decree, in ink, on rolled parchment, with a wax seal. Then Sherlock nailed it to the pub wall, and though Arthur's now dearly departed, the order still stands, far as the Aussie's concerned."

What an amazing ride this is, you think. But you wonder why an outside service is being used in your case. "Stephen, um, not to sound rude, but doesn't the manor have its own chauffeur?"

"Yes, that would be Savannah Reddy, the American who's seriously into motocross. Has made quite a name for herself on the local circuit."

"Really?" you exclaim. "Didn't know about the motocross. Saw her on the local news. Seems to be a stanch environmentalist as well."

Stephen then half turns and winks at you. "But you'll soon find she's quite fit, that one."

Your driver then informs you that he needs to pull off and make a brief stop for petrol.

You try to check your phone for messages but there's no service out here. The surrounding countryside is nondescript, but it feels good to get out, inhale the night air, and stretch. Odd, though, that the gas station's name is scripted in an alphabet you don't recognize.

Hey, Storyteller, isn't this England? ***Indeed! Merry Old England it soon shall be!*** *What the heck does that mean?* you try to project to the jovial, distinguished-looking male visage floating above, but this time there's no reply.

The sky is overcast, the breeze stirring, the air humid, the temperature falling—heralding a change in the weather. The short break allows you to collect your thoughts and consider what else you'd like to bring up with Stephen, since he is such a fount of information. You study your driver from a distance. Again you think he somehow looks familiar.

Your journey resumes and you ask, "Stephen, is it possible we've met before?"

"Oh, I should think not, m'lord," he answers hurriedly.

"That gas station back there had a giant neon sign I couldn't read at all. It looked like some Asian script."

"Oh yes," he replies. "So many of the petrol stands these days are foreign-owned and operated. Difficult to keep track."

Then you remember something else you've been meaning to ask. "Does your son know Thomas Sutherland, the current headwaiter? I saw him interviewed on a BBC program, and then at the airport, I picked up a *Wine Spectator* and, surprise, there he was."

Stephen turns toward you. "Do you still have it?"

"Yes, it's right here in my briefcase."

"Mind passing it up so I can have a look?"

He scans the article while masterfully steering. "I'll tell you a secret, m' lord, since you seem the trustworthy sort. Lad was down visiting Colin just last month, in fact. Anyway, 'Sir Thomas,' as we've nicknamed him, wants to be a head butler himself one day. He's saving to attend one of those proper butler schools."

Interesting. You'll keep him in mind as a possible replacement for Mr. Knives and Forks if it comes to that. "Sounds ambitious. Can't wait to meet this Thomas," you tell your driver.

"In that case," Stephen replies, "how about inviting Thomas to ride along with us for a spell?"

"I'm sorry, Stephen, I don't believe I heard you correctly," you say. "Are we stopping to pick someone up?"

"No, we're not required to stop anywhere." Stephen struggles to keep himself from laughing. "Here, use this to summon him." He hands back a flat black remote controller with the roles of the manor servants printed on the buttons.

"I take it I should press the HEADWAITER button?"

"Correct, but first, brace yourself."

You guess that pressing the button will trigger some sort of video clip on the DVD player you see attached to the limo's ceiling; a screen will unfold or slide down, and Thomas will burst into view and introduce himself. Nice touch if that's what happens.

But that's not what happens at all. Not even close. It's something straight out of a Disneyland ride. A silvery funnel-shaped cloud whirls like a silent tornado, then disintegrates. Your jaw drops. Sitting beside you is Thomas Sutherland himself. In the flesh!

Well, not exactly. After a few more seconds, you recognize it as a full-sized holographic image. But not ghostlike, nor possessing the ethereal quality of an apparition. It is utterly lifelike. "Well, hello, Thomas!" you call to the holo. "Stephen, this is incredible. Who did this?"

"His Lordship arranged it, of course," he informs you. "A few weeks back, he sent a holographic projector and a library of 3D clips to Browns and instructed them to have it available. I hooked it up just before I set about to fetch you. The setup is fairly intuitive. It utilizes Bluetooth, point-to-point Wi-Fi, and personal hot spots." Your IT background enables you to picture the device configuration. But the projection technology itself? Unbelievable.

"I believe we are glimpsing the future of motion pictures," Stephen exudes. "Scenes that are richly projected in near space. Scenes we can circumnavigate and view from every angle. Scenes we can walk right into if fancied."

You nod in agreement while exclaiming, "Stephen, are you really a chauffeur? All of a sudden you sound like a tech wizard. Anyway, my TV already does all this."

Stephen turns and gives you a wink, saying, "But does it do this?"

Now Holo Thomas turns to face you. He hoists an imaginary champagne glass to offer a toast, saying, "Greetings, my lord. Looking forward to meeting you in person." He pauses to glance down at his watch. "In about an hour and a quarter's time."

You're blown away. "Stephen, did you hear that! It spoke to me."

"I heard, m'lord. Why not say something back?"

"Um, Thomas, how do you know exactly when we'll arrive?"

"I have a sixth sense when it comes to time," he replies. "Particularly on special occasions."

"Okay, Thomas," you say, "it's a pleasure to make your acquaintance, but you're getting to be a bit spooky." You press the HEADWAITER button again, blinking Thomas out of existence.

Stephen resumes his assessment of the headwaiter's prospects. "Afraid Thomas won't last long, though," he says. "From what I hear tell, Farnsworth and Van Scoy have run off four of 'em in the last twelve months."

You press BUTLER on your remote. He's now sitting on your left. Steely eyed, arrogant-looking, and downright scary. After a moment, the holo turns and speaks to you with a cold expression. "So you're about to arrive. I wouldn't assume that all's settled with Arthur's estate, if I were you." Evidently, this projection is trying to intimidate, frighten you. Not going to happen.

"Mr. Farnsworth," you call out, "you are dismissed," as you re-press the button. In the front, Stephen is snickering a little.

Next, you press CONCIERGE, who materializes on your right. Regal, commanding, gorgeous. She appears to be regarding you with interest. She leans in and speaks softly, "He doesn't think your claim to the title is legitimate."

On impulse, you reach for her, hoping to lightly touch her shoulder. But, of course, your hand goes straight through. You feel silly but have no intention of turning her off. At least for now. From your window, you notice lightning flashes, followed by a roll of thunder.

You mention to Stephen that, when you telephoned recently, you spoke with a woman named Penelope Stratton. Stephen snaps his fingers, reaches into his satchel, and pulls out another remote, which he hands back. You power it on, and the DVD screen above unfolds.

"Welcome to the Hanover Manor Estate and Galleries," greets Penelope, with the voice of a seasoned performer. She's standing in front of the massive oak doors of Manor House, palms lowered and extended in a welcoming pose, bidding entry to one and all. She's stunning, reminding you of any of a dozen top models you've seen.

"Beautiful young lady, but a bit of a scatterbrain, I'm told," says Stephen. "She's got prowess as a long-distance swimmer, aiming to do the Channel in summer."

"Impressive. Let's double up on her," you reply happily as you press the RECEPTIONIST button.

The young lady, in addition to holding forth on the screen above, now materializes beside you, turning her lovely head to face you and smiling ever so winsomely. "Everything has been arranged. Do enjoy your stay with us," she says to you.

Storyteller, this may be the best ride ever. ***Indeed, immensely enjoyable.***

When you resume the video, you see Farnsworth acting all high and mighty and snobbish, while beside you sits the refined Adrienne Van Scoy. You pause both, mentally composite the images, and are forced to admit that the butler and the concierge are indeed an extraordinarily attractive and aristocratic-looking twosome.

Sure hope they're not *a couple.* ***If so, you must endeavor to "decouple" them, heh heh heh.*** The wicked-sounding directive from an elderly male causes you to smile and nod conspiratorially in reply. ***Don't listen to that old troublemaker***, a mature female voice interjects. ***It would be quite bad form to engage with the private lives of servants.*** *So do you people always give contradictory advice?* ***Incessantly, we're afraid.***

The video is now featuring one Noël Elle Léon. It might be your imagination, or all the rumors you've heard from Stephen, but the chef certainly does look cunning in these frames. You press the Chef button. He materializes in the middle of a row of seats behind you, looking quite debonair in a distinctly French sort of way. Almost as if he's read your mind, his holo says, "Do I, like, look like I do?"

In the video clip above, the chef is shown serving a green salad, hot Indian bread, and a juicy steak to Lord Hanover. "Kayak salad, Alaska yak, naan!" The chef beams. "Sir Hanover, my lord, are you thrilled you are my Lord Hanover, sir?"

To which His Lordship laughs and replies, "Am I? Noël Elle Léon, I am!"

Are you catching the palindromes, Storyteller? A young Britisher responds, ***Yes, highly amusing repartee, we think.***

Next, Bruce Sherlock appears in the clip, singing karaoke while tending bar. So you press Publican, and the gregarious and good-looking Aussie is placed beside Noël in the limo. "Evening, mate. Me and some of my manor mates are waiting to welcome you good and proper."

"Sounds great," you tell him. "What time?"

"Soon as you're in, settled, and thirsty," he says heartily.

In the video program, you now see that the estate has a significant repository of paintings that hang throughout the hallways of Manor House. "The galleries are open to the public free of charge," narrates Penelope, "as are guided tours of the estate and grounds provided by the staff." Lord Hanover then appears to offer commentary on the collection, which is captioned on-screen as:

LOOKING AT ART—BEHIND THE CANVAS

"When I first consider a painting, I endeavor to look behind whatever is being depicted on the surface. There can always be another realm that lies beyond the painted image, one that is alive with people and their stories—if only one knows how to truly see and hear them. Whether this other place emanates from the soul of the artist, or is engendered by the nature of the work, or springs from another origin entirely, I have never learned. I only know that some works reveal more hidden places than others."

For some reason, his disclosure seems important, like something you should keep in mind. An elderly dark-skinned face shakes his head vigorously from side to side. ***It is. You should.*** *Ah, I know that mannerism. You're Indian!* The Storyteller smiles broadly while nodding up and down. ***No, Your Excellency, but close. Pakistani!***

Keeping Adrienne, Penelope, Noël, and Bruce in place, one by one you press the remaining buttons on the remote to fill the seats beside Stephen, who chuckles, and all the empty places behind you. HEADWAITER, for the charming Thomas Sutherland who was here earlier; CHAUFFEUR, for Savannah Reddy, the sexy blonde expatriate who races motorcycles; DOORMAN, for the irrepressible Reggie McCabe who sports a different coat of colors each and every day; HOUSEKEEPER, for Mildred Simmons, the head housekeeper and outspoken naturalist; and GUEST, for Mildred's grandson, Christopher Robin—now gazing out the window looking like he's immensely enjoying the ride. In the video, the lad appears to be bright and alert but with no official role. He's just *there*, you suppose, living a charmed life, commiserating with the local flora and fauna.

Now the limo is packed with servants as the hum of conviviality fills the air. You survey the interior; all seats are occupied. No place for Farnsworth. Good. The DVD program has reached its end. You pause the final frame. In three rows of smiling faces, the entire household has lined up as a stage family might.

Stephen has plugged in his phone and is streaming music, filling the cabin with mesmerizing synths of disguised guitars, electric piano, and drums, along with dreamy, layered vocals you can barely make out. "Stephen, what's this music?" you ask. "I vaguely recall hearing these songs some years ago."

"Don't quite know," Stephen replies. "Colin sent me a playlist filled with songs like this. Said it was a collection of 'neo-psychedelia,' whatever that might mean. It's titled 'Aughts/Teens Classics.'"

Stephen now suggests you press the SYNC button for some "additional merriment." As soon as you do, you quickly receive a jolt. The holograms temporarily freeze, then after another moment, they all start rhythmically swaying to the music and bobbing their heads to the hypnotic beat. A fantastic sight! It feels like you're in a motorized disco. Dozens of smiling Storytellers appear above.

One of them says, ***All gathered here love psychedelia too. Reminds us of us.***

You freeze the passengers and take pictures with your phone. Then you unfreeze them and take videos.

You slap the console, exclaiming, "Stephen, I swear this trip is starting to seem like an extended Disney ride."

Stephen turns slightly and says, "Just wait till you get to the manor! His Lordship loved theme parks. Toured many, was inspired by them all." He gestures at the passengers, now rocking back and forth to an increased tempo. "These joyful riders are all waiting for you in real life."

Ecstatic but nearly exhausted, your mind drifts, as you are barely able to keep your eyes open. You start to doze off, fantasizing about meeting the concierge for the first time. Should you do something quaint like kiss the back of her hand and say, "Charmed, I'm sure"? You need to get this right!

Right! A declaration from an authoritative-sounding woman above startles you out of your reverie. ***As they say, you never get a second chance to make a first impression! But I would skip the hand kiss if I were you.***

Too sleepy, though, to further fantasize a proper salutation, you nod off.

After a while, you hear another voice, Stephen's, calling from what seems far away in this cavernous limousine. You slowly shake your head and rub your eyes. Coming to, you ask Stephen to please repeat what he just said. "We've arrived, m'lord," he calls. "Hanover Manor."

The main gates are shut for the night. The Bentley can go no farther than the sweeping cul-de-sac. It halts in front of massive iron gates emblazoned with the Hanover coat of arms. Seeing this large, exquisite bronze shield, you note its most prominent symbol, the solitary white dove of peace. Even the fine detail of the bird's olive branch is discernible in the pale moonlight. The shield is lovely to behold, but you can't picture your ancestors marching into medieval battles behind such a pacifistic emblem surrounded by tiny images of tableware. You don't understand the origin of "Manner House," but it seems quite funny now that you see the shield up close.

After stopping the vehicle, your driver gets out, walks around, removes your baggage, and opens your door. Still drowsy, you emerge, fumbling with your cell phone only to find there's no service out here either. Still, it feels good to be outside looking at this incredible scene. No stars are visible in the thick overcast, but a full moon has found a patch of clear sky. Occasional flashes backlight the clouds, and thunderclaps echo in the distance.

The closed gate bars vehicle entry to a long driveway, and an open expanse of manicured lawn stretches on both sides. Then, looking over the roof of the Bentley, you see the massive outline, at once foreboding and welcoming—Manor House.

Stephen picks up your shoulder bag and starts wheeling your luggage. Although the storm keeps threatening, it's a pleasant walk up a slight incline of smoothly paved surface. Looming ahead are the white stone walls of a modern castle and the redbrick sides and arched tiled roofs of its auxiliary buildings.

Several yards in front of the main entrance lies a short wall of rough brown rock and stone. It extends as a midline across the lawn, from manor arm to manor arm, interrupted only by the driveway itself. The wall incrementally rises to columns, which buttress each side of the road. Atop each one, a stone lion stares across the lawn. At this point, the road becomes a large oval driveway. A large bronze statue is set in the island the middle of the driveway creates. The figure is seated, hunched forward on a chair.

Drawing closer, you see he's holding a quill in one hand and balancing a writing tablet with the other. Now standing before him, you see that you'd guessed right—the plaque identifies WILLIAM SHAKESPEARE (1564–1616), BORN IN STRATFORD-UPON-AVON, WARWICKSHIRE, ENGLAND.

Stephen has set your bag and briefcase on the ground. You catch a glimpse of him removing a small object from his vest pocket, seemingly counting to himself, and then aiming it. Just as you've walked around to examine the back of the statue, you catch sight of Stephen's thumb depressing a button.

Suddenly—music! A deep, prolonged pounding on kettledrums followed by rapier thrusts across bass cellos.

"What the—?" you shout.

Now a tingling of piano chords and a stir of rising violins enters the fray. The instruments create a powerful and dramatic overture. A full-blown orchestral arrangement blasts out across the lawn. Might be Beethoven. Might be Tchaikovsky or Mahler. Heck, you don't know.

Nature kicks in.

Thunder and lightning erupt over the manor sky, illuminating Shakespeare, the lions, the annexes. The lions rise from their haunches, shake and toss their mighty manes up and down and side to side, and let out deafening roars before quieting, then slowly settling back into sitting positions.

Whoa, Storyteller, scary! ***A bit frightening for us too! But my goodness—now look!***

Shakespeare is rising from his chair, yawning while stretching his arms outward and clenching his fists. Slowly, he reseats himself. You cannot see if his lips are really moving when he intones, "As my good fellow Puck would say, 'If we shadows have offended, think but this and all is mended. That you have but slumbered here while these visions did appear.'"

You're tingling, involuntarily rising to the tips of your toes as the short recital ends and a giant visage of Arthur Hanover, shown from his head down to the crest of his ascot, appears in the gray-black sky.

The music segues into a violin solo that falls gracefully aside to make way for an approaching voice. Lord Hanover's eyes are filled with mirth, his smile radiant as he rolls his head back and laughs uproariously, then speaks with the force of a prophet thundering from the heavens:

"My beloved child, at long last you have come. I am your uncle, Arthur Hanover. May I extend to you my warmest welcome to this place and time, which I dearly hope you will find in your heart to accept as your new home and your new life. I have prepared everything necessary to secure your ownership and title. If you encounter difficulties, I will assist you when I am able. I have told you what I can in a letter you'll find in your room. Good luck, my child, for incredible discoveries await you at Manor House."

For a few moments, his image lingers, a clear-eyed gaze of warmth and bemusement.

Then it slowly dissolves into the night sky, like a film or computerized transition. The refrain comes back up, holds another moment or two, offering some final flourishes of strings and woodwinds, then fades on a single extended note as the weather takes its cue: the thunder now only a distant rumble, the lightning vanished.

Along with Stephen.

CHAPTER FIVE

You blink at the spot where he was just standing. Turning around slowly, you cast long squints at the stone wall, at the statue, around the driveway, across the green. But there's no sign of your driver. As you turn and face the manor doors, you wonder if he slipped inside. Except, had the doors opened, you would have noticed. Your suitcase and bag are on the ground where he placed them.

You call out his name repeatedly. No answer. Try to think this through. Stephen obviously triggered this short concert and holographic show with whatever he was holding. He did this, likely, in cahoots with Arthur Hanover, which means they were actually close pals. Probably planned it all out as their way of giving you a big, dramatic, unforgettable welcome. It sure worked. Even got a guest appearance from Mother Nature. Okay, so Hanover Manor has large external speakers mounted up high somewhere. And access to a powerful projection system, probably laser based. It's too dark to spot anything now, but you can check tomorrow.

From the opening measures until Lord Hanover faded away, Stephen would have had ample opportunity to slip off into the shadows and down to the gate. He's surely on the road by now, probably replaying the spectacle over and over in his head, immensely satisfied with himself and how he kept his promise to his old friend and benefactor. This spectacular event has jogged your memory. Now you realize where you'd seen "Stephen" before—in photos, on websites, on TVTV News. Only those images showed an undisguised Lord Dennis Rollinsby, sans muttonchops and handlebars.

"What a pair," you chuckle aloud. They had time, money, and tech to burn all right. You walk over to the base of the statue to reach up and touch the top of Shakespeare's shoe. It's as cool as the night air.

Equally puzzling is why the musical extravaganza failed to attract any attention. Why didn't any staff or guests step onto the porch, or at least poke their heads out? Golden lights shine through the windows of the main building, silvery ones from the resort spa on the left, and a flickering soft glow—probably candlelight—emanating from what you assume must be the dining hall opposite. Here, above the entrance, are wall-mounted lanterns, now burning brightly. People are obviously at home.

High time you go inside, get settled, find that letter, and see what it says. That's your plan as you mount the granite steps to ring the bell. Only there isn't one—no elegant brass or gold knocker like you'd expect. There isn't anything at all, except your clenched fist, which does no good when you pound on the stately oak door. Feeling foolish, you call, "Anybody here?"

Light rain is starting to fall. The porch is uncovered, and there's no portico above the driveway. You're about to get drenched. Where is everybody? All these servants you're supposed to meet? *Hey, where* is *Reggie McCabe, the world's greatest doorman?* A bald man who looks to be in his nineties appears, his bright face illuminating the night sky like a starburst. ***Heh heh heh, good one. Keep looking.***

That's when you spot a shiny silver card at the end of a granite ledge beside the manor steps. You walk back out to the driveway, retrieve your baggage, then hoist your suitcase up the steps. You don't see any slot, so you merely hold up the card. The massive doors open by themselves.

After walking in and setting your bags down on a gleaming white-and-gold-speckled marble floor, you hear the solid doors close behind you. Dreamy, neo-psych music, same as the limo's, is playing softly in the background. The place is trippy. You catch a lyric fragment, "Time's still circling me," as your gaze becomes a movie camera.

It shifts from mahogany walls with protruding gold candelabras to enormous white sofas near a roaring fireplace on the right. Your gaze pans slowly up to a massive chandelier suspended from an etched, pearl-colored ceiling, then down to an oversized diamond-shaped bench upholstered with burnt-orange crushed velvet.

You call, "Hello, hello? Anybody here?" but get no response. Behind the bench stands a massive ceramic vase minutely decorated with Chaucerian scenes of everyday life in the Middle Ages. From where you're standing now, you can look left and right down identical mahogany-paneled hallways interspersed with numerous carved doors and laid with forest-green and auburn carpet. Several large paintings give the hallways the effect of a narrow gallery.

"Good evening . . . Hello . . . Anybody here?" Again no replies. Over to the left, there's an official-looking area with an arrangement of rosewood desks and chairs and other paraphernalia—including several antique silver telephones. This feels like a hotel lobby in an intimate, ultra-exclusive boutique establishment—one, given the background music, that might cater to guests in altered states.

Except you've been wandering around for some time and haven't seen a soul. Returning to the entrance, you now hear strong wind and driving rain outside. You decide to crack the door for a quick peek. But when you pull, then push on the large gold handles, all you hear is the thud of whatever it is that's now barring both doors.

What is this—Hotel California?

Might as well explore and see if you can find someone. You want to call home, tell someone that you've arrived safe and sound, that all is well—except it isn't, exactly. You pick up one of the receivers but hear no dial tone. Checking your cell again, you see there's still no service. However, sitting on this desk is just what you need: a solid-gold summons bell. You jingle it.

A young woman you instantly recognize as Penelope Stratton emerges from a door behind the reception area. Her expression is troubled. "Good evening," she greets you. "So sorry to have kept you. I've so much to attend to in this place. Now let me see . . . if I'm not mistaken, your room is all made up."

As gorgeous as her picture in the brochure, Penelope wears a navy-blue sweater-and-skirt ensemble of cashmere, finished with classy gold accessories that scream money. She looks like a poster child for finishing school.

"You'll find your key just inside on the table."

"Excuse me, Miss, but . . . which room?"

"Miss Stratton, I need you immediately," an authoritative male voice calls from the direction of the room she just came from. Summoned, Penelope gestures in the direction of the left hallway and rushes off.

Stephen—better think Rollinsby from now on—was right about her being a looker. That perfume . . . You're no expert, but you think you know "very expensive" when you catch its scent.

In the hallway, you pause to look at the gold plaque mounted on the first door on the right. It reads The Armory. That can't be it. You move down to the second, which is identically inscribed. The third door reads The Cottage—but is locked. As is the last one, likewise labeled The Cottage. There aren't any doors on the left side, only paintings and large windows with drawn drapes. At the end, there are unmarked double doors that are locked as well. Exasperated, you leave your bags, try the armory doors, find them locked as well, and so head back to reception. But no matter how many times you ring the bell, Penelope never reappears. Nor does anyone else.

Terrific. Now what? You return to the spot where you left your bags—oh no, now they're gone! Yet all the doors remain locked.

Matters seem to be turning seriously bad. But you're determined not to panic. You walk the length of the hallway to another set of double doors. They're locked. You walk a third of the way back to inspect the first of two doors you passed. It reads Office of the Concierge. You knock, but no one answers. The second door would be the hall entrance to the office from which Penelope emerged a while ago. It reads Office of the Butler.

You hear muffled voices and knock several times. No response. Now you're highly irritated since you're sure they're in there. Attached to the wall is an electronic ten-key numeric pad. To vent your frustration and annoyance, you tap in some random numbers and press the Enter button.

All hell breaks loose.

CHAPTER SIX

A loud buzzer alarm blares followed by an announcement: "Unauthorized entry is being attempted. You are advised to desist immediately. Failure to do so will result in a police summons. All staff should remain where they are."

Startled, you freeze on the spot. A moment later, the alarm stops blaring. The door opens, and out steps the personification of the correct English butler—the handsome and impeccably groomed James Farnsworth. And he is furious.

"So, you've finally arrived." His eyes fairly burn.

You nod and attempt to speak, but he interjects—as a superior addressing a subordinate: "This letter arrived for you. I chose to deliver it personally." Farnsworth hands you a wax-sealed envelope, whose signet you recognize as your uncle's. "No doubt you have questions about the general situation," he says haughtily. "I cannot attend to them now. See me in the morning." He practically slams the door in your face.

A woman's voice, cultured and British, sounds on the PA. "All is well. We apologize for the interruption. Carry on." The background music switches to light classical.

Purposeful strides help calm you down as you return to the opposite end of the hall. Your bags are still missing, and the doors remain locked. You're about to return to the lobby when suddenly Noël Elle Léon, in checkered trousers and a towering chef's toque, emerges from the second cottage door. He carries a covered serving dish and appears nervous, as if caught in some illicit act.

"*Pardonnez-moi*. I am sorry, we have closed the kitchen for the evening." He quickly locks the door.

"I was just looking for my room. Is this—"

The chef interrupts. "But *mais oui*, I can arrange a late supper if it pleases you, and *mais oui*, even now I am in the very midst of composing in my own head something so very, very *spéciale* for your breakfast tomorrow. It will be perfect, *extraordinaire. Je vous assure!*"

Again, you try to explain your predicament. But the chef doesn't understand—or pretends not to—that you're not sure which room is yours, you have no key, and you've lost your baggage. The more flustered you get, the more rapid, colloquial French he employs. Eventually, he shrugs as if at a total loss.

"But, Chef, my door is locked!" You twist the knob rapidly so he can see for himself what you mean.

"No, it is open on one position," he calls out enigmatically, then disappears through the double doors.

He just spoke in palindrome, says an adolescent Storyteller. *So?* ***Probably dig it if you answered in one too.*** *Don't know any.* ***We can prompt you when the time comes.***

You shrug—you're back at square one. Probably no chance you'll get that late supper either. Maybe things will improve if you try upstairs.

Mounting the staircase, you pause to examine the towering window that dominates this wall. HANOVER MANOR is etched in a broad arc above the frame. All around the lettering are medieval scenes like those on the large vase downstairs.

From the landing, the stairwell branches left and right. You start up the left side, pausing when you hear the concierge announce, like a highbrow deejay, that for the next hour the musical program will consist of selections by the late British composer Simon Jeffes and his Penguin Cafe Orchestra.

You pause, thinking, *Now that's a coincidence, Storyteller.* ***It is not. There are no coincidences.*** The young male is no longer visible; you only hear him.

You recall how just last week you happened across an old *Rolling Stone* article about the group. You'd never heard of them, but apparently, the British sextet was popular in the nineties for its unique blend of art rock and traditional chamber music.

Jeffes, the article went on, was enamored of penguins. Constantly saw them everywhere he went—in Parisian cafés, on LA streets, along Hawaiian beaches. The birds always graced his album covers. Even the jokes he told were generally inhabited by penguins. You chuckle as you recall the one quoted in the article, thinking it might be a good one to tell some evening when you're socializing with the others:

> A London constable spots an old bloke driving a convertible around Piccadilly Circus with three penguins perched on top of the backseat. He motions him to pull over.
>
> "Sir, might I inquire about those penguins?"
>
> "Your Honor, I just spotted these penguins a ways back, looking all lost and forlorn, so I picked 'em up," the motorist, a tourist from Bristol, explains.
>
> "Well, sir, you should take those penguins to the London Zoo straightaway."
>
> "Jolly well right, Officer. I'll do it this minute."
>
> The next day, the bobby spots the same motorist in the same convertible with the same penguins—only this time, they're all wearing sunglasses. He waves the car over again.
>
> "Sir, I distinctly advised you yesterday to take those penguins to the zoo!" the constable declares.
>
> "I did," explains the tourist. "Had a wonderful outing, too. Today we're headed for the beach."

You step on to the gleaming hardwood floor of the giant rotunda and spot Mildred Simmons, the housekeeper, dusting the top of an antique table down the hall. She's wearing a maid's outfit—full skirt, white apron, and a lace cap, and her bright hazel-green eyes and reddish-gray hair enhances her rosy complexion.

"Excuse me. Hello . . . Mrs. Simmons?"

"Oh, hello, dear, I've just prepared your room. Do hope you'll find it comfortable until we can secure you better accommodations. The receptionist has the key." She glances around and adds confidentially, "Don't forget to mind your valuables whenever you're away."

"I'm so confused," you tell her. "I'm not sure where my room is, and every door downstairs is locked."

"You're to be temporarily housed in the cottage," she tells you. "I'll tend to matters immediately." Mildred points toward the hallway branching left. "Take that hallway all the way down to the Falstaff pub and wait for me there. And why not grab a bite? You must be famished."

"Sounds good! Thanks."

You start toward the hallway. On your right, beneath a sign labeled The Library, stand massive carved doors. You recall reading that it houses one of Europe's largest collections of rare books, some thirty-five hundred volumes, not a few of which are centuries-old first editions. The library's locked, but you're looking forward to going in there, perhaps tomorrow.

Like downstairs, the walls here are lined with paintings—Dutch masters, still lifes, pastoral scenes. There's a very surprising arrangement of a cluster of five paintings, laid out star-shaped, of Native Americans. And at the star's center is a portrait of an old, bearded White man who clearly lacks any Native American features.

You study the Native American faces, momentarily wondering if you'd seen these paintings before. The old guy, though, looks somewhat familiar. It's funny. He actually looks like what you'd imagine you might look like if you age well into your eighties. Kind of spooky, though.

Storyteller, did my uncle do this? ***Yes.*** *How come?* ***You'll find out when the Time comes.***

There are two doors in the hallway between the rotunda and the pub. The closer one is labeled Her Majesty's; the farther one, His Majesty's. Ah, yes, you recently learned what that's all about: in earlier times, noblemen had to reserve their estate's best rooms for visiting royalty, even though the royalty rarely showed up. Noting details like these makes you think you're starting to relax.

You try to push open the doors labeled The Falstaff, whereupon the door bursts halfway open, bringing you face-to-face with a grinning Bruce Sherlock, the publican who is literally foaming at the mouth.

"Evening, mate," he roars. "Keg just up and exploded, whole place got flooded. Had to close her up earlier this evening." Sherlock looks exasperated. "Ah, come back later and—" Suddenly he slips and loses his grip on the door, which slams shut. You hear Sherlock falling along with the clank and clatter of a crashing mop and pail. "Be all right, mate. No worries!" he yells through the door.

You decide you'd better try to find Mildred, but before returning downstairs, you'll check the opposite end of the hall. There's only one door on the left, another locked entrance to the library. Numerous portraits hang on both sides of the hall, all of European noblemen and military types: conquistadors and brigadiers, cavalrymen and swashbucklers. Some of your ancestors?

You move on to the room marked BILLIARDS ROOM & WHISKY BAR. Surprise—it's open. Disappointment—it's empty.

The room is dimly lit, conical lamps overhanging the three billiard tables across the room. On a far wall, a wide-screen TV silently displays a plump woman with flowing blonde hair riding a small white pony around in circles in what appears to be a small courtyard. It looks as though the rider may be nude. You squint to make out the screen caption, which says:

COMING SOON—LOCAL LADY GODIVA SUES CHOCOLATIERS

Storyteller, is that lady nude? ***Indeed, she's gallivanting while lacking any attire. Purposely, I might add.*** This twenty-something Storyteller seems highly amused. Intrigued, you press 3DHOLO, watch for another moment, then, laughing out loud, collapse the image.

Crazy. Lady Godiva. Whatever it is, you'll definitely try to catch that full report.

At the long oak bar fronting an array of silver goblets and crystal tumblers, as well as a collection of every spirit imaginable, the lighting is subdued. And there's something else about the place—the music is completely different.

As "Someone to Watch Over Me" begins to play, you take a seat on a high stool. Something to drink would be nice. Then you hear a warm "Good evening," which sounds like your wish is about to be granted.

Recognizing his voice, you've already guessed who this must be. You swivel around and face Headwaiter Thomas Sutherland, who is balancing a silver tray containing a bottle of wine in a leather bucket. He looks fabulous in his short-jacketed tuxedo, ruffled white shirt, and black bow tie.

"Happy birthday! I'm Thomas; I believe we met on your journey up. May I offer you a sincere welcome with this selection from our private reserve?" Thomas sweeps the tray in your direction. "Lord Hanover left instructions to provide a bottle the moment you arrived." He senses your hesitation. "Well, if not now, you might enjoy it before retiring this evening . . . or perhaps at your official birthday celebration."

"Thanks, Thomas," you reply amusedly. "But I'm afraid today's not my birthday."

"Ah, but don't you feel somewhat 'reborn' tonight?" Thomas is disarming—he reminds you of that cliché: "the epitome of well-scrubbed British manhood."

"I see what you mean," you concede, then tell him that the housekeeper is looking after your accommodations but doesn't know you're in here.

"Relax, I'll see to it straightaway," he reassures. "May I bring you something light, some hors d'oeuvres perhaps?"

"That would be great," you tell him as he removes the wine and departs.

And never returns. After what feels to be about twenty minutes, you poke around behind the bar but can only find a tray of small gelatin squares. Famished, you devour nearly the entire assortment, even though they taste rather odd, and a few moments later, you began to feel a little odd yourself. Not a bad feeling, but definitely one with a strange afterglow.

Settling into a leather chair, you open your uncle's latest letter, which, as before, is beautifully handwritten. The top line once again materializing does not surprise you. Not after your encounter with Farnsworth—you almost expected it.

This sentence will appear only if the seal on the envelope has been broken and then reattached.

Like before, the script momentarily flashes.

My beloved child,

I offer my fondest and heartiest welcome. I know you have journeyed far and, though tired, must be absolutely bristling with questions. It is perhaps my greatest regret that I cannot be there to answer them in person. Still, I shall do what I can in this all-too-short missive to enlighten you about the unusual—one might even say unsettling—situation you find yourself in.

First, however, there are some things that must be said. I want you to know beyond the shadow of an angel's doubt that I am, in every legal sense, your uncle. Three of the four documents now in your possession will provide ironclad proof of that. To wit: my last will and testament; the findings of the court; and the report from the Genealogical Society, which establishes that there are no other claimants to my properties or title.

The fourth and final document is the deed to Hanover Manor. All four must be presented to the local court before you can assume your inheritance.

Let me reassure you that there is absolutely nothing sordid about our connection. Furthermore, I have observed you at various times during your life and found much to praise, even more to admire. My love for you remains unaffected by time, distance, and, yes, even death.

Now as to me. Why, you may ask, do I not simply tell you everything about our family ties? In partial answer, let me say that my entire existence has been reflected by a simple mirrored principle: life is discovery, and discovery life.

None of the things I have invented would have taken shape had I not persisted in looking beyond the obvious and the possible. From my observations, I know you also possess this overwhelming degree of curiosity. That is fortunate, because I foresee the likelihood of certain obstacles—perhaps even active interference—during your quest.

My wish to have you overcome these difficulties comprises the other part of my answer to your question of why I've offered no forthright explanation of our relationship: I want you to one day embrace the entire manor staff as new additions to your family. For years, they gave me loyal and devoted service, and I cherish them all.

Yet now you have arrived in their midst as a stranger and a potential threat; never was any guest so utterly unexpected at Hanover Manor. But if you come to know my servants well, and they you, I am confident that strong new bonds will emerge to replace those that were severed with my passing.

I believe that humans best establish close ties by resolving conflicts and working together towards a common purpose. This is what I hope you will accomplish in the early days of your new life at Hanover Manor. I devoutly hope that you will win the entire staff over and that together you'll discover the truth about my work, my life, and us.

Affectionately,
Arthur Hanover
Lucerne, Switzerland

Warm and reassuring, to be sure, but so many unanswered questions. He refers to the vital documents in your room. Given tonight's events, though, you wonder if they'll still be there, if ever you do get inside. But even if they are, how do you file them? Who can you trust to help with these formalities?

Why the manor staff was never alerted as to your existence is puzzling. As is the fact that Lord Hanover chose not to explain your relationship to him. Interesting, though, how he did say there's nothing scandalous about it. But how can that be? You're touched by the old man's genuine affection for you, but these tantalizing letters in flowery prose don't address your most pressing concerns. Namely, why did your uncle not invite you to visit him and the manor prior to his passing?

Oh well, as your uncle says, "Life is discovery, and discovery life." You decide to return downstairs to see if you can "discover" whether there is an active conspiracy afoot to keep you up all night or if it's just an unfortunate comedy of errors.

But while in the hallway, you hear the hum of conversation and laughter coming from the Falstaff pub. Looks like it's now open. Maybe you can find someone who can help you get settled. You stride down the hall and push open the pub door.

"Surprise! Happy birthday! Surprise! Happy birthday!"

Stunned, you freeze momentarily but are soon mobbed by high-spirited servants who rush over and guide you to a stool in the center of the pub. Bruce, seated at a honky-tonk piano, begins to play as the crowd sings:

"Happy birthday to you! Happy birthday to you! Happy birthday dear new lord. Happy birthday to you!"

Everybody applauds, and several rush over to offer individual welcomes and congratulations. You'd love to stay and get acquainted, but you can hardly stand up or keep awake.

Relax, a female Storyteller says. ***Say to them what I say to you. Got it?*** *Got it.* ***Now, stand up.***

You rise to address the gathering. "Thank you so much, everyone, for your warm welcome on this my 'rebirthday.' I look forward to getting to know each and every one of you and to many boisterous nights in this establishment."

The gathering applauds.

"But for tonight, I'm afraid I shan't be the last one standing, as I've been traveling all day and now need to get settled. I do hope you'll understand if I bid an early adieu."

"We do, my lord!" several call out. "Get your rest, m'lord," cry others.

With that, you depart, projecting a big thank-you to the Storyteller who came up with those well-received lines for you. ***At your service, . . . my lord.***

As soon as you descend the last flight of stairs, you spot two individuals, one of whom you instantly guess is Reggie McCabe, a.k.a. the world's greatest doorman.

"Evening, m'lord!" he hails from across the lobby. "Sorry to be away when you arrived. Oh, you'd never want to be out on a night like this." A short but powerfully built man, he removes his raincoat, revealing a blue-and-cardinal-red doorman's coat with silver epaulets. "In truth, we've been outside for the past two hours—battening down the hatches and shutters, boardin' up windows and doors and such."

Okay, Storyteller, that explains it. Not Hotel California after all. ***True, but still, you can't leave.*** *Ha ha very funny.* ***We know all the songs.***

"Reg, I've just heard on the HAM that the road to The Village has been washed out," his tall female companion calls out. You regard the young woman now taking off her raincoat. Underneath is all charcoal and black—blouse, vest, and pants tucked into knee-high patent-leather boots. She removes her rain hat, and you are struck by the contrasting splash of bright cascading blonde hair. Of course—Savannah Reddy, the beauty who caused that stir at Browns and who is, your driver reported, an idol on the local motocross circuit.

You nod hello and inform her, "I'm supposed to be in the cottage, but both doors are locked and my bags are gone."

Reggie and Savannah exchange knowing glances. "Savannah, why don't you go see what the chef's up to?" the doorman suggests. "I'll check on His Majesty Farnsworth."

"On it." Savannah saunters off in the direction of the kitchen.

Reggie pats your shoulder. "Not to worry, m'lord. We'll locate your bags and have you in your room in no time."

You stifle a yawn, saying, "Sorry to put you to all this trouble."

The doorman shakes his head and points to the sofas near the fireplace, bidding you to make yourself comfortable while he straightens out "old Knives and Forks this minute."

You take his advice and collapse on one of the sofas, figuring you've probably seen the last of those two as well.

You're right.

CHAPTER SEVEN

You're sleepy but determined to remain awake until somebody returns. The music has become an ensemble of piano selections. "Moonlight Sonata" is the current one. Beethoven, deaf yet able to write all those symphonies.

Storyteller how could he possibly have? Says an elderly woman, ***We played the notes in his head. That's one of our capabilities. We have many.***

So maybe old Ludwig actually heard the music and simply transcribed the notes. Yes, but first he had to think the notes, you surmise, as you pick up a nearby remote and idly switch on the wall-mounted TV.

"Was Beethoven any good at music?" a young woman is asking.

"Yeah, I mean, he's considered to be the best composer of Western classical music ever," replies a scholarly looking woman identified in a chyron as a music professor at a British university.

The young interviewer continues, "Did Beethoven write that song that goes, "Da da da dum . . . Da da da dum? What do those lyrics mean?"

You chuckle, noting the BBC logo in the top left corner and the show's name, *Cunk on Earth*, printed on the right. Of course! You remember this mockumentary from a decade ago. Absolutely brilliant stupidity.

"Well, it's a really strong orchestral motif—" the professor starts to explain.

Cunk interrupts with, "But it's just the word *dumb* over and over again." Her expression is earnest as she wonders, "Is it a dig at his audience, or is it German or something?"

"With the Beethoven symphonic music," the professor patiently explains, "it's all just instruments, so there are no words to these pieces at all."

Hearing this, Cunk asks pointedly, “No lyrics? How are we supposed to know what the song’s about if it doesn’t have lyrics? It’s literally meaningless.”

The segment ends.

Storyteller, you and I were just discussing Beethoven and then—you point the remote at the TV. ***You should ask Carl Jung about that. We shall try to make him available at some point.*** *Okay, Storyteller. Sure. Whatever.* ***Oh, we’re quite serious, I assure you.***

Next, you click around, hoping to find that same local channel you watched back home. Soon, you spot the familiar anchors, Michael and Meredith, in their usual places behind a long news desk. In the upper right corner of the screen, the semitransparent TVTV logo revolves like before.

“And now for football.” Meredith turns to her right. “Jake, we hear it was quite *greasy* on the Surleigh pitch earlier tonight just as the storm hit,” she leads.

A young hooded sports reporter appears standing on a concourse underneath the stadium. The screen caption reads:

SURLEIGH GREASES GLOBBED
YOBS 5–2 IN “GRUNGE” MATCH

You’re not a diehard fan of the sport but are interested in how the local teams might be faring. You stand, turn up the volume, press 3DHOLO, and immerse yourself in the broadcast.

“That’s right, Meredith,” Jake replies. “Yobwell’s footballers staggered onto the pitch an hour late Friday night for their grudge match with Surleigh after the club’s chartered coach was stranded for three hours on the notorious M375 ‘loop from hell.’ They found themselves literally mired in traffic when a large lorry overturned and spilled its used cooking oil near Hanover Manor, causing trailing vehicles to slide into a massive, slimy pileup.”

Ah yes, you recall, those “great rolling beasts” Mildred, Savannah, and Christopher complained about on the broadcast you watched back home. And this on-scene reporter, who you’re now seeing up close, this Jake guy, he looks just like *The Hollywood Reporter* dude you saw in the UFO story. Does Jake have an American twin brother?

A player now appears in the shot. A chyron reads, "Liam Hamstoke, Yobbler Captain."

"We couldn't get any traction whatsoever," says Hamstoke. "Me and the lads got off and tried to push but ended up falling down and getting quite mucked up."

The camera returns to Jake, who narrates highlight clips now being shown. "After the match began, Yobwell's troubles continued. Surleigh striker Denny Doorwort headed home a winner in the twenty-fourth minute as Yobwell goalkeeper Reggie Spift had his vision obscured by globs of congealed oil dripping from his dreadlocks." A close-up shows the blinded goalie wiping grease from his eyes as an opponent's ball rolls harmlessly between his legs for a score. Jake now reappears. "Apparently in response to the Surleigh jeers, Spift then dropped his pants." The camera moves right to reveal the player in question, his face mud-splattered, his dreadlocks drenched and greasy looking. The chyron reads, "Reggie Spift, Yobbler Goalie."

"That's nonsense," the keeper says. "I'd just been struck hard on the hip by a foreign object hurled by those Surleigh rowdies. Was only checking to see if there was a mark."

Match highlights continue. The storm has struck, and mud-soaked players are shown slipping and falling all over the pitch, some kneeling and trying to stave off uncontrollable vomiting. Jake continues: "The Yobs rallied valiantly, equalizing in the fifty-eighth minute on a penalty kick by sleek German import Horst Glock, then seized the lead briefly when striker Bruce Sherlock headed in a beaut two minutes later."

You're impressed by the publican's technical skills. *But, wait, Storyteller, how did he get back up here afterward?* ***Amazing, isn't it?*** *You're no help.* ***Oh, be patient, you'll find out soon enough.***

Jake continues: "But the rest of the second half was pure disaster as two goals apiece were struck by Surleigh midfield stalwarts Cyrus Twoffley and Donald Ewart."

Yobwell manager Reggie McCabe is now captioned and shown in a close-up defending his side's collapse. "The lads were quite nauseous at the end. Throwing up all over the field and each other. That cooking oil was nasty stuff. Feeling a bit off myself."

Reggie too! Storyteller, he was down there and now back up here? ***Amazing, isn't it?***

On-screen, Jake concludes his report with, "Well, Meredith, it's become quite a slippery slope out here, so I'd better head out for drier spaces. Back to you."

Michael, the male anchor, apparently has a related story. "Hooliganism, which historically has marred Surleigh-Yobwell matchups, was not in attendance tonight." A shot shows empty stands on one side of the field. "Surleigh supporters looked across the pitch and found their Yob counterparts absent from the fray. It seems the visitors' club bus got lost on the motorway and eventually delivered the notoriously hard-drinking Yobblers to the wrong match. Thomas Sutherland, team bus driver, is here to tell us about it."

Your jaw again drops as Thomas appears on camera, standing outside the stadium, where the roar of the crowd inside is accompanied by loud samba music. Again, you're perplexed by the time disparity between tonight's match and your encounters here in the lobby and upstairs in the bar and pub a short time ago.

"Ha! Storyteller," you call out loud. "Did they all teleport back or something?" ***No, they did not . . . on this occasion.***

On-screen, Thomas says to Michael, "The drunken Yobblers were in a highly confused state when they staggered into an international friendly between top clubs representing Thailand and Brazil." Thomas pauses to smile mischievously. "They were given a hugely warm welcome by both sides, but really didn't know what to make of the Latin dancing and carnival atmosphere."

"I'm sure they didn't," Michael replies with a knowing smile of his own. "Thank you, Thomas."

Savannah reappears in the lobby and joins you outside the holographic stadium where highly inebriated Yobblers are attempting samba steps with several of the locals. Laughing out loud, she says, "Ah, dancing and football, two of my favorite things after moto." She then joins the dancers in a furious cha-cha.

Finally, she pauses and gazes at you. "Sorry, still no luck finding the Frenchman and sorting out your room . . . Say, if you'd like to go somewhere tomorrow," she says huskily, handing over a small walkie-talkie, "or whenever the weather clears, use it to summon me. I can have a motorbike out front in three minutes' time. Or a touring vehicle, if you prefer."

With that, she departs.

You fiddle with the device Savannah gave you—a charcoal-black unit with G, R, D, H, B, and P labels over depressible buttons. They probably stand for GARAGE, RECEPTION, DINING, HOUSEKEEPING, BAR, and PUB. Pressing G triggers a prerecorded message from the same voice you heard on the PA, the concierge's. "Chauffeuring service is not available at this time due to the storm and conditions of the road. We deeply regret any inconvenience." Pressing any of the others produces either a busy signal or an intermittent ring that is never answered.

A commercial break has ended and a new story begun. You walk over to stand behind the news desk between the two anchors. "Turning now to events transpiring earlier today," Michael says as the screen caption now reads:

LARGE REWARD OFFERED FOR DOGNAPED ROTTWEILER

"A local pet owner is offering a sizable cash reward for any information leading to the recovery of his stolen pet rottweiler, Crunch, which was taken from a farm in Flogway Down just outside of Nuttey between eleven thirty p.m. on Wednesday and five thirty a.m. on Thursday."

The camera briefly displays a LOST DOG poster with Crunch's face prominently displayed. The snarling rottie wears a black patch over one eye.

Ah yes, Storyteller, the dog they were talking about in the road rage story the other night. The leader of the pack. ***Bingo!*** says an elderly gentleman with a strong American accent. ***Is it vital that you notice every detail and try to make connections? Yes siree, Bob!***

Tired of standing, you collapse the room-size image and return to the sofa to watch in normal mode. Michael continues, "Owner Nigel Wanton is concerned for the thieves' welfare. Crunch, who is about ten years old, has a nasty temper, he tells us."

Wanton, a balding middle-aged man with droopy eyes and a sad expression, now appears in a scene at his farm. A tall forty-something reporter is extending a microphone toward him. "He's a bit blind in the left eye, and if they approach him on that side, he'll likely snap off an appendage," says Wanton. "He's only got three legs, so he's sensitive on that topic as well, most particularly in the company of urinating dogs. He's also not in the best of moods if not fed sufficiently."

"You must be frightfully worried," the reporter sympathizes.

Replies Wanton, "I am, but frankly, I'm more concerned about possible lawsuits."

The shot returns to the male anchor. "To hasten the dog's recovery, Wanton says he is prepared to offer a modest reward to anyone able to give information leading to Crunch's safe return, including the dognapers themselves."

"The nappers themselves! Really, Michael?" His coanchor has interrupted to express her genuine surprise.

"Indeed, Meredith. Moreover, Wanton stated that if the abductors had already been bitten, he'd be open to negotiating a lump settlement that would cover the ransom they presumably want, damages for any injuries suffered, and expenses the thieves may have incurred for Crunch's care during his incarceration."

"I'm simply speechless," Meredith says, shaking her head.

The camera quickly returns to Wanton for a closing comment. Looking forlorn, he says, "I'd like to avoid litigation at all costs."

Michael reappears with a bemused expression. Meredith is still shaking her head.

"Well, we shall certainly keep a sharp eye cast on that story," Michael says as an illuminated "The Village News at 11" graphic spins into view, settling just below the news desk.

Meredith nods and smiles, then looks directly at the camera. "That concludes our broadcast for April first. We do hope to see you back tomorrow. In the meantime, dear viewers, don't get too fooled out there!"

From the top of an end table, you pick up several pages of what looks like a fax transmission or a computer printout. It's the newspaper from the local village. The masthead says *The Village Journal*, with the subheading *April 1 Afternoon Edition*. The main headline reads:

THE ICE AGE COMETH? CLIMATOLOGISTS FEAR EARTH SOON COVERED BY GLACIERS AND PERMAFROST

The wire-service story is an alarming account of a recent worldwide meteorological conference at which leading experts in the field predict the coming of a new ice age—despite the global warming trend. New weather satellites, recently positioned, have revealed this impending catastrophe. One of them is shown hovering above the Earth in the photo that accompanies the story. It's scary all right, and you wonder why you had not previously heard of this momentous development in climate change.

On the next page, Lord Hanover's "Looking at Art" passage is repeated in the Thought for the Day column. You stand up to stretch and walk around. Coming to a halt in front of the fireplace, you gaze at the painting above the mantel. "Uh-oh," you blurt out, detecting movement. Slowly, the pastoral scene begins to move. Hills and valleys and farmhouses blur as the picture morphs into the image of Arthur Hanover. Your uncle's face comes into clear focus. His lips begin to move.

"Someone was in your room and locked your door when they left. I've arranged to have it unlocked. Quickly, go now!"

CHAPTER EIGHT

The painting morphs back to its original scene. You glance around—nobody. Crossing the lobby and walking down the left hallway, you try the first cottage door. Locked. Continue on to the second. This one's unlocked.

You open the door, spy your luggage and briefcase, and rush over and confirm that your passport, currencies, and airline tickets are all there. On an oak desk, several documents are laid out next to a gold key with a green-turquoise sapphire at its base. A bottle of wine is bucketed in a wrought-iron stand. Nearby, a video phone's blinking red message light prompts you to press the button. On-screen, the face of a middle-aged male sporting a dark brown bowler appears.

"Hallo, sir or madam. This is Franklin F. Farnsby from *The Village Journal* calling. We're seeking confirmation that you are Arthur Hanover's heir apparent, and that you've already arrived and taken up residence. If you receive this message and are in fact that person, would you kindly get in touch with us. We are prepared to offer a handsome sum for an exclusive interview—ah, but on second thought, if you are who we think you are, I don't suppose money would matter much, would it? And if not, I seriously doubt we'd be prepared to pay anything. Oh dear, I'll have to sort all this out and call you back! Sorry to be a nuisance."

Chuckling, you examine the wine bottle, *Aligoté de Bouzeron Bourgogne*. There's an illustration of the Manor House in the center of the label and the inscription "Special Reserve of the Hanover Estate, February 29, 1978."

You flip through the title pages of the court ruling and official reports from the genealogical societies. Lord Hanover's letter refers to four sets of documents—there are only two. The will and the deed are missing.

According to the papers, your uncle's official death and burial certificates arrived from a sanatorium in Switzerland. The blood relationship between the two of you has been legally certified. You note that the court went out of its way to characterize all the data it received—tissue samples, DNA profiles, and laboratory reports—as "incontrovertible evidence" that you, the heir apparent, and your uncle are, "by every modern medical and scientific measure," related.

"Storyteller, how did they get my samples?" you call out. ***We're looking into that***, an elderly male with an Irish accent replies. "I thought you folks knew everything that's happened, happening now, and going to happen." ***We don't always know everything at the exact moment. Often, we are required to turn to it and review multiple scenes. Be patient.***

There are separate findings from Britain's most revered genealogical organizations, certifying that your uncle never married or sired offspring. There are no other possible claimants. In addition, the estate taxes are paid, there are no outstanding debts, and he hadn't sold off any of his titles.

There's so much paperwork—forms if you want to register the title, others if you want to disown it. There's a copy of every twentieth- and twenty-first-century Acts of Parliament relating to "hereditary" and "life" peerages. Yours is a rank near the top of the pecking order. You take out a pen and underline it on the list:

1. Duke, Duchess
2. <u>Marquess or Marquis, Marchioness</u>
3. Earl, Countess
4. Viscount, Viscountess
5. Baron, Baroness

You realize from your prior research that you've got a hereditary rank that can be passed on and entitles entry into the House of Lords, where you can make speeches, be eccentric, harangue your fellow peers, and hurl insults and rejoinders. Terrific. But what to do about the missing documents? Of course the chef took them, using that dinner tray as a prop and a pretense for entering your room.

Right now, though, you're exhausted. In the adjoining room is a welcome sight—a king-size bed. You don a pair of brand-new silk pajamas you purchased on your pre-trip shopping spree, climb beneath the quilts, and lay your head on an oversized goose-down pillow—pure luxury.

You expect to immediately fall asleep, but too many thoughts are still buzzing around. Like how Farnsworth and the rest probably weren't left a penny. The butler surely feels that his family's long service entitled him to at least something. As if this weren't stunning enough, he's probably worried that you may even decide to put him out of a job. Worst of all, there's nothing he can do to prevent this.

Or is there? Is this your real-life manor mystery—the heir done in and the butler did it? And to think about it—you followed Lord Hanover's instructions to the letter: Not a single person you know knows exactly where you are. Or why you came.

Frivolous thoughts enter your head: When Bruce's pub reopens tomorrow night, will you fit in? You're not great at karaoke. Better stick with easy ones like "Michelle" or "My Way." You've just inherited all this wealth, yet here you are fretting about social skills. Maybe it's true what they say about money making no difference. At the end of the day, you're still the same old you.

"Right, Storyteller?" ***No, not here. Not now. You're now the new you! Enjoy.***

Will Savannah be able to drive us around tomorrow? Mildred, Thomas, Reggie, Penelope—why didn't they ever come back? Lord Hanover, will he appear often, as in the painting, and how did he do that last trick anyway, if he's dead? Who unlocked the door? Did they take the other documents? Who around here can I trust?

"Storyteller, can things get any stranger?" ***Of course they can—and of course they shall! But as I said, enjoy!***

A chime signals a phone call. You throw on a robe and stumble into the drawing room, where you see the red message light again blinking. The caller looks Indian and speaks with a strong accent.

"Good evening. Evan Aesheed here. Terribly sorry to call so late, but we're in a bit of a panic. I'm an associate editor of *Burton's Peerage*. In preparing an entry for you in our next edition, I'm afraid we've drawn a complete blank concerning your background. To be perfectly candid, we don't even know your name, where you're from, your ethnicity, your age, your gender, and, therefore, whether we should list you as a marquis or a marchioness. And we've absolutely no idea of any deeds you've done. It's vital that you inform us on these matters. Our deadline is fast approaching, and the court records in your case are sealed for the time being. I'll try to reach you again later. Thank you for your assistance."

You crawl back in bed, musing that if *Burton's* can't get back in touch in time, they can always make something up. But still, you're unable to sleep, so you roll over to the nightstand and pick up the TV remote to see what's on at this late hour.

Not much. Eventually, though, you do find a *Monty Python* rerun on Netflix and settle back to enjoy their zany slapstick once more. You start to watch but don't get very far into their Spanish Inquisition skit before, unexpectedly, you hear loud footsteps tromping toward your door, filling you with dread. Slowly, the bedroom door swings open.

It's Farnsworth! In costume! He's wearing a red galero, red robe, black boots, and holding something long and silvery. A weapon? Your dread intensifies, but somehow you manage to speak.

"Mr. Farnsworth! How did—"

"Silence," he commands. "Tonight, I'll ask the questions. You'll supply the answers."

The butler quickly dashes across the room, rolls a desk chair to the side of your bed, sets a small gooseneck lamp on the nightstand, and then plops down in the chair. He leans forward menacingly. "So! You claim to be Arthur's sole heir? So! You have journeyed to England to lay claim to his title and fortune? Well, we shall have to have a conference."

You are petrified, unable to move. Your heart is pounding. Farnsworth switches on the lamp and swivels its neck toward you. The white-hot light illuminates your face, nearly blinding you to your inquisitor. But you do see his silhouette putting on what appears to be thick leather gloves, which increases your panic twofold.

Dear God, Storyteller, what's he planning to do? No reply.

"So, thought you could just skulk off tonight with no explanation of who you really are, eh, Masa?"

You shut your eyes tight. Lowering and shaking your head no, you stammer, "My name's not Masa."

Your interrogator is undeterred. "What's that? Your name's not Masa? Don't give me that. Here at Hanover Yard we aren't so easily put off. You're in the hands of Inspector James L. Farnsworth, Flying Squad, Special Manor House Investigative Division now, me boy. Of course, at this hour, or any time, actually, *no* one expects the Manor Inquisition!"

From behind him, you hear a shouted line from the program, "*No* one expects the Spanish Inquisition!" followed by a burst of canned laughter. Farnsworth turns the glaring lamp away from your eyes. Your fear slowly dissipates. This scene is no longer so frightening; in fact, it's starting to seem comical. Is the butler trying to scare you out of your wits or leave you in stitches? Or both?

This is crazy, Storyteller. Still no reply.

"Inspector" Farnsworth resumes his line of questioning. "So talk, Masa."

"My name's not Masa."

"It is now." Farnsworth adopts a softer tone. "So talk, Masa Ginza. Or we're going to sit here until you do, stopping only for tea and bickies at about three. No choccy Hobnobs for you, though. And no milk or sugar in your tea, either."

More laugh tracks from the TV. The inspector elevates an arm and adjusts its glove before going on. "Yes, it's the new England, and now that we're divorced from those lily-livered Jerrys at the European Union, impostors like you will learn just how tough we've gotten. After tea, you'll lie right back in that bed until you talk, or until six o'clock rolls around, when you'll be confined to another room—dark, dank, dreadful, and far below—with nothing but BBC 1 to watch. No Sky TV and Channel 4. And no bloody Netflix!"

Again, the canned laughter.

"But, Mr. Farnsworth, I don't think—"

"You don't *think*? We at Hanover Yard don't give a tinker's cuss what you or, for that matter, what Amnesty International or what the Human Rights

Watch or what anyone else *thinks*. Now, are you going to talk, or do we have to get really tough?"

From the TV, more laughter, eerily in sync with your live interrogation. In the distance, you hear studio applause and the *Monty Python's Flying Circus* theme that closes the show. Farnsworth switches off the lamp, and you blink several times to readjust to the now dimly lit room, illuminated solely by show credits rolling up the screen.

But not only is the show over, Farnsworth has vanished as well. Slowly, you rise from your bed and walk tentatively into the living room to check the door. It's locked. Your sigh of relief, though, quickly turns into a worrisome realization for which you seek counsel.

Farnsworth is entirely unhinged. He might do anything, right, Storytellers? Several faces appear, all with puzzled expressions. Finally, one of them says, ***We've no idea what you're talking about.*** *But he was just here, questioning me.* Says another, ***We saw nothing of the sort.*** And a third, ***You'd better get your rest.***

Guess you'd better, as you collapse back into bed completely exhausted.

CHAPTER NINE

You have no idea of what time you awaken, but you don't feel like you slept at all well. Is it morning, or already afternoon or evening? Last night—was Farnsworth really carrying on in here, or was it all only a dream? Or maybe one of Lord Hanover's Disney-inspired apparitions?

An elderly Storyteller appears. ***None of the foregoing, I'm afraid***, she says. "Okay, Madam Storyteller, what was it, then?" ***The bar snacks perhaps, but we're not certain.*** "Why not?" ***If you experienced hallucinations, your visions would be outside our range of perception. Sorry.***

No idea what that means, but you do remember feeling somewhat aglow after munching on the gelatin.

There's no shower, just an antique bathtub, a washbasin, and a mirror in the water closet. You unlock your living room door and step into the foyer to find a breakfast tray, coffee and teas service, and bucketed champagne on a provisions cart, which you roll into your living room. The message button is blinking again. Piped-in harpsichord—perfect morning music—surrounds you. You lift the cover on the tray to croissants, bacon and sausage, eggs benedict, friands smothered in mushrooms and béchamel, assorted jams and jellies, and fresh fruit piled high. The spread is a welcome sight. Chef Noël really did make an effort.

One thing, though—you hope the food and drink are safe to consume. Still, it wouldn't do to starve. You sample a croissant as you retrieve your phone messages. There are three. *The Village* reporter and *Burton* editor have called again, urgently requesting interviews, followed by a message from a striking redhead. She speaks in an upper-class British accent:

"Hello. Are you there yet? My name is Cynthia Rollinsby. My brother Roland and I urgently wish to speak with you. Our father, Dennis Rollinsby, was your uncle's best friend. We already know that no one can call out from where you are. We'll continue to try and reach you. In the meantime, for your own safety, we caution against experimenting with any of our father's devices should you run across them. At least not until we've had a chance to speak with you. We'll call again. Good day."

Not sure what to make of that. Something related to Hanover's appearances in a painting, perhaps? You finish breakfast, then get up, intending to run bath water. As you near the bathroom, you hear your uncle's voice calling, "My beloved child." You roll your eyes, muttering, "Here we go again."

Lord Hanover, looking chipper, is there in the mirror. "If you've already found the gold key with the red jewel," he says, "use it to enter and explore the other rooms within your quarters. It is essential that you learn their contents, and there is something you must find, which you will later need. It appears to be an ordinary thing, yet it is very special indeed. Good luck!"

His image fades in the wisps of steam. You'd like a bath, but first you'll have more tea and think about your uncle's latest appearance. It occurs to you that this place may be some kind of funhouse. Or maybe some sort of real-life game is at play.

"Storyteller, any thoughts?" Says an elderly voice, ***Remember how inspired Lord Hanover was by Disneyland?*** "Go on." ***He may have been intent on transforming this place.*** "So I just relax and enjoy the rides and attractions?" ***What have you got to lose?***

You nod in agreement. Returning to the matter at hand, though, you confirm that your room key's inlaid jewel is green, not red. Since there is another entrance marked The Cottage, there's apparently more to your suite than you've seen so far. And Uncle just said there's something in there you need to find. Checking the hall and seeing no one around, you test your key on the other door. The notches and grooves line up, but it doesn't work.

Back inside, the piped-in music is interrupted by the concierge: "The butler has informed me that the Manor House Art Exhibition, scheduled to open to the public today, will, regrettably, be unattended due to the inclement weather. He reports that the condition of the road makes the manor unreachable by car or carriage and therefore recommends the staff acquaint themselves with the newly hung works when they are free from their duties. Carry on."

You mentally cross off sightseeing with Savannah from today's activities. With an ear cocked for the phone, you quickly unpack, then double-bolt the front door and enjoy a long soaking bath. Afterward, clothed in a luxurious robe with the Hanover Manor monogram, you feel great.

Eventually, you head for the lobby, determined to get some answers.

Nobody's around. You tap on Farnsworth's door. No answer. Same with the concierge's. Since the spa is just down the hall, you try its door and literally step into a different world. Cool jazz piano and saxophone plays softly, and the decor and furnishings are modern in soft, muted colors. Several wide-screen TVs are mounted on the ceiling and tilted forward for easy viewing. The sets are all muted, but on one of them you see Michael and Meredith breaking for commercial. The promo featuring the naked lady riding in circles atop a diminutive white pony is replayed.

Notices on bulletin boards tell of upcoming golf tournaments, procedures for checking out croquet equipment and reserving tennis courts, and suggested scenic walks about the estate, and there are sign-up sheets for skiing and camping excursions in the North of England and Scotland. A formal-looking placard lists dress codes to observe when using the saunas, jacuzzis, and swimming pool.

This is a huge facility you're standing in. The beige-violet carpet is striking. You see numerous seating areas with round glass tables surrounded by chairs with cushions in bright floral patterns. Ideal spots for daytime reading, sharing tropical drinks and conversation, or perhaps a game of whist. The room is alive, though no one is present. At least it seems so until: "Oh, good, finally found you." The new arrival is Mildred's grandson, who impressed you mightily the other day on the local news. Dressed in woolen knickerbockers, long stockings, and an oversized sweater, he's holding an artist's sketchpad and a plain white box.

"Hullo, I'm Christopher. Been looking all over for you. Grandmother asked me to bring you this." He hands over the box. "Says to remind you to *always* keep your valuables with you whenever you're out." He gestures toward the box. "Inside, there's a gadget Uncle used to carry about. Haven't a clue as to how it works. Perhaps you can sort it out."

"Sure. I'd be glad to take a look," you tell the boy. "But don't count on—"

"Oh, I'm sure you'll do your best." Christopher arches an eyebrow and grins slyly, as if he hasn't told you quite everything. The two of you engage in getting-to-know-you banter. Christopher says he and his parents live in London, but he's just this year gone off to boarding school in France. He spent his entire childhood at the manor and returns every chance he gets. Right now, he's on midterm holidays. You tell him you saw his appearance on the news recently. "They hoped to have you back—did they?" you ask.

"Twice," he replies. "I'm always chuffed to talk on about plants and such."

You get the impression that your uncle and he were very close and that Christopher misses him terribly. He refers to him as "Uncle," though technically Lord Hanover was not his uncle. And you're aware he recently lost his real grandfather too. You recall reading a glowing tribute to Mildred's husband, the late George Simmons, the manor's head groundskeeper for forty-three years. He was credited with having brought the estate's gardens to the forefront of the great residential grounds of Europe. You leave this sensitive topic by expressing curiosity about that sketchpad Christopher is carrying.

"Would you care to see some of my drawings?" His expression, already bright, is now glowing with enthusiasm.

"By all means," you enthuse. The boy flips to a page and hands you the pad. The pen-and-ink drawings demonstrate incredible talent. You immediately recognize the style of the characters as being from the Winnie-the-Pooh series. However, there's something else here, and soon you grasp it. None of Christopher's illustrations are of the actual characters. Yet they're so similarly drawn in that distinctive line style that you see what the lad has brilliantly achieved; he's simply added to the cast of Pooh Bear and all the rest. They're perfectly accented, here and there, with a mere clump of grass, a small stand of trees, or the bare outline of a hillside in the minimal style of the originals—settings that leave everything else to a child's unbridled imagination. Christopher has added an English bulldog, a squirrel, a raccoon, a beaver, some birds, plus, unaccountably, a South African aardvark to the Pooh menagerie. "So, Christopher, about the aardvark—"

"Well," he explains, "it was the first one in the library's encyclopedia when I started the drawings years back." Then, thoughtfully, he adds, "Besides, what's a tiger, a kangaroo, and an elephant herd doing running loose in England anyway?"

"I see your point." You observe that Milne's main character is Christopher's namesake.

"The whole name," he says, with another grin. "Both my parents were gone on the books." But now he's got to dash. "I have to tell my grandmother that I found you."

You get the feeling he'd like to become friends, and in parting, you invite him to find you anytime he's free. Nodding and smiling, he departs.

You sit down and open the box. One item is a passkey in the form of a plastic card for the pool area. There are numerous brochures and pamphlets about sightseeing attractions in the Lake District. You've also received a "Drinks on the House" invitation for tonight. The last item, apparently the one that Christopher added, looks like some kind of remote controller. But what it operates is by no means clear. It's a cream-colored handheld device, grooved along its top surface and rounded at the edges. At one end is a large glassy blue orb raised from the base. When you touch it, it lights up, emanating a soft bluish-white glow and emitting a low techno-sounding hum. Remove your thumb, and the sound ceases and the illumination fades. There's no switch or any other buttons. No power supply or cord or any compartment for batteries—it's all one elegant piece.

You walk over to the pool entrance to try out the plastic card. The door slides open. You step onto the tiled floor on the upper level of a double-deck facility. The area is silent, save for the intermittent hiss of steaming jacuzzis. Below lies an Olympic-sized pool with potted palm trees between circular columns along the length of its right walkway, floor-to-ceiling picture windows, and columns along the left. You descend the steps.

In one of the far corners is an electromechanical timing device that swimmers apparently use to train or compete. The hands of the timer are frozen at fifty-nine minutes and four seconds—a reading that suggests training for long-distance events.

*The receptionist, Storyteller? **Who else?** Is that time important? **Every detail is important.***

At the steps, a flat marble ledge extends out from the wall, on which is a potted flower. Lying beside it is a small, shiny object. It's a gold key identical to your room key but embedded with a ruby. Mission accomplished. That was easy.

You're about to mount the tiled steps when you see her. Adrienne Van Scoy is planted at the sauna entrance, her arms folded. She's tall, striking, imperial—and even more beautiful than her hologram. You call out, "Hello there," and wave, but receive only a look of disdain.

"It is not permitted to enter this area in the sort of attire you're wearing," the concierge informs you. "You can be provided with approved swimwear." She pauses, switching on a cold smile and adopting a clipped, rehearsed tone. "And if there is anything else we can do to make your stay with us more pleasant, see Miss Stratton at the front."

You start to mumble an apology, but the woman walks away. You cannot believe the rudeness, the condescension. Stephen may have been right; this could be someone to avoid like the plague. You hope not, though. Her beauty took your breath away.

Returning to the butler's door, you knock, but again there's no answer. The world's greatest doorman is absent from the main entrance, and the receptionist is not at her post either. You think you could run this place better than whoever's in charge. Maybe soon you'll give it a go.

With nothing to do, nowhere to go, and no one to talk to, you may as well look at art. There's a still life of a bowl of fruit hanging on the wall beside the kitchen doors, so you begin there. Upon inspection, you judge the painting to be too still, too lifeless, unworthy of public attention or any more of yours. In the spirit of the game you seemed to be trapped in, you flick the remote at the offending bowl. It's still there of course, but the device does something different. The electronic hum doesn't stop even after you release your thumb. Nor does the orb dim. Then you look back at the painting. The scene inside the frame is *changing*. It fades to reveal Chef Noël speaking and gesturing to someone you cannot see. "*Tenez, monsieur*. I have already looked everywhere, examined every single thing, checked all the belongings, so I am certain our guest does not have them."

Off-camera you hear Farnsworth asking, "Did you search the cottage's kitchen and living room?"

The chef is quick to reply. "*Certainement*! But our visitor cannot get into those rooms. The deed hidden in there? *C'est impossible*, I swear it to you, *monsieur*." With that, he walks out of camera range while Farnsworth mutters, "As far as Arthur was concerned, nothing is impossible."

The will and the deed, Storyteller. So they don't have them either. ***Seems like it.***

The scene remains silent and empty, as the two have presumably walked away. In another moment, the screen fades back into the painting. You look at the remote admiringly. So that's what it does—incredible. But is this the gadget Rollinsby's daughter warned you against? You check yourself for any ill effects. Ridiculous—all you did was watch two guys talking. Nothing has happened to you as far as you can tell. So off you go in search of more "wired" works of art.

Nothing happens when you aim the remote at the Rembrandt or the Reubens that hang across from your cottage doors. Or when you target the Renoir, the Monet, the Manet, the Cézanne, or any other Impressionist works that line the walls all the way down to the opposite end. Too bad nothing hangs outside the offices of the butler and the concierge.

Returning to the still life, you find the painting dissolves as before, but this time the camera pans the chef's empty office. It reverses, returns to its original vantage point, and shuts off automatically as the painting is restored. Okay, you're beginning to get this. Encounters with your uncle were prerecorded, but scenes involving others occur in real time.

You make a quick reconnaissance of the second floor and find there are many more paintings upstairs than below. You wonder if any were prepared as observation posts. But your observations are interrupted by voices coming from the stairwell—Farnsworth's and Van Scoy's. You do need to speak with the butler, but now's not the time.

You spot a small alcove with roped-off velvet drapes near the rear of the rotunda. Voices and footsteps signal they've reached the landing and are now starting to climb the remaining flight. You rush over, untie the sashes, and yank the sides closed just in time to slip behind the curtain, tugging to align both ends. The voices draw nearer.

"How are you going to—" Farnsworth starts to ask but is quickly interrupted.

"Just leave it to me, James. The less you know, the better—there's bound to be some sort of inquiry."

"Tonight, then?"

"I just told you—don't ask."

"Are you using Noël's brigands?"

"How many times, James . . . How many times must I—"

The voices recede, and you can no longer discern their speech.

CHAPTER TEN

You risk a quick peek out. Upon reaching the landing, the pair enter the library. A few moments later, they pop back out and promptly descend the stairs. They never looked in your direction. Your prospects with her aren't looking so good. She could well be one of those femme fatales like in some movies you've seen.

Possibly, says a young female who looks to be in her twenties. ***She's lovely, though—well worth taking the risk, don't you think?*** Then, sounds the voice of someone distinctly older. ***There are so many reasons, on so many levels, why you should not pursue a relationship with the concierge.*** *Why not?* ***To begin, she is in your employ.***

Once again, your Storytellers don't agree, but you're relieved you weren't discovered. You sit down on a bench in the alcove. This puts the entire rotunda, plus the hallways branching left and right, within your field of vision. In your diary, you make a diagram of the paintings on both floors, placing an *X* inside the boxes of the hot ones downstairs. Ready now to test the ones up here, you first try one of the pictures outside the pub—and hit a bull's-eye. The painting fades to reveal Bruce Sherlock behind the bar, polishing glasses. He's singing "Blinding Lights" accompanied by synthesizers from his karaoke machine. The landlord is quite a crooner. He lifts the pint he's poured himself and offers a toast, "To Savannah, letsgetpist!"

Nearby, a landscape painting turns out to be a window to the room labeled His Majesty's. But you get only a silent pan of an empty room. Seems a shame nobody ever uses this well-appointed suite. But now, suddenly, the camera detects movement and begins to whirl. It focuses on the massive bed in the center of the suite, then zooms in to reveal a most unexpected sight: nestled under the covers with only his grinning face popping out is Chef Noël!

The chef calls out, *"Dis Google! Jouez de la musique française sexy."* To which Google replies, *"Certainement! Jouer de la musique française sexy."* The room fills with a lovely female vocal—the melodic equivalent of a heavy erogenous whisper. You recall reading somewhere that French songs can be more stimulating than kissing and touching. Even while standing outside the scene, you find that soft susurration to be highly titillating. You wonder what might happen next and cast quick glances in both directions, but no one is in the hallway. Guiltily yet pleasurably you resume your new role as manor voyeur. Now, detecting more movement, the camera whirls to His Majesty's entrance, where the door opens, and—*OMG!*—Farnsworth himself emerges.

Storyteller, this is getting good! A young man from above laughs. ***We're riveted.***

Farnsworth explodes: "Good God, man! What are you doing here? How did—"

The chef holds up a remote controller identical to yours except its orb is red. "Waiting for you, James," Noël coos. "I am *always* waiting for you." Noël pauses, then smiles seductively, lowering his voice to a purr. "Now—or later? We could talk first if you like." He flutters his eyes and assumes an exaggerated coy expression.

The butler is momentarily speechless. Finally, he lowers his voice and says softly, "Noël, I've told you before, I'm not quite ready. I'm confused. I don't know what to think at times."

"But *at times*, James, you think you want me. It is true, yes?"

"It is true," Farnsworth sighs. "Sometimes I do." He motions toward the connecting door. "But then there's her."

Noël rolls to the side and beckons him. "Won't lovers revolt now?" He sings along to Édith Piaf's classic *"Johnny, Tu N'es Pas Un Ange."*

You're no angel, the storyteller translates. *Yowza! Storyteller, did you catch his palindrome?* ***We did not. Too engrossed in the scene itself.***

Farnsworth, his eyes unexpectedly vulnerable, approaches Noël. The way the light hits him, his face glows and reminds you of any number of young men in Renaissance paintings with halo effects.

But from farther down the hall, footsteps sound, causing you to step back, close the scene, and seek partial cover by crouching down behind a giant floor vase. Then you see *her*, gorgeous as always, striding up the hallway toward Her Majesty's room. She's holding some document and reading intently. Van Scoy never looks up. She unlocks the door and enters the suite. Glancing over, you find three wood carvings depicting fairy tales mounted on the rotunda wall outside Her Majesty's room. The middle one works. The camera finds the concierge knocking on the adjoining door and calling out, "James, are you in there? I have found something and must speak with you." She receives no reply.

You quickly dash back to His Majesty's portal, where you catch sight of powerfully built and scantily clothed Noël leaping out of bed, grabbing his chef's outfit, and scampering toward the bathroom. The camera whirls and finds Farnsworth heading toward the connecting door. "Sorry, dearest." He struggles to catch his breath. "I was a bit indisposed just now."

"James, are you well?" you hear her ask. "Your voice sounds terribly odd. And why is this door locked?"

The butler looks worried as he replies, "Adrienne, I am feeling slightly out of sorts and require a brief respite. Can we converse later on, perhaps at tea?"

"Of course, darling," she replies. "Lie down and get some rest. We'll speak later—I've much to tell."

You depart the area, hoping this tryst you just witnessed blossoms into full-fledged romance—less competition for *her*.

Humming happily, you resume your expedition. None of the other paintings—including the Native cluster with the old man in its center—in this immediate section is active. Nor are companion carvings on the wall fronting the library. You turn right and walk to the end of the hallway and take aim at an Italian explorer in front of the whisky bar. Another bull's-eye. You catch the tail end of a conversation Mildred Simmons is having on her walkie-talkie. "That's right, Savannah. Starts right after dismissal . . . Oh, I know you can hardly wait." The housekeeper pauses to listen, then says,

"No, I haven't a clue. I'm certainly not about to directly inquire, either—or snoop." Again, she pauses, then asks, "What does Reggie think?" She listens for a moment. "Reggie thinks he's straight—and a straight arrow to boot!" Another pause. Mildred giggles. "Oh, I see. All right then. It's a secret between us girls. Bye-bye, love."

Somehow you get the sure feeling they were talking about you. You wonder if they know about Noël. They probably do. But how about Farnsworth? They probably don't.

Ha ha, Storyteller, it's a secret between us boys. ***Heh heh. Good one!*** *Were the two ladies talking about me?* ***What do you think?***

You now realize your chauffeur may have an interest in you. *Adrienne or Savannah, Storyteller? This could get complicated.* ***Oh, but it will! Enjoy!*** *But these are manor servants. It may not be appropriate.* ***Indeed, but if your intentions are honorable . . .***

You continue exploring. Near the bar entrance, the sea captain and the cavalryman are normal. But the third painting is live. The scan reveals shelves of bound volumes, a long conference table around which a dozen or so thick leather chairs are placed. There's a fireplace with statuary and sculptures on its mantel. You activate the scene several times because there's so much to see. And it's lucky you do—on your fourth or fifth try, the camera, detecting something, whirls. Penelope Stratton is facing you, balancing a large book with one hand while holding something folded in the other. She begins talking to herself, musing aloud. "He told me to keep it safe until I'm asked. Well, easy to remember that time and pace. Oh, Penelope, what a clever girl you are."

Oh, Penelope, how incredibly beautiful you are. But you don't know about her—she seems awfully young. A teenage girl appears. ***True. But you might be surprised.*** *Really? Does she go out with guys my age?* ***You'll never know unless you ask.***

Penelope inserts the papers in the book and ducks out of the scene. Too bad—if only she'd kept congratulating herself, the camera would have stayed focused on her, and you might have seen if and where she shelved the book.

Farther down the hall, the sixth painting is hot. Nothing, however, is going on at this end of the library. You don't expect the remaining three portraits to be wired, since they face the same area, which proves to be the case.

Then, in a burst of insight, you rush back to the bench where you left your briefcase. You pull out the manor brochure and reread Lord Hanover's "Looking at Art—Behind the Canvas" passage. Now you're certain. If interpreted literally, it spells out the purpose of your remote: "For in art, there can always be another realm that lies beyond the painted image, one that is alive with people and their stories—if only one knows how to truly see and hear them." And: "Therefore, I am only rarely concerned with the painting itself, but instead focus on its ability to evoke that other world behind the canvas and the frame." Blah, blah, blah—but brilliant!

You only got the remote working by accident, so you're resolved to read the paper more closely from now on. But your reverie is interrupted by another PA announcement: "The butler has asked me to announce that he has completed his evening inspection of the premises and finds everything to his satisfaction at present. The day staff is therefore dismissed and may retire to quarters. The main gate of Hanover Manor has been shut for the day and will remain so throughout the evening. Therefore, it will not be possible to leave the estate by motorcar this night. Good evening."

People will soon be coming. You'd better get out of here.

Back at your room, Thomas Sutherland has left a note saying he hopes to see you tonight in the pub. He challenges you to a game of darts. Both journalists have continued to try and catch you in—and lamented to your vid mail every time they couldn't. Cynthia's brother, Roland, has left an urgent message:

"Roland Rollinsby here. You must not touch a beige-colored, hard-shell controlling device with a green orb that my father was experimenting with in the Hanover labs." You have to laugh—you're not radioactive, your face didn't fall off. He's even got the color wrong.

Someone has dropped off the afternoon edition of *The Village Journal.* The top headline reads:

FOUR COUNTY SWIMMERS ADVANCE

HEARTIEST CONGRATULATIONS to the following county residents:

K. O'Leary, PCHS; R. Snowcross, St. Albans's; P. Stratton, HM; W. Tewksbury, King's College. These swimmers have all qualified for the regional level of competition in the All-England Endurance Trials. They now join a select group to compete in the Channel Championships next summer. The event is expected to bring together the best long-distance swimmers from around the world.

That probably explains the timer you saw.

You grab a remote and turn on the large wall-mounted TV in your living room. It looks as though you've caught the tail end of the weather report. The meteorologist concludes with, "Meredith, I'm afraid there'll be no letup in this storm for the rest of today and likely tomorrow as well."

The screen caption changes to:

DOGNAPERS REMAIN AT LARGE

Says Michael, "Coming up after the break, we'll update the Crunch saga all you viewers have been calling and messaging on social media about since we broke the story yesterday evening. So stay with us."

A short run of ads concludes with one that sparks a pleasant memory of your stopover in New York. It's a Fountain of Youth Mushroom Serum ad, and—whoa!—there they are: Megumi, Reiko, and Namiko, the kimono-clad trio you met on the Fifth Avenue sidewalk and spotted the next day at Piccadilly Circus. Today, they're decked in party dresses and performing the cosmetic company's jingle under a neon enlargement of the mushroom at the center of its logo. They're singing and dancing around like exuberant teens in a TikTok video.

The newscast resumes with Michael leading in: "Crunch, the fearsome yet beloved rottweiler and unofficial mascot of mini-Henge who was recently abducted in Flogway Down near Nuttey, remains in the hands of his captors despite dogged attempts by local authorities to locate farmer Nigel Wanton's handicapped pet. We go now live to Witless Station, where Chief Constable Thomas O'Bannion is updating the press on the case."

The chief stands behind a podium and speaks into a mounted mike. Reporters are seen crowding around. "We've hunted the nappers high and low but haven't found them. I can assure the public that all officers are unrelenting in their searches. We've given this case our highest priority."

A nearby reporter from *The Village Journal* asks, "Chief O'Bannion, many local pet owners are now voicing concerns that Crunch's seizure may signal a new wave of crimes against canines. Are their worries warranted?"

O'Bannion nods gravely in agreement. "They are," he says. "If nappers are now even nabbing elderly, three-legged, half-blind doggos, then I'd say all owners should remain particularly vigilant until we can bring the perpetrators in."

The shot returns to the news desk, where Meredith picks up the story. "Crunch's owner, Nigel Wanton, is with us via Zoom and says he has more pressing concerns at the moment: Wanton fears Crunch's captors may sue him . . . Good evening, Mr. Wanton. Tell us, why are you worried about legalities at this point?"

Wanton looks nervous. "It's been past forty-eight hours now," he says. "I cringe o'er what havoc Crunch's wreaking in unfamiliar surroundings. I'm just back from the courthouse to see if anyone's filed. So far no one has, but I'm holding my breath."

The camera abruptly switches to Michael. "Meredith, sorry to interrupt, but Mr. Wanton's fears may be well founded. I've just been told that the station received a call, two minutes before broadcast, from the alleged dognapers, who promised they would soon send a letter outlining their demands."

The shot returns to Meredith. "Who are these nappers? What will their demands be?"

You'd like to watch more, but now it's time to freshen up and change into one of your chic new outfits and hit the pub. It will no doubt feel foolish lugging your briefcase up to the party, but that's how it's got to be.

You plan to ask Cynthia or Roland Rollinsby—if you can ever catch one of their calls—to call home for you and let people know you're in England and everything's fine.

Fine—except the manor phones don't work; there's no Wi-Fi or cellular reception; you're locked inside the weirdest place imaginable; the butler, chef, and concierge are plotting against you; and you're half wondering if your deceased uncle has lured you into another dimension.

But this seeming real-life episode of *The Twilight Zone* or *Fringe* notwithstanding, you'd like a message relayed to everyone back home—that you're having a wonderful time and you wish they were here!

You take a long, final look in the mirror and think you look fabulous in your burgundy sports coat, untucked light-gray dress shirt, and tailored navy slacks. Ready now to head upstairs, you stand and open the bedroom door but are stopped cold. From somewhere, the theme from *The Twilight Zone* actually begins to play over the PA followed by: *Whoosh, whoosh . . . whoosh, whoosh, whoosh.*

"Draw, O coward!" You cast a sidelong glance and are terrified to spy Chef Noël standing in front of the fireplace, wildly wielding a rapier.

"How did you . . . Why are you—" you stammer.

No answer. Noël extends his sword, shouting, *"En garde! Oh! Souffrez-vous d'aibohphobie?"* while cavorting around the room pantomiming an intense duel with an imaginary foe—but not advancing in your direction.

Storyteller, what does it mean? ***Aibohphobia? Fear of palindromes.***

You laugh. This bizarre scene hardly seems scary now; instead, it's wildly comical. Just like when "Inspector" Farnsworth barged in and conducted an "interrogation." Is this also a dream? Another Pythonesque skit? Spiked tea?

"Chef Noël, are you okay? What's going on here?" you call out.

Now, switching to English, the chef declares, "I was once known as Zerimar Ramirez! Reviled did I live! Evil I did deliver!" With an exaggerated final flourish, Noël places his sword in a scabbard attached to his belt and smirks triumphantly. *"Est-ce que tu comprends?"* ***Do you understand?***

No, you don't, but you've had quite enough of this absurd charade, so you retreat to the bedroom and lock the door. You'll sit on the edge of the bed and try to collect your thoughts while waiting for the crazy chef to leave or this crazy waking dream to end.

After a quarter hour or so, having heard no more sounds from the adjoining room, you unlock the bedroom door and tentatively peer out. No sign of the mad Frenchman.

"Hey, Storyteller, what in the world was all that?" ***Ailihphilia perhaps?*** "Very funny. Is that a real word?" ***Yes, 'tis, and means just what you'd expect!***

Okay, so the chef simply adores palindromes, just like that BBC manor tour narrator said. Maybe you should follow that teen Storyteller's advice and start employing some whenever you can. Get, and stay, on his good side. After all, he's in charge of your meals.

We can help with that if you like. "How, Storyteller?" ***We can feed you palindromes you can say to the chef.*** "Sounds great, thanks." ***Our pleasure, my lord.***

CHAPTER ELEVEN

To sounds of an acoustic guitar and an Irish harp, upon entering the Falstaff, you're greeted by Reggie McCabe, who's smiling broadly and carrying two pints of ale.

"Least we could do for keeping you cooped up all day."

You clank steins. Reggie is interested in hearing about your meeting his former colleagues at your New York hotel. You fill him in. "So, what caused you to take a job here, of all places?" you ask.

Reggie grins. "That's easy. Here at the manor, I can don a different costume every day!" He turns slowly to give you a full view of his white doorman's coat and puts on a hat with Peninsula embroidered in gold. "From Japan," he says.

Above the bar, you see a giant television. The sound is muted, but you can see the conclusion of highlights of a recent cricket match between India and Pakistan. The screen caption now reads:

GROUP FORMED TO OPPOSE SUMO-THEMED PUB

Bruce rushes over saying, "G'day, m'lord." He then summons everyone nearby. "Mates, you gotta see this. Saw it on the afternoon cast. It's epic." He unmutes the TV and presses the 3DHolo button to blow up the scene to room size. The camera returns to the familiar female anchor as the TVTV logo revolves in the top right corner, tonight in crystal blue. Meredith begins: "A local citizen's group is trying to legally block a Japanese restaurant chain from turning the historic three-hundred-forty-year-old Hog & Snout pub into a sumo-themed restaurant complete with sumo ring. Our reporter is at the scene. Jake, what's all the fuss about?"

The football reporter is back, this time standing under the Hog & Snout's protected entrance with another man as heavy rain falls. "Meredith, standing beside me is local resident Cyril Twoffley, who heads up the newly formed Preserve Independent Gastronomy Society or PIGS for short. Mr. Twoffley, tell us why you felt compelled to undertake this protest."

The camera moves to a close-up of Twoffley, who looks like an average bloke. "It's a crime, what they're doing. Once the Hog & Snout's gutted, there won't be a decent place left in these parts to lift a pint in," he complains.

"There's always the Falstaff, mate!" Bruce shouts as he comes out from behind the bar and walks into the scene.

Reggie is laughing uproariously. "If the stout and the stew were decent, I wouldn't mind having a go. Think they'll have any lady wrestlers in diapers?" he asks you. Before you can say you doubt it, Savannah Reddy sidles up to the bar. Reggie fills her in on the news story, saying, "Savannah, I challenge you to a match on opening night."

The chauffeur laughs. "I hope you wrestle better than you shoot pool, Reginald," she says. "Otherwise you may as well hand over your wallet here and now."

On-screen, the shot returns to the reporter, who continues, "Mr. Twoffley has indicated his group will soon mount a public relations campaign to warn local residents of the pitfalls of dining in a sumo atmosphere. Isn't that correct, sir?" Jake extends his mike.

"All that gorging and slurping and stamping about—it'll be a horror show," Twoffley scoffs. "And you won't catch any self-respecting bloke prancing about in a big diaper, either."

Michael, the coanchor, appears. "Thank you, Jake. We have in studio Osoroshi Saigo, who is Seibu Corporation's liaison for this project and begs to differ." A giant still of a lone sumo wrestler crouched with one foot elevated prior to the beginning of a match forms the backdrop.

You nudge Thomas, saying, "They're pretty decent anchors. Personable. Don't sound angry all the time."

Thomas nods and replies, "Superior to most cable news."

On-screen, Michael greets his Japanese guest. "Good morning, Mr. Saigo. Tell us why your company thinks the time is right for a sumo pub here in The Village."

The camera shifts to a young, smartly dressed Japanese businessman brimming with enthusiasm, now seated between the two anchors. "We've studied this district quite closely and feel it is the right place," the corporate spokesman begins. "We are sure that people here will find the *chanko-nabe* stew sumo wrestlers eat appetizing. It goes very well with beer, as any wrestler will tell you."

Michael continues, "We've heard you plan to import a licensed referee and a stable of young sumo wrestlers to get things rolling, in hopes the locals will soon join in."

Saigo-san nods in affirmation. "Yes, Michael, and may I state that Seibu has no plans to change the name of the restaurant. We believe Hog & Snout to be very appropriate. Finally, I'd just like to add that, since karaoke has succeeded so grandly in British pubs, why not sumo?"

"Thank you, Saigo-san!" says Meredith. "Meanwhile, Twoffley and fellow PIGS have vowed to boycott indefinitely the refurbished and repurposed Hog & Snout. So Seibu Corporation may have a real fight on its hands. Perhaps the warring parties should settle this in the ring!" The broadcast then goes to commercial.

"So, Savannah," Bruce teases, "what color's your diaper gonna be when we collide?"

Savannah drains her mug and plops it down with a mighty thud. "Sherlock, you wouldn't last a minute with me." She pauses and smirks. "In any physical contest."

Watching them go at it, you're reminded of when you first searched for her back home and found her on a Harley-Davidson fan site. The clip showed her leaping off her bike just after she'd crossed the finish line to win a competition, the camera zooming to a close-up as she peeled off her helmet. Despite her grease-stained face—easily offset by that billowing hair and white smile, not to mention the perfect figure and flare of sassiness—she had looked and sounded like a Hollywood actress. "I enter, therefore I win," she quipped to a reporter who'd shoved a microphone in her face and asked a dumb question. Now the doorman is challenging her to billiards tomorrow night and proposing a sum. She accepts. You wouldn't bet against her.

The next arrival is Mildred Simmons, who sits down beside you and orders two pints. She leans over and whispers, "Mind your valuables, dear," nodding in the direction of your briefcase. Mildred is matronly all right, but simply gorgeous, too.

You're amazed at how soon you're staring at another drained stein. Feeling a bit wobbly, you turn to greet Thomas Sutherland, who is out of focus but seems to be extending yet another pint, saying, "You're empty. Can't have that. Positively against pub regs."

You start to ask about the fan bus mishap, but the sound of scattered applause preempts Thomas from explaining in detail. "Had a wager with Reg and Bruce," he calls out as he's moving toward the stage.

"That you wouldn't deliberately transport your own rowdy fans to the wrong match?" you guess. Thomas grins and flashes a thumbs-up.

Onstage, Bruce is announcing that his song will be fellow countryman Tame Impala's classic tune, "Yes I'm Changing."

Wow, that's the song Stephen/Rollinsby played on the drive up. What a coincidence! From above, a youthful Storyteller shakes her head and scolds, ***How many times must we tell you?***

Savannah hums along, smiling at you. You think Bruce's rendition is quite good. He finishes to enthusiastic applause and returns to his post. Pints are poured, steins clinked and drained. The conversation is lively as more members of the manor staff arrive. You attempt to initiate a bit of conversation by inquiring about current attitudes toward smoking in pubs over here. Sherlock shakes his head and points to an exit that leads to a smoking lounge outside. "Mate, before His Lordship put a stop to it, we had two sections for the patrons—'Smoking' . . . and . . . 'Chain Smoking'!"

Good one. From above, several Storytellers are chuckling too.

Bruce now informs everyone that he has an amusing story to share but it must be acted out. "Who's game to perform this one?" he asks the crowd. Numerous hands are quickly raised.

"Bruce does this often," Savannah whispers. "Actually, they're usually quite good. Everyone here loves role-play."

Bruce hands notecards to the "cast members," instructing, "Mildred, you're the narrator. Reggie, you're the tourist. Thomas, you're the constable."

Thomas scans his lines and says, "Oh, this looks like fun."

Bruce motions toward the karaoke stage, saying, "Mildred, you stand off to one side. Over there, perhaps." She moves to the edge of the stage.

"Perfect," says Bruce. "Now, Thomas, you pretend you're in your constable's car." Thomas sits on a pub chair, pretending to drive. Bruce goes on. "Reggie, you're the tourist." Reggie sits on a chair, placed ahead of Thomas, in an imaginary car with his hands on an imaginary steering wheel.

"Places, please," calls Bruce. "And action!"

Mildred: "A London constable pulls over an old man driving a convertible in Piccadilly Circus with three penguins in the backseat."

Thomas makes a noise like a siren. He gets out of his "car" and walks up to Reggie.

Thomas: "Good day, sir. Might I inquire about those penguins?"

Reggie: "Your Honor, I spotted these penguins a ways back, looking all lost and forlorn. I picked 'em up."

Thomas: "Well, sir, you should take them to the London Zoo straightaway."

Reggie: "Jolly good, Officer. I'll do it this minute."

Thomas returns to his place.

Mildred: "The next day, the bobby spots the same motorist in the same convertible with the same penguins—only this time they're all wearing sunglasses."

Thomas gets up from his "car" and waves Reggie's "car" over again.

Thomas: "Sir, I distinctly advised you yesterday to take those penguins to the zoo!"

Reggie: "Officer, I did. Had a wonderful outing, too. Today, we're headed for the beach!"

Savannah, you, and the others laugh and applaud. Reggie, Thomas, and Mildred take bows.

"Hey, Bruce, that was great!" you call out above the hum, adding, "I read that joke just last week and here you've staged it."

"Rolling Stone?" he asks.

"Why, yes," you reply. "The issue was at least forty years old. What a coinci—" You catch yourself, not wanting to be reprimanded from above.

"By the way," you say to the barkeep, "I was exploring today. I'm impressed at how the estate observes the tradition of reserving bedchambers for visiting royalty."

But instead of offering a nod of agreement, Bruce cracks up. "Hey, Savannah, you've gotta hear this!" he yells. When she and others move within earshot, he turns back to you. "Let's have that last bit again, please."

You repeat your observation, wondering about the cause of all the hilarity. Thomas clues you in. "After receiving the official notification of Lord Hanover's death, Mr. Farnsworth, fully expecting to be named as inheritor, committed the single most outrageous act in memory."

"Oh tell us, do tell us what he did!" Savannah, Mildred, and several others recite in unison. They sound like a Greek chorus.

Says Thomas, "He abandoned his quarters, moved into his deceased master's bedchamber."

Savannah leans in and whispers, "Farnsworth's playing for keeps." Hearing this, you get a slight chill.

Bruce takes up the tale. "He didn't stop there. One day later, he gave Ms. Van Scoy permission to occupy the adjoining suite."

Yes, and the door between them is usually left unlocked. Not a good sign, right, Storyteller? ***Indeed, it is not . . . Well, as far as you're concerned.***

"One that had not been used in decades because His Lordship never married," adds Mildred. The housekeeper then mimics the concierge out loud: "The manor, the money, the title—I want it all!" She receives a round of applause.

She may get her wish, you muse. Her precious James may not be the man she thinks he is. Maybe you will "decouple" them, heh heh.

Storyteller, if she wants it all, she might have to include me! ***Really? I'd be quite keen to see that!*** calls a young British female overhead with a sultry voice.

Thomas continues, "The entire household was appalled, but it was our heroes McCabe and Sherlock who expressed everybody's outrage with a brazen deed of their own."

"Which was?" sings the chorus.

"At first opportunity, our lads rushed local craftsmen onto the scene and had them mount those tasteless His and Her Majesty markers on the bedroom doors." Now that you think about it, those plaques are slightly different from the others, and a bit tacky.

"But if sarcasm and humiliation were the intended effects, it failed utterly," Thomas concedes. "His and Her Majesty didn't blink an eye."

Grouses Reggie, "Neither of them has said a word . . . nor made any attempt to have them removed."

"One suspects they rather like them." Everybody nods in agreement with Mildred's assessment.

All the backbiting makes you realize how deeply alienated the staff is from management. Your uncle has urged you to win the servants over. Tonight seems like a good start. You consider yourself fortunate to have not known all this earlier. Might have decided much differently—and not necessarily for the better as far as their collective well-being goes. These people may be counting on you.

"Penny for your thoughts, dear—and mind your belongings." Mildred nods at your briefcase, which has been accidentally kicked over.

Your welcome party rages into the night. There's conviviality, crowd hum, and constant bursts of laughter as your circle widens with new faces, and more stories of life in the manor are recounted. The karaoke plays nonstop. The balcony air is blue with cigar smoke. You lose miserably at darts. Your appetite returns, and you demolish a bowl of Irish stew. You appreciate that no one treats you special beyond the occasion of celebrating your arrival.

Storyteller, they all seem to know and accept who I am, yet no one pries. ***They like you, my lord. It's obvious.*** *I like them all too.* ***They know. It's obvious as well.***

Bruce is clearly smitten with Savannah and all night has been challenging her every chance he gets. You see that he's about to take another shot. "Tell you what, Savannah." He props his elbow on the bar. "Next sunny day, take the Harley, give me any other hog in your garage, and I'll race you down to the village—loser buys dinner." He offers his hand to seal the wager, proclaiming, "Back in Oz, they called me 'Heaven's Angel' when I rode through the outback."

Savannah rolls her eyes and tosses her head. "Sherlock, trust me. You never want to know what they used to call *me* back in CA." Everybody around them nods in the chauffeur's direction to award her "points" in the exchange.

You decide to break into the topic. "Savannah, just how many motorcycles do you have?"

She smiles and points at you, saying, "No, it's how many *you* have . . . Bruce, do you mind summoning our holographic friend?"

"Not at all, mate." Bruce reaches under the counter and retrieves a small wireless microphone. "Okay, Google, show Manor Bike Collection."

On the far side of the pub, an entire wall revolves, revealing a hidden partition—a curiously imposing sight, as it consists of a floor-to-ceiling grid in which twenty or so black fans are embedded. The fan blades are beaded with pulsating LED lights. They all start to spin at once, which produces a whooshing sound and propels a cool breeze into the immediate vicinity.

A riot of pure color envelops the space in front of the wall. The blades spin faster and faster. Finally, the palette achieves clarity and resolves into a single image—a giant, gleaming motorcycle slowly revolving 360 degrees in midair. Absolutely mesmerizing. You recall seeing displays like this at trade shows, but never in an intimate bar. And never so close, so large, and in such high definition.

Bruce hands Savannah the mike. She clips it to her lapel and uses her voice to narrate and her fingers to enumerate, allowing ten seconds or so for each image to slowly turn and vividly display.

"You've been viewing the Ducati Monster . . . Okay, Google, two, the Honda . . . Okay, Google, three, the Kawasaki . . . Okay, Google, four, the BMW . . . Okay, Google, five, the Harley." She pauses and smiles, seemingly to check if you're suitably impressed. You are. Not only by the bike holos but also by her vocal control of their display.

"Then there's Lord Hanover's antique collection." Savannah itemizes them as well. "Okay, Google, six, the Pierce Single . . . Okay, Google, seven, the BMW R60/2 . . . Okay, Google, eight, the Indian Board Track Racer . . . Okay, Google, nine, the Harley Two-Cam Racer. And now, my personal favorite. Okay, Google, ten, the Captain America Chopper . . . Okay, Google, pause." The last image freezes.

"Easy Ridin', Santa Cruisin' Savannah!" quips Bruce.

She face-palms, murmuring, "Somebody give me a break."

Now a couple of facts from your research pop into your head. "Savannah, did you know the motorcycle was invented here? And the first motocross—"

"Camberley, Surrey, in 1924," she says, finishing your sentence.

Impressive. "So did you study motorbike history in college?" you ask with a teasing smile.

"Nope, I majored in philosophy at UC Santa Cruz," she replies. "Also played a lot of soccer. Back then, I was a rootin' tootin' Banana Slug. But my professors didn't quite know what to make of me." Savannah contorts her expression and twirls an index finger beside her head in loco mimicry.

You laugh out loud. "Okay, so you were a little crazy back then, but what do you mean they didn't know what to make of you?"

"They were always probing," she replies, "asking me what I intended to do, to decide, to find, to become on my life's journey. How will I ultimately be, in their terminology, 'arranged' philosophically?"

You're not surprised. "Of course—they're philosophy profs," you tell her. "Their questions are bound to be deep; that's what they do, right?" Still laughing at her loco gesture, you press on. "How did you answer them?"

Savannah assumes a serious demeanor, points up to Captain America, her nose theatrically in the air, and adopts a snooty tone. "I told them I had long aspired to become . . . 'a motorist.'" Savannah, awaiting your reaction, repeatedly winks while simultaneously flicking her tongue.

Bruce leans over, smirking. "We just got Savannah's patented French wink, mate." He straightens up, adding seriously, "But I can attest that she's also a highly skilled mechanic, enjoys tuning and servicing all the vehicles as much as operating them. His Lordship often raved about this."

You nod, further impressed. "So, Savannah, tell me more about your soccer days. Been seeing TV news reports about Reggie's and Bruce's recent misadventures."

Before she can answer, Bruce interrupts, "Savannah manages the women's team down in The Village. They always win their league. Tell him, Savannah, your secret, what you learned at uni."

"Back in college, I played on the men's team," she replies matter-of-factly.

Your jaw drops. "Wow! Savannah, you must've been really, really good."

"Good enough," Savannah replies with a crooked smile.

"Did you start?"

"I did."

"You must've been a stud."

"I was."

"Scholly?"

"Full ride."

You fist-bump her. "So, what's that secret Bruce was alluding to?"

"Oh, that one," she muses. "Yeah, when I took over the team here, I told the ladies that, from here on out, we would only play our preseason friendlies against men's teams. We often scrimmage against Bruce's and Reggie's squad."

"It really works well—both sides gain," Bruce affirms. "We show her sheilas what ferocity on the pitch feels like."

Adds Reggie, "They show us what unselfish team play looks like."

Savannah reflects. "In most matches, Bruce and his guys knock my gals around pretty good. But when league play officially starts, guess what I've got?"

Reggie answers for her. "A battle-tested, pissed-off pack of rough-and-tumble lassies is what she's got. Ready to storm the pitch and take out pent-up frustrations on unprepared opponents."

You can really picture such a strategy. "So, Savannah, what's the name of your team? Can I, like, buy a jersey somewhere?"

Again Bruce pipes up. "That's another thing Manager Reddy does quite differently. Every season, she changes the team's name, colors, logo, signage—everything! And no namby-pamby mascots like Molly Magpie or Finnick Fox either. This past season they wore all black, had a ghostly football as a logo, and called themselves The Haunting."

You laugh. "And before that?"

Says Savannah, "Our uniforms were two-toned—a decayed lime green and a putrid brownish yellow. Somewhat unnerving to the opponents, particularly when they first read the print on our jerseys."

You take the cue. "Which was?"

"Toxic Slime!" Bruce calls out, then guffaws. "And the year before that—Gang Green!"

Savannah looks at you dreamily. "Wanna know next season's?"

You nod eagerly. "Sure."

"We'll don navy blue for the night sky, trimmed in silver for a lustrous full moon," she says. "Our logo will be a high-heeled, diamond-encrusted glass slipper kicking a white ball patterned with navy-blue stars." She pauses to peer directly into your eyes. "We'll call ourselves Midnight Passion . . . What do you think?"

You're all in on the logo—and on her. "Love it! Your fans will love it too. That's definitely the jersey I want. You know, support the team." Savannah smiles broadly, stands, stretches, then says she's got to find Mildred. As she saunters off, she turns and blows a kiss in the barkeep's direction. And then a second one in yours. You're thoroughly charmed by your chauffeur and can't wait to take some spins with her. Maybe you should give good ol' Bruce some healthy competition for her affections.

Giddy at the prospect, you swivel around to fully take in your surroundings. The pub's atmosphere is warm and inviting. An upright honky-tonk piano takes up one corner. Everywhere you look there is wood—the kegs, the exposed ceiling beams and solid arches overhead, the thick cedar posts planted throughout the bar area. The columns are posted with notices, menus, adverts, coasters, plaques, and photographs—the same as bars the world over. There's brass everywhere, on the railings, stands, and the woodwork trim. And of course that magic holographic wall.

The shelves and mantels are lined with beer steins and seidels, along with whimsical figurines, souvenirs, and curios. Except there are no clocks. You ask Bruce what time the bar closes. "When the last one standing ain't," he replies with a wink. He staggers in circles, flailing his arms to mimic the final customer collapsing. His hand brushes against one of the posts, knocking loose several tacked-up paper items, which flutter down on the counter. You help him gather the name cards and pin them back up. He hands you one that has apparently caught his eye. It's a snazzy card with a 3D logo from Japan. One side is in Japanese; the other, English. The person listed has an unusual job title.

"Bruce, do you know this company, imagine21?"

"Vaguely recall hearing about it," he replies.

"Ever meet this Megumi Kondo, with the job title, untitled-7?" you ask.

"No, but, until recently, there were lots of workers here from abroad, including many Japanese. Could have been one of them." Bruce thinks the company name is intended to evoke the new century. "So maybe this imagine21 is some kind of tech outfit," he says.

Reggie peers over your shoulder and examines the card, saying, “I think it invites me to imagine what it would be like to be twenty-one again—but know everything I know now. If that’s the case, whatever this outfit’s selling, I’m buying!” He bangs his cup resolutely.

Mildred’s impressed. “There’s an entire sentence embedded in a single word, imagine21. I do like economy of expression. Wish more writers would tidy up!”

“Oh, I know *all* about i-two-one,” Savannah says devilishly as she edges toward you. “Trust me,” she continues, now fixing your gaze with a smile and an arched eyebrow, “I’ve been . . . all . . . the . . . way . . . through it.”

Though you have no idea what to make of that remark, you sense from the group’s expression that they all get what she means. You decide not to press.

Thomas figures the word is a copywriter’s creation but says he’s attracted to its creative typography and poetic absence of capitalization in the style of e. e. cummings. “I believe the missing space between the end of the alpha and the onset of the numeric is as vast as the universe,” he says. “Yet its omission is the key to the space-time continuum.”

“Huh?” You’re confused.

Thomas gives you a wink. “Remember Newton’s apple? How all Sir Isaac had to do was look at an everyday phenomenon in a certain way—then *bang*, the world’s got gravity? Well, my friend, this one’s even simpler.”

“What’s simpler?” You’re hooked.

“Why, the space-time continuum,” he says. “The inner big bang. No beginning and no end. Circular time flow. Imagine two-one.” The headwaiter bows to his listeners, signifying he’s finished. Everyone applauds.

Bruce snaps his fingers and calls out, “Okay, Google, show i-two-one.” Magically, the logo, identical to the one on the name card but giant-sized, sparkles, then crystallizes into view and begins to slowly rotate—displaying the shiny red-and-blue 3D alphanumeric characters set in relief against a 2D matte silver disk. “Huge . . . huger . . . hugest! Good on you, mates,” Bruce calls in tribute to whoever created holographic projection.

Inspired by Thomas’s space-time riff and the revolving i21 holo, Bruce rushes over to the piano and begins to play. “Roll over, Eye-yin-stein. Dig these physics and views,” he sings. A sizable crowd joins in a sing-along while clapping and stomping their feet as Bruce continuously improvises new verses.

When he finishes, several faces in the gathering turn to you. Apparently, it's your turn to voice your interpretation. But given your intoxicated state, you think you're at a loss for new ideas or words to describe them.

Relax, just listen, say what I say, and do what I project.

It's the mature female Storyteller again, apparently ready to direct your spiel.

You take a deep breath, intending to comply. Somehow, wondrously, you're immediately awakened, highly energized, and thrust into character. Fixing your audience with a peculiar and protracted stare, you call out, "Think I may be one or two, or two and one?" Nobody answers. Everyone looks puzzled. You sound like Hamlet.

Now, act like a deranged person. Roll your eyes. Smack your lips.

So, after another pause, you become wild-eyed, smacking your lips repeatedly. "Indeed, I suppose I could be a forgetful alien that assumes it isn't an alien while mindlessly abducting humans and taking organs."

The audience gasps. It almost seems as though you're now possessed.

You raise your arm up high and jab your finger at the i21 holo. "Or maybe I'm one of *them*—you know, the twos who only come out at the fin de siècle, wreaking havoc at the outset of each new century." ***Pause. Let it sink in.***

Everyone is riveted. There's not a single additional sound throughout the entire pub. You now lower your voice and, while adopting a conspiratorial tone, motion your audience to move closer and listen more intently.

"And, folks, since you weren't around for Y1K, well . . . you . . . just . . . can . . . not *imagine* who turns up when a *millennium* turns. We started arriving three decades ago, and there's many more twosomes on the way—real *Apocalypse Now* joy riders, straight out of Mad Max's wasteland, screeching and howling, and tenfold wilder than the standard-issue centurial ones." Out of the corner of your eye, you spy Bruce silently pumping an enthusiastic thumbs-up to Reggie and others.

Storyteller, thank you. They seem to be enjoying this. ***You've got them. All yours. Now let's give them the big finish! Jump on that bench.*** *And I'm so energized now.*

You leap atop a nearby bench, bang your fist on the bar, and shout, "Or, hey, I might be only one—Nostradamus reincarnate, here to say, 'That's all, folks!'" Then you jump down, dash to an empty table directly under the hologram, lay your head down, loll one arm off the side of your chair, then swivel to fully face the audience. Whereupon you roll your eyeballs, raise a solitary index finger high, and shift your tone to falsetto.

"Or maybe, I'm just the original April fool who arrived just last night." You cackle maniacally then add your middle finger to form a pair. "Or both." Then you quickly hop off, stand straight up, extend both arms, smile fiendishly, and shout, "Am I two or one? You decide."

After a moment, you relax your pose. Your expression returns to normal. Smiling and waving, you turn and bow several times to every corner of the pub.

Thunderous applause. Standing ovation. Jump arounds. Shouts of "Hurrah! Hurrah!" and "More! More!" fill the air. Thomas and others mob you with congratulatory outpouring. "Your soliloquy was as good as any I've seen on a London stage," the headwaiter gushes. "I do hope you'll reprise it one evening for those who had duties elsewhere tonight." Smiling, you tell him you'll try but only if you can remember it.

"Indeed," he says. "Often the price one pays for spontaneity. But don't worry, I've committed it to memory and will write it out for you presently."

"Thank you, Thomas."

Thank you again, Storyteller! ***You're welcome. We didn't know if you'd take to temporary possession. But you were superb.***

There is conversation, laughter, ditties, improvisations, and hip-hop like that all night long, interspersed with karaoke breaks, in which you decline participation on grounds you don't know any of the songs. The interludes give you time to enjoy your new circle's performances and further reflect. You decide "ol' Reg and Millie" would make great grandparents for Christopher. You ask Thomas how well he knows the boy.

"I'm always so busy," he replies. "Scarcely had any chance to make his acquaintance."

"I understand he was quite close to Lord Hanover," you venture.

"Arthur loved having him around, even when he was working," Thomas informs. "That said, I'm sure Christopher has been to parts of the manor that nobody else has and knows things about the place that nobody else does."

"I've read a little about Lord Hanover's inventions," you tell him, "but still don't know much."

Thomas shakes his head. "Nor do any of us; it was always hush-hush," he says. "As was any discussion of his trips abroad. But as I say, Christopher is the one to ask. He's the only one besides Lord Rollinsby who was allowed back in the laboratories."

"Where are they?"

"Just beyond your quarters, actually," Thomas replies.

"What was it like when the manor was getting its theme-park makeover?"

"Extremely busy for me," Thomas says. He relates that there were German and Japanese engineers around for months, with new arrivals occupying guest bungalows as fast as the locals could build them. "Had the full run of the place, they did. In the dining hall, or up here every night singing their silly heads off. That's how karaoke got started here, by the way. And those gentlemen were the origin of Bruce's crack about our former 'Smoking' and 'Chain Smoking' sections."

"How did the two groups get along?"

"Rather famously, from what I saw." Thomas chuckles at the recollection. "The Germans tried their best to sing Japanese *enka*, while the Japanese had a go at all the football songs. They attempted to converse in each other's language, too. But with scant success, I'm told." Thomas places his hands over his ears to indicate how painful the parlando had been.

"They had competitions over which group could make things smaller," Thomas recalls. "The losing side had to pay for drinks and dinner in The Village. The Japanese had devised a new circuit board that could be seen only with an electron microscope."

"So did they win?" you ask.

Thomas laughs. "Oh, they were quite confident they'd soon be treated to a night on the town when they sent the board over to the Germans and asked them what they thought of it, and if they were ready to pay up."

"So did they?"

"Hardly," Thomas replies. "The Germans promptly returned the board with a note saying *nicht viel*, meaning they didn't admire its miniaturization, and, no, they weren't conceding anything."

You attempt a guess. "So, the Germans had their own board, a smaller one, maybe?"

"No, even better," Thomas replies with a chuckle. "The Japanese were puzzled so they put the board back under their microscope. The Germans had drilled three holes in it."

Great story. The pub gets more crowded as staff members just getting off duty begin to arrive. You try to remember the names of all the new faces you meet, but when it gets to be dozens and dozens, the task becomes impossible. Everybody addresses you as "my lord." Nobody asks your name. Which suits you fine.

Finally, at around what you imagine could be close to dawn, after hearing every manor saga from time immemorial, after exchanging armchair opinions on everything under the sun, after sharing antiestablishment sentiments and irreverent asides with Bruce, ol' Reg, Millie, Thomas, Savannah, and with passersby on their way to the john who overheard something that caused them to linger and edge closer to listen to you and the others hold forth or deliver punch lines, finally, after all is said, done, and undone, it turns out that *you*—now alone beside your bar stool—are the "last one standing."

Feeling highly intoxicated and exhausted, you stagger away, raining thank-yous and good nights on Bruce. By golly, stayed up all night until everyone else passed out or went home, you did. By gum, still jet-lagged and confused, outlasted them all, you did.

You turn and weave toward the door and are just about to exit when you snap your fingers, remembering. You dread turning back around because, somehow, you already know.

Your briefcase is gone.

CHAPTER TWELVE

You and Bruce scoured the pub for nearly a quarter hour to no avail. Now you're a wreck, physically and emotionally. You collapse in a booth, forehead in your hands. Numb, you can hardly think straight.

Your passport, currencies, airline tickets—all gone; the vital documents your uncle entrusted you with—all gone. You've still got some small cash and credit cards in your billfold, but so what? You can't get out of the country for the time being. And now you wonder how much longer you'll be able to stay here.

Bruce says he can't vouch for every person who was there last night. But he's sure one of Noël's kitchen staff nabbed your briefcase. "Remember how everybody crowded round in the end?" You do—and feel like an imbecile.

"No worries, mate," Bruce says. "Your crew will see you through this. Give us the particulars, and we'll take it a step at a time. Call your embassy, get the new passport going. Call British Airways, tell 'em what happened. It's a hassle, I know, but not the end of the world."

You oblige by agreeing that it isn't. But you know well what's really at stake, especially in his and Reggie's case; it could spell the end of their manor careers. You ask him to call your room, to pound on the door if necessary if he finds anything out.

"Just get some sleep, mate," he replies. You exit the Falstaff and trudge back to your quarters.

"Storytellers," you call out after entering, "please tell me who took it!" A young man with a bemused expression appears. ***Ah, but you must sleuth the manor yourself!***

Okay, then. Still wiped out but at least functioning, you seize on an idea. You steal a glance down the hallway, hoping to see nobody.

Nobody's there.

You head toward the lobby and mount the stairs. Nobody's around on the second floor, either. You remove the remote from your pocket and aim it at the painting that looks into His Majesty's bedroom. Pay dirt! The camera finds Farnsworth in the midst of a conversation with someone, surely Van Scoy. "The karaoke is abominable. Thank goodness they've shut it off," he says. "Noël and I finally got Arthur's computer set up in my office. But we can't log on because we don't know the password."

The concierge, wearing a full-length periwinkle nightgown in a hydrangea pattern with capped sleeves, steps into the scene. "And you've absolutely no idea what it might be?"

As always, gorgeous. And what a shape.

An elderly woman appears with a scolding expression. ***She's a person, not a mere pretty-pretty or a shape***, she says, shaking her head. ***Anyway, what are you going to do about making her acquaintance?***

Farnsworth shakes his head. "None. We've tried every keyword we can think of, but no luck. We think it's something Arthur would never write down but have no trouble remembering because it's printed or posted somewhere around here. The old man was funny like that. I've been up all night making a list of possibilities."

"Well, better luck tomorrow, darling," says Van Scoy. "I'm turning in. Good night."

Farnsworth steps out of range. You hear the sound of an interior door closing, and the scene darkens as the light is switched off. The painting reappears. You move around the corner to the wired wood carving on the rotunda wall. Your luck holds. Leprechauns and forest nymphs melt into the scene inside "Her Majesty's," where the concierge is pacing while whispering into her walkie-talkie. Now she's listening. But to whom? Definitely not Farnsworth. You're getting nowhere watching her nod, make small sighs of affirmation, and utter an occasional "And so?"

On a hunch, you make a break for the chef's office downstairs. Your luck turns out both good and bad as you catch the tail end of their conversation.

Good, because Noël continues to do all the talking—loud and clear. Bad, because his frantic narration is mainly in French, which at first you can only get the gist of but later, again thanks to your psychic companions, you understand somewhat. Good, because you get confirmation that the chef indeed sent some of his helpers up to steal your briefcase. Bad (and here is where it gets murky) because apparently, they failed, or so the chef claims—he has no idea who got there first, much less where the case is now.

"Souvenez-vous, je suis toujours avec vous, Adrienne." ***Remember, Adrienne, I am always with you!***

Hearing this translation, you're now certain that something is going on between those two—and whatever it is, it's going on behind Farnsworth's back. You wonder if both are secretly cheating but with the same person—the chef!

Storyteller, this is getting so complicated. ***But enticing, wouldn't you agree?***

You do.

Notwithstanding, something more may be happening with the chef that the concierge isn't in on. Or vice versa—a scenario where the chef is telling her the truth, not realizing that she sent her own crew in to steal the case. Or, possibly, one set of flunkies is now in possession of a stolen briefcase, which *they've* lied to their boss about and are now trying to figure out *their* next move. You shudder considering the possibility of minions satisfied enough with redeemable items, who then simply discard or destroy everything else.

Returning to your quarters, you decide to run a bath, but, just when turning the handles, you hear a rustle from the drawing room. Your pulse quickens when you hear it again. Slowly you edge back into the bedroom, inch toward the connecting door, open it slightly, and cautiously peer out.

Nobody's there. But standing upright on the coffee table is your briefcase.

You rush over and open it. Every item is there. Your video phone chimes. It's Mildred, looking highly agitated. She's beside herself over what she says she and Reggie have unintentionally put you through. Her explanation is simple: "Oh dearie, while you were carrying on up there, we 'stole' your briefcase to teach you a lesson." She goes on to explain that they intended to remove it for a short time, then stroll back in and issue a "see how easily this could happen" reprimand.

"It's okay, Mildred," you reassure her. "All's well that ends well."

The housekeeper still looks highly distraught, her eyes darting back and forth as she continues: "As soon as we got outside, however, Reg sensed that we'd been shadowed by a couple of 'snafflers,' as he calls them, who were now barring the pub entrance. I hurried away with the case and, thank goodness, reached here safely."

"What happened to Reggie? Is he okay?"

"Oh, trust me, he's tip-top," Mildred replies. "When he returned, he said there'd been a bit of an altercation but not to worry, for it was the snafflers who were worse for the wear."

You're still puzzled. "So how did the briefcase get here?"

"Christopher brought it back," she says. "He said he knows a secret way to your room. Again, Reg and I are dreadfully sorry."

You wave her off. "Mildred, it was a lesson I needed to learn. Besides, it turned out lucky, don't you think? You two swiped it before they could."

The conversation is cut short by a knock at the door. A grinning, solicitous Noël has brought breakfast. *"Bonjour, monsieur!"* he greets heartily.

The chef seems much too eager to sweep through your room to find the perfect spot to set down the tray. You take it out of his hands while deftly moving him back toward the door, all the while lamenting about the weather and how cooped up you are. You set the tray down and lift the lid as a Storyteller suggests a frivolous, palindromic response.

"Evil olive?" you say, pointing to the garnish atop the omelets.

Noël's expression registers surprise—and approval. *"Aucun, je vous assure monsieur."* A Storyteller quickly translates: ***None, I assure you, sir.*** Noël pauses, then asks, *"Comprenez-vous le français?"*

Do you understand French? "None, I assure you, sir," you reply straight-faced. The chef nearly cracks up as he beams wholehearted approval and departs.

But soon, there's another knock. You open the door and beckon Christopher inside, telling him, "I just spoke with your grandmother. Any trouble getting here?"

The boy's eyes grow wide. "I was accosted by ruffians. Men of the kitchen, who came in the night." His expression tells you he thinks you're falling for his dramatics, but then his nose begins to twitch.

You, too, catch a whiff of the aromas coming from beneath the stainless covers. "I take it that's my cue to offer you breakfast."

"Umm." Christopher smacks his lips. The two of you eat heartily but hardly make a dent in the provisions, even though you couldn't get enough of the scones and fresh mushroom omelets garnished with delicious black olives—none of which looks or tastes "evil."

After breakfast, Christopher departs, saying his grandmother has chores for him to perform. You were sleepy before, but three cups of that odd-tasting yet addictive pink tea changed that—you're fully charged. There's a new message on your machine.

A distinguished-looking gentleman pops into view. "Hallo there. This is Harold Hornsby from the Genealogical Society phoning. Sorry to bother, but I'm afraid we're a bit stuck this morning and could do with some help. We're trying to reconstruct the Hanover family tree, so to speak, and find we cannot continue until we learn if one of your parents was Lord Hanover's brother or sister, or if he was in fact your father. Or your brother—and if so, forgive me, but are you half or whole? If you could possibly shed some light on these matters, we would be most grateful. I'll call again. Thank you."

It's amusing in a way. First, the guy from *Burton's* asks if you're a he or a she, now this Hornsby character's wondering whether you're "half or whole." But it is disturbing that he thinks Lord Hanover is perhaps your father. Sounds like they're confused and don't know what to think—so they're raising any and all possibilities. But still, you've never come up with an explanation for this constant "my beloved child" form of address.

Your room phone chimes. It's Bruce sporting a mischievous grin. "Free after dark?"

"I am. That is, if I can figure out when *dark* is in this place."

He laughs, then says, "Then join us in the billiards room when the day shift's done. Reckon it could even get moderately boisterous if ol' Reg gets his dancin' shoes on! Really give 'His and Her Majesties' something to whinge about!"

"Love to—what time?"

"Oh, right after dismissal," he says. "Heard from Millie you got your gear back. Cheers."

You disconnect and see that a note has been slipped under your door.

I don't want to disturb you, so I'll tidy up your room later.
Here's an odd thing I think you should know about. Early this morning Farnsworth told me to go down to the wine cellar and write down all the dates on the labels of the estate collection and bring the list to him straightaway. Why do you suppose he asked me to do that?

Sincerely,
Mildred Simmons, Housekeeper

You have no idea. But looking over at your estate bottle, you think you might like to see what a sixty-thousand-dollar vintage would taste like. Maybe invite a few of the others to an after-party tonight to share.

You pick up your walkie-talkie to tell Mildred she can do your room anytime, but instead of pressing H, you accidentally push G and unexpectedly find yourself overhearing what seems like the tail end of a conversation between the concierge and the chauffeur. "So what I want you to do, Miss Reddy, is this: make a list of all the vehicles in the garage with their license plate numbers and leave it with Miss Stratton at the front."

"Yes, madam."

"Do this right away."

"Of course, madam."

"I'm counting on you."

"As always, madam."

"That will be all."

"Thank you, madam."

Now that, you surmise, is a completely different tone from Savannah—so respectful, so ingratiating. You wonder momentarily, and unhappily, whose side she may really be on.

When you step out and set down the breakfast tray in the hall, a PA announcement comes on. This time the concierge sounds especially condescending:

"The butler and I would like to remind everyone, particularly our guests, that only approved swimwear may be worn in the pool area. And we would also request that guests returning late from our restaurants and bars proceed quietly through the hallways. Thank you for your cooperation."

What a statement! The nerve of that woman! You are the only "guest" currently in residence. Now you get Bruce's wisecrack about His and Her Majesties whinging on the PA; they've probably been making this same announcement all morning—their petty attempt at psychological warfare.

You're torn between conflicting emotions, but you allow your rage to take center stage. Ha! After you secure your inheritance, we'll see how quickly Ms. Adrienne Van Scoy changes her tune and her tone. Still shaking with anger and embarrassment, you step back into your room and shut the door. Your briefcase is gone. You cast wildly around the room, hoping against hope that somehow you've just overlooked it.

"Ahem," calls a voice from your bedroom. You peek inside. Christopher wags his finger at you, tapping your briefcase. "You realize, of course, that I must inform Grandmother," he says and frowns. He folds his arms. "She'll probably send you off to bed without your supper." With his unruly mop of hair hanging down on his forehead, his shy smile, and the fact that he's wearing short pants and high stockings, he really does look like Christopher Robin reprimanding a semi-naughty companion in the Hundred Acre Wood.

"Well, it's not like I can walk out to reception, request a safe-deposit box, and check my valuables" is your lame attempt at an excuse.

Christopher bounds across the room. "Come along," he says matter-of-factly. "I'll show you how I got in here." He leads you over to the fireplace, puts his hand under the mantel, then lets you feel where a button is. You press it and step back. The fireplace rotates ninety degrees clockwise so that the unit now stands perpendicular to both of you. Peering through, you can see an identical fireplace, likewise rotated, and the room on the other side. It's simple to walk in and press a corresponding button. You watch the fireplaces revolve to their original positions.

With your door securely bolted and your briefcase welded to your hand, the two of you return to explore the new rooms in your cottage. There are two—the living room containing the fireplace, and beyond it, a cottage kitchen.

The living room has a front door, the one you expect that your red-jeweled key opens from the hallway. You show it to Christopher but hold off telling him that you got this info from Lord Hanover in a mirror yesterday. Christopher takes the key out to the hallway to test it, and you start looking for whatever it is that "appears to be an ordinary thing yet is very special indeed."

But here in the alternate living room, there is nothing besides the furniture, the mantel, and the fireplace—no decorations or anything lying loose; nothing on the shelves or inside any drawers. In fact, this room is *too* devoid of everyday objects; somebody's been in here and cleaned it out. Somebody like Chef Noël Elle Léon, who was telling his boss yesterday that he'd thoroughly searched these rooms.

The kitchen displays pots and pans hanging over wood-burning stoves, and wide countertops with an assortment of cutting boards and knives. But beyond all the utensils, there's nothing at all. Anything nonfunctional has been removed. Except for one item—a yellowed paper, thumbtacked to a bulletin board, entitled "Chef Emil's Recipe for Manor House Scones."

Ah yes, Emil, the chef who preceded Noël—the Hungarian who reportedly served highfalutin guests magic mushrooms and mescaline tea.

We adored Chef Emil. You're startled—the voice sounds like a warble not a human one. Now, above you, is a most extraordinary sight—a large cactus plant adorned with a white flower rotating slowly in its center.

"What are you?" you call. ***Breakfast.*** "Okay, Mr. 'Breakfast,' should I worry?" Again the warble: ***Never worry. It never helps.***

Well, your vital signs seem okay, no nausea nor any discomfort so far. Actually, your senses have become noticeably heightened. And now, astonishingly, you're listening and talking to a plant. "Something in that pink tea?" you ask. ***Clarity.***

You take the recipe down as a reminder to bring up the subject of the ex-chef at tonight's party. You'd like to get the full scoop from someone who was here back then.

A recipe for scones—they're sensational here, as you learned this morning. Then a realization hits—Christopher never came back from testing the key.

CHAPTER THIRTEEN

When you head up to reception to see if by chance you can call home, you don't expect to find Penelope. But this time she's actually at her post. She looks perplexed until she spots you, whereupon her face registers a look that you were just the person she wanted to see. She extends a folded sheet of paper, saying, "I think this was left for you, but I don't know by whom . . . Oh, I do wish people would at least sign the notices they leave here . . . It's a list of the manor's vehicles. I'm sure it was made up especially for you."

"But I didn't—"

"Well, if it were me, it would be something I'd want to find out about." Her face brightens at the prospect.

"Miss Stratton," you say to her, "I still can't get any cellular reception, or Wi-Fi."

She shrugs. "It's on in some places, off in others, but I haven't a clue."

"What about the manor phones?" you ask. "Callers leave vid mail but never call when I'm in the room. And I can't call out."

"I'll check on that," she says, rising and heading toward the connecting door to the butler's office, "and get back to you straightaway."

You turn away, unfolding the paper. This must be the list you overheard discussed a short while ago. Apparently, Savannah brought it to the front desk as instructed and left it unaddressed when she could not locate the receptionist. Now Penelope has given it to you. Should you perform a good deed by finding the concierge and politely saying, "Excuse me, but I rather think this was meant for you?" Though it might serve as a pretense for approaching her, you decide to resist the temptation for now.

The length of the list is astonishing. In addition to all the motorbikes

Savannah ticked off last night, the garage has an Aston Martin, a Bentley, a Rolls-Royce, a Lamborghini, a Jaguar, a Bugatti, a Land Rover, a Maserati, a Ferrari, and a Porsche.

Oh dear, Storyteller, I'm at a complete loss over which vehicle to select for today. ***Heh heh. Good one***, says an elderly British male approvingly as you head back to your quarters.

Christopher is finally back and breathless. "Too many people around, couldn't test the key," he explains. "So did you find whatever it was that Uncle Artie instructed?"

You nod and hand him the recipe. "Christopher, did you ever meet this Emil?"

"No, but I've heard many wild tales about the 'Mad Hungarian,'" Christopher replies. "He was very popular with the townies who came up at weekends. It was rumored he served magic mushrooms and mescaline tea at Sunday brunch. We should keep this recipe."

It's been nagging at you all morning, a kind of quid pro quo for all he's shown you. "Christopher, remember this?"

His eyes widen at the blue remote. "You got it working? Brilliant!" he exclaims. You explain how certain paintings in the hallway will turn into a kind of screen on which live images from hidden cameras are rear-projected with sound.

Christopher points to a large blank wall across the room. "Let's pretend there's a painting hanging over there." He presses the remote's orb—and you both nearly jump out of your skin. The wall is illuminated with representations of all the wired art, lined up in three rows of four, similar to thumbnails on websites. Christopher hands you back the remote, saying, "You didn't know it did that?"

"No way." You aim at the top left image, the still life in front of the chef's office, and click. The two conversations you witnessed zoom out to life size and replay as the audio is delivered through speakers you now see embedded in the wall.

Christopher's jaw drops. "Blimey!" he shouts.

You learn to point the remote away when you want to shut down the grid, and that you need only point and press at another image whenever you want to interrupt the current playback and start a new one. You also discover that the system will cycle through whatever recordings are associated with a given thumbnail until you switch to a different one or shut it off. If nothing's been recorded, you get a silent, continuous pan of the room.

There are some puzzlements. Represented here are a painting and a wood carving, both from the second floor, that you thought were not wired. Sure enough, nothing happens when you point and click at them—no recordings or silent pans. "The painting is on the wall of the hallway opposite the library," you remind the boy. "That means nothing would be behind it. Which makes no sense if this is a surveillance system."

Christopher immediately grasps this, adding, "Right. The wood carving is in the rotunda near the library entrance. But that makes no sense, either. Just around the corner, the painting of the Russian nobleman monitors the same scene."

He stands and walks toward the grid, saying, "Another confusing thing—every thumbnail shown is of artwork except two, the mirror in your bathroom, which we now understand, and a top-down view of the swimming pool, which we don't. Nothing happens with this latter image, either, when we try to enlarge it."

"Okay, Christopher, what's your theory?"

"I think it's because you'd previously experienced the event live at its source, your mirror, but not yet at the pool. This grid seems to be no more than a repository of past events." After reviewing the daytime recording of Noël and Farnsworth, the predawn exchange between the butler and the concierge, and the concierge's secret conversation with the chef, Christopher can see that this is serious business.

His knowledge of past manor events elicits more details about the concierge's and chef's machinations—like how they ran off servants that Arthur particularly liked for fear these favored ones might replace them. You get the impression that this young lad is genuinely worried about you, which only causes your uneasiness to return.

Glancing again at the recipe, you're reminded of Chef Emil's proclivities. "But what about those mushrooms we ate earlier?" you ask. "You don't suppose . . ."

Christopher only shrugs, saying he didn't eat any of the omelets. But, given the warbly voice you heard earlier, you start to seriously wonder. And for good reason. The magazine story about Christopher's grandfather also told of his startling views about intelligence in plants. George Simmons claimed to have had communications with many of them, which was also alluded to on the newscast you saw back home. The article is in your briefcase. You pull it out and begin summarizing it for the boy.

"Christopher, this article says, according to your grandfather, the plant kingdom, like animals, maintains a hierarchy. It says here that *Psilocybe mexicana*, or magic mushroom, is an example of a genus so highly evolved that its members can actually communicate thoughts and feelings. 'Without any capacity for speech,' Simmons asserted, 'they manufacture substances to temporarily alter the minds of the creatures that ingest them—then beam their messages.'"

Christopher merely nods as if all this is common knowledge. You continue. "It says that plants talk, socialize, share."

"Grampy spent all his time growing things. There are many varieties all over this manor," Christopher says.

"That reminds me," you tell him. "When I saw you on the news, you said that some plants told you about what birds and bees said. How is that possible?"

Christopher nods knowingly, his expression confident. "Grampy explained that what these plants manufacture isn't the by-product of seeding or pollination, or photosynthesis or reproduction . . . or any life-sustaining function. The plants sent him a kind of 'Why else would we make it?' message."

You point to a nearby window. "So, Christopher, do you ever, like, eat the plants out there?"

The boy smiles. "Yes, I do on occasion forage in the nearby woods. Especially after rainstorms." You're highly intrigued, but the boy doesn't elaborate further. "Anyway," he surmises, "if Noël had served us poisonous ones, wouldn't we be ill-stricken or dearly departed by now?"

Above, a brown mushroom rotates and sounds, ***Don't worry, there were no nasty ones amongst us.*** The lilting voice, like the warble you heard earlier, does not sound human. *Hey, Storyteller, that wasn't you just then, right?* ***No, my lord.*** *But a plant apparition just now reassured me that the mushrooms were not poisonous.* ***Sorry, but we can't digest what plants think or say.***

Why not? ***We can't digest what we can't ingest.*** *Ah yes. Of course. Sorry. Forgot about that.* **No worries.**

Now you decide you've had enough of going through this alone, so you take the letters out of your briefcase and tell Christopher everything. It makes you feel unburdened. While he reads, Christopher wags his finger at you and snickers over certain passages, probably those recounting episodes from your past. When he finishes, he hands the papers back with arched eyebrows, a headshake, and an expressive grin. "If good old Uncle Artie has named you as sole inheritor, then it's fine by me." He offers his hand to shake on your newly formed investigative team, adding, "From what I just read, you're quite a character in your own right. You must be in his bloodline."

For a kitchen that may be trying to do you in or drive you bonkers, it sure serves great food. Today's lunch, again delivered by an overly solicitous Chef Noël, is an assortment of small soufflés, mushroom quiches, dessert crepes, flasks of red and white wine, bread, an assortment of cheeses, and a rather odd-looking assortment of yellow pastries.

Getting a suggestion from above, you point to the tartlets with a quizzical expression and ask, "Stressed desserts?"

The chef smiles blissfully, blurting out, "No lemon, no melon, *je vous assure, monsieur.*" You can see Noël appreciates the effort you're making to get on his wavelength.

You and Christopher lunch and continue talking things over. When you describe Uncle Artie's dramatic welcome the night you arrived, he laughs out loud. "He did that incessantly at outdoor parties," he says and confirms that his uncle had a fancy laser projection and sound system installed, and, yes, he was able to film himself—or anybody—and then project the image gigantically into the sky. "Apparently, Uncle Artie," he says, "was so impressed by Disneyland and Universal that, after several trips, he had a lot of similar attractions, laden with special effects, installed on the estate."

"Like lions roaring and Shakespeare coming to life?" you ask.

"Those bits too?" he replies. "My, but you did get the royal treatment."

You tell him about the trio on the way up, the holographic passengers, and how you're certain Stephen was Uncle Artie's accomplice that night. That he was actually Dennis Rollinsby in disguise. Christopher agrees, but now he wants you to try and recall every detail of every event—before and after your arrival—no matter how insignificant it may seem.

"Well," you tell him, "there was all the confusion the night I arrived—people suddenly appearing, then disappearing, then gathering to sing 'Happy Birthday' to me when it wasn't even my birthday . . . And since then, nobody's said anything directly about my being heir apparent—that's really odd, don't you think?"

Christopher pauses to consider. "Not necessarily," he eventually replies. "Servants are trained to be discreet, not to pry."

Christopher continues with more questions, and you can see that he's trying to connect disparate events. You're impressed with this kid's analytical mind. He makes connections a lot of older people would miss, including you—well, before you started drinking that tea. Which causes you to wonder if the boy's insights are likewise achieved by ingesting psychotropic plants.

"Congratulations on correctly parsing Uncle's nutty quote," Christopher says when you show him the "Looking at Art" passage.

"This is all like some weird game," you tell him.

The boy claps his hands. "Right, this whole scene is something straight out of several immersive games I play in my spare time. Do you know any?"

His question sparks a memory from long ago. You recall your enthusiasm for *Myst* as you spent untold hours playing it instead of meeting some work deadline. You remember once reading that *Myst* along with Steven Hawking's book *A Brief History of Time* are works that only fifteen percent of purchasers actually finish. Yet both were and remain international bestsellers. "I remember *Myst* being artsy and difficult," you tell him. "You may not know it, though. *Myst* is from the early nineties."

"Oh, it's considered a classic among gamers," says Christopher. "As Uncle says, it's still 'the One' . . . One of Uncle's favorite sayings is that he knows real rocket scientists who can't work *Myst* out." His facial expression turns to sadness. "After he went off to Switzerland, we shared several game sessions on

Twitch. But then one day, he sent me a letter saying he was sorry but he had to stop. Maybe that's one of the last things he did. I do hope he could finish the games."

"I hope so too, Christopher."

Christopher nods and observes, "The best thing about these games is how a lot of characters don't exist until you the player encounter them. After which they come to life."

Oddly, this puts you in mind of *Burton's Peerage*. You suspect their editors have been up to something similar in this country for a long time. "Yes, I remember that from *Myst*," you tell him. "The player's job is to figure out what's happened to these people. Find them and try to help, right?"

Christopher nods, indicating you're correct, and explains there are multiple outcomes, things can turn out differently depending on what you do in the game. "As the player, you must be careful," he says, then adopts a more serious tone. "As here, you should be careful too."

"So, the best way to look at this," you ask, "is that we're trapped in my uncle's real-life game scenario? Where multiple outcomes are possible?"

Christopher answers quickly. "Yes, I do believe we are." He glances around as if fearful of being surveilled. "We need more clues. Maybe there's some in here." He picks up a copy of *The Village Journal*. After a brief perusal, he says, "There's just this one bit about Penelope in the swim competition. Don't quite know how that fits—but hang on!" He points the remote and replays the receptionist talking to herself in the library.

You're the one who gets it first. "Christopher, she's not saying 'time and place.' She's saying, 'time and *pace*.'"

"Brilliant!" he shouts. "Only we don't know what she's hidden, in which book, and whether it's still there." He says he's going to see if the *Journal*'s afternoon edition has come.

The boy soon returns with the paper. You both spot the item, though neither of you has any idea how it fits in; it just does.

KITCHEN CORNER: CHEF NOËL ELLE LÉON'S RECIPE FOR MANOR HOUSE SCONES

WEEKEND BRUNCH at the Grand Dining Hall at Hanover Manor is a time-honoured county tradition. And who among us hasn't arisen on a Saturday or Sunday with an absolute craving for Manor House scones? Now, for the first time, *The Journal* is proud to publish Chef Noël Elle Léon's special recipe for those incomparable delicacies.

¼ cup butter

1 ¾ cups flour

3 tablespoons sugar

2 ½ teaspoons baking powder

½ teaspoon salt

2 eggs, beaten

½ cup raisins

4 to 6 tablespoons half-and-half

Heat oven to 220 degrees Centigrade. Cut butter into flour, sugar, baking powder, and salt. Mix with pastry blender until mixture resembles fine crumbs. Stir in one egg, the raisins, and just enough of the half-and-half so the dough no longer sticks to the side of the bowl. Turn dough onto lightly floured surface. Knead it lightly 10 times. Then roll or pat until it is about 12 millimeters thick. Cut with floured circular cutter. Place on ungreased baking sheet; brush dough with second beaten egg; bake 10–12 minutes or until golden brown. Immediately remove from sheet. Split scones. Spread with butter and serve with raspberries or preserves if desired. Makes approximately 14 scones.

You compare Chef Emil's recipe to Noël's and see that the Frenchman has generally based his on the original but with several differences—key ingredients and condiments, units of measure and baking utensils, or the number of scones that result. As Christopher reads them out, you enter comparison lists in your diary:

NOËL'S RECIPE	EMIL'S RECIPE
raisins	currants
half-and-half	cream
Centigrade	Fahrenheit
millimeters	inches
baking sheet	cookie sheet
circular	round
raspberries	strawberries
fourteen	fifteen

Christopher leaves you to deliberate on all this while he takes the remote to go "look at art." He thinks the servants will pay him less notice than they would you. He also wants to drop by the library for any sign of Penelope's book, though he thinks that's a long shot.

You turn on your TV to the local news channel, hoping for a Crunch update. You're in luck, and you immediately enlarge the broadcast to fill the room.

CHAPTER FOURTEEN

DOGNAPERS THREATEN OWNER

Michael, the male coanchor, reports on a ransom note.

"On-screen, you can see, unedited and in its entirety, the letter we received this morning from Crunch's captors, who enclosed the dog's collar to authenticate their claim."

You pause the broadcast and scroll the note slowly.

> To Nigel Wanton, Owner of Crunch,
>
> We are the blokes what tuk your doggo away last evening. First we must say what a vile, naste pet you raised up what doesn't even know how to kuntrol itself after eating and drinking and then bits my younger bro suverely about his leg and thy and arse and somewhere else to and for no good reason, either, while the lad was only having his bathe, and you shood be ashamed of yourself Mr. Wanton for owning such a huribble doggo. This paper sed yesterday you will pay us muny for our trubles. Now tell how much or we shall force you to take steps. We won't wait long so you must answer shorty!

Michael's voiceover continues: "Crunch is easily distinguishable by the fact that he has only three legs and by the black patch he normally wears over his blind left eye. Anyone with information about this case is advised to contact the Witless constabulary."

Meredith returns, looking amused. "Ah, the plot thickens. We're reaching out to Mr. Wanton to see if we can learn what his response to these demands might be."

Christopher returns, breathless. "Just caught something at the fruit bowl," he says, bringing up the image grid. He wants to know if you found something in the paper or saw something on the news. "Well, there are these dognaper demands," you tell him, rewinding the program to the Crunch segment.

After a cursory glance, the boy offers a dismissive reply: "Don't get any connection. And it's not even a proper ransom notice." He pauses the video, collapsing the image, and aims the blue remote at the wall and presses the orb. The window opens and shows Noël with his back to the camera. He's holding his walkie-talkie, listening intently.

"Who—butler or concierge?" you ask.

"Her," Christopher replies.

The chef raises his hand in a gesture of exasperation and interjects, "'Oh, Monsieur Noël,' you ask me, 'where did you leave such *une petite* thing?' Do you think, madam, if I knew that we would even be having this conversation *maintenant*? *Mais non*, I would be back in those rooms searching and searching once more. No trace; not one carton!"

Christopher pauses the playback. "Did you catch his palindrome?" You smile and nod in affirmation as the boy resumes the clip.

On-screen, the chef listens and then replies, "I was many places yesterday. How can I remember them all? *Ce n'est pas possible!* Wait, perhaps there is something—at the pool, when I was . . . *Chérie*, allow me to check and ring you back." He switches off and steps out of view. A door slams.

"I got away from the painting just in time," Christopher says, certain that the chef never looked his way as he flew through the double doors and sped down the hall.

You agree that what Noël is searching for, but is not going to find, is the key he now believes he saw or left there. And that will raise the possibility in his mind that you have it and were able to get inside the other cottage rooms. Christopher wants to know if you spied anything else at the pool.

"Just a large stopwatch that swimmers use. I suppose to keep track of—" You smack your forehead, exclaiming, "Of course—'time and pace!'"

"Brilliant! What time was on the timer?"

"Don't remember."

"Think you'd recognize it if you saw it again?"

"Maybe."

"I'll dash down to the pool. Be back in a jiff."

Returning to the paper, you find an item to circle—Adrienne Van Scoy's name in a gossip column that lists the astrological signs of well-known villagers and asks readers if they think the notables exhibit the traits of the sign, in her case Virgo. You make a note in your diary.

Christopher returns, reporting, "The timer reads fifty-nine minutes and four seconds. Here, look at my phone."

"I'm fairly certain that's the time I saw," you tell him. "But I can't be a hundred percent sure until I see it up close."

Says Christopher, "I also checked the chef's office and was a bit surprised to see Farnsworth passing through somewhat furtively on his way to the kitchen. No one else was around. He looked nervous. Like he was up to no good." He turns to you. "Find anything else in the paper?" You show him the concierge's name circled, and he brightens. "That fits with what I just got upstairs."

Christopher points the remote at the wood carving, which dissolves into a scene showing Van Scoy facing the camera, engaged in a conversation with Farnsworth. "I rang the chauffeur and asked her to bring the numbers to Miss Stratton. But I was just at the front and couldn't find any list, and our little receptionist, as usual, was nowhere to be found," she tells him. "Shall I call Ms. Reddy and ask for another before she brings the vehicle round?"

Replies Farnsworth, "No, we've got to get cracking on those inspections. Let's just leave yesterday's in place. We can start using the new sequence tomorrow. How does it go again?"

Van Scoy answers with, "Day, month, year, two digits for each, six numbers in all." Then she asks, "James, is this blouse okay? How do I look?"

"Smashing," Farnsworth says with a sensual growl. "You always were a tigress, darling. And you're certain nobody around here knows?"

"No," Van Scoy replies, turning in his direction. "A woman in my position never reveals her true age."

Farnsworth laughs. "Well, you don't look a day over . . . overdone." Then he says, businesslike, "Right. There's a bit of a break in the storm, so let's be off."

You're anxious to pinpoint the concierge's date of birth. You'd like to show your young friend here he's not the only one with an agile mind. "We know the format—two digits each for day, month, and year. From the looks of her, she'd be midthirties, which means born in the late nineties, right?"

"Carry on," Christopher encourages.

"From that astrological chart in the gossipy news story, we can narrow the month and date down to—what does it say?" He hands you the paper. "Somewhere between August twenty-first and September twentieth," you read aloud. "Christopher, what steps should we take next to narrow it down?"

The boy just grins. "Easier if I just ask Grandmother. She knows everybody's birthday around here. Always sends a card."

"But will she know the year?"

"Likely not. We shall have to ferret that bit out." He reaches Mildred on the walkie-talkie and relays the information that Adrienne Van Scoy's birthday is September fifth.

You cannot suppress your amazement. "Wow, that's my birthday too. What a coincidence!"

"It's no coincidence," Christopher replies with a lopsided grin. "Perhaps you two are star-crossed!"

You wonder if he suspects your crush, though you don't think you've let on to anything.

Storyteller, do you think he suspects? A middle-aged man appears and offers, ***Perhaps he does but is being discreet, as a well-bred English lad should.***

"So that's the zero-five-zero-nine," you say to Christopher. "Any idea on the year?" Christopher smiles and replays the clip. "Nothing clicks for me," you tell him.

He pauses the frame. "Look at that Oriental blouse she's wearing."

"So, okay, it's got tigers on it," you reply. "Still don't get any connection."

"She might be consciously, or unconsciously, attracted," he observes.

"Attracted to tigers, like in the Chinese calendar?"

"Could be," Christopher replies and pulls up the Chinese horoscope on his phone. He then ticks off years and animals working backward to the year he assumes she was born in. "So, if we've reasoned it properly, she must have been born in ninety-eight."

You're very impressed you tell him. Will be even more so if that combination actually works. "Obscurities are typical of immersive games," he says.

You rub your chin and offer an observation: "If so, then this is too much like them. We find a recipe, then right away its companion is in the newspaper. We spy on people, and they drop hints."

Christopher nods and says, "This probably means that Uncle Artie really did dream all this up, figuring you and I would play it out. But we should proceed without letting whoever's helping know we know." The boy seems adamant.

"Why? Why not?"

"Because, we might disturb a history Uncle might have written. We might dislodge Uncle's future from our own timeline."

Storyteller, I've no idea what he means. ***The lad is prescient. He intuitively understands Time. Pay him heed.*** *Yeah, yeah, yeah, but what does he mean?* ***He thinks you should proceed with caution.***

All these admonitions, guesswork, and deductions have made your head spin. You feel like you need a break. "Christopher, I'm going to take a walk, try to clear my head. I'll go down to the pool and check that timer." Christopher nods, saying he'll wait for you here.

It's good to stand, stretch, and walk around. As you head to the spa, you realize you're once again in violation of the dress code, but you couldn't care less. If Van Scoy appears and scolds you, you'll show her—oh yes, you certainly will—who's now in charge. As the new lord of the manor, you'll stride right up, take her in your arms, bend her back, and give her the most romantic kiss she's ever tasted!

Your fantasy appears to unnerve one of the British Storytellers, who appears looking quite distraught. ***We don't recommend resorting to such improprieties. Bad form really. Moreover, you rarely get another chance to undo a bad impression.*** *Oh, Storyteller, I was just spoofin' you all.* ***Heh heh. Brilliant. You put one over. Well played!***

Opening the spa doors, you're reminded of how the atmosphere in this facility is so completely different from the rest of Manor House's main floor: ultra-modern furnishings, cool jazz music, giant overhead TVs tuned to channels from all over the globe. At the opposite side of the stylish lounge, one of the monitors is replaying the friendly between Thailand and Brazil from the other night. You stroll over to watch for a spell.

Thomas was right—the whole scene, despite the rain, looks more like the Rio Carnival than a soccer match. You laugh when you catch sight of a few fans staggering around in Yobbler shirts looking dazed and confused, trying to cha-cha in the rain.

But suddenly there are voices at the entrance—the chef and the concierge. Quickly, you duck into a nearby storage closet. Once inside, you spy a step stool and place it so you can see out the transom window above. It is open slightly, allowing you to hear hushed voices, now only a few feet away. You peer out into the well-lit spa. It's the chef and the concierge all right. And neither looks happy.

At first, you hear Van Scoy say, "I don't have much time because I've got to—"

Noël interrupts with, "I know, I heard the announcement." He moves closer to her. "Did you summon me because lately we've had no chance to—"

Van Scoy, frowning, replies, "No I did not. Not this time, Noël. Not at all." She clears her throat, then continues, "Noël, I want you to tell me something, and truthfully. Are you seeing James?"

Noël looks flustered as he proclaims, "Why do you ask such things? *Ma chérie*, I dream only of you and the life we can have together."

Van Scoy's expression turns to anger as she exclaims, "Oh, do tell me about this life, Noël. I'm just so keen to hear all about it." She stands erect, folds her arms, and glares at the chef.

Noël is quick to respond. "It's simple. First, we get rid of the pretender, as James calls him."

Storyteller, that must mean me. Is this guy serious? ***Hmm, sounds like it.***

"And then?" Van Scoy prompts the chef, who continues, "James lays claim to the title and the estate. After all, he and his family have served for generations. There are no other claimants. There is precedent for this, I've learned. I have people looking into—"

Van Scoy interrupts with, "Who—those lowlife barristers from The Village?"

Replies Noël, "Why yes, dearest. They are eager to assist."

Good God, Storyteller, is she going for this? ***Let's see how this plays out, shall we?***

Van Scoy asks, "Then what?"

"Then you marry James, and after some time, we get rid of him."

"And then?"

Noël gesticulates wildly, shouting, "We are together, as is our destiny. And we shall have all of this."

What! Hey, Storyteller, where's the broken English? The patois, the palindromes? This is a totally different guy. A young man with a French accent tries to respond. ***Perhaps, monsieur, he is a man of many charms and talents.***

Van Scoy looks frustrated as she stammers, "Noël, I did not bring you here to listen to your crazy talk." She jabs a finger at him. "Now, look at me, and tell me—are you intimately involved with James?"

Noël places a hand over his heart and says, "No, no, *chérie*, I swear it to you."

The concierge vigorously shakes her head, saying, "I do not believe you. I can see it in your eyes."

Oh, Storyteller, Adrienne doesn't know how right she is. I saw with my own eyes. ***Possibly, though, she does know. A woman's intuition perhaps?***

"But what about us?" Noël cries out.

Van Scoy's tone is measured. "As far as I'm concerned, Noël, there is no longer *us*."

Noël now seems desperate as he pleads, "So you will remain with James? He cannot get you what you want. Or give you what you need. Only I—"

The concierge's walkie-talkie rings, quieting the chef. Van Scoy listens for a moment, then speaks into her device. "Time to go? Yes, James, I'm coming. But I'll need to make an announcement beforehand."

She ends the call and turns back to the chef, saying, "Noël, we are finished. And I'm going to pretend I never heard your foolhardy scheme."

Noël again pleads, "Do not do this, Adrienne!" He whirls around threateningly. "What if I tell James all about us?"

Van Scoy looks completely unperturbed. "Do as you please," she replies evenly. "But be sure to update your CV beforehand. Besides, I've got someone else in mind . . . Anyway, I've got to get back."

The two walk away. You can no longer hear them, but the chef's continued frantic gestures indicate he's imploring the concierge to reconsider. After a moment, you slip out of the closet and exit the spa.

Hurrying back, you can't wait to get Christopher's take on the butler-concierge-chef love triangle. As soon as you open the door, Christopher asks about the timer. "Did the numbers match your memory?"

You explain that you never made it down to the pool. "The chef and the concierge suddenly popped in and were having a lovers' quarrel!"

"Oh, do tell!" the boy exclaims. His eyes widen as you recount in detail their conversation. You ask him if he thinks you should worry about Noël getting rid of you.

"No, I don't think so," Christopher calmly observes. "Look, you said she told him she wouldn't go along with it. Our chef would have nothing to gain."

"What if Noël makes good on his threat to tell all to Farnsworth?" you ask.

Christopher shakes his head. "Oh, I don't think Farnsworth would confront her, given his own duplicity. But if he did, I'd expect Ms. Van Scoy would deny it. Then it would be he-said, she-said. Mr. Farnsworth would likely let his heart decide whom to believe."

"So do you think it would be her he'd choose to believe?" you ask.

"I do," says Christopher. "From what we've earlier observed of Mr. Farnsworth's and Ms. Van Scoy's interactions, I think our chef is merely a dalliance."

Once again, your young master analyst here seems to have sorted this out. You decide not to worry about the chef. At least for now. "But Christopher, there's one other thing: when Noël spoke, it was almost entirely in English, unaccented, like a native speaker."

"Hmm, I'll have to give that some serious thought," he says nonchalantly. For several moments, Christopher looks like he's lost in thought. Finally, he cocks his head and says, "Care to know what I think their next moves will be?"

"Of course. Spill it. I'm all ears."

"Our passionate chef will make a strong play for Farnsworth, force him to choose." Christopher's mouth curves into a knowing smile. "Noël may even insist on being allowed to move into Her Majesty's."

"Hmm," you murmur. "And our Ms. Adrienne Lynn Van Scoy—what's her next play?"

Christopher doesn't hesitate. "You—she'll make a strong play for you. She wants it all. What other route can she take?"

God, you hope he's right.

Again, the two of you go over everything that's happened, this time focusing on your interactions with the servants. The first thing that comes to mind is Thomas Sutherland's presentation of that bottle of wine, saying, "Happy birthday," and telling you Lord Hanover requested it be bestowed the moment you arrived.

Christopher retrieves the bottle. "There something wrong here."

You stare at the inscription. Thinking of the current year, you mentally calculate leap years back to 1980, which causes you to exclaim, "But 1978 wasn't a leap year, right?"

Christopher snaps his fingers. "That's it!"

So this rare and expensive wine from Hanover Manor's special reserve has been mislabeled. Deliberately so? Perhaps, knowing Uncle Artie's penchant for quirkiness. And money being no object, he could have directed the winery in Bordeaux to print one special label on just one bottle. "So all we'd have to do," you explain, "is type in a six-digit sequence, such as 290278, or maybe an eight-digit one, like 02291978, to log on to the computer?"

Christopher replays a clip from the wall, then pauses the frame, observing. "Like Farnsworth was telling the concierge last night that he and Noël have been trying to do."

"But hold on—I nearly forgot. Christopher, your grandmother mentioned earlier that she'd been ordered by the butler to inventory the wine collection."

"When did you speak with her?"

"Didn't talk to her, at least not at first. She mentioned it in a note, which came when you were off changing clothes."

"Where's the note?"

"Must have thrown it away."

He looks around for a wastebasket, but you tell him you think the waiter took the trash away after lunch. "That's not good for Grandmother if Chef Noël reads it. He'll likely inform Mr. Farnsworth." He looks slightly distraught. "You ought not to discard anything. Even if it seems unimportant. It might contain a clue."

The boy's right—again. "It now seems clear," you tell him, "that Uncle knew that Farnsworth and his cronies would cause trouble over the inheritance. That's why he's got Rollinsby or whoever working behind the scenes, telling 'our helpers' what to do, but not necessarily why."

"What's the one thing they all have in common?" Christopher asks.

"Like I said earlier," you reply, "after I saw them once, they all disappeared for the rest of the evening. Finally, I went to bed and had a weird dream about the butler in a red costume."

"And nobody's mentioned anything about it since?"

"Well, maybe somebody said something last night, but I don't remember—with all the pints and lack of sleep."

"I know, I heard," says Christopher, lifting an eyebrow. He remains silent, but he laughs when you tell him the penguin joke from last night. "Penguins shall be my next additions to Pooh Bear and friends," he declares. "Along with Mr. and Mrs. Magic Mushroom, Miss Wildflower, and Sir Peyote Button." Then he says, "Carry on. You may be onto something."

"So, Christopher, these people may be scripted. Think Rollinsby or someone told them to go away and not return that evening?"

"Yes—I now think so. You?"

"I do. From that very first night, I think Uncle wanted to lay the groundwork, get me used to the idea that he's still going to be around, taking care of me, especially when I'm stymied. Come to think of it, reading about Farnsworth on the flight over was quite a coincidence—don't you think?"

Christopher's expression brightens. "Hmm. Tell me, have you ever read Carl Jung?" he asks.

"Do you mean the collective unconscious, human psyche, all that deep, hidden stuff?"

He's talking about us, you know. *Yes, I know. But I'm by no means ready to tell him about you people just yet. Especially since he can't see or hear you.* ***Good thinking.***

"I don't know about Jung," you say. "Always get him mixed up with that other guy—what's his name—Sigmund Freud."

Says Christopher, "I haven't studied Jung either, but do you know anything about Jung's ideas on coincidences—what he called 'synchronicity'?"

"Can't say that I do."

"That's okay," Christopher assures. "All you need to know is that there are no coincidences—everything's connected."

You're curious. "So is this what they teach you kids in France?"

Christopher shakes his head. "Oh no. Not at lessons. Uncle Artie explained it to me. He spelled out Jung's ideas in simple terms when we first began to play games. Said it would help me solve all the puzzles."

You nod, saying, "Sounds like it sure did. You're quite adept at this, young man."

"That's how I learned never to overlook anything," he says resolutely. "There are signs and symbols everywhere—but one has to make the connections. What Uncle Artie really wanted me to learn was that this is true in real life, too." He raises his two index fingers high in the air, then slowly brings them together, offering, "There's just more to look at, to consider, to connect."

Christopher's tone now changes to resignation. "But sadly, most people never do. They meet a stranger and don't stop to figure out that person's role in their life. Or vice versa. Things happen to us, or we make things happen, but few of us think beyond what happened—and try to figure out why."

"So, Christopher, do you often talk to strangers?" you ask.

"Any chance I get."

"And what do you study at your school?"

"Just before the holiday, our French class read *Waiting for Godot*, which is *En Attendant Godot* in French." Christopher explains that the characters mostly go around shouting easy phrases like "Such is life," or "Nothing to be done." So it's a good one for studying French.

A chime signals a PA announcement. "May I please have the staff's attention. The butler and I shall be away from the manor this afternoon. We will be down in the far residential area inspecting some recent renovations to the guest bungalows and appraising any storm damage in the area. Miss Stratton can reach us if you need to speak to us. I regret to announce that the road down to the village remains closed. Carry on."

With a look of serious mischief, Christopher inquires if you're ready.

"To do what?"

"Go to Mr. Farnsworth's office. Have a go on Uncle Artie's computer, of course!"

You take a deep breath. "Like Uncle's real-life scenario intends us to?"

Christopher rubs his hands and shouts, "Right! No time like the present!"

"Another Godot-ism, Christopher?"

"No, this proverb's courtesy of John Tresler, an Englishman."

CHAPTER FIFTEEN

You reach the butler's office without incident. Christopher wants you to do the honors on the door lock. You whisper, "Don't you realize we're probably breaking some law?"

"Crime of the century." Christopher seems not the least bit apprehensive. You punch in the concierge's birthdate, hold your breath, and press ENTER. No alarm sounds. The door opens, and the two of you slip inside.

Farnsworth has a beautiful office, with a large maple desk, oversized leather chairs, a conference area with a round table ringed by upholstered chairs, and a wet bar. There are two other doors inside. One connects to the concierge's office, the other to the lobby. A computer monitor is on the conference table, with a CPU and printer underneath. Farnsworth and Noël have set up Lord Hanover's system hastily, as evidenced by a tangle of power cables and extension cords strung to an outlet across the room.

"Right, let's get cracking," Christopher urges. A press of the power button starts up the machine, and a dialogue appears for password entry. Christopher keys in the first leap year combination but gets an "invalid password" message. He repeats the same sequence—in case he mistyped it—but access is again denied. Next come double and triple tries on six-digit variations. No luck. The minutes pass. He tries the eight-digit variations, ones that include the full 1978. Still no luck. Another quarter of an hour. You're getting nervous. Christopher now tries alphanumeric combinations, like 29FEB78, but to no avail.

Then you both freeze at the sound of footsteps approaching from the lobby. Your heart starts pounding at hearing the jingle of keys, followed by the sound of one being inserted into the lock. In the lobby, a telephone rings. The key is withdrawn, but another is quickly inserted. The ringing stops. You sense it was answered as a third key is inserted. Your eyes grow wide as the knob starts to turn. Then you hear Penelope calling from the lobby, "Monsieur Noël! Mr. Farnsworth wishes to speak with you."

"Oui, j'arrive." The key is withdrawn, and the chef's footsteps recede.

You wipe sweat from your brow. Pacing the room, you look on as Christopher frantically types, forgetting that you should remain silent. "Christopher, it makes me angry—that label clue, all the deductions we made, all worthless; they've given us no advantage over the opposition."

"True," he replies in a hushed tone. You're especially annoyed and disappointed because it seems to mean that this part of the game is poorly designed!

But then strong encouragement comes from an adult male Storyteller. ***Think deeper. You can do it!*** *Can't you just tell me?* ***And deny you the satisfaction? Surely not.***

Your gaze falls upon *The Village Journal* lying on Farnsworth's desk opened to that Ice Age story from two days ago. You stare at the accompanying photograph and your agitated mind suddenly achieves a new insight—you've solved it! Christopher is nearly knocked off his chair as you lean over and hurriedly type in the password, press ENTER, and watch Windows sign on.

So there, Uncle Artie! So there! ***We're certain he is delighted.*** *Did you plant the answer in my thoughts?* ***No, you got it all on your own. Congrats!*** *Yay me!*

Christopher looks blown away as the screen desktop appears with two folders, one labeled INTERNET, the other DOCUMENTS. The latter opens to reveal eight items whose file names are ACCOUNTS, DEBTS, DEED, LETTERS, REPORT, TAX, TITLE, and WILL. Eight in total. During the startup, you scribbled a note, which you now push under Christopher's gaze:

The password = AprilFools

He mouths, "Awesome," and gives you a silent high five.

You open your diary to the page listing the discrepancies in the scone recipes—eight in total—and hand it to Christopher. You're sure that these files will be individually password-protected. You first point to Chef Noël's, then to Chef Emil's side of the list, mouthing, "Which?"

Christopher leans in and whispers, "Child's play." He double-clicks the Deed file, sees the password dialogue, and types in the third word, *Fahrenheit*, from Emil's list. Of course it's going to work the very first time, you reckon, because Deed is the third file in the folder list.

Emil's recipe holds the keywords, you realize, because there is, presumably, a single copy, whereas *The Village Journal* is lying around everywhere.

Ha! Embryo's play, Storyteller. ***Heh heh. Embryo play. Good one.***

As soon as the file pops up, Christopher clicks the Print icon, and you both heave a sigh of relief when a blinking light signals data being received, then another when the laser printer outputs the pages.

Next, Christopher opens and prints the Will file using the password "fifteen." What a treasure trove! You stuff the papers into your briefcase as soon as they enter the tray. As expected, the remaining passwords—currants, cream, inches, cookie sheet, round, strawberries—are each used once in accordance with their chronological appearance in the recipe vis-à-vis the document's alphabetical listing in the folder. Your luck even extends to the printer not running out of paper during the session. But luck does run out when Christopher tries to open the other folder on the desktop, the one labeled Internet.

Every attempt fails. None of the keywords from either recipe work.

We've gotten what we came for, though. Much more in fact—so why continue hacking away? Especially since we don't know what we're looking for, whether it's needed, or why we're still risking discovery when we've already had a close call. Via sighs, whispers, and sign language, you frantically raise these concerns. When they have no effect, you scribble, *Why???*

Christopher scrawls back, *Got the deed, Now the greed! Too much is never enough!*

Without thinking, you break the silence, blurting out, "Christopher, Florence and the Machine—really? You weren't even born yet!" The boy tries to shush you, but it's too late. Having heard only a faint click, certainly no door sound, you are astonished to turn around and find yourself face-to-face with the butler himself—and his pistol aimed right at your forehead. You're frozen in place, terrified to be confronting an individual who has somehow entered the office without making a sound and is now standing right beside you.

He bellows, "This is an outrage!" You flinch violently. Farnsworth looks crazed, waving his gun wildly, continuing to yell. "I shall summon the authorities at once, and then we'll see how much you enjoy assisting our local constables with their inquiries." He points his gun at you and commands, "Leave my office at once and take nothing with you. I insist that you remain in your quarters until this matter is resolved."

Wheeling around to Christopher, Farnsworth, still seething, drops his voice to a tone that carries controlled rage. "As for you . . . I suggest you hurry to your grandmother's side. Stay with her. Comfort her. You'll need each other soon enough." Christopher seems about to stand up when, suddenly, he ducks underneath the table and yanks the power cord.

"Why you little—what's the password? I demand you tell me!"

Christopher hurries to his feet, steps back, and says cooly, "We never got that far."

Without a word, you snatch your briefcase, put your arm around the boy, and quickly depart as the daily dismissal comes over the PA:

"The butler has asked me to announce that he has completed his evening inspection of the premises and finds everything satisfactory at present. The day staff are therefore dismissed and may retire to quarters. The main gate of Hanover Manor has been shut and will remain so. Good evening."

"Well, not everything in the manor is 'satisfactory at present,'" Christopher says ruefully, "but Ms. Van Scoy doesn't know it yet."

"But hold on," you assert. "I'm the heir to the estate; Farnsworth can't threaten me that way. Besides, how are constables to get up to the manor? The road is impassable."

Christopher's reply is succinct. "Mr. Farnsworth has shown himself to be a determined foe." You unlock your door, and Christopher trudges inside. While you watch him, it occurs to you that the butler never entered the room through any door—all three entrances were well within your field of vision.

Storyteller, he came out of nowhere. ***Ah, but did you not notice the object he was holding?*** *A gun, right?* ***We saw no such thing.*** *What was it then?* ***The boy knows.***

Christopher looks at you, as if about to say something important. "Grandmother and I shan't be in peril as long as you're here with us. Please say you will be."

You feel close to the boy—yet uncomfortable dealing with this. His request represents an ultimate choice, one that you're not quite ready to make. You pull the documents from your briefcase, muttering, "Let's have a look, shall we?"

"Well, think about it, won't you?" the boy asks.

"Christopher, I will, I promise—I just can't right now. I'm too shook up from having a gun pointed at me."

Christopher's eyes widen as he says, "What? Are you certain? I never saw any gun. All I saw was a remote in his hand, much like the one we have."

Okay, you don't know for absolute certain. Maybe you were seeing things. You shrug and turn back to the stack of documents.

There is a mountain of legalese to leaf through. Finally, you reach the bottom of the pile and find your uncle's will and the deed and conveyance forms entitling you to Hanover Manor Estate and all its adjoining lands "in perpetuity." The other two documents are copies of those you had all along—the court ruling and societal findings. But those don't truly represent anything tangible. Not like what you're examining now. You flip through the pages until you reach the last one—where your eyes receive a jolt. There, on the bottom line of an otherwise all-black printed property deed, is bright-blue handwriting: "Arthur Reynold Hanover." This is not a computer font. There's no question that this is your uncle's signature in real ink from a fountain pen. You've seen enough samples in his letters to know.

You call Christopher to your side. "Have you ever heard of Uncle's 'advanced ink technology,' whatever that means?" He shakes his head no. "For example, this." You point to Arthur Hanover's sure hand in royal blue.

Christopher looks at the signature and offers congratulations, but as for the technology, he has no idea. "But you certainly strove hard to obtain these," he says. "And I assisted."

"Never could have done any of this without you, Christopher."

"Nothing I did compares with your rebirthday bit—where did that come from anyway?"

You snap your fingers. In all the excitement, you'd forgotten to explain. You hand him the newspaper story. Christopher glances at it and shrugs. "I don't get it."

You pat him on the shoulder, saying, "Look closer. Tell me what's wrong with the picture."

It takes a few seconds, but he spots it. "That's no picture of Earth as seen from space." He laughs out loud. "It's a fake! Look, the so-called Earth has 'England,' 'France,' 'Spain,' 'Germany,' printed on the countries."

Christopher can't stop laughing. "Of course!" he shouts. "Now I get it. April Fools' Day—the night you arrived. February twenty-ninth was a false trail." Christopher is mightily impressed. He looks up and calls out, "Very good, Uncle Artie. Only premier creators can pull that off."

You certainly agree. "Christopher," you exclaim, "these puzzles are getting to be way too much fun! I'm getting addicted."

"Oh, by the way," he says, "I've been allowed to attend tonight's billiards match. So . . . what are you going to do—come along or stay in your room without supper as Mr. Farnsworth insists?" Savannah versus Reggie—you wouldn't miss it for the world.

"One more thing," says Christopher, "now that you're titled, feel free to change your first name if you like. You may want to use Hanover as the surname, but it's up to you, actually."

"Great suggestion, Christopher. I'll choose a new name to go with my new life!"

Yes you will. Especially sincc you're so hazy about the name you came with. Then you slap your forehead, now thinking that your holdings were never really at risk.

"Don't you see, Christopher? There's nothing Farnsworth and Noël could have done even if they had located the files first."

The boy slaps his own forehead, mocking you. "Are you quite certain about that? Couldn't all of the files simply have been placed in the rubbish bin and zapped?"

Touché.

CHAPTER SIXTEEN

Naturally, all the phone messages came while you were out burglarizing. But there's nothing new—the same callers imploring you to call them back. Wish you could—especially Lord Rollinsby's son and daughter. You snack on a mushroom casserole and sip pink tea left by the kitchen while reading over your uncle's last will and testament.

Hey, Mister Magic Mushroom, is the casserole okay? ***Have no fear***, it warbles.

It took only a short time to become accustomed to the Storytellers. Now you're starting to get used to communicating with plants. Amazing—the paranormal now seems so normal.

Again, you see "heir apparent" written throughout the will. As you guessed, you inherit everything; nobody else is even mentioned. There are more material riches enumerated than you could have ever imagined. This document says you're rich, fabulously rich, filthy rich. You bathe with your briefcase beside the tub, change into another spiffy outfit you bought for the trip, and leave your chambers in high spirits.

As you mount the staircase, a premonition hits—*something's about to happen.*

At the landing, your eyes fall on a wood carving on the library wall. You recognize it as one of the nonwired ones that nevertheless appears on the grid but does nothing when you try to activate it. You step in front of the Fairy Queen, and what seems about to happen—without any pressing of the device—happens.

The scene has dissolved to a headshot of Lord Hanover exuding enthusiasm.

"My beloved child, Hanover Manor shall soon be all yours, and my ancient title passed to you. And thus, you may claim your rightful place among your peers if you so desire. It is critical, however, that you make haste and attend to the remaining formalities. Have the chauffeur drive you and the documents to my solicitors in The Village early tomorrow morning. They will take care of matters concerning the probate. Then, I beg of you, turn your attention to more pressing matters. Endeavor to assuage concerns and reconcile differences amongst all my devoted servants. Good night, and rest well."

His image is covered by the descent of a red theater curtain. After a pause, the curtain rises, and the wood carving is restored.

You hastily return to your room. As expected, the thumbnail now works. You missed it the first time, but now that the image is life-sized, you see that the outdoor scene behind him performs a 360-degree panoramic rotation. You can see he's been perfectly composited into a day full of sunshine and blue skies.

While he is speaking, the background scene pans across the breadth of Hanover Manor. As the panorama rotates toward the open green down to the main gate, your breath is taken away by the vista of woods and lakes and valleys beyond. And what look like snow-capped mountains in the far distance that are taller than what you would have expected in northern England.

By the time Uncle finishes speaking, the panorama has made a complete rotation, and you're back at the base of Shakespeare. Whew. You can't wait to show Christopher.

Arriving at the whisky bar, you step into lively conversation mixed with piano jazz and the sounds of a billiard game in progress. A crowd has gathered around the center table. You can't see the players, but bursts of applause are followed by frequent calls of "Nice shot, Savannah" or "Great leave, Miss Reddy." You hear nothing crowd-pleasing about her opponent, Reggie.

Bruce is tending the bar. "Evenin', mate," he hails. "Savannah's been cleaning ol' Reg's clock. He's never gonna hear the end of this."

The match concluded, an ebullient Savannah calls for attention. "Reginald, the alleged pool shark," she announces, "has turned out to be a fraud. At first,

I thought he might be hustling me, but, oh no, he . . . actually . . . is . . . a . . . cue-challenged player." There's a guffaw from Bruce and mumbled protests from Reggie.

Separating herself from the crowd around the pool table, Mildred joins you at the bar. She observes that you have your briefcase close by and beams approvingly.

You glance down the bar at Thomas Sutherland, who is sliding a glass in your direction. "Got some of the house's best single malt. You may need some fortification for the spectacle you're about to witness." You take a swallow of what is a mighty stiff drink.

Christopher has entered the bar and is standing across the room. He has on an oversized bowler. Apparently, he has been commissioned to be part of the entertainment and just been given his cue. As master of ceremonies, he delivers his lines in a loud shout.

"Ladies and gentlemen, your attention, please. Tonight's command performance will now commence. Direct from his favorite haunts in London, Glasgow, Edinburgh, Belfast, and Dublin, please welcome the one, the only, Reginald McCabe!"

To applause and the opening strains of an Irish fiddle, a shoeless, costumed Reggie breaks into an Irish jig on top of the billiard table. The overhead lamp serves as a spotlight. His body rigid, his arms folded, he flits back and forth with high, choppy steps and occasional leaps.

"Crickey!" yells Bruce. "Ace! Good on ya!" You can't tell which Bruce is enjoying more: his friend's performance or the fantasy he's probably having about Farnsworth and Van Scoy raging on tomorrow's PA. The music and cheering crowd becomes thunderous. Now he's yelling above the din, "Hey, Savannah, back in Straya they used to call me 'Fast Track Bruce' when I won all the motocross championships. So how about—"

Laughter from a nearby table prevents you from hearing the rest—or her invariable, more macho rejoinder. You've been here only ten minutes or so, but already it looks like quite a party. You glance up at the TV and are intrigued by the screen caption on TVTV news for an upcoming story.

BELOVED PARAKEET TWIMBLEY SUCCUMBS

Before you can even request it, Bruce unmutes the volume, blows the image up to 3D, and calls out to all those nearby, "This is must-see TV!"

The camera shows Michael, who is looking somber as he begins his report: "Twimbley, the ten-year-old talking parakeet, much beloved by village residents, died Tuesday after a long illness common to parakeets." He pauses to suppress a sniffle of sadness. After a moment, he continues: "Nearly the entire village turned out yesterday to see the small green-and-yellow bird laid out beautifully and lovingly in a miniature coffin at Dear Pet Cemetery. Several moving eulogies by Twimbley's neighbors were given."

Reggie leans over to say, "Bruce and I served as pallbearers. That bird was one of our village favorites."

"But how did you get—"

Reggie doesn't hear you, as he's moved away. The scene changes to a filmed report shot inside the cemetery's viewing facility. A chyron identifies "Emma Tophan, Director." An elderly British woman in funeral attire is standing beside an open coffin displaying the deceased bird lying on its back. You stand and walk into the scene to get a closer look at Twimbley.

"We shall miss dear Twimbley—deeply," Tophan says while placing a garland of white roses round the coffin. "Those who daily passed the parakeet's window were charmed by his sayings." She manages a slight smile while looking away wistfully.

The camera returns to Michael, who has regained his composure. "Charmed, indeed," he says, "but many of the bird's utterances were a bit salty at times, said other mourners who attended the rites, though not disapprovingly."

You return to your stool as Michael continues, "Twimbley reportedly spent his formative years in Liverpool and was raised by a pair of seafaring brothers. As such, the bird learned to talk by mimicking the speech of sailors and dockworkers who frequented the residence, and by imitating nearby parrots in the brothers' aviary."

Meredith breaks in. "Liverpool. Sailors. Parrots. I can just imagine Twimbley's upbringing and vocabulary!"

Michael, now smiling faintly, concludes with, "Yes, Meredith, and The Village Television regrets that it is unable to repeat Twimbley's best-known greeting, as it is unsuitable for a family broadcast. Still, we deeply regret the loss of one of our most illustrious and loquacious citizens."

The story ends, and Bruce again mutes the sound. You spot Reggie, who has changed back into his doorman's getup, an orange-and-gray ensemble. "Hey Reggie," you call out. "So, how did Twimbley usually greet people?"

"Ahoy, matey, ever been buggered at sea?" he shouts back in his best pirate brogue. Hilarious. You can just picture the shocked and dumbfounded expressions of passersby. Now it looks as if some group activity is about to begin. Looking up, you notice the wall containing the holographic projector array is already visible to patrons.

"Okay, Google, text mode. Dreams ampersand Schemes," Reggie announces. A giant 3D rendering of the phrase appears in midair and begins to rotate. You're transfixed. But there are no gasps from those assembled. Nobody seems at all surprised. So you figure they've seen this before. Last night it was revolving motorcycles; tonight, it's glowing neon signage. The font selection and aliased edges of the rendered text are fantastic. Speech to text—love it!

Reggie begins the game. "Okay, Google, Smokes ampersand Jokes." The phrase is quickly rendered and begins rotating high above. "Waitstaff are veteran performers at improvisational comedy clubs, and, in between lighting your Cubans, they crack one howler after another. They've all got their specialties. Tonight, you may wish to be attended by one adept at insulting you and your guests à la Monty Python. Tomorrow, you may choose to be seated next to a table being waited on by that same person to enjoy a reprise at someone else's expense."

As more servants settle into the chairs around a large table, you are invited by Thomas to participate in one of the pub's fantasy games, called Dreams & Schemes, that the manor staff apparently enjoys playing from time to time. Tonight's rendition is inventing, then selling, your ideal pub restaurant to the group. Holography is used to provide graphical support to accompany each entry.

"The rules are simple," Thomas explains. "Your fantasy pub restaurant name must be short and descriptive, two rhyming words separated by an ampersand. You are expected to briefly describe your dream pub's decor, staff or clientele, menu, or other sales points. We players decide whether we would wish to patronize the place. At the end of the session, we'll all vote to determine the overall winning concept."

You nod. Sounds creative and fun. *Storyteller, maybe I'll take a shot later.* ***I'm here to assist if you like***, says the talented woman who directed last night's performance. *Oh. Absolutely. I think we make a great team!* **Indeed we do.**

Savannah now takes her turn. "Okay, Google, Drugs ampersand Hugs. Would work well in California. The employees are all trained psychotherapists and counselors," she explains, "including a doctor to prescribe legal stimulants and antidepressants. Everything is touchy-feely. No matter what your problem is, after you confess, you get a hug to go with your Prozac and cab." Hearing this, most think they'd probably pass on the place but agree with Thomas that it has "excellent franchise potential among affluent neurotics."

Bruce looks at Savannah and tells her that his place is similar to hers but "a little kinkier." He then offers, "Okay, Google, Drinks ampersand Shrinks. All of my bartenders and waitstaff are ex–mental health professionals permanently disbarred from practice—and able to withstand my rigorous background check to verify this." He grins devilishly. "Or they can still be licensed but must show that they've lost at least one major malpractice suit in their career, preferably recently. Of course, they're bound to dispense weird, dangerous advice to the sad sacks, which will serve to keep the atmosphere charged."

The consensus is that this pub would be closed by the authorities within its first week, but everybody says they'd try the place at least once out of curiosity. "Would expect to witness one complete breakdown per quarter hour," estimates Reggie.

"Ye Olde Stout and Gout," offers Mildred. "World-class pints, all-you-can-eat gourmet buffet. Enough said." The housekeeper has summed it up so quickly she didn't bother to invoke any holographic signage.

"You've got to give more details, Millie, if you expect to compete," Reggie grouses.

"Hearts and Flowers," pipes up Penelope, who has wandered over to join in, blissfully unaware that her entry is in violation of the rhyming rule. She, too, does not summon the projectors. You hear a couple of groans but hope nobody will be so unkind as to challenge her. Penelope says dreamily,

"My pub has a beautiful bouquet at every candlelit table. Soon as they enter, ladies are pinned with lovely corsages, while gentlemen receive boutonnieres. We always bid them farewell with a gift of fine chocolates in a golden heart-shaped box tied with a red satin ribbon."

"Doesn't sound like any pub I've ever been in," says Bruce. "But, hey, I'm open-minded."

"Your idea is exceptionally sweet, dear," says Mildred with expansive matronly warmth. Thomas nods in enthusiastic agreement.

"I'm going to invest all of my future pool winnings in your enterprise, Penelope," Savannah declares. "Which should be substantial seeing as how some people never learn."

Once again you are treated to the chauffeur's barroom style: stroke and support any underdog; zing and zap all top dogs. You like it. You like her, too, and again wonder if it was you she was pressing the housekeeper about in the conversation you overheard earlier.

Thomas proposes an exception be made and that "Penelope's meritorious entry not be disqualified." He says he'll explain the rules to her so she "can be up to speed on the next go." She looks grateful and gazes at him soulfully.

Christopher announces, "I'm getting sleepy, but before I go, may I offer this entry. Okay, Google, Dames ampersand Games—where you shoot billiards, throw darts, and play Dungeons and Dragons all night with beautiful women who serve excellent bangers and mash. That's it. Someone can tell me in the morning how much I won."

Reggie and Bruce are ready to declare him victor right now, but Penelope timidly reminds everyone, "We've yet to hear from Thomas . . . and from our guest of honor."

Prompted, Thomas announces, "Permit me to offer for the group's consideration." He clears his throat for effect. "Okay, Google, Beers ampersand Rears."

Penelope's hand covers her mouth in embarrassment as Mildred voices an objection. "Thomas, that may be a bit too scintillating. Some might take offense." But Reggie, Bruce, and Savannah quickly come to Thomas's defense. They love the name and want to hear more.

Sensing he's been given a green light, Thomas expands. "It is true that the primary qualifications for staff at Beers and Rears are visually compelling derrieres. But I'm only trying to be practical here, give many pub goers what they truly want. After all, isn't a formula for a successful enterprise part of what we're after here?" His question is obviously rhetorical.

"I envision a delicious bill of fare," he goes on, "but the pub's layout will be the main consideration." He wants everyone to picture this. "There will be a 'delicious' amount of distance between the bar and kitchen and the customer seating area. Every seat in the house is one with a view, the real reason everybody comes."

Thoughtful silence indicates the group is impressed with his marketing savvy. He continues, "Of course, all customers are welcomed as long as they're 'bum-loving' . . . gays, straights, bicons, celibates—all with glutolatrous appetites as their common denominator. An all-star, callipygian staff, naturally, will be recruited from every corner of the globe." Loud applause follows. Game over?

"Forget the lad," Reggie exudes. "I'm switching my vote to Thomas here."

Bruce opens his wallet and offers pound notes. "Take as much as you need to get started. More where that came from."

But Savannah interjects, "Give me your chump change, Sherlock, and I'll invest it for you—in another startup I know of. It's called Mikes on Bikes. Might be a bit rough—but honestly, I think you're cute enough to chain up and drag around the parking lot."

As usual, Savannah gets the big laugh—the biggest coming from Bruce himself. You can see how much those two enjoy going at each other.

Penelope is clearly smitten with Thomas, but the headwaiter's difficult to read. As for Reggie and Millie, you sensed the first time you saw them together that they'd soon be ordering wedding invitations.

Now it's your turn. You can feel the pressure—even if this is only a bar game. People at nearby tables have turned their chairs toward yours while others drift over to hear. Anticipation is in the air. Those who were here last night well remember your wild soliloquy. Those who weren't have heard about it—and they can't wait to see you perform.

Storyteller, you ready? ***Yes!***

You slowly rise, ready to repeat verbatim what she dictates. "Ladies and gentlemen!" With just that intonation you feel that you've been transformed into a genuine toastmaster, in the vein of Ivor Spencer himself.

This is so much fun. ***Good! You know the drill. Just say what I say.***

"After lengthy deliberation, I've chosen the name of our pub. It shall be entitled as follows . . . Okay, Google, Endangered Species!" The sign spins into view, surprising the gathering. Quickly, you acknowledge that once again the rules have been transgressed. "But Penelope was allowed, and her entry established a precedent. It should not matter that she didn't know the rules beforehand or that I did."

Murmurs of interest fill the space. "While ignorance of Dreams and Schemes's ancient precepts is no excuse, either a nonrhyming entry is allowed or 'tisn't. Thankfully, in dear Penelope's case, it was. As follows, so mine should be. Ladies and gentlemen, I rest my case."

Reggie pipes up, "I say, the lord of the manor is only beholden to the rules he fancies."

Nods of agreement encourage you to go on.

"As for the pub itself, Endangered Species shall be an establishment with an international flavor, its staff hailing from all over the world. Special hiring preference will be given to anyone who has received asylum on this nation's hallowed grounds. Special consideration is given to those who lost their positions because their occupations no longer exist. And to anyone who is, or ever was, an orphan."

There are murmurs of approval from the crowd as you continue. "Our menu will consist of synthetic meat based on animals that have been designated as endangered. It will likewise consist of foodstuffs derived from plants facing survival challenges. This will also apply to any decorative plants in the pub. Endangered Species ale will be brewed according to special recipes well worth preserving, which only requires consumers to ensure that they are."

"Ancient recipes for stout?" Thomas looks amazed.

Now, walk through the audience, patting shoulders as you speak.

"Our target customers will be members of vanishing breeds, especially those who are the last of their line. To anyone whose native tongue is dying or who speaks a dead language. To anyone who walks or bicycles to work."

Look over and smile at the chauffeur.

You look over at Savannah and add, "Or anyone who motorcycles at work!" This causes her to blush.

Now gesture towards the housekeeper.

"Anyone who writes letters by hand in fountain ink." Everybody points at Mildred, who smiles warmly.

Sweep your hand to the doorman and waiter.

"Who shines their own shoes," you proclaim, which prompts Reggie and Thomas to stand and take a quick bow.

Nod warmly to the receptionist.

"Who uses a handkerchief." Penelope quickly waves hers. "Indeed, the pub will reach out to all who are rare and unique. Our sign will proclaim Eccentrics Most Welcome."

Shouts of "Hear! Hear!" from everyone.

You look at all with great fondness and come to a realization: your new family is being born tonight. Your voice grows louder, the oratory stronger, your gesticulations more pronounced.

Ready for your big finish, really drive home your message?

You are as you shout, "Every person here tonight would be welcome at this pub. Precisely the type of staff member or customer we're seeking. Because, at the end of the day, all gathered here, servants on a remote English estate—are, by definition, an endangered species. Hence, our true purpose: To honor you and your kind. To preserve and protect. For merry old England. God save the king!"

The audience erupts in spirited applause. "Thank you one and all for your attention and your support," you call out. More applause.

The group's choice is quick and unanimous. Endangered Species is tonight's runaway victor.

You are gracious in your acceptance speech, claiming you had an unfair advantage by going last and apologizing for the lengthy harangue—perhaps that was unfair as well. "Thank you again!" you call out in parting. "And a very good evening to all of you indeed!" Taking measured steps toward the door, you turn and wave to a standing ovation amid a chorus of cheers and shouts of encore.

Exit stage right.

CHAPTER SEVENTEEN

Heading back, you think it was a good sign that Penelope joined in tonight and seemed to be enjoying herself. Maybe the tide is turning downstairs.

So why did you—and that amazing Storyteller—turn a silly bar game into an over-the-top address? It must have been because, despite your inherited status, somehow, you feel you've got to *earn* their allegiance. And maybe, too, because, odd as it seems, you've developed an affection for these people. You hope they'll accept you, to somehow become an elected heir.

Back in your cottage, you're slightly surprised to see there are no new messages. You'd like to listen again to the ones from *Burton's* and the Genealogical Society, but your telephone line is dead. Maybe you should use your walkie-talkie to see if you can get someone to make a test call. But you don't really want to draw anybody into this besides Christopher, who's likely sound asleep by now. Besides, this could be a normal malfunction due to the storm, nothing untoward about it.

You look forward to a long overdue good night's sleep. But first, a bath and some reading in the tub. You want to finish what you started on the plane, *Errors to Beware of in "Burton's Peerage."*

The manuscript lists mistakes in innumerable family histories and attempts to unscramble the mess. Comfortably reclining in the bathtub, you read that *Burton's Peerage* is no more authoritative on ancestral details than *Burton's General Armory* is on the legitimacy of coats of arms.

The mention of a companion volume reminds you of the rooms next door. The armory has always been locked whenever you've walked by and jiggled the knobs. You have never seen anyone go in or out.

You hear a faint sound, look up, and are nearly startled out of your wits to see the bathroom doorknob slowly turning. The door creaks open—and into the bathroom, of all people, steps Savannah Reddy, dressed in a satin-belted trench coat and holding a matching half mask on a stick to cover her eyes and forehead. The chauffeur looks like she's on her way to a masquerade ball.

"My God, Savannah, what are you doing here? And how did—"

Savannah places a finger on her lips to shush you. "I'm here, strictly, to pleasure you. Save your chitchat for the pub," she commands huskily, tossing back her head and running her free hand powerfully through her lustrous blonde mane while locking your gaze with hers.

Storyteller, can this possibly be happening? ***Sorry, we are not seeing anything out of the ordinary.*** *So this is not happening?* ***Maybe it is to you, but not to us.***

Samantha walks to the edge of the tub, places her hands on her hips, and assumes a playful expression. "So are you ready for Reddy?" she asks, twirling a lock of hair between her fingers.

Seeing as how you're trapped nude in this oversized tub at the moment, you guess you are, or might as well be. You nod faintly with a slight but not unpleasant feeling of helplessness.

Savannah takes a few steps back, pulls out a mini-speaker and a small incense burner from her coat pocket, and sets them on the sink counter. She lights the incense, then begins to unfasten her belt, purring, "Would you like to see?"

You're dumbfounded, but again you nod. You're starting to tingle inside.

Savannah sets her mask on the counter and allows her coat to slide off her shoulders and fall slowly to the floor. She's stunning, a version of Savannah you could never have imagined.

The room fills with the pulsating rhythms of Indian dance music, sounds that grow ever more wild, sensuous, and intense as Savannah gyrates forward offering her rendition of Hindi dance. Explosive quick steps. Random leaps. Sudden spins. Followed by gymnastics. Backflips. Half twists. Somersaults. Savannah pauses in the steam to allow you to admire her costume.

You're mesmerized. And holy smokes! You cannot believe her costume. She's gone full Bollywood, with a red sari and sheer blouse. Heavily bejeweled with necklaces and finger rings, bracelets and bangles, earrings and anklets, she has henna tattoos on her hands and feet and a gleaming red dot on her forehead.

The music segues into high-pitched Hindi vocals, which she lip-syncs flawlessly.

You slap the bathwater repeatedly, obviously excited. Savannah's lips are full. The steam makes it a sensual, hazy, dreamlike scene. Like the steam room of a harem or a Turkish bath. Incense billows throughout. Reddish, pretty, romantic. You inhale deeply.

She speaks, "Listen . . . believe me . . . I've been there . . . I know exactly what a man wants. Watch, I'll show you!" She unfastens her sari, leaving her clad only in a fringed costume belt with side drapes, showing her toned, athletic body off to perfection. She remains still until the music changes.

Bollywood meets bolero! Savannah starts belly dancing, gyrating in infinity loops, figure eights, and serpentine flourishes. Upon the climactic finale of the piece, she spins across the room, arriving at the counter. You sit up, breathless, to see what will happen next.

Savannah spins back, offering only a salacious grin. Then she abruptly gathers her garments, speaker, and incense, and dashes silently out of the room, flinging only a blown kiss in your direction.

Completely unnerved, you cannot, cannot, *cannot* believe what just happened here. Did that woman cast a spell or something? You never touched her nor touched yourself, but the bathwater is discolored, and you are spent and aglow. Smiling broadly, you're ready to get up, get dressed, and get back out there to find whatever else this magical evening may yet have in store.

You're not certain, but while toweling off, you think you hear a tapping noise in the vicinity of the drawing room's front entrance. You throw on a robe, walk in, unbolt the door, and try the knob. It doesn't turn. You jiggle it violently. No movement.

You run back to the bedroom, rush through the fireplace passage, and try the other door. Same result. It's bolted from the outside. You're locked in.

You rest your head against the door and sigh. Things have become scary bad. Is Savannah a party to this? Was she here to distract you while they bolted the doors?

CHAPTER EIGHTEEN

Another sleepless night.

No way you can get any rest after confirming that you've been literally "confined to quarters." Nobody answers your poundings or calls for assistance. Your room telephone service was never restored. The walkie-talkie gets only static.

You have no luck finding the secret way in and out that Christopher sometimes uses. Your worry mounts when you replay Uncle Artie's latest message. So impressed with its production values, you had forgotten to do as he instructed—arrange transportation to The Village. You could kick yourself. While he didn't say that you'd lose your inheritance if you don't file today, he did attach urgency to doing so.

Hours of tapping on walls, looking for secret buttons, feeling for hidden recesses have yielded nothing that would indicate an escape route. You had supposed that Christopher would eventually show up, via whatever secret means he knows, but as time goes by, you suspect that some "palace coup" may have restricted his comings and goings as well. Maybe all of your associates are locked up somewhere too. Maybe Rollinsby has even been apprehended. Game over?

You stand before the bathroom mirror and hope Uncle will again appear. Then you're struck by an idea. It may not help you escape, but it will pass the time. You've been curious ever since Lord Hanover first appeared, and now you intend to take the mirror down, tear it apart if necessary, and find out what's hidden behind. If you find no sign of cameras, circuitry, projection equipment, or something physical, then, well, you'll give up—you're in another dimension, Uncle Artie's a real ghost, and the men in the white coats might as well come and haul you away.

Right, Storyteller? ***You're not mad. No white coats will be coming for you this night.*** *How can I get out of here?* ***Be patient.***

A heavy gold frame surrounds the mirror. You don't know if it is attached to the wall or built in, whether you can pry it off or if you'll have to smash it. Turns out neither is required. On the right side of the frame is a small raised octagonal shape without a corresponding one on the left. Looks like a button. Feels like a button. Voilà! It's a button.

You heave a sigh of relief when the frame swings open, revealing AV equipment stacked on the shelves of a cabinet. You examine the power supply. No surprises. Standard cords run through an opening in the back of the cabinet. Several cables interconnect the units. You reason that these components are connected to more equipment—most likely the heavy-duty, theme-park stuff stacked up in the room beyond, behind the big projection wall in the drawing room.

Standing flush against the cabinet shelf is a large leather box inscribed with a title.

Three Families
The Paisleys of Abercorn
The Ogilvys of Airlie
The Frasers of Lovat

Each name is printed on a large sash that drapes over the handles of two crossed swords. Balanced in each vortex is a coat of arms emblazoned on a shield. This is the heraldry you saw in all those library books—thick lines in chevrons or saltires circumscribed beside decorations of rings, roses, crosses, mythological creatures, or scientific instruments. This looks authentic. Not at all like the flying dove and silverware on the Hanover crest.

You remove the box to examine its contents and soon recognize what it must be—a game, and from the looks of the materials provided, a simple one. There are several dozen plastic name badges and a supply of blank cards. Along with the same number of leather pouches, each identified with the emblem of one of the three families. There are hundreds of colored coins—gold, silver, copper, rust, and gray—in roughly equal amounts. Each is inscribed with COIN OF THE REALM and indicates a denomination between five and fifty. On rolled parchment paper, there are four guiding principles:

> The Wealthiest Pretender Shall Be King or Queen
> All Others to Be Destitute
> Allegiance to Family Is False
> Play to Know Thy Fate

The next item is a gold crown encrusted with jewels. Beneath it, a booklet and a short note instructing you to take the box and close the mirror.

As soon as you do, Lord Hanover appears in it.

"My beloved child, I trust you are enjoying thus far the game of succession I arranged for you. At the earliest opportunity, use this one to reverse the roles—from game player to game master—and in so doing endeavor to win over the hearts and minds of the entire household. For they are not merely your servants, my child; they are your family. And it is my fervent wish that you keep and cherish them all. Good luck!" His warm, smiling countenance gradually fades away and is replaced by your dumbfounded face in the mirror.

Well, that confirms it—Lord Hanover really has turned all of this into a game. You shake your head.

"Storyteller, this guy has taken 'eccentric' to a level beyond imagining." ***But enjoyable, right?*** "Most of the time, yeah, but being locked in isn't much fun." ***Ah, but look what you've found.*** "Should I stage this sometime if I ever get out of here?" ***By all means.***

The booklet contains detailed instructions for the nonplaying "game master." As you begin to read, you find that as leader, you will require an assistant. Of course, you'll choose Christopher. It doesn't call for any fancy equipment, only a sizable group and time. The language used in the instructions is quaint, but the concept is quite modern. You haven't the faintest idea when the "Rules of Engagement" were written or by whom. Lord Hanover himself? You wouldn't be surprised. Uncle's right—it might be the perfect activity to resolve conflicts around here. Only problem is you're locked in a fancy cell, starving to death.

Your room phone chimes. It's the receptionist, looking fetching as always. "Good afternoon. I hope you've rested well. I want to thank you for allowing me to join in last evening. I had such a lovely time, the best I've—"

"Hey, Penelope," you interrupt, "I'm locked in here! Can you get me out?"

She giggles. "You can't possibly be locked in. They haven't brought you breakfast and lunch because there's a Do Not Disturb sign on both your doors."

"I don't know anything about any sign."

"I was asked to make them as soon as I came on duty," she says. "They're nicely decorated and exceedingly polite. They say, 'Please do not disturb' with 'pretty please' in parentheses and swallows and tulips at the edges."

"Penelope, I'm really—"

She exclaims, "Oh dear me! I've just remembered you're not to be disturbed, and here I've just rang. I'm dreadfully sorry."

"Penelope, I'm really locked in!"

"Oh my, but you *are* a jokester!"

You sigh, giving up. "Have you seen Christopher?"

"Oh yes, he's right here in the lobby reading the paper. Been waiting for you to get up."

You sigh deeply. "Please put him on."

In no time at all, Christopher emerges from the fireplace, grinning at you. His secret way turns out to be simple, and he shows you. When the fireplaces rotate to open the passage, there's a button on the panel between the double walls. At the press of the button, the panel slides sideways; you walk a few steps and reach another panel with an identical button. You press it, the panel slides, and you're in the laboratory.

Christopher says he didn't try your door lock when he went by earlier; he just saw the Do Not Disturb signs. "Everything's normal here," he assures you. "No one's been dragged off in chains."

You show him Uncle Artie's latest appearance, and he agrees that Savannah must be brought into this but doesn't think using the walkie-talkie is a good idea. "The lines get all gummed up, and then they often cross. I'll go find her. Want me to stop by the kitchen and pick up something?"

"Yes, please." Your incarceration has left you famished.

As he leaves, he hands you the paper. "Lots of good bits in here today."

You settle down intending to search for clues but decide first to turn on the TV in 3DHolo mode, hoping for an update on Crunch. "The Village News at 1" graphic, accompanied by sign-on fanfare, spins into view, settling just below the news desk. The familiar faces of anchors Michael and Meredith are smiling as the camera moves in. The screen caption reads:

CRUNCH FOUND; DOGNAPERS FILE SUIT

"Good afternoon, Villagers," greets Michael. "It's April fourth, Crunch has been found and reunited with his owner, and in just a moment we will go live to the courthouse where Magistrate Winston McConnell has been hearing opening arguments in an extraordinary lawsuit brought by two village brothers, who are . . . the dognapers themselves!"

Michael continues: "Tug and Timothy Skaddle are seeking redress over Crunch's recent run amok inside their Witless cottage. The brothers lodged a formal complaint in district court yesterday, including a £2,000 request for punitive damages from the dog's owner, Nigel Wanton. The Skaddles are members of Runaway Dogs, a rugby club based in Witless. Pleading before Magistrate Winston McConnell, here's what Tug the elder had to say just an hour ago."

A video replay shows Tug Skaddle speaking to the judge. "Your honor, we only 'borrowed' the dog for last evening's match. The lads were gutted on account of the side's won no games. Me and Timothy hoped Crunch could serve as mascot, inspire the team a bit."

The magistrate nods empathetically. Michael voices over as Timothy Skaddle is shown approaching the bench: "However, neither the Skaddles nor Crunch made it to the pitch that night."

The younger Skaddle is now shown testifying. "Soon as we got 'im home to give 'im his supper, the monster destroyed the place." At that point, Timothy shocks the proceedings by dropping his drawers. The screen, however, remains frozen on a still of Timothy from the waist up. "See what Crunch's done," he says, pointing to what the viewer can assume are numerous bites and scratches about his lower extremities.

The shot then returns to the news desk as Meredith takes over. "A half hour ago, owner Nigel Wanton was called upon to explain his pet's behavior. He profusely apologized to the Skaddles in open court."

The video shows the repentant farmer testifying, "Had the brothers only consulted beforehand, I'm certain the trouble could have been avoided. But I realize that's no excuse."

The anchor continues: "The Skaddles told our on-scene reporter that they were approached by a local barrister anxious to take their case. James Prance, who now represents the plaintiff dognapers, has joined us."

Prance is shown standing outside the courtroom, wearing a loud checkered sports coat. To you, he looks sketchy, like an ambulance chaser. "Good morning, Mr. Prance," the anchor begins. "What can you tell us about this complaint you've brought?"

"Good morning, Meredith. We are petitioning the court for compensation for the suffering my clients were forced to endure, and we're asking the magistrate to incarcerate Crunch for an indefinite period of time. Upon his release, Crunch should be made to attend a reputable obedience school in order to learn manners and not to discharge his leavings in other people's cottages."

Meredith pinches her nose, then replies, "*Eau de bowwow*. Not a pleasant scent nor sight indeed . . . Michael, are we ready for Magistrate McConnell's preliminary ruling?"

Michael is shown intently listening through a tiny earpiece. "Yes, Meredith, I believe we now are."

The scene switches to a live shot of the magistrate sitting behind his bench. He's addressing the Skaddles, "Lads, I can see you've been through an ordeal. I promise swift deliberations and a final ruling soon."

The judge turns to Wanton and Crunch, who is leashed and muzzled. The farmer leans down to gently pet the top of the rottweiler's head.

"In the meantime, the pooch may be discharged to the care of its owner," McConnell rules.

"Thank you, your honor," Wanton says. "Crunch'll be less nasty when he's back in familiar surroundings."

Michael closes the segment with, "We're certain there's much more to come, and we'll be keen to learn of each new development. As I'm sure all of you out there are as well." Meredith nods in firm agreement. The newscast enters a commercial break.

Christopher returns. He hasn't found Savannah, but he's put the word out for her to get in touch. He's brought you tea and some steak-and-kidney pie smothered in mushrooms. He wants to know what you've figured out from the newspaper.

"Well, I saw the dognaper update but couldn't find—" Your walkie-talkie rings. This time the dining hall D button is blinking, and you wonder why the chef would be calling, but no, it's Savannah. She speaks in a near whisper, as if afraid of being overheard. "I can't talk long. The road's still closed, but I think I can get through on one of the bikes. Can't risk taking you along, though, so just slip the docs to Reggie, and he'll get them to me. I should leave ASAP so I can be back while it's still daylight." The connection breaks off.

At some point, in private of course, you need to ask her about last night.

But, Storyteller, was she part of a plot? ***Don't ask us. Ask her.***

You tell Christopher the gist of her message. "Why was she calling from the dining hall?" you ask. "And why do we first have to give these documents to Reggie?"

Christopher shrugs. "Just have to trust her, I guess."

You nod, gathering the documents. "Once I'm in the lab, what's the best way out from there?"

Christopher draws a quick diagram, which you easily follow as you depart. You end up in a storage closet underneath the lobby staircase. If you hadn't been in such a rush, you'd have enjoyed exploring the laboratory. As you passed through, you spied a lot of AV equipment and several high-end workstations, the kind Christopher said are used to make Pixar animation hits. You now understand how Uncle Artie is able to make his mystic appearances. The racks of servers and rows of workstations are serious gear.

You exit the closet but don't see Reggie at his post. Seeing no one else either, you bound up the stairs and head for the Falstaff, hoping to find the doorman in his favorite haunt. You cross the rotunda and enter the left hallway. So far so good.

You hate having to walk by the royal suites, though; one of these doors may suddenly burst open. Which happens as you pass His Majesty's. "Halt!" Farnsworth shouts, again seemingly with some object in hand. Ignoring him, you rush into the pub.

Bruce hails you with, "G'day, mate! Ol' Reg's been looking everywhere for you. Just left, in fact. All business today, Reg is—could be the first time in pub history he popped in and didn't stay for a pint."

You jerk your thumb behind and mouth, "Farnsworth."

"Ah, no worries. This is your sanctuary. He'd never set foot in here." Bruce points to the parchments affixed to the wall, the edicts that authorize karaoke and bars the butler from the premises.

"But I think I just saw him with a gun!" you tell him.

"Must be your imagination, mate," says Bruce. "Ol' Knives and Forks is never armed. Almost nobody in this country is."

Help me out here, plant friends. Am I hallucinating again? A pink mushroom appears overhead, warbling, ***You're projecting fear. We are merely the projectors.*** *What can I do?* ***Dispel your fear.*** *Easier said than done.* ***Try it. You might be pleasantly surprised.***

Bruce reaches underneath the counter and produces a manor floor plan. "I reckon Reg is in our other establishment." He shows you how to leave by the rear exit and use the underground passage to reach the other side. He tells you you'll find another set of stairs that leads to the whisky bar; it's how the public goes back and forth. "By the way," he adds, "your Endangered Species toast was huge. It's all they're going on about this morning."

You tear out the exit and bound down the stairs, across the passageway, and up another flight then into the bar. Nobody's there. But soon you hear the door open and close. It's the housekeeper. "Oh, hello, dear. Was just across at the library. Didn't see you come in. Reggie was just here looking for you. He seemed rather frantic and went off to check the spa." Her smile is maternal as she reaches up and straightens your collar. "Reg and I were enormously proud of the talk you gave last night. It really rallied the troops."

You depart, shuddering at the prospect of having to pass the offices of the butler and the concierge. But your mad dash is uneventful aside from the PA announcement you hear while crossing the rotunda:

"Attention, please. Mr. Farnsworth reminds the staff that his regularly scheduled seminar will commence promptly in the assembly hall after dismissal. This evening he offers us a special treat—a complete video tour of the grounds. Light refreshments will be served. Perhaps these inviting summer scenes will put us in better spirits, since, we regret to inform you, the village road remains closed and a second storm is reportedly fast approaching the county. Carry on."

You suppose the bars won't be up and running early due to the seminar. If you weren't such an unwelcome guest, you wouldn't mind dropping in and catching the tour.

As soon as you enter the spa, you spot Thomas arranging tropical drink cards on tabletops. "Ah, you've just missed one Reginald McCabe," he tells you.

"He just left?" You're exasperated.

"Right. Been searching high and low for you," he says. "Mentioned something about needing to obtain sensitive documents before dispatching Chauffeur Reddy on a secret mission. Said he'd try the pub next. You should have no difficulty catching up with him there. Once inside, he rather tends to linger."

The pub? You're too exhausted for any more of this wild-goose chase.

Thomas suggests a drink and a bite of something. He hurries away. But almost immediately, you hear the doors at the pool entrance slide open and the voice of the concierge. "He's not down here, James. Where should I look next?" She's standing still, staring at her phone; she doesn't see you. You spring from the chair, seize the packet of papers, and make for the door. As soon as you step into the hall you see doorman Reggie McCabe standing, of all places, at his assigned post, looking fabulous in his green-and-gold ensemble.

A door slams, and Farnsworth emerges from his office, again waving the same object. You're sure you're not seeing things. He sees you and bellows, "Now stop right there!" Behind Reggie, you spot Noël coming fast up the hall.

The spa door flies open, and the concierge steps out, crying, "James! James! Do something!"

Fearing gunshots any second now, you grab your packet of documents and make a run for it. You sense Farnsworth closing in. He's shouting, "You cannot escape!" You desperately hope he's not going to actually shoot.

Signaling Reggie with your eyes, you rush toward him, hoping he understands your intent. Still no shots. As you speed by, you feel him snatch the packet from your hand as though it's a baton in a relay race.

Let's surprise them. Do as I tell you. Say what I say. Once again, it's your "drama coach." *Of course. It always works so well when you're in charge.*

Embrace the chef and kiss his cheeks.

You call out, "Bonjour, Monsieur Noël Elle Léon! *Comment allez-vous?* Léon Elle Noël Monsieur bonjour!" Reaching the chef, you embrace him and kiss both of his cheeks while catching a blast of howling wind and hearing the heavy thud of the manor door closing.

Spin him around.

You spin the startled chef around, gushing, "My dear chef, keep sending me those magnificent mushrooms! I adore them. What is your secret?" You continue raving over the magnificent food and drink.

Lock arms and march him forward.

As instructed, you march Noël up to a dumbfounded Farnsworth, who does not display any weapon. Inwardly, you heave a short sigh of relief and continue with the Storyteller's spiel.

"Good day! Good day, Mr. Farnsworth! Was just telling our dear Chef Noël here how splendid his kitchen's repast is." Van Scoy arrives, and you nod amiably, neither halting your stream of delirious chitchat nor waiting for any replies. Then, glancing at your wrist as if you're late for an appointment, you bid them adieu. "Oh dear, I simply have to get going. Running a manor this size never stops. But you three are just splendid. Do carry on."

As you depart, they observe you with the same stupefied expressions they wore when they watched you consult an imaginary wristwatch.

Turn back and call to the concierge.

Suddenly you turn back as if you've forgotten something and call out, "Adrienne, mind doing me a favor?"

Van Scoy looks jarred as she stammers, "I beg your pardon."

"If I'm not around when my New York office calls, tell them to *buy*. If Paris calls, *sell*. And should my man in Rio check in, tell him he's fired. Give a twelve percent raise to all staff at the Prague branch. Got all that?" The woman is speechless, her mouth agape. "Thanks, Adrienne. You're an angel."

Now, walk briskly to reception.

You stride over to Penelope, who, remarkably, is also at her post. Pleasantly, but loudly, you inquire, "I say, has outside telephone service been restored?" She regrets that it has not. "Well, in that case, is the afternoon paper in?" She hands you a copy. You point to a sofa near the fireplace. "I'll be right over there should any calls come through or guests arrive."

Now, go and relax in that sofa by the fireplace.

You settle in, pick up the remote, and unmute the volume while keeping the trio, still astonished and frozen in place, in the corner of your eye.

Oh, Storyteller, you're the best. ***So are you, dear. You were smashing just now.***

CHAPTER NINETEEN

The screen caption now displays:

UN PALINDROME POUR LA SAISON

Meredith introduces her next story, for which the backdrop is a large photo of the Manor House chef looking especially striking and debonair.

"Chef Noël Elle Léon has been faithfully serving residents and guests at Hanover Manor for several years. But have you ever wondered how he got his start in the culinary world? Earlier this week, we visited the manor's famed Michelin-starred restaurant to find out. We first spoke with Butler-Administrator James Farnsworth." You press the 3DHolo button to enlarge the broadcast.

The scene changes to a taped report. Meredith is in the lobby standing next to Farnsworth. To the camera, she says, "Monsieur Léon caught Butler-Administrator James Farnsworth's eye when he read in *La Cucina Italiana* a decade ago of the young man's virtuoso preparation in the apprentice division of *Le Prix Culinare International*, a European competition for chefs." She turns to Farnsworth. "Mr. Farnsworth, you reportedly called *Le Cordon Bleu*, then interviewed and hired their passionate, precocious student over the phone. Is that true?"

Farnsworth replies, "It is. Though under ordinary circumstances, I would not have taken such an impulsive and seemingly foolhardy gamble on hiring a key person I had never met. However, I was desperate, as I had just dismissed our Hungarian chef who had disturbed many of his diners."

Meredith asks, "Chef Emil? I've heard he hosted rather extraordinary fetes outdoors after rainstorms when the sun reappeared."

Replies Farnsworth, "Indeed, but some far exceeded the bounds of propriety." The butler clears his throat. "As I was saying, I was under the gun because the annual Manor House Christmas Ball was only ten days away, and the number of qualified and available chefs in all of England at that time was probably less than aught."

The camera now picks up Van Scoy and Noël who have walked up to join the scene. Meredith gestures welcomingly and says, "Let's hear the chef's own account of the competition. Monsieur Noël, was it anything like those pressure-filled contests we often see on television where master chefs are unremittingly yelling at apprentices?"

The camera moves to the chef. *"Oh non, madame."*

Meredith interrupts. "But Chef, at times you are such an avid diva in your kitchen, are you not?"

Noël laughs, then replies. "*Oui, madame.* But *Le Prix Culinaire International* is *not* a competition for *les gens ordinaires*. I no longer remember the precise details of many of my dishes, much less the ingredients or preparation methods I used. I only recall the audacity of my presentation."

"Noël dearest," Adrienne purrs as she brushes his shoulder, "please try to recollect for us the items on your menu that day."

Oh no. Storyteller, is something going on between those two again? Has she taken him back? This prompts an immediate and mischievous observation from one of the older males. ***Perhaps you should ask her precisely that question. Getting rather late in the chase, you know.*** *Does Farnsworth suspect?* ***We don't know his mind, only yours, and only when you summon us.***

Noël snaps his fingers, brightens, and exclaims, *"Oui, je me souviens maintenant."* ***He said he now remembers.***

"I first served the judges a leafy salad with crusty bread, an assortment of sharp cheeses, then a fish entrée in a tangy, slightly sour sauce. My main dish—what it was I cannot be certain, but possibly *Chateaubriand*—came next, followed by the same fish but presented in a creamier, sweeter sauce. I then made a repetition of cheese, but in a milder selection. I closed with a serving of sweet bread to accompany a fruit salad."

The chef beams and bows. The group offers polite applause.

Meredith now addresses the concierge, whom she seems to know personally. "Adrienne, I heard you were coincidentally present on that occasion too, as an observer representing a Dutch culinary society. Why do you suppose the chef chose such a radical bill of fare?"

The concierge places her index finger on the side of Noël's head and speaks to the camera. "His mind adores the palindrome. It's literally how he thinks, speaks, creates, approaches life. Our dear chef goes forward, reverses, then forward once again, then reverses course once more. It's how, I've gathered, he manages time flow. I believe the phenomenon is known as 'chronesthesia,' if memory serves."

Says Meredith, "Adrienne, that term may be unfamiliar to some of our audience. Do you mind explaining?"

"Chronesthesia, as I understand it, is the capacity of an individual to be constantly aware of the past and the future."

Adrienne, you really should join us in the pub some evening. You'd fit right in. ***Dude, why don't you just invite her?*** The pesky preteen has returned to egg you on. *Okay, kiddo, watch this.*

You beckon the concierge, who stands for a moment, perplexed. "Ms. Van Scoy, you're on the news."

"Yes, I can see that," she replies.

"Come watch with me."

"I really haven't got time." She looks torn.

"With chronesthesia you do!"

Van Scoy seems nervous but manages to say, "Well, that's quite witty."

"That's nothing," you quickly reply. "You should join us in the pub some evening. Witticisms, hilarity, improvisations abound."

"Thank you, but I'm usually occupied elsewhere."

You're undeterred. "Have you ever heard of i-two-one?"

"Why, yes," she replies, seeming a bit surprised.

"Then you should come."

Van Scoy exchanges glances with Noël and Farnsworth, then walks through the news story to stand beside you. Farnsworth is left fuming. Noël looks stunned. The shot returns to the news desk where Michael addresses Meredith. "Hmm. So while you were out there, Meredith, did you sample some of the chef's famous entrées?"

"No, unfortunately," replies the concierge on-screen, "we were not present for lunch or dinner, but at tea, Chef Noël did offer us sweets. One of his original creations. 'Stressed Desserts,' he called it."

Noël looks at you, and you both share spontaneous smiles. Looking confused, the concierge returns to rejoin her colleagues.

The segment ends. But after viewing the next round of stories, you are disappointed that there was no Crunch update. You mute the TV and open the paper. There's another contribution by Uncle Artie in the Thought for the Day column.

A THOUGHT FOR TODAY: "LOCATION, LOCATION, AND LOCATION!"

LOCATION, LOCATION, and location? Why, this whole Internet thing has quite knocked the stuffing out of that old business axiom, hasn't it? Now you've got virtual this and virtual that, virtual storefronts with goods and services online in living colour for immediate purchase, and electronic cash to buy them with. And I've no doubt there are even more technologies on the way that will render moot the entire point of anything's or anybody's physical or temporal location.

Storyteller, I'm almost certain a clue is embedded in that one. Must think on it more. ***Indeed there is. And indeed, you must.***

You sense the trio has finally departed. Ducking back into the stairwell closet, you negotiate the passage and head toward your room. In the laboratory, you pause to admire the vast array of equipment. On impulse, you switch on a nearby monitor.

"Oh my God!" you involuntarily shout as you see your mad i21 soliloquy from the other night being replayed. After a moment or two, you pick up a nearby remote and fast-forward to the next segment, which shows the Dreams & Schemes pub game from last night. Following that are several clips of scenes you and Christopher captured with the blue remote:

Farnsworth's tryst with the chef, Van Scoy's angry breakup with him, Savannah and Mildred musing whether you might be gay. Plus a half dozen other encounters you watched before either live at the portal or on the grid in your room. You conclude that the manor must have an elaborate security system and somehow you've stumbled onto some of the recordings.

You're just about to turn the monitor back off when you start seeing new scenes, ones you hadn't seen before involving intrigue and machinations you didn't know about until now.

The first one shows Savannah in Farnsworth's office, seated in front of his desk. Standing behind the butler's chair with her arms folded and wearing a serious expression is Van Scoy. Farnsworth is seated and is riffling through a stack of forms spread out in front of him.

"Ms. Reddy," Van Scoy says after a moment, "as you may know, it will soon be time to renew your work visa here. Mr. Farnsworth has received the forms from immigration."

"Yes, madam, I know," Savannah replies. "Lord Hanover always provided the Certificate of Sponsorship in the past. I love my position here more than I can express. I sincerely hope I'll be allowed to stay on."

Farnsworth looks up and says, "As long as you continue to perform your duties satisfactorily, your position here will remain secure. But you must know we also require unflinching loyalty from staff."

Savannah places her palms on the arms of the chair, leans forward, and says, "Mr. Farnsworth, whoever's in charge here can expect no less from me."

At that point, Van Scoy walks from behind the desk to stand beside the chauffeur. She places a hand on Savannah's shoulder, leans in, and says softly, "Savannah, I must say you've made quite a name for yourself over here. You're quite the talk of The Village, with your achievements in motorcycle racing and the success of your football teams."

Savannah coughs nervously, looks up at Van Scoy, and says, "You are correct, madam. My life over here is one I could only have dreamed of, thanks to Lord Hanover and the two of you."

Farnsworth straightens the papers and says, "Miss Reddy, we've come upon some intelligence that leads us to believe that the so-called heir is not legitimate after all, and as such, we intend to dispute any and all of his claims to Arthur's title and estate. You may soon be handed some important documents and asked to courier them down to The Village. If that happens, we want you to inform us straightaway. Can we count on your cooperation in this matter?"

Savannah hesitates before replying, "I'll do my best, Mr. Farnsworth."

The clip ends.

You don't know when this was recorded, but now that Savannah actually has the documents, you're worried about their fate. Has she informed them? Are the documents safe? Will they really be delivered as promised?

Storyteller, any advice? ***You have no choice but to hope for the best.*** *And be prepared for the worst, right?* ***Always, that's life.***

The next clip is even more disturbing. Inside the kitchen, Chef Noël has assembled several of his cooking staff. The discussion is heated and entirely in French, but a young male Storyteller translates the rapid-fire exchanges. You get a chilling picture of what may befall Savannah should she try to make it down to The Village—what may be transpiring at this very moment if she is already en route. Initially, Noël wants to know who among the cooks and other helpers knows how to operate any of the high-performance bikes in the manor garage. Several hands go up. Noël then divulges that he needs one or more of them to follow Savannah, should she depart the manor soon, and intercept her because she has stolen vital documents and must be prevented from handing them over to undisclosed parties in The Village, scoundrels who seek to gain control of the manor.

The group's reaction is shock and disbelief. Several state that they know Savannah well, like and admire her, and cannot believe she was involved in anything nefarious. Most are not in favor of pursuing the young lady. But others press Noël for more details, asking if their livelihoods and visas would be endangered if these documents fell into the wrong hands. Noël replies convincingly that they would, that, for everyone's sake, the chauffeur must be stopped. Just as the clip ends, you get the impression that one or two of the chef's "brigands" are going to volunteer for the mission.

Storyteller, have I completely misjudged the chef? He was starting to seem harmless. ***As you've seen, the chef has multiple desires and designs and does tend to oscillate between them.*** *What does that mean?* ***That he has a palindromic personality.*** *Did Savannah decide to go down to the village? Did she* *make it safely? Did she deliver the documents? Is she still on our side?* ***So many questions! Again, we must remind you, no spoilers!***

You return to your quarters, frantic with worry, and fill Christopher in on your escapade with Farnsworth et al. along with a digest of the surveillance tapes in the lab. "Now all we can do," you tell him, "is hope Savannah's on our side and she makes it down to The Village."

Christopher says now that you're back, he wants to go on a reconnaissance mission of his own. But first he wants to know what happened to Uncle Artie's wine. "Mega pricey—did you consume the entire bottle last night?"

"No I didn't—what do you mean?"

"Well, it's gone." You cast glances all around. It's gone, all right, and you've no idea how or when. It was the last thing on your mind as you tried to escape from the "Tower of London." If somebody took it, they probably did so while you were in the whisky bar dreaming and scheming. Maybe the chef has decided there's something about the label that's important. You hope so; it'd be good if the opposition runs down that false trail.

From his expression, you know Christopher brings big news. And he's brought more pink tea. Lad thinks of everything. Now he points the remote at the fruit bowl on the grid. The life-sized window opens to reveal the chef examining a wine bottle. *"Qu'est-ce que c'est? Le vingt-neuf février, dix-neuf-cent, soixante dix-huit? C'est impossible! Léon, émir cornu, d'un roc rime Noël!"* he mutters to himself.

Noël stews for a moment more, then suddenly hollers like a madman. He yanks his walkie-talkie from inside his apron and blurts, "Monsieur, I believe I know how we can—how do you say?—*enregistrer* the computer."

He pauses to listen. "*Oui, oui*, I'll meet you there." He rushes out of the scene. But a moment later, Farnsworth rushes through the office on his way to the kitchen.

"Don't know what Mr. Farnsworth's up to," Christopher observes, "but Chef Noël has definitely figured out the wine label. He said, 'What's this?

February 29, 1978? It's impossible!' He finished with a silly palindromic aside about how his name rhymes with Christmas."

"Christopher, think they'll figure out April Fools'?"

"We shouldn't underestimate them," the boy replies, sounding serious.

"So what if they somehow log on to Windows?" you remind him. "They can't open the files without the passwords. And we've got the only copy of Emil's recipe."

"They'll see what's there—maybe incinerate the entire folder," the boy reminds you. "Savannah could disappear with the only copies we know of. Or be intercepted. The weather could clear, the road reopen, and Mr. Farnsworth could summon the constables up here and have you arrested."

A long pause allows all this to sink in. Christopher's right on all counts. "And there's more." He points to the remote. His expression is grim.

"Bad news?"

"No, maybe better actually." Christopher grins. He knows his flair for the dramatic has once again sucked you in. Now he's ready to show two snippets he captured before Noël's. At the third painting on "Military Row," the camera picks up Van Scoy in the library on her walkie-talkie speaking to Farnsworth. She sounds resigned as she tries to persuade the butler to give up his campaign against you.

"James, listen to me. If there are copies of the documents on the computer, and worse, if they've found them, then it's all over. You've got to accept that. If that's the case, we need to think about surviving, salvaging what we can here, about staying together. Don't you see?" The concierge appears to be on the verge of tears. "This can't go on. I say we try to repair the damage and start anew with Arthur's heir, who, as you've said, isn't a bad sort. James, promise me you'll think about it." Adrienne ends the call and collapses in a chair.

Indeed. You're a "good sort," if only she would give you the chance to prove it! Again, the teen girls appear. ***Well, you keep talking, talking, talking . . .***

"Christopher, this is a positive sign, but do you think she'll get her nerve back if Noël manages to crack the code?"

Says Christopher, "Put that thought on hold until you see Farnsworth." You will, but you sure didn't like hearing that "staying together" bit.

Says the elderly British male you first met on the ride up, ***As some of us***

have oft stated, you should endeavor to "decouple" them. *Yeah, but some of you don't agree. They scold me for even thinking about approaching.* ***Don't listen to those fuddy-duddies.***

"Remember how angry he was yesterday?" Christopher asks. "Well, we're not the only ones who caught it." The new window opens to reveal the butler pacing in a small circle, obviously agitated, listening to his walkie-talkie. Exasperated, he shouts, "Noël, you went completely beyond the pale." A pause. "Don't interrupt me! Yes, I *know* I told you last night I'd ordered our guest confined to quarters, but I certainly never gave you any direct instruction to jam those locks! Or to make those absurd signs."

Farnsworth pauses to listen, but again soon interrupts: "Have you gone completely mad? Even if they could get up here, what would they do, arrest the heir apparent to the Hanover estate? No, the only thing I want you to do, Noël, is fix those locks, and quickly. Call off your brigands. And while you're at it, go to my office and change the entry code. Use one of the numbers from Miss Reddy's list. Tell us later which one."

Christopher, pointing to Farnsworth, who's listening intently and at length, sighs and says, "Oh dear, here's where it gets amusingly dicey."

After another moment the butler again explodes. "Noël, listen to me!" he cries. "We are not going to 'get rid' of anyone. It's too late."

Storyteller, does the chef really want to get rid of me? ***We have no way of knowing what he thinks.*** *But you do know how it turns out.* ***True, and soon enough so shall you.***

Farnsworth's expression changes to melancholy as he listens to the chef's reply. "Noël, I do understand how you feel, but I've made up my mind," he says in a much softer tone. "There can no longer be *us*." Now Farnsworth's jaw literally drops. He seems unable to believe what he's hearing. "An *official ménage à trois*, you say! Never! Never! Never! To *extend* this ancient lineage? No! No! No! My good man, you must be—"

Farnsworth, apparently interrupted, stops speaking. He listens for just a moment longer, then exclaims, "Noël, the times may be changing, but the country would never accept any redefinition of the noble classes, such as you are suggesting. Listen to me! You must abolish that idea forever. It is revolting and blasphemous. Besides, I would not share Adrienne with any other man."

Alas, he already has, Storyteller. ***You'll soon witness the denouement of this love triangle.*** *Can you at least give me a hint?* ***What! And spoil the ending? Never! You must live it. It's your story, not theirs!***

As the butler listens further, his expression changes to controlled fury. His reply is measured but emits like a low hiss. "Say what you will, Monsieur Léon, but know this: the moment you do, you'll forfeit your position here. She'll terminate you on the spot." Farnsworth disconnects and, with a disgusted sigh, steps out of the scene.

Christopher says he wants to get his hands on whatever list he's talking about. You pull it from your briefcase, explaining how Penelope mistakenly gave it to you the other morning. You unfold it.

Motor Cars

Aston Martin	HM 536851
Bentley	HM 500124
Bugatti	HM 164475
Ferrari	HM 621006
Jaguar	HM 077887
Lamborghini	HM 992996
Land Rover	HM 992996
Maserati	HM 181926
Porsche	HM 254452
Rolls-Royce	HM 379188

Motor Bikes (Current)

BMW	HM 149725
Ducati	HM 149724
Harley-Davidson	HM 149721
Honda	HM 149722
Kawasaki	HM 149723

Motor Bikes (Classic)

BMW	HM 070116
"Captain America"	HM 182301
Harley-Davidson	HM 001982
Indian	HM 000613
Pierce	HM 108765

Nothing jumps out. You hand the list to Christopher, who, after only a moment, snaps his fingers and exclaims, "I've got it!" You motion him to give it back, saying not to tell because you want to see if you can get it yourself. Returning to "game mode," you recheck the list and the surveillance clip where Farnsworth mentions it.

You glance at the TV. "Hey, Christopher," you call out, "check out the news." A screen caption reads:

ROAD RAGE RAGING ON

"Freeze that, please," Christopher calls out. "Okay, unmute and play, please."

Michael is narrating from behind the news desk. "Last week, we told you the constable's report found Rabblesnare Lane was used by 452 vehicles per day, of which 254 were large trucks. This week's count, the constabulary has told us, will be significantly higher, as it already exceeds the previous tallies just three days in."

"Hmm," Christopher muses, "I wonder if Noël used the list or saw this report." Then he jumps up, exclaiming, "Tonight's the night—Mr. Knives and Forks!"

"So?"

"They'll all be at the seminar, and we'll get another crack at it!"

"At what?"

"Mr. Farnsworth's office! Open the INTERNET folder. Snatch its contents!"

"Christopher, have you gone mad?"

"We are all born mad; some remain so."

"Godot again?"

He nods yes, then spreads his palms. "Show me a sane man . . . and I will cure him for you."

"Another one?"

"No, that one's courtesy of Sigmund Freud." Wow. This fourteen-year-old is really something else, you conclude—for the umpteenth time.

And, oh yes, that reminds you of your great discovery from your recent incarceration. You fetch the Three Families game box. Christopher's eyes widen as he reads the instructions. "Are you really going to stage this?" he asks.

You nod affirmatively. "But, Christopher, do you regret reading it? Spoils your chance to experience the succession, to possibly be crowned king."

"I'd never win anyway," he replies.

"So how do you think you'd have ended up?"

Christopher consults the outcomes section of the guide. "Oh, storming the Bastille, probably." He laughs, adding that he'd much rather be running the game with you than actually playing.

The PA chimes. "Good evening, residents and staff. This is Adrienne speaking. I do hope you've had a pleasant day. Everything at Manor House seems perfectly in order at present, thanks to your efforts. James's presentation will commence shortly, but attendance tonight is not mandatory. However, if you are free and would like to come along, we would be more than delighted. Thank you."

"Such a friendly tone—what in the world should we make of *that*?" you ask. Christopher thinks it may be a ruse to keep you off balance.

"But could it possibly be," you wonder, "that she's had a genuine change of heart and is trying to adopt a nicer persona?" Christopher sticks his finger in his mouth and makes a gagging noise. You gather he doesn't think so.

You rise. You want to go for it. The sequence Noël selected to set the door lock is clear to you. As is the password Uncle Artie used to protect the INTERNET folder.

CHAPTER TWENTY

You head for the door, giving Christopher a so-don't-just-sit-there look.

The hallway's deserted. Everybody's probably at the seminar.

You punch in the Porsche plate number from the vehicle list and press ENTER. No entry, but thankfully, no alarm. "Okay, reverse it," Christopher instructs. When you do so, the door unlocks, and the two of you duck inside.

Christopher bounds into the center of the room, unsheathes an imaginary sword, and points it at an aristocrat in a wall painting, calling out, "Murder for a jar of red rum!" You roll your eyes.

While waiting for sign-on, which is taking a long time due to an update Windows has messaged it's running, Christopher shakes an impatient finger at the screen, exclaiming, "Dammit I'm mad!"

"Okay. Okay, Christopher. I get that you got it."

"Of course Chef Noël would choose those particular plate numbers, maybe even unconsciously," Christopher surmises. "His mind naturally parses everything for palindromes."

"So you're saying he chose the Porsche's numbers and then decided to reverse them?"

Christopher cups his chin. "Maybe he got some bright idea from the news after realizing the traffic numbers matched those of the plate, only backwards. Or maybe he didn't see the news but just did it on his own as a final flourish."

"Or maybe, Christopher, somebody behind the scenes—you know, the ones we think might be secretly helping us—planted that story to point us in the right direction."

Christopher laughs. "On live television? My, my but we are ruminating way, way outside the box, aren't we now?"

But you don't consider it to be far-fetched. It's the most likely of explanations to your way of thinking, which at the moment seems sharp as a tack. Did Rollinsby plant it? you wonder.

The desktop appears. The INTERNET folder is there. The DOCUMENTS folder is gone. You're not surprised. It's what you'd expected them to do—if they could ever log on.

"Amazing," you whisper, "*les saboteurs* worked out April Fools'."

Christopher looks at you quizzically. "Funny name, that. Where did you get *les saboteurs*?"

"Don't know, Christopher. It just popped into my head a moment ago. So, no DOCUMENTS folder. Now Savannah's got the only copies," you say.

Christopher turns to you, confiding, "Still not sure about her, either." You chuckle inwardly. If only the boy knew how much more there is about Savannah to not be sure of.

Right, Storyteller? ***We've no idea what you're talking about.*** *C'mon, you know, the night she burst in doing full-on Bollywood.* ***We witnessed no such thing.*** *Really, did I dream it, then?* ***We do not know the content of your dreams.***

Christopher double-clicks the INTERNET folder and asks for the newspaper when the dialogue appears. It is such an easy word, one that most kids his age could readily spell, so you're surprised that he needs to check. Oh, now you get it. He wants *you* to identify the password—so *he'll* know you know. You point to the key word three times in succession as he grins and taps it in.

The folder opens, revealing a single icon, a stylized "HM" in purple and gold, which Christopher double-clicks. There's no sign-on, no splash screen that titles or credits the program. An instant of cursor animation, and suddenly it's all there.

A full-screen graphic on the oversized curved monitor puts the viewer in a front-row theater seat that looks out on an elevated stage—a gold-tiled floor delineated by green lines and small diamonds at the corner of each square. The front ledge, suggestive of an Elizabethan motif, is convex and curves to a center point. On each side, pillars arch toward the top of the screen, enhancing the 3D effect of the scene. The rear of the stage is dominated by a drawn theater curtain, the same one that dropped last evening to close Uncle Artie's rotunda appearance. It is a feat of graphics skill, with every ruffle and fold meticulously rendered.

Now come the sounds of an orchestra tuning up and the stirrings and murmurs of an audience anticipating a performance. There are no on-screen directions. You intuitively know that a mouse click will raise the rear curtain or bring a costumed actor onstage. You nod to Christopher to proceed.

To a violin background, the curtain rises to reveal Arthur Hanover standing in the center of the lobby. He's dressed in a blue blazer over a white shirt with a red paisley ascot. His slacks are dark gray over tasseled loafers. He is smiling magnanimously, arms outstretched, palms upturned.

His image speaks. "Welcome to Manor House. Please feel free to wander freely about the premises. Explore . . . discover . . . linger . . . enjoy. I'll be right here and will speak to you again before you depart."

This greeting isn't for you. It's for anyone, everyone. Why?

Any idea, Storyteller? ***They've devised a game based on your current adventure here.*** *Who's "they"?* ***Perhaps those unseen who are helping you and the boy?***

The entire lobby rotates, erasing Uncle Artie from the scene. It settles on a view of the fireplace and stops. For the first time, a mouse cursor appears. Christopher brushes the mouse back and forth on the pad but doesn't click on anything just yet.

He holds down the mouse and drags it across the pad. The scene rotates à la Google Earth; it's a virtual video tour, and the manor scene zooms in or out. Christopher "walks" in different directions. In the background, virtual servants go about their duties and occasionally make eye contact and nod in your direction.

"Hey there, hello!" you call out to one passing by.

The servant stops, smiles, and replies, "Hello to you too, kind sir."

Christopher calls out, "How's the weather shaping up for tomorrow morning?"

The servant pauses for a moment, then says resignedly, "More storms, I'm afraid."

Both you and Christopher are enchanted as the servant turns and goes on his way.

"This isn't 3D," Christopher whispers. "It's 4D. I think the Windows update included its AI extensions."

"How does he know about tomorrow's weather?" you wonder.

"Oh, that's easy. The interface consults the web forecast. Didn't you notice his slight pause before he answered?"

You nod, saying, "Yeah, it's like my sprinklers back home knowing when to water the lawn. So cool to see that applied to a game."

Despite the magical scene, there's the unpleasant reality of this room. You cast nervous glances at both doors, then over at the massive bookcase—the only place from which Farnsworth could not possibly have come. Yet he did. Yesterday's scary feeling returns. It must show on your face because Christopher gestures at you to relax.

"This is great," you concede, "but we'd better go. There's nothing to print. Let's get out of here."

"Another minute, please," the boy requests. "We've all seen this kind of 360-degree interface before," Christopher marvels, "but I've never seen photorealistic people walking about reacting live to sounds *we* make. Spot on, Uncle Artie!"

But it's time to leave—Oh! Too late.

Whoosh! The bookcase revolves, and Farnsworth strides into the room. He's holding something. You hear another whoosh as the bookcase rotates shut. Terrified, you watch the butler raise what might be his pistol and bear down on you.

Fear not! a plant warble commands.

Abruptly, Farnsworth stops. "So sorry. Didn't mean to startle you," he says softly. "I wanted to give you this device of Lord Hanover's . . . And I've something to tell you as well." You could have sworn he was holding that pistol again.

Above, the cactus warbles, ***You dispelled your fear. Thus, it can no longer be projected as an illusionary item.*** *Okay, thanks, plant pal. Think I'm starting to get this.*

The butler hands you a remote, identical to your blue one, except its orb is red. This is what your fear mistook for a pistol. "It's what allowed me to come upon you so unexpectedly just now and last time—and I do sincerely apologize for my outburst on that occasion."

Aha! Storyteller, that's how Noël got into his bedroom that time. ***Bingo!***

Farnsworth pauses. This seems difficult for him. "Apparently, Arthur has left intact an ancient network of hidden passageways that connect rooms and floors here at the manor. A few weeks ago, I found this amongst his things and must confess to having tried it out on a few occasions. I'm certain your uncle would want you to have it."

He turns to Christopher. "What I said to you yesterday was unforgivable. Yet I wish you to accept my sincerest apology." The boy, eyes bugging out, simply nods. Turning back to you, Farnsworth announces, "A text attachment has arrived, which I've printed and placed in your room."

That reminds you. "Thank you, Mr. Farnsworth. I'm curious. You can text, but I can't?"

The butler merely shakes his head and stammers, "Sometimes progress isn't progress." Then brightening, he informs, "But the locks are fully repaired, and again I must apologize for another inexcusable act on my part."

You notice that he's covering for Noël. Or maybe you should credit him for taking full responsibility. "I wanted to inform you of it straightaway," he continues, "but you weren't in your room. Noël has changed the combination here, but I haven't seen him to learn what it is." Farnsworth refrains from stating the obvious—that you two have learned it. He points to the remote. "That is why I entered with that." He bows and departs through the hallway door

Christopher and you exchange shrugs, not knowing what to say. The boy turns back to the computer and rotates the panorama to face the front entrance. Whereupon Lord Hanover steps forward once again. "Thank you for visiting Manor House. Please know that you are always welcome here, whether your visit is virtual or real. Farewell."

Impulsively, Christopher shouts, "I miss you, Uncle Artie."

To which Hanover replies, "I miss you too, lad."

The theater curtain falls, the music fades away, and the screen goes blank.

You and Christopher depart and head straight for your quarters. Your key works, and inside, all is in order. Sitting on your night table is a printout confirming that your documents were received and filed, and that the court accepted them "in absentia." The final sentence advises that the documents will soon be in the public domain.

In other words, Storyteller, I should get ready to be hounded by the press and others? ***It could well be a mob scene all right.*** *So happy and relieved that Savannah made it.* ***So were we.*** *But you knew all along.* ***Still, we are, were, will be relieved each and every time.***

You hand the paper to Christopher, expressing the hope that now you can get a decent night's sleep, happy that Savannah turned out to be "on our side" after all and made it to the law offices safely. But Christopher isn't ready to call it a day. He wants the two of you to make a trip upstairs, then, if necessary, down to the pool. "I want to see Uncle Artie appear live," he explains, "and I bet he will because we've made another game progression."

You suppress a groan. But since you've stayed awake this long, another few minutes shouldn't matter. The two of you stand for a few minutes before the painting of the French nobleman on "Military Row." Nothing happens. It's late now, and you can hear music and a hum from the bar and the pub. But you don't have the energy for either tonight.

Descending the stairway, you meet Savannah on her way up. She smiles enticingly, like she's especially glad to see you.

"I'm so sorry I didn't have the chance to tell you earlier that I'd delivered your docs," she informs. "Had to dash straight into Farnsworth's lesson. Wasn't so bad tonight, actually, and it was over rather quickly. Good thing too—I'm ready for some food, drink, and relaxation."

Her expression suggests she hopes you'll join in too. You're tired but sorely tempted. "Savannah," you tell her quite seriously, "we were worried that you might be followed. That someone might try to stop you." The chauffeur laughs derisively.

"Might I venture a guess?" Christopher interjects. "You hopped on Cranky Causeway, right?"

"Exactly. When I sensed they were after me, I veered onto the causeway, full throttled Captain America, went around a bend, then jumped off-road to hide behind a clump of trees. I waited until they zoomed by, then doubled back and headed down to The Village on the back road."

Christopher looks thoughtful, then says, "The causeway ends at the motorway, thirty miles away. Think they went that far?"

Savannah says she wouldn't be surprised. "They're such amateurs." Her expression hardens. "They'd better not have messed up our bikes, though."

Suddenly Christopher gestures. "Hang on, Grandmother's ringing on the walkie-talkie." He answers and holds up the device so that everyone can hear.

Mildred sounds concerned. "Christopher, have you seen Savannah?"

Replies the boy, "Why, yes, Grandmother, she's right here with us at the staircase."

Mildred speaks rapidly. "Tell her that Noël has been frantically searching for her. Two of his young helpers took bikes from the garage, and now they're stranded down at the end of Cranky, as they've run out of petrol and don't know what to do. Noël wants to know if Savannah can help them, bring petrol or something. Neither of the lads speaks English or has any currency or cards on them."

Savannah calls out, "Hi, Mildred. It's Savannah. I'm sorry, but I wouldn't want to venture out at night in a storm like this. They should hang tight, and I'll head down with gas cans at sunrise."

"Okay, dearie, will do. It's going to be a long, wet night for those lads."

Savannah's reply is stoic. "Could be worse. Could be winter."

Mildred agrees. "Indeed, much worse . . . I'll tell Noël . . . Night, dearie."

Savannah turns back to you both, saying, "Serves them right. Don't you think?"

Christopher merely smiles and says, "We're just relieved no misfortune came your way, Ms. Reddy."

The chauffeur continues: "Had a rough return trip on that bike in the dark—very mucky—so I got back late." Excitedly she adds, "The Village is in quite an uproar, you know. Everybody's dying to find out who you are. But I think they're more interested in uncovering some deep, dark secret—like you being some undocumented child from Lord Hanover's past."

"Oh, did my uncle have a love interest that you know of?" you ask.

"No idea. I certainly was *not* his confidant," she says laughingly. She hands over a sealed envelope and continues up the stairs.

You watch her ascent, fondly reminiscing—you'd really like to ask her about last night. ***What do you mean?*** You're jolted. Somehow, incredibly, you've received a sort of telepathic reply, as you're certain you just heard Savannah's own sultry voice outside your left ear!

You look up. No Storytellers visible. Nor cacti or mushrooms rotating above. You feel the need for privacy. "Christopher, why don't you go ahead. I'll catch up."

Christopher shrugs and darts down the stairs.

CHAPTER TWENTY-ONE

Savannah, you can actually hear me?

Savannah, descending back down, stops at the landing and nods. ***Kind of weird, and I should be freaked out about now.*** You blush, then project, *Have you been able to hear me the whole time?* ***Oh, don't look so horrified.*** *Hard not to!*

Savannah looks at you intently, then projects, ***Well, what were you saying about last night?*** *Savannah, let's not play little games. You came into my room while I was having a bath! You danced around.* Savannah shakes her head. ***No idea what you're talking about, but it sure sounds like fun. Want me to, sometime?*** With that, she turns around and heads back up the stairs. It takes a moment to fully recover your senses. You note that you heard her loud and clear. Beyond that, you don't know what to think.

Storytellers? Plants? A brown mushroom revolves overhead as the plant warbles, ***We think she may have ingested something.*** *What—some of you guys?* ***Something like us but not us.*** *Well, if you find out, I'd sure like to know. Really enjoyed conversing like that.* **Bar snacks?**

You rush back to your room to inspect the contents of the envelope.

Christopher's waiting at the entrance. He seems unperturbed; you're pretty sure he didn't notice anything odd earlier. And you know by now that others do not hear what the Storytellers or the plants say. But now it seems another entity—neither Storyteller nor plant—has been added to the mix.

Storyteller, can things get any stranger? ***Of course they can. And stranger they shall become.***

Impatient to get to its contents, you open the envelope. A short accompanying note reads:

> *My beloved child,*
>
> *Be sure to examine the two discs I have prepared for you. One of them contains excerpts from my personal diary before I departed on my last journey; the other holds my laboratory notes, as well as those from my closest colleague. I have edited them both from my original written sources to spare you a plethora of cumbersome details and the wandering ruminations of an old man. Play them through, and much that you have been curious about will be revealed.*
>
> *Affectionately,*
> *Arthur Hanover*

You show the note to Christopher, who immediately states, "There's only one disc here."

You shrug. "Sounds like another Easter egg hunt." He points to the pool thumbnail on the wall. You nod in agreement, and you're off.

Down at the pool, the two of you stand around for several minutes, but nothing happens. "Let's go check the timer, so that you can see the position up close," Christopher suggests. Now, standing before the device, you're certain that the hands are where they stood before, at fifty-nine minutes and four seconds.

As you start back, preparing to call it a night, the lapping of the pool suddenly becomes a pronounced churning. The water ripples and forms the countenance of Lord Hanover. He gazes fondly up at you. "My beloved child, you have done superbly! The documents were all in order and are now in the hands of the court. Tomorrow the staff will be officially notified by my solicitor of the impending transfer of title, funds, and property. But much remains for you to accomplish here. I want you to enlist the help of all your newfound friends, as well as your former foes, to discover the secret of our relationship. I am counting on you, my child, for in your discovery there is something else, something important, something the world must know!"

Lord Hanover ripples away, and the pool is once again calm. Christopher turns and looks at you intently. "Looks like it's still game on. Are you up for more?"

"Hell yes. You?"

"Hell yes."

But for now, you're exhausted. "Well, Christopher, I think I've had enough excitement for one day."

"Right!" he exclaims. "We'll need to be well-rested with sharpened wits in order to find whatever it is the world must know."

"Good night, then," you call to him as you walk up the hallway toward the lobby. But just as you pass by the butler's office, the door bursts open and Farnsworth steps out. His appearance is disheveled, his expression distressed. He may have been drinking, but at least he's not waving a pistol.

You tense up but manage to say, "Mr. Farnsworth. Is everything—"

Farnsworth interrupts, bitter and slurring his words. "You have prevailed. I should say, 'Congratulations,' or, 'Well played,' or the like. I'm afraid I cannot." You nod, understanding. Farnsworth goes on, "In all my years of service, Arthur never, not once, mentioned he had a living relative, an heir apparent. He must have known I believed I would inherit at least a good portion of his wealth and estate . . . He was so bloody clever."

"I know he valued you," you try to assuage. But this only angers him.

"Please. Don't patronize me," he says forcefully.

"Fair enough."

"You do not keep such secrets from people you 'value,' as you put it. How cruel he was to hide this from me."

"Mr. Farnsworth, I really don't know what to say. I do understand how you must feel, though."

"Again with the psychobabble patronizing you Americans love."

You decide not to respond.

"And now it seems I'm in dire straits," he confesses. "I had planned to ask Adrienne's hand in marriage soon, but this turn of events could very well change things."

"Have you had a chance to speak with her tonight?" you ask.

"No, not yet. I'm sitting here in my office mulling over what I should say. Worried about how she will react. Summoning my courage, to be perfectly honest."

Storyteller, should I tell him about his breath? A forty-something male with a strong Jersey accent replies, ***Up to you, boss—depends on whether you wanna help or hinder the guy.***

"Again, Mr. Farnsworth, I don't know what to say. This is all a big shock to me as well," you tell him.

"A *shock*? Why would you say that?" Farnsworth shouts with exasperation. "Surely you must have known all along you would inherit. Arthur was your uncle, for God's sake."

You remain silent, with a neutral expression, holding Farnsworth with a steadfast gaze. The butler coughs nervously, then clears his throat, seeming hesitant to speak. "Earlier, this afternoon," he chokes out, "I saw the way you looked at Adrienne, and she at you. So I'm compelled to ask, do you have designs on my beloved?"

Storyteller, how does he know? He can't read my mind, can he? ***No, but you did make a small gesture while watching her on TV. Just say to him what I'll say to you. Ready?*** *Yes, yes, tell me and I'll say it.*

"Mr. Farnsworth, I've never communicated on private matters with the concierge."

The butler looks relieved. "Truly?"

"Earlier, I was merely trying to be friendly in an attempt to diffuse some of the tension we've all been experiencing these past few days. It's no different from socializing with everyone in the pub."

"But you invited her to the Falstaff . . . where I am banned."

"Let's focus on one barrier at a time, Mr. Farnsworth."

"Not that I'm begging to get back in with Sherlock, the bounder . . . and that abominable karaoke!"

"Yes, I know that there is . . . a history."

"It doesn't matter," Farnsworth mutters. "They have their world, I have mine. Maybe it's for the best."

You continue to repeat the Storyteller's dictation. "People can come together in unexpected ways."

“I do not care about the pub. Hear me out, I beg of you,” Farnsworth cries out. “Tonight I’ve learned I’ve lost the manor, the title, the inherited wealth I always thought would be mine.”

“I understand, perhaps better than you think.”

He obviously knows Savannah made it to town. ***Obviously.***

“Then quite possibly you’ll be able to grasp this: if I lose Adrienne, I’ve lost everything. And that I could not bear.” His face becomes flushed with anger as he looks into your eyes and says threateningly, “And will not abide.”

“Mr. Farnsworth, try and get some rest. That’s what I intend to do. We can talk about your future here in the morning.”

“I cannot rest until I receive assurances. I will prepare myself and go to Adrienne straightaway.” Distraught, Farnsworth returns to his office. You head on down the hall toward your quarters, feeling like you’ve deceived him.

Overhead, a sophisticated-looking lady appears. ***Tsk. He claims he cannot live without her after what happened with him and Noël? And he doesn’t even know about her and Noël.*** *But that’s their business, and maybe I do have designs on . . .*

Yes indeed, as some of the younger ones have been encouraging. *So what should I do about all this? Better yet, what did I do?* ***Well, if you didn’t take chances on occasion, yours wouldn’t be much of a story, now would it?*** *You mean the one I’m reliving? The one you’ve already seen?* ***Precisely. Speaking of which, another one of us is waiting for you in your quarters. Let Mr. Farnsworth sort himself out for tonight.***

You return to your room, brimming with curiosity. As soon as you step inside, you’re greeted by a lively male Storyteller who sounds like an impresario. ***Welcome to Soon! Behold a preview of your forthcomings.***

Suddenly, a giant holographic movie begins playing in the middle of the room. A 3D image depicts you rushing across a room in response to persistent knocking at a door. “Yes, yes, who’s there?” your holo calls out.

“I seek admission to your quarters,” replies a sultry female voice. While muffled, the voice sounds familiar—possibly the concierge’s—but you’re not sure.

Abruptly, the scene changes to an outdoor gala. All of the manor staff are crowded around Thomas and Penelope, who appear to be cohosting some sort of magic show.

Thomas is dressed in a black tuxedo and a black top hat while Penelope is adorned in a flowing gown and a cone-shaped hat with a star atop.

She points a sparkling wand at the statue of William Shakespeare, saying, "Observe poor Shakespeare over yonder, sitting in the moonlight, toiling over his sonnets and plays. Do we not suppose he tires of eternal confinement? William, hear me. I grant thee a brief respite."

Before Shakespeare can respond, however, the scene dissolves into one that at first glance seems somber. You, Christopher, Farnsworth, and Van Scoy are huddled around the butler's desk with remorseful expressions.

Then shock!

Lord Hanover, life-sized, materializes into a chair behind the desk. He opens a volume entitled *Diary of Arthur Hanover* and begins reading.

"After all these decades of despairing that the Hanover line would end with me because of this abominable affliction, there is salvation. At a high price, yes, but one I'm prepared to pay for the chance to—" His recitation is cut off in midsentence.

"Storyteller, are you there? He didn't finish. Do you know what he meant to say?" An elderly woman replies, ***Of course we do. We just wanted to whet your appetite.***

Lord Hanover's image is replaced by a noisy, crowded scene in which twenty or so manor servants are all dressed in choir robes and seem to be involved in a group activity, possibly a role-playing game. You spot all your manor friends along with, surprisingly, Farnsworth, Van Scoy, and Chef Noël. Off to the side, you see yourself and Christopher, with the Three Families box.

Without warning, an incensed Savannah bursts into the middle of the room, yelling at Reggie and Bruce. "Hey, Lord Reggie! Hey, Lord Bruce! Why are you holding back? Go ahead and announce your final edicts. A bit shy, are we? Or maybe you're just cowards! Permit me to elucidate your points eight, nine, and God knows what else you'll come up with next."

There are guffaws of laughter, cheers of derision. Supporters stamp their feet.

You're shocked. "Storyteller, was that . . . Three Families? If not, what in the world?" ***Oh, such a grand night of fun and games awaits.***

The fiery group scene is replaced by one showing Adrienne sitting at her desk in what appears to be her office. Her video phone chimes. You're pleasantly surprised to see yourself start to rise from your chair, but floored by the sight of Megumi, Reiko, and Namiko, the mushroom serum trio.

"Konban-wa. Aduri-chan genki?" Reiko shouts.

"I'm fine! And you girls?"

The trio nods enthusiastically, indicating they are all in high spirits.

"Hi, Adrienne, what time is it there?" Namiko asks in English.

Smiling, the concierge replies, "Nami-chan, don't you remember? There are no clocks here. We don't keep track of time at the manor. Ladies, I do want to catch up, but would you mind terribly if I ring you back in just a few? I have a visitor." The call ends.

Adrienne smiles in fond remembrance, saying, "Oh indeed, those i-two-one lovelies. We became fast friends when they were here for the renovations."

You're stunned to see this new side of her. Such warmth, such genuineness. "They filled my days with sweetness and energy. And my goodness, how hard they worked till all hours," she tells your holo.

Your holo calls out, "I can't believe this!" Adrienne smiles and wants to know why. You try to explain: "Adrienne, I ran into that trio, purely by chance, in Manhattan, the day before I flew here. Then once I arrived, I saw them again in Piccadilly Circus. I can't figure this out."

The concierge muses, "Really? Well, they do get out and about quite a bit."

You continue, "Both times, they were dressed in kimonos, promoting mushroom skin-care products . . . Really."

Adrienne's expression turns quizzical. After a pause, she brightens and says, "Manhattan, then London, you say? Well, those three truly are Japanese dolls come to life, and isn't it a small world after all?" At that moment, the floating scene dissolves.

"Storyteller, you still there?" you call aloud. "I just watched myself in the future, and Adrienne and I . . . well . . ."

You're not still worried about that butler, are you, mate? replies an Australian youth. "No, but how did this meeting in her office come about?" ***You finally listened to those kids. Made your interest known.*** "But my now knowing this, isn't that changing the future?" ***No, not at all. When you actually live these moments inside Time, you won't remember previewing them. That's how it works, mate.***

"How is seeing the future even possible—because I'm 'outside' time?" ***Chronesthesia, mate, it's in a nascent stage in your consciousness but developing rapidly.*** "Now that I've seen some of it, I can't wait for tomorrow!" ***Neither can we, mate . . . So by the way, how do you like your story so far?*** "Love it. some parts are scary, some funny, some pretty steamy. Never know what'll happen next." ***Like a good book or movie?*** "Exactly."

PART TWO

THE PROMISE

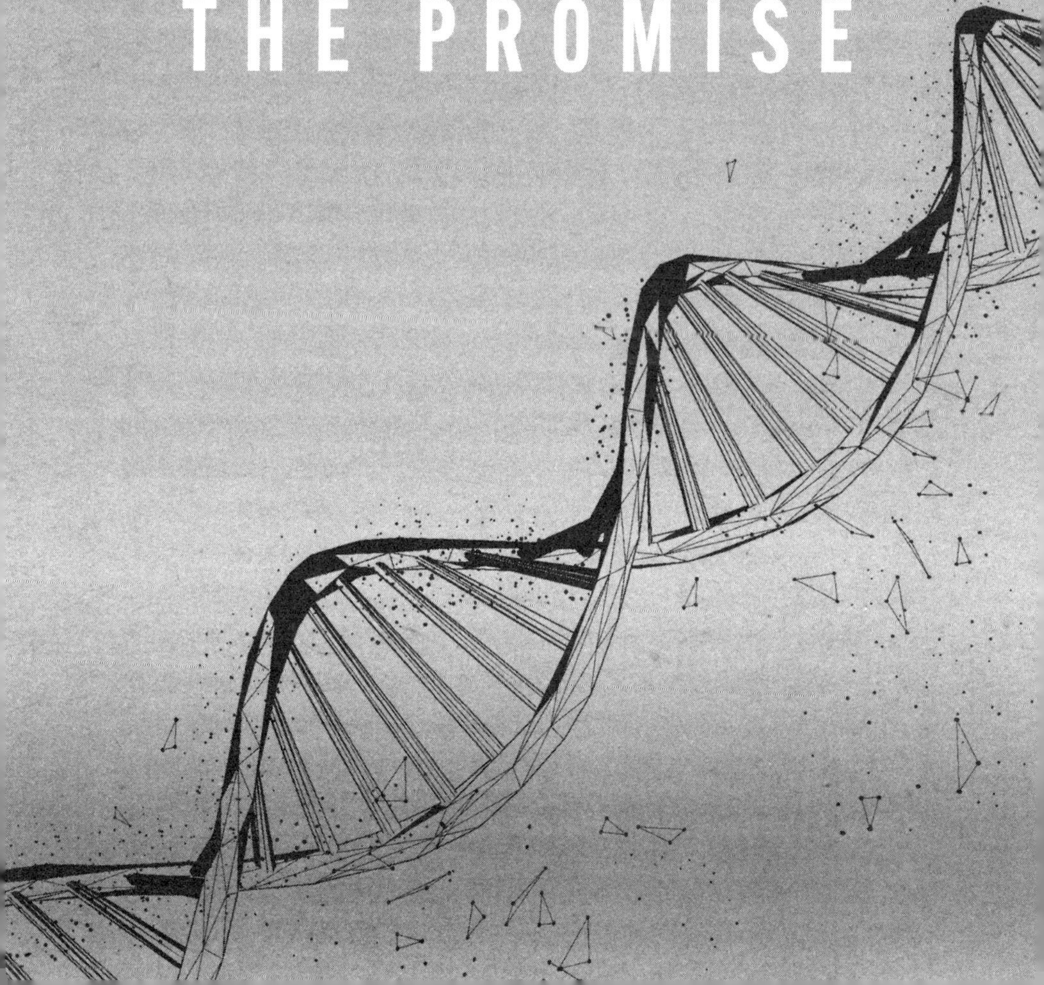

CHAPTER TWENTY-TWO

When you finally awaken, it doesn't take long to realize everything has changed.

You pad into the drawing room and remove Penelope's Do Not Disturb sign that you, desperately needing sleep, placed back on the doorknob last night. You spot several envelopes underneath the door.

The first note is from Mildred.

Congratulations and best wishes to you, dear.

Mr. Farnsworth instructed me early this morning to prepare the royal bedchambers for you, as he is sure you'll want to relocate there straightaway. I have done so, and the rooms are ready now. Miss Stratton will have the key, and Reggie will fetch the rest of your belongings.

Sincerely,
Mildred Simmons, Housekeeper

This is followed by one from Bruce.

Good on ya, mate—you did it! Soon as the weather clears let's roll some kegs of amber fluid out on the lawn, fire up the barbie with fish and fowl, and celebrate in dinky-di Oz-style.

Bruce

P.S. Now that you're the Top Thingo around here, can't you order Savannah to take me for a spin on that Harley of hers?

Next, is an engraved invitation from Noël.

The Honour of Your Presence
Is Especially Requested
This Evening
For a Dinner
To Be Prepared by Noël Elle Léon
And a Recital
To Be Performed by Adrienne Van Scoy
In the Manor House Grand Dining Hall
In Semiformal Attire

S'il regret repondez, s'il vous plait

Okay, so you need only RSVP if you're not coming. You chuckle—another party without a starting time.

The last one is a printed note from Thomas:

Well, I'm positively stunned. First this whole business with your inheritance getting sorted out, and then just this morning, Mr. Farnsworth informs me that from next term he'll grant me a leave of absence so that I may attend the British Butler Institute in London. He also told me that I shall (with your kind permission, of course) be promoted when I finish! I cannot believe my good fortune, as I suspect you may be having difficulty believing yours. Again, my heartiest congratulations.

Sincerely,
Thomas

Wow. Each note has topped the last. Farnsworth's really going to help advance Thomas's career? Noël's hosting a dinner in your honor? Adrienne performing especially for you?

"Storyteller, what's the world coming to?" ***Congratulations! The tide has turned***, calls a young Irish-sounding voice from above.

It's probably safe to assume that room service has been restored. You've no idea what time it is, but breakfast suits your mood. You call on your walkie-talkie, and an encore of those fresh mushroom omelets, hot buttered scones, and pink tea service is delivered almost instantly.

Your message light is blinking, which means they've restored incoming phone service as well. There are three new ones. You play the first, and the butler's smiling face appears. "Good morning, Farnsworth here. I am preparing to move my office to the annex, as I'm sure you'll need a comfortable place to attend to the estate matters sure to come your way. We have reset the code on the door to 1234321 and await your instructions about whether to remove the alarm altogether. I wish you a pleasant day."

The second is from the concierge. "Hello, this is Adrienne Van Scoy calling. I would just like to say how sincerely sorry I am for all the confusion and unpleasantness we may have caused during the early part of your stay. And, well, I'd also like to tell you I've been composing a short musical piece and would like to play it this evening in your honor. So, naturally, it would mean a great deal to me if you could attend. Thank you."

You smile because you know, in her case, you're completely willing to forgive and forget!

Next, you see the chef's cheery face. "*Bon jour*, I am Chef Noël Elle Léon *à votre service*. I hope you have rested well. I have this a.m. been able to revise the number to *enregistrer* the computer. It is 1234321. But, *je regrette*, we have not discovered the location of the password for the Internet."

Funny, the chef's ironic choice of phrasing about the Internet password. They're sharp cookies all right but not quite as sharp as you and your man Friday!

If everything has turned around overnight, it might extend to outside calls. You call reception, and Penelope seems sincere when she says that service has not been restored. On that count, maybe they've been truthful all along. You throw on some clothes to make a quick trip to the lobby for the paper and to ask the receptionist if perhaps she can text messages back home for you.

Halfway up the hallway, you spot Reggie at his post. He's startled when he sees you, apparently thinking you intend to go outside. "Top of the morning, m'lord, but believe me, you don't want to be venturing out till it dies down a bit. Still a torrent, and now there's hailstones to boot. Had to bar the door again, because of all the blowing debris."

"That's okay, Reg. I'm just looking for the paper."

You spy the stack on a nearby table but don't see the receptionist. "When do you think it's going to let up?" you ask the doorman.

Reggie has no idea. You nonchalantly inquire if he has any plans for this evening and are glad to hear he's been invited to Noël's soiree. This probably means the rest of your newfound circle will be there too.

As you start to go back, you again spot the nude lady riding a small pony around in circles on the lobby TV. Damn, it seems you're never in time to catch that story. This is followed by a spot for an upcoming wildflower festival that evidently folks in the tri-county area are quite excited about.

A PA announcement begins. Surprise—it's Penelope speaking. "Good morning! It's my first time to make an announcement, and I'm a bit nervous, so please bear with me. Ahem. Today, a new storm has advanced to the county, and I am sorry to report that the road to The Village remains closed. This evening, Miss Van Scoy shall play her new composition, and everyone is invited!"

Can't wait for tonight, Storytellers. ***Neither can we.***

Penelope goes on. "And thank you very much, Adrienne, for letting me have a go at what I've always wanted to try. I would like to dedicate this hour's program to our headwaiter, Thomas Sutherland"—she giggles—"who always works so hard and does such a marvelous job. Have a glorious day, everybody!"

You have to smile. Yesterday, Manor House was the Tower of London; today it's Camelot. Penelope's playlist offers a collection of saccharine love songs, starting with, no surprise, Olivia Newton-John's "Hopelessly Devoted to You."

Not finding Penelope herself, you return to your living room. It's nice to plop down on the couch to enjoy your paper with more pink tea and scones.

A knock at the door comes just as both the room phone and the walkie-talkie start chiming. You call, "Come in," then pick up the walkie-talkie and press the flashing C button. Christopher sticks his head in the door, and you gesture for him to answer the phone.

From the walkie-talkie you hear, "Good morning. This is Adrienne speaking. Um, did you rest well?" The concierge sounds nervous and tentative. You thank her, hoping your friendly tone puts her at ease.

"Do you mind stopping by my office sometime this morning at your convenience?" the concierge asks. "I've a few matters I'd like to discuss with you."

Overhead are two tittering teenage girls. ***Here's your chance. Go for it***, one says.

Your pulse quickens as you try to mask your excitement. "How about now?"

"Certainly. I'll be waiting at the door."

Isn't this exciting? *It is, but did I sound too eager?* ***Yes, but so what?***

To Christopher, you mouth, "Be right back."

Standing in the hallway outside her office, the concierge dazzles in a white silk blouse with a corsage of pink carnations, a canary-yellow long skirt—tight around the bodice—accented by a wide satin lavender belt. It's early April, and you think Ms. Adrienne Lynn Van Scoy, concierge and curator of Hanover Estate Galleries and Gardens should be crowned Goddess of Springtime!

She really is stunning. But you should endeavor to know the person, admonishes a female thirty-something. *I will, Storyteller, I promise.*

You reach her entrance and are bewitched by her radiant smile and scent. She takes both of your hands and greets you with, "Welcome. I am always at your service. Please come in." Upon entering, she motions you to take one of the two gray low-profile leather chairs. They are positioned in front of her sit-stand desk—a parabolic-shaped top set upon a white titanium base. There is nothing on the desk save a video phone and a laptop.

The concierge's office could not be more different from Farnsworth's. The furnishings are modern, Scandinavian. The decor, save for several giant ferns in white ceramic pots, is minimalist. There is no sign of clutter anywhere. The sole decoration is a large abstract painting hanging on the far wall.

You walk toward it. "That is a spectacular work of art. My gosh, is it an *original*?"

The concierge laughs. "It is, but it's not mine—nor yours. It's part of a collection on loan from the Tretyakov, which will comprise our May exhibit. One of the perks of my position is that I can hang a new masterpiece in my office nearly every month."

She glances briefly at her laptop screen, then turns back to you. "I wanted to confer with you because Miss Stratton and I are being deluged with inquiries, and we're wondering if you would care to speak to the press or issue a general statement."

"I don't know. To tell the truth, Ms. Van Scoy, I just woke up. What would you suggest?"

"Oh, please call me Adrienne."

You nod agreeably; it'll be easy because you already do in your fantasies.

She goes on. "I recommend you let me continue to handle them. Until you've had a chance to sort matters out. Later, I'd like to outline some options for you."

"Fine. I trust your judgment," you tell her.

Adrienne's expression changes to hesitancy. She clears her throat. "Do you think you'll be able to, I mean . . . can you attend tonight?"

"Of course," you quickly reassure her. "I'm so looking forward to your performance!"

Why not propose an aperitif before. Or a nightcap after? *Storyteller, I don't want to rush things.* ***Why not?*** *She may want to keep things strictly on a professional level.*

The concierge's video phone chimes. "I'm so sorry," she tells you, "I have to take this."

You walk to the painting to give her some privacy. The plaque reads:

COMPOSITION VII BY WASSILY KANDINSKY

Born: December 16, 1866, Moscow, Russia
Died: December 13, 1944, Neuilly-sur-Seine, France
Kandinsky is widely considered to be the Father of
Abstract Art.

The concierge is speaking to someone in Russian. Apparently, you discern from your internal translator, the caller is concerned that the last shipment of Kandinsky paintings is stalled in a nearby township. Adrienne is explaining about the storm and the road, and reassuring the curator that it will reopen soon and all is well.

If she's talking to someone in Moscow, maybe she can call home for you?

And another bright idea flashes just as you see she's ended the call. You reseat yourself and ask, "Will all resident staff be attending tonight?"

"Everyone's been invited, and a big turnout is expected among those off duty," the concierge replies.

"In that case, may I have some time with the group after dinner?" you ask, hoping to enlist her help in setting up the Three Families game.

"Certainly, but we do have a small, special after-dinner event planned especially to honor you. Should only take a quarter of an hour." She looks excited merely contemplating it.

"No problem," you tell her. "Can we gather them afterward?"

"Of course. Should I arrange for a microphone in the dining hall so you can address them?"

"No, that won't be necessary. But is the assembly hall available?"

"Certainly—how would you like it set up?"

Recalling the instructions for Three Families, you tell her you'd like three conference tables, each supplied with eight chairs, in three areas of the room.

"I'll attend to it personally," she says enthusiastically. Her phone again chimes. You start to rise but are floored by the sight of Megumi, Reiko, and Namiko, the mushroom serum trio.

"Konban-wa," Reiko calls in greeting.

"Aduri-chan genki?" asks Megumi. ***Good evening! Are you doing well?***

"Mina, genki desu-yo," Adrienne tells them. ***Everyone is fine.***

Namiko says in English, "Hi, Adrienne. What time is it there?"

"Nami-chan, don't you remember?" Adrienne replies teasingly. "We don't keep track of time at the manor? Ladies, I do want to catch up, but would you mind terribly if I ring you back in just a few? I have a visitor."

"Mochiron-yo! Ato de mata hanashimashou!" they call out in chirpy unison. ***Of course! Let's talk later!***

The call ends. Adrienne smiles in fond remembrance. "Oh indeed, those i-two-one lovelies. We became fast friends when they were here for the renovations. I simply adore those young women. They filled my days with sweetness and energy. And my goodness, how hard they worked till all hours."

"I can't believe this!" you exclaim.

"Why do you say that?" Adrienne asks, puzzled.

"Adrienne, I ran into that trio, purely by chance, in Manhattan, the day before I flew here. Then once I arrived, I saw them again in Piccadilly Circus. I can't figure it out."

"Really? Well, they do get out and about quite a bit."

"Both times, they were dressed in kimonos, promoting mushroom skincare products. Really."

The concierge's expression again turns quizzical. After a pause, she brightens and says, "Manhattan, then London, you say? Well, those three truly are Japanese dolls come to life, and isn't it a small world after all?"

"But, Adrienne, haven't you seen their ads here on the local channel?" She shakes her head no. Confused but charmed nearly to death, you thank her and head back to your quarters—realizing you totally forgot to ask about calling home.

Or asking her out, one of those familiar teens calls impatiently.

CHAPTER TWENTY-THREE

Christopher reports that it was Roland Rollinsby on the phone, warning about a green remote. "I told him that everything is in order. There's a red remote that opens special doors and a blue one that opens special windows, and they're not dangerous. And that we've not yet found a green one."

"Did you ask him what the green one does?"

Christopher nods and says, "But Roland did not want to discuss it in case the lines are not secure. He said if he and his sister, Cynthia, can make it up here and it can be found, they'll show us."

You show Christopher all the thank-yous and fill him in on the conciliatory messages from Farnsworth and the others. "At some point today they want me to move upstairs, they said."

"Right," Christopher says as he picks up the blue remote and heads for the door. "In the words of a Russian proverb translated for a famous American president we studied last term, 'Trust—but verify.'"

You chuckle as Christopher departs. Ronald Reagan was a showman with a penchant for espionage, and this lad, Christopher, seems cut from the same cloth. You open the paper and glance at the headline. Well, well, speaking of Russia.

WELL-DRESSED MARXIST WELL FESTIVAL SPURS CONTROVERSY

THE MEDIEVAL art of "well dressing" is being revived Wednesday through Sunday as the village holds its three hundredth annual wildflower festival.

Right, you saw a promo for that on last night's news. Wondering if there's an on-air story, you turn on the TV and press 3DHOLO. The morning news is now airing, the screen caption identical to the headline in the paper. The backdrop features fields of gorgeous wildflowers in a riot of color.

Meredith is seated in her usual position behind the news desk. Above her are four separate windows populated by talking heads and hairdos. You look closer. Your jaw drops. In two of the windows are the smiling faces of Farnsworth and Van Scoy! You think you see the butler's office in the background of each frame—they must be video conferencing. Again, you wonder why the Internet is seemingly working for everybody else in the manor except you.

You walk closer to listen more carefully in case someone drops a clue. Meredith is introducing her panel: "This year's pageant, designed by Emily Poutcastle, has an ambitious and somewhat controversial theme—the rise and fall of communism. This departure from tradition has sparked a lively debate among residents. James Farnsworth, Hanover Manor's butler-administrator is with us now. He is highly critical of the choice."

The frame around Farnsworth's window is illuminated. He's sporting a boutonniere fashioned from a single blue-starred wildflower as he says, "I'm having none of it, mind you. Not only is it completely out of character for the festival, but if we were going to portray this particular subject, I think we're awfully late in the chase, historically speaking."

An Anglican vicar whose chyron identifies him as "Reverend Ramsay Emswiddle, St. Quispin's Church" is shown wearing a Hawaiian-style lei of bright petals. He also has reservations. "Water is an essential part of life and plays a central role in Christianity," he says. "As such, I cannot fathom our young designer's theme."

Emily Poutcastle, a twenty-something who is wearing a bucket hat ringed with a variety of pastel wildflowers and a hippie-era blouse badge that reads FLOWER POWER, defends her choice: "Oh, gentlemen, I'm of no political bent. It's just that the hammer and sickle, and the curvature of the numerals in 1989, particularly lend themselves to this type of floral presentation." You make a mental note about the year.

Meredith addresses Van Scoy: "Adrienne, I understand most of the flowers actually come from the fields within Hanover Manor proper and are donated to the festival. Can you describe the process for our viewers?"

The concierge, adorned with a lovely corsage that matches Farnsworth's boutonniere, is keen to explain. "Yes, Meredith, I'd be much pleased. Each year, we transport hundreds of flowers to the old vicarage on Slugmoor Lane. The large well, within the walls of the residence, is 'dressed' by forcing different-colored flowers into clay to create a vivid panorama. It's been going on here for three hundred years!"

"Interesting, thank you," Meredith replies and returns to the pageant's designer with another question. "Emily, we understand the festival is adding a new spectacle this time round. Can you preview it for us?"

Poutcastle becomes highly animated in her window. "Oh yes! We're quite excited. This year, we'll have floral-decorated floats, a marching band, and equestrians festooned with wildflowers that parade through the town, leading one and all to the vicarage. And just outside the grounds, kiosks will offer wildflower salads consisting of poppies, daisies, dandelions, borage, and one more . . . Oh dear, I forget."

"Forget-me-nots?" the concierge ventures, looking down at her corsage.

"Yes, those. They are most essential to the recipe."

Meredith looks surprised. "Emily, I knew most wildflowers are edible. I did not know there are actual recipes for their concoctions."

"Oh my, yes," says Poutcastle. "We shall follow to the letter the recipes my parents obtained from a former Hanover Manor chef."

"Emil?" the other windows call out in unison and with amazement.

"Why, yes," the designer affirms. "I've been sampling quite a few of them myself lately. Emil's dishes are tasty and inspiring! Please regard the designs they've sparked." The backdrop switches to a slideshow of artist renderings of the planned floats. You watch in utter amazement as Poutcastle provides commentary.

"The first is a long trailer on which our theme, 'The Rise and Fall of Communism,' is scripted with bright-red field poppies set against a background of white primrose, and with a brilliant-yellow kingcup forming the ampersand that strongly accents the title." This may well be the most bizarre image you've ever laid eyes on. Poutcastle goes on,"You can see that our second one depicts the 'Berlin Wall-1989' in a broken-cement-block motif fashioned out of magenta corn cockles with mauve cuckooflowers spelling out the title."

Nope, this float takes the cake when it comes to strange.

Another slide is projected as the designer continues, "Here you see the 'Founding Fathers' float with busts of Marx, Lenin, and Trotsky perched atop pedestals with garlands of yellow cowslips and fragrant honeysuckle adorning their heads. In the parade, their heads will revolve as the fully decorated trailer presses forward!"

You guess this would be what a Soviet Disneyland would have looked like had the Russians won the Cold War.

"The last trailer," Poutcastle continues as a new slide appears, "is my personal favorite. You can see it carries a long banner entitled 'The Tractorium Period in Soviet Architecture' and will feature a giant columbine-decorated tractor surrounded by multicolored depictions of heroic buildings from the 1930s constructed of bluebells, chicory, foxglove, musk mallow, daffodils, buttercups, violets, and scarlet pimpernels. To script the title, we'll use peach geraniums. Won't it be grand?"

Actually, it probably would be, eh, Storyteller? ***It really should be.***

This final image appears to unnerve Farnsworth, who breaks in with, "'Tractorium Period'! I must confess, I'm at a complete loss here." He tosses both hands into the air in futility.

Replies Poutcastle gently, "When I studied the USSR at university and examined old photos, I found everything in that era to be dull, drab, depressing, and uniformly gray. One day, after tea, an inspiration struck. It said I should endeavor to *colorize* Russian history a bit. And try to increase its olfactory appeal as well. Thus, most of the flowers chosen for the floats will be both beautiful to behold and heavily scented as they pass by."

At that, Reverend Emswiddle bangs his palms against his temples several times but somehow manages a final question. "Ms. Poutcastle, you propose to theme this year's festival, on its three hundredth anniversary no less, around the very antithesis of Christianity. Tell us, do any of these recipes of yours, by chance, specify mushrooms?"

The designer nods enthusiastically. "Why yes, nearly all of them do. I follow them religiously nearly every day. But, as Chef Emil states, they must be wild and freshly picked. Never store bought." With that, Meredith thanks the panel and announces a commercial break.

Reagan, communism, Christianity, mushrooms. So many things to connect here. Maybe this is one of those Jungian synchronicities Christopher's always going on about.

You scan the printed article, scouring for potential clues. You believe "1989" is the top candidate with "hammer" and "sickle" as secondary choices as you set the paper aside.

Christopher's back, breathlessly pointing to the image grid. "Oh, I've got good ones," he says as he brings up the wall and plays the first clip. At first you don't see anyone. Clothes are piled high on Her Majesty's bed, and open suitcases are on the floor. Somebody's in the midst of packing, and the camera cannot decide where to track.

Off-camera, you hear the concierge. "We did the right thing, James, bowing to the inevitable. It's better this way. We were never meant to *have* all this."

Replies Farnsworth, who is also unseen, "I suppose you're right. Though I am deeply hurt that Arthur didn't remember me at all—none of us, actually. But I'm doing my best to put it aside."

"Hmm. I just hope we can repair our relationship with Arthur's successor," says Van Scoy.

Farnsworth replies, "Quite. I'm doing what I can, as I'm sure you are as well."

At this point, Van Scoy steps into the scene with both arms extended, palms up. "James, I hope we can concentrate on our relationship, now that everything else is more or less decided."

Farnsworth appears and clasps her hands. "Yes, dearest, I hope so too."

The couple lingers together while Christopher mock-sniffles, tosses his head, and pantomimes playing a violin. They step out of the scene. It seems as though these two will attempt no further harm. But you're highly disheartened seeing this. Should you try to get her alone and tell her how you really feel, make a move before it's too late?

Not surprisingly, another adolescent appears. ***How many times do we have to tell you? Go for it.***

Christopher says he didn't intend to capture the next one. He was trying to catch Farnsworth at His Majesty's—before finding them both at Her's later—but he accidentally pointed the remote the wrong way, which activated the nearby pub window. The next scene is vintage Bruce. The barkeep is facing the camera and listening on his walkie-talkie. Before he says a word, his salacious grin reveals whom he's likely chatting up. "Aw, what makes you think I couldn't handle a go on one of your bikes?" His smile widens as he explodes in mock indignation. "Whaddya mean, 'couldn't handle the rough road'? Back home, all the sheilas idolized me. Called me 'Captain Straya, Wizard of Oz'!" He guffaws at his own humor. "Right," he goes on. "Soon as the weather clears, you're on, mate."

His expression changes. "You don't say? . . . What else did they tell you? . . . Really? That will set the whole village into the stratosphere . . . Tomorrow's TV news and the paper? . . . Right, I'll speak with you later." He switches off, whistles a sigh, and steps out of the scene.

It's discomforting. If what you've just heard means the press is about to have a field day, they're probably ready to portray you as Lord Hanover's illegitimate child.

Christopher now points the remote at the fruit bowl. "I caught up with Noël on my third attempt."

The window opens to reveal the chef on the walkie-talkie. "*Mais oui, madame, bien sur.* I want to surprise him with this *spécial* one I've just seen in *le Journal du Village*." He pauses to listen and then says good-naturedly, "All right, *madame. Je jure à vous*, I will not . . . ever again."

Noël walks away, giggling and murmuring a ditty to himself. *"Léon a rasé César à Noël!"* He puts the walkie-talkie away, smiles, and departs.

Somehow you get the feeling that whatever it is he's up to now, it's good, not bad, which causes you to smile too. But after a few seconds, once again Farnsworth appears in the scene. He casts a few quick sidelong glances and rushes into the kitchen.

Now what to make of that? An elderly male voice speculates: ***Up to no good, we think.*** *You read my mind, can't you read his?* ***Afraid not. You're special.*** *How am I special?* ***You now have an ancient mind, a bicameral one. Yet it is also a rational mind, a hybrid. You may be the first of your kind.*** *Is that good?* ***Only Time can tell.***

"Looks like there's no way we can peer into the kitchen," you tell the boy. Christopher supposes not. You call the butler's office, but there's no answer. Anyway, you know the new access code—thank goodness; you're a little weary of puzzles for the moment. "So why don't we stroll down there and get on the computer?" you say to the lad. Christopher thinks it's a grand idea.

"Duh." You're standing in front of the butler's office, pretending you've forgotten the code.

"One-two-three-four-three-two-one," Christopher reminds you.

"Duh." Could he repeat it again, this time more slowly? And where in today's paper is it, anyway?

"Okay, you got me," Christopher says.

After he keys in 1234321 to log on, you notice that the DOCUMENTS folder is back on the desktop. Christopher points to an external drive on the floor. "Whoever did that," he observes, "was clever."

There are simultaneous knocks from the two connecting doors. You call, "Come in," and into the room steps Van Scoy from her office and Farnsworth from the lobby. They both have something to say. "Ladies first," you propose.

The concierge wants to bring several inquiries from the genealogical societies to your attention. You tell her you've been getting their messages. "Anything to say at this point?" she asks.

You shake your head, hoping the disc will shed some light on matters. "Can you check back in, say, a couple of hours?"

"Certainly," she replies, handing you a diagram. "And is this seating arrangement for tonight satisfactory?" You notice she's placed all your buddies—Reggie, Bruce, Savannah, Mildred, and Christopher—with you at the table of honor. Thomas will be your waiter. She's put the butler and herself at one of the lesser tables off to the side. You nod, indicating it's fine. She shows you another diagram of how the assembly hall can be arranged.

"Just what I had in mind," you tell her.

"All staff are coming, so you can count on twenty-four attendees," she says.

"Terrific."

"Lastly, I'm still stonewalling the press," she reports. "But for your information, the London-based tabloids are starting to call. They've caught a whiff of something big. When the road reopens, expect a rat pack." She departs—businesslike but relaxed. This woman is back in her element, seems on top of everything.

And watching her walk away is always such a delight! ***Enough of this objectification!*** a strident female voice interjects. ***Grow up!*** *Storytellers, you already know how Adrienne and I will turn out, but you're not going to tell me, are you?* ***Oh no***, one scholarly looking gentleman quickly replies. ***We can never reveal anything definitive about your future. If you knew in advance but then decided otherwise, that might wreck the event chain and cause serious harm.*** *How?* ***Some events would be duplicated, some would not occur at all. Some would occur before they should, some after. People would go mad.*** *Okay, okay, don't tell me, then.*

Farnsworth doesn't have much, simply wants to apologize for not having cleared out sooner. He's been busy moving his personal belongings from upstairs and thinks he can get to his office things very soon.

"Mr. Farnsworth," you try to assure him, "it's not at all necessary for you to vacate your office." You explain that you only need to use the computer from time to time. The butler starts to object, but you insist. He seems grateful as he starts to leave. "If you can spare the time, Mr. Farnsworth, why not stick around and watch this?" You figure he must be as curious as you are about Lord Hanover's diary, and maybe he can fill in some blanks.

"I'd be most honored . . . if you're sure you don't mind," Farnsworth says agreeably.

Christopher asks you for the DVD and pops it into the drive. A window opens, revealing an "MH" icon identical to the one you saw yesterday, but this one's labeled MH UPDATE.

"Right. This update will probably install new stuff to the theater business we saw yesterday," Christopher supposes. "Maybe more AI stuff as well."

While waiting for the update to finish, Farnsworth mentions that Lord Hanover used a Japanese firm to create his virtual walkthrough. "I remember that crew," he says. "Hang on. Let me check." Farnsworth pulls open his desk drawer and retrieves a business card. It is another imagine21 card, this one reading "Namiko Idabashi," who's listed as "untitled-5."

"There were three of them, all lovely ladies in their late teens or early twenties, I'd guess," Farnsworth recalls. "Worked with Arthur nearly every day until just before he left for Switzerland. Highly energetic lot."

"So, these are the people who actually wrote this program? Three young Japanese women?" you ask, as you're mightily impressed.

"No, I rather think they were the designers," says Farnsworth. "The ladies were mostly concerned with the artwork and music. *Assets* was the buzzword I believe they used."

All this has evidently brought back pleasant memories. Farnsworth recalls the young women were extremely polite and considerate. Filming was always in the middle of the night so as not to disrupt the manor. They asked if they could attend his seminars on table manners because they were interested in learning new social graces while on extended assignment. They taught him the Japanese word *genki*, which means happy, fine, contented, and *"O-genki desu-ka?"* the standard Japanese greeting for "How are you?"

"I don't recall ever seeing a 'genkier' bunch" is his summation of the trio. He pulls out his phone and shows you a picture of the girls, apparently taken at one of his etiquette seminars. You chuckle. It's Namiko, Reiko, and Megumi—the Fountain of Youth trio, once again, this time all outfitted in semiformal attire and wearing serious expressions.

Christopher signals that the installation is over and calls out to Windows to open the INTERNET folder. He looks at you when the dialogue box appears, requesting the password.

But Farnsworth beats you to it and calls it out, adding that last night they finally figured it out. He looks at Christopher and says admiringly, "It's obvious that once again you were way ahead of us."

On-screen, Arthur Hanover is standing in the lobby just as he was yesterday. He's dressed the same. But he doesn't step forward and welcome one and all to Manor House. This time, he spreads his palms and simply says, "My beloved child."

CHAPTER TWENTY-FOUR

Christopher holds the mouse down and rotates the lobby scene to face the hallway that leads to your cottage suite. He rotates farther to the main entrance and clicks on one of the door handles. The "clunk-clunk" sound effect signifies the door is locked. Just like here in the actual manor.

But now he discovers something. Lying on one of the lobby tables is a small black case. The cursor changes when he passes over it, indicating a hot spot. He clicks down on the object, drags it onto the stage, and releases the mouse button, and the case slides away. It is now absent from the virtual lobby.

"Blimey! Looks like we've 'found' something," notes Christopher with a chuckle. "Uncle has come up with yet another game within this game. Why are we not surprised?"

When clicked on, the case doesn't open, but wherever he goes in the mansion, it remains lying on the stage. In the spa lounge, the musical program switches to jazz, just as it does in real life whenever you go in there.

Christopher slowly pans over every scene, looking for anything "collectible." Finally, he finds the key card to enter the spa and pool. It, too, is automatically placed on the stage.

He moves over to the purple doors and aligns the panorama with the entry slot. He clicks and drags the card up to the opening. A buzz sounds as the door slides open. Once you're inside the pool area, the music stops, and there is only the hiss from the jacuzzis and the lapping of the pool. The water is rippling. It's an utterly convincing scene.

You look over Christopher's shoulder and spot the gold key with the red jewel. It's lying on the shelf, right where it really was a few days ago. He zooms in and clicks on it. The key animates from its position and falls onto the stage. "We're on an Easter egg hunt." He laughs.

He circumnavigates the pool, and you exchange glances when you see the timer frozen at the same position it was yesterday: fifty-nine minutes and four seconds.

A few minutes later, on the second floor, the Falstaff pub is open.

Inside, Christopher pans the wall decorations, looking for a telltale cursor change. He sees one when he passes over the top of the player piano, and now drags another black case onto the stage. "This really isn't a performance stage," he says. "It's more like a shelf to hold the items we're supposed to find. Bother! This is a lot of work!"

You offer to switch places, and Christopher scrambles out of the chair. You sit down at the computer and are immediately drawn into this incredible re-creation. The high-definition picture is like watching a moving photograph—seamless, with colors and a picture so sharp that the writing on pub items tacked on the wall is perfectly legible. Now, traversing the pub seating area, you notice a gradual increase in volume as you approach the large speakers mounted on the stage. And the karaoke machine actually works. "Wow, those designers thought of everything!" Christopher raves.

Then you catch a familiar refrain. Bruce's vocals for "Yes I'm Changing," the song he performed live the other night. But now it's embedded here. Things are starting to get weird.

Farnsworth offers a suggestion that distracts you from further speculation. "Let's go in here. This room. The room we're actually in."

Sounds like a good idea.

You exit the virtual pub and hear the classical music interrupted by a routine manor announcement in the concierge's voice.

Adrienne is startled. "That's my voice but I've never recited that particular announcement."

Christopher says he thinks he knows. "The program's AI has your voice samples; it likely authored that announcement itself."

The concierge sighs, saying, "Soon I may no longer be needed."

When you position the mouse at the hallway entrance, you see the electronic pad. Clicking on it brings an enlargement of the device to the center of the screen. You key in the concierge's birthdate, press the ENTER key, and watch the door spring open.

It feels strange to be moving through an exact replica of the office you're in, with even a computer set up. You pan around but don't notice any hot spots.

Christopher asks you to click on one of the boxes—he's got a hunch. You do, and this time the case pops open. Inside is a silver disc, which you drag and insert into the on-screen DVD slot. The mouse cursor disappears as the scene begins to rotate on its own, the panorama adjusting to allow a direct view of Farnsworth's desk and chair. Lord Hanover is seated here, perfectly composited into the scene. He opens a leather-bound volume and says, "Good morning, everyone. I have much to disclose now that you're all gathered here. May I now begin?"

The room falls silent. Everyone merely nods tentatively.

"Right . . . so, after years of dealing with bureaucrats, I've learned how to baffle them. My genealogical records will be altered, and at a fair price. And because they can't work out precisely why I'm doing it, they're at a loss to take further advantage of the situation—beyond the bribes they've extracted. They obviously think I'm just another rich eccentric. Perhaps they're right. Well, at least all this will spare the authorities the expense of having to dig me up after I'm gone."

He laughs, closes the book, and shimmers out of view. The cursor is restored. You switch discs. Lord Hanover appears as before, finds his place, and reads.

"Blood tissue analysis successful. Inherited ABO antigens showing up as expected. Next step: some saliva samples that stand up to the most rigorous scrutiny. Read a fascinating piece in *Nature* today about the use of DNA profiling in UK courts. Seems it's all the rage in paternity and criminal cases. Ah, but if they only knew what I'm certain I shall soon prove, courts worldwide would have to throw that evidentiary procedure out with yesterday's newspaper."

Puzzled, you watch the two clips again and again, noting that Lord Hanover's initial greeting is not included in the replays. Turning to Farnsworth, you ask if he knows what Lord Hanover's talking about.

"I've no idea," Farnsworth says, then he clears his throat. "As I've said, this renovation project was all out in the open. But as far as Arthur's scientific experiments were concerned, none of us were ever allowed in the lab when serious work was underway."

"There's got to be a way to save this," Christopher says, referring to your progress in this "game." He reaches over and moves the mouse to the top, where a menu is normally placed. When it reaches the folds above the panorama, the curtain lifts the short remaining way up, revealing a control panel.

On one side, there are five gold buttons labeled New, Open, Save, Print, and Close. You wonder aloud why the menu has a print function. Christopher says you'll probably find out as you go along.

In the middle is an ear icon with two buttons, one labeled On and the apparent default, Off. Beside them are three more labeled Low, Medium, and High. At present, Medium is depressed. Quick experimentation confirms that you can raise or lower background audio. You decide not to fiddle with the ear icon right now.

On the far right, there is a final two-button set, whose icons are a pair of smiling masqueraders. Live and Screen are the choices; the latter is currently depressed. You start to click Live, but Christopher stops you, cautioning that since you don't know what it will do, you should save the file first.

You click Save, but a dialogue pops up requesting a four-digit pass code.

"Piece of cake," you call out, recalling the wildflower news story. You input the year, click Save, and name and save the file in the standard Windows fashion. After that, you click Close and then relaunch.

"Well done!" exclaims Farnsworth. "How did—"

Smiling broadly, you pull out the paper, roll it up, and tap your head with it.

Nearly a half hour passes, but you find no more black cases. You do find more keys, some graphic representations of crucial documents like the deed and the will, even a facsimile of *The Village Journal* in its usual place in the lobby.

The legal documents fill most of the screen when enlarged, but the writing is not legible. Aside from a title—"Deed" or "Last Will and Testament" or "The Genealogical Society: Report of Proceedings"—written in bold script, there is nothing to actually read. You guess the idea is to merely suggest their existence for the game.

That is until Christopher instructs you to click on PRINT. The whole document prints out with your status as heir apparent in all the appropriate places and signed in blue ink by Lord Hanover.

"So it wouldn't have mattered if we'd—" Farnsworth mutters, then catches himself.

Moments later in the cottage, you find another black case in a kitchen cupboard beside a bulletin board holding Chef Emil's recipe for scones. You see the cursor change when the mouse passes over it. Farnsworth's got a sharp eye. "Hang on. I think there's something. There, on the notice board." You click on it, and the recipe fills the screen. "I see," Farnsworth says good-naturedly. "Once again, well played."

Returning to the office, you play the next installment. Lord Hanover appears agitated as he reads.

"Blast heredity! Having ruled out adoption, it falls to me to divine the solution. Current published research is only mildly promising; I'll not be getting most of what I need from outside sources. Oh, there is that famous Italian case with the alleged half sister of one of my peers, but I plan to go much further than merely having it all proved in court. Our records will even bear up under the most intense scrutiny of the genealogical societies."

He seems to be talking about an heir. Somehow your connection with him is bound up in his research. Christopher looks puzzled, and you can tell he's put on his thinking cap. Farnsworth is guarded. You sense that he's distressed by all this.

"I've checked my real desk drawer," Farnsworth says, "but we haven't checked my virtual one." He's right. You rotate the panorama so that you can click on the drawer. It slides open with a rolling sound effect. Inside, along with usual desk items, is a replica of the red remote the butler handed over yesterday. You click and drag it onto the stage where it slides to a preordained spot.

"Mr. Farnsworth, you know all about this, so would you like to take over?"

The butler is eager to change places. A short tutorial from Christopher gets him used to operating the panorama smoothly. Soon he is rotating the scene, zooming in and out, and changing nodes with alacrity.

Ready now to show how the red remote works, he travels to the bookcase. He places the cursor over the red orb and clicks. The bookcase revolves with the same whoosh you heard before and reveals a staircase behind. The butler clicks into the node, goes up the stairs, clicks again, and whoosh—the library appears.

"This is exactly the route I take, down to the last detail," Farnsworth says admiringly.

"Any others?" you ask.

"Yes. From my—excuse me, from *your*—bedchambers," Farnsworth says as he leaves the library and moves down the hallway in that direction.

His Majesty's door is locked, but the purple-jeweled key unlocks it. There's a bookcase in the room flush against the wall. Just before Farnsworth clicks the remote, Christopher spots another black case on the mantel above the fireplace.

Farnsworth retrieves it and returns to the bookcase. A click of the remote revolves it. He makes a quick descent to the cottage's living room and exits via another bookcase.

"Well, let's examine our latest find, shall we?" the butler says.

Behind him, you and Christopher risk eye contact that seems to transfer your thought: How are we going to explain a virtual blue remote that's sure to be around here somewhere?

Lord Hanover shimmers into view, looking pensive. He seems to be mulling over something. Finally, he speaks. "Of all the individuals I've considered, this one seems the most promising. Bright, affable, curious, self-confident, and with sufficient amounts of self-control and humility. Apparently not afraid of change, either. Besides, something beyond those obvious traits—intuition, perhaps—tells me I've found who I'm looking for."

He closes the diary and speaks to the camera.

"Yes, I do believe I've decided. Now to the indelicate task of obtaining my heir's medical records and samples, followed by the delicate task of announcing myself."

Christopher and Farnsworth look at you. Shaking your head, not knowing what to say, you ask to see it again. You keep requesting more replays, needing more time to think.

Okay, Storyteller, he's clearly talking about me. It seems like this recording was made some time before he first made contact. ***Correct.*** *What's this about medical records?* ***He's referring to yours.*** *So what's Farnsworth thinking?* ***We can only hazard a guess that he thinks somehow he's been cheated.***

There's now a palpable feeling of tension in the room.

Farnsworth turns to you with a cold stare. "Excuse me, but I must ask: Did you and Arthur ever actually meet? Do you or anyone in your family actually *know* him? Your alleged *uncle*?" It is clear that Farnsworth always considered you a genuine blood relation, albeit a closeted one.

You shake your head. "No, I never knew him. Never even heard of him before he contacted me. And I've never discussed this with my family."

The butler refuses to believe this. "I cannot imagine you not informing your own family of this relationship, of your purpose for coming to England." Now he's on his feet, waving his arms and yelling, "So, you're an impostor. This is all a hoax. Your scheme to deny me what is rightfully mine!"

Now, in your opinion, the man has gone too far. He frightened Christopher last time, and you're not about to let it happen again. *Storyteller, any suggestions?* ***Yes, repeat what I say.*** *Yes, of course.*

You clear your throat and once again allow a Storyteller, this time an elderly male with an upper-class British accent, to dictate your reply. "Mr. Farnsworth, have you ever considered the possibility that Lord Hanover may not be my uncle?"

The butler wheels around to face you. "Indeed I have—I am now considering that as being the *most* likely case!"

"I mean—"

"The entire household is clamoring to know what you *mean*." Farnsworth's voice is a sneer. "So why don't you become a bit more forthcoming?"

Lower your voice. Adopt a confidential tone.

"But have you ever considered the possibility that Lord Hanover may actually be . . . *my father*?"

This stops Farnsworth in his tracks.

Now slowly stand up.

You rise, spreading your palms, and recite, "That perhaps this 'uncle' business is a ruse to keep innocent people from being hurt."

Pause for a moment. Good. Now continue.

"To prevent, or at least lessen, the scandal certain to arise? . . . To protect the Hanover name? . . . That Lord Hanover also did this out of consideration for *me*, Mr. Farnsworth? Tell me, did you even consider that possibility?"

For a moment, Farnsworth says nothing. Then he stares hard at you.

"Frankly, I did not." The admission comes reluctantly. "So. Is that the case? Is he your father?"

Become circumspect. Gesture toward the cases.

"Perhaps you should consider that these recordings may be part of a cover story. So that nobody gets hurt," you offer silkily. "How might you have handled this if you were Lord Hanover?"

Any conjecture the butler may wish to offer is interrupted by the concierge, who sticks her head in the room. "Sorry to bother," she calls. "Anything new?"

Storyteller, did she overhear? An elderly Storyteller wearing silver-rimmed bifocals replies: ***Don't think she heard a thing.***

"We won't be able to decide anything today," you inform her. "We've learned some, but we're certain there's more to uncover here."

"I see. Well, good luck, then." She starts to close the door but turns back. "Oh, by the way, I've been screening your calls, but there was a gentleman a few moments ago who insisted on leaving a video message. I know who he is. He's a very important person in this country."

"Is it possible to retrieve it from here?" you ask.

"Certainly." You lift the receiver and press the button. A distinguished-looking elderly man appears.

"Good day, my name is Professor Garfield Gatsby. I'm a member of the Royal Society, UK Academy of Science. We have just come into possession of a most extraordinary account detailing the late Lord Hanover's research. In it, he asserts that if you've been legally certified as heir to his title and estate, it will prove that a final experiment he performed on himself has succeeded. So my question is simply this: Do you in fact exist? If not, please disregard this message. I'll ring back later to confirm. Goodbye."

Mincingly, Christopher repeats, "Do you in fact *exist*?" He's not a bad mimic, sounding almost as dry as the caller. You think it's funny too, but Farnsworth is not amused. The concierge only looks confused.

The butler gets up, saying he's had enough for the day. You'd like to continue exploring the virtual manor but need time to get ready for dinner. Christopher saves the file, and powers off the equipment.

The four of you silently depart.

When you're back at your cottage door, Christopher asks, "Do you have some reason to think Uncle Artie actually is your father?" He sounds hurt—as if you haven't shared everything with him.

"Not a chance," you reply, slapping him on the back as you unlock the door. "At that particular moment, I got a brainstorm that it was a possibility our friend in there should at least *consider*."

"But how do you really know?" he persists.

You explain that you fretted about it that first night at home, then realized that you bear too much physical resemblance to be any man's child other than your own father's. And Lord Hanover looks nothing like him.

But the old man in the hallway portrait might be, eh, Storyteller? ***He certainly does bear a resemblance.*** *Why is he even there? Makes no sense.* ***It will eventually.***

"Well, your little bombshell worked," Christopher says. "I was gobsmacked. Where did it come from?" Well, you're not quite ready to tell him that your impromptu misdirection was dictated by a being hovering above. One of many only you can see and hear. You wouldn't want to give Christopher cause to believe you belong in the funny farm.

The boy departs. You'd like to take a bath and think more about the phone message. "Do you in fact exist? I'll ring back later to confirm." Funny, very funny indeed—classic British drollery.

But also, quite disturbing.

Do I, Storyteller, exist? Serious question. I can't even remember my name. ***Of course you exist if you think you do. You do not only if you think not.*** *Huh? Sometimes you're all mumbo jumbo, Storyteller. But, hey, thanks for all your help in there.* ***Always at your service, my lord.***

CHAPTER TWENTY-FIVE

Soaking in the tub, mulling everything over, you regard Uncle's latest revelations to be something completely out of the blue, something that never occurred to you in the countless hours you've spent trying to figure out this relationship. It's obvious, too, that this is the "something important, something the world must know" of which Uncle Artie so passionately spoke from the pool.

But why is he turning this real-life scenario that mimics a computer game into an actual one? And, good grief, how is this being done—and so quickly? And Farnsworth? Under surveillance this morning, he seemed like he'd thrown in the towel. In the office, at first, he almost seemed endearing, going on and on about those spirited Japanese designers and such. But then he became increasingly suspicious and finally exploded.

Storyteller, what's next from this character? A middle-aged man appears. ***You'd be surprised. Or perhaps not.*** *I see, I have to find out myself since it's my story.* ***Correct.***

You climb out of the tub, towel off, and throw on a robe. For now, you'd better put all this aside and think more about tonight's game. In light of the butler's change of attitude, the Three Families ending might be particularly volatile. But you don't want to permanently alienate Farnsworth or anyone. On the contrary, you hope Three Families will bring the entire household together as your uncle desires. You recall his instruction: "Use this to reverse the roles—from game player to game master—and, in so doing, endeavor to win over their hearts and minds."

The thoughts give way to a young exuberant Black voice. ***Yo! Wassup!***

Lil' 'Teller here. Hey, new lord, why not give them all a big surprise tonight! Check it out!

Suddenly, a panorama of scenes shimmers into view. You spin around and around, marveling at all the exhilaration depicted. You see delirious expressions on the faces of dozens of manor servants, including not only your inner circle but also the butler, the concierge, and the chef! You stare, mouth agape, when you spot yourself in one of the panels, wearing an ecstatic expression in this carousel of near-future scenes.

Have you really become clairvoyant? Or is it yet another of Uncle Artie's zany theme-park effects? Or just a garden-variety hallucination?

As the panorama slowly dissolves, you grasp that this is an event you can append to Three Families, a bombshell ending that you believe could very well channel pent-up emotions—from both the game and real manor life—in a new, positive direction for one and all!

Wow! Lil' 'Teller, this looks great. Can hardly wait. ***Gonna be a rave-up, baby.***

Excited, you call housekeeping and get Christopher on the line to talk over your brainstorm. He listens, says it's way out there all right, and oh yes indeed, he can provide all the gear you'll need. "Did you get the inspiration because of an event from your past?" he asks.

"Yeah, maybe." You're not sure. Maybe you just want to show everyone here that you intend to be every bit the showman and bon vivant your uncle was.

A few moments later, Christopher knocks at the door to tell you that he's come up with an embellishment of his own. Says he's on his way to the chapel to pick up vestments they store for visiting choirs. "There are sets in at least three colors, and probably enough for each 'family' to wear. If everyone's in costume, it will lend atmosphere, don't you think?" he asks. You absolutely do. Man, this kid thinks of everything!

You call Adrienne. She confirms that the assembly hall lighting is on dimmer switches, so you can brighten or darken the room at will. And, yes, there's a sound system that can stream audio from any device, and, yes, there's a holographic projection system embedded in the back wall. Signing off, you note that she didn't sound upset about anything she may have overheard or learned from Farnsworth, but then, she might be professionally skilled at hiding her true feelings.

To kill time before dinner, you turn on TVTV news. After a flurry of storm reports interspersed with ads for Fountain of Youth skin care starring the *genki* girls, more promos for the upcoming wildflower festival, and notifications about Lady Godiva's chocolatier lawsuits, you get an unexpected surprise. The screen caption reads:

WHERE'S CRUNCH? AUTHORITIES BAFFLED BY SECOND DISAPPEARANCE

As you tap into 3DHolo mode, the camera moves in close to Michael, who adopts a serious tone. "Lost then found—the half-blind, three-legged pooch from Flogway Down is lost again. According to Chief Constable Thomas O'Bannion, owner Nigel Wanton reported his pet rottweiler missing at dawn."

The screen cuts to a prerecorded clip of a morose Nigel Wanton standing near one of his cows while chickens run about squawking in the background. To the camera, he says, "Crunch's remaining evil eye helps keep the cows in line during milking and the hens orderly during egg collection. But this morning he was nowhere to be found."

The screen backdrop now displays stills of the Skaddle brothers as Michael continues: "Suspicion immediately fell on Tug and Timothy Skaddle, confessed dognapers of Crunch, who returned Wanton's pet yesterday after a court proceeding in which the brothers filed suit against the owner for personal injuries and property destruction inflicted by the rottie during its brief incarceration. However, O'Bannion's office has cleared both Skaddles in the dog's latest disappearance."

A prerecorded video clip of Constable O'Bannion speaking fills the screen. "The lads spent the entire night scrubbing floors and making repairs, our investigator told us. The officer also presented detailed photos. From the looks of young Timothy, I believe him when he says he'll have nothing more to do with the dog."

The camera returns to Michael, who continues: "Wanton has offered a £500 reward for any information leading to his pet's return, claiming the last thing he needs right now is another legal contretemps over Crunch. Magistrate Winston McConnell, who was expected to rule today on the Skaddles' request for Crunch's incarceration, has postponed his decision due to the canine's inability to appear."

The camera moves to Meredith, who has a related development. "We reached out to Barrister James Prance, who represents the Skaddle brothers in their lawsuit, for his reaction to these extraordinary developments."

Prance is now seen on-screen. Dressed head to toe in lavender, offset by a hot pink necktie, he looks cartoonish, not at all like an attorney. Nevertheless, his tone is grave. "I hope anybody out there who has also been victimized by Crunch will contact me, as I am, trust me, experienced in all matters of legally confronting this particular pooch, which is as nasty as a canine can be."

Meredith closes the segment by observing, "Michael, I don't believe we've ever reported a story with so many twists and turns."

Michael nods in full agreement. "Meredith, I certainly cannot recall any. What can possibly come next?" He pauses briefly. "We'll be right back after these messages."

Outside, there are sounds of footsteps and muffled voices heading for the dining hall. You regard your briefcase lying on the bed and decide you're not about to lug it around all night. You compromise by removing your valuables and stuffing them inside the game box. With a parting glance in the mirror, you decide you look great in your silver tux, white shirt with diamond cuff links, and black bow tie.

You've resided in the manor for several days and have entered—or peered into—several spectacular rooms. But nothing could have prepared you for the grandeur, the sheer size of the grand dining hall.

You pause at the entrance to take it all in—the sea of white linen, with vases of flowers, ice sculptures, and candles atop each table; the towering cathedral ceiling; the crystal-adorned chandeliers and brassy candelabras; the gleaming hardwood floors; the tall palms and ferns in pearlescent ceramic containers. A strolling violinist threads between the tables. The concierge, looking regal in a flowing evening gown, her hair exquisitely coiffed, is ascending to the elevated dais.

And now Chef Noël Elle Léon is standing before you. "Ah, *enfin*! The guest of honor has arrived!" His voice projects through the entire room as you observe the tiny microphone clipped to his tuxedo lapel.

A spotlight suddenly illuminates you both. Noël escorts you to the centermost table, and as you walk arm in arm, polite applause fills the hall. To the gathering, Noël announces, *"Je vous en fais mes félicitations! Ce soir, la concierge du château seigneurial, Adrienne Van Scoy."* He turns back to you, exclaiming, "She will play *une composition musicale* especially to honor you. *Bon appétit*!"

The chef seats you with Bruce, Savannah, Reggie, Mildred, and Christopher. They all look fabulous in their tuxes and gowns. Thomas is circling the table pouring champagne.

You look up at the dais where the concierge is now walking toward a grand piano. She looks stunning in her botanical silk chiffon gown with its form-fitting bodice and floor-grazing skirt. Thomas fills your glass, leans over, motions toward the concierge, and whispers, "Oscar de la Renta."

"Of course, Thomas," you quip. "I would expect no less."

From the opening chords, you sense that Adrienne's recital will be a powerful, passionate performance. The allegro wastes no time in reaching a high plateau of sustained emotion and drive. Her playing is furious, awe inspiring, with every note commanding attention. You are equally amazed by her composing skill. She finishes her piece to loud applause and cheers from every corner of the hall.

Your heart is pounding. *She wrote this for me! Maybe there's a chance after all, Storyteller.* A smiling young lady appears, shaking her head slowly from side to side and singsongingly says, ***Not if you don't approach her in earnest.***

A toast to you is proposed. Christopher catches your eye and signals that he's brought everything you asked for.

Now Chef Noël is back to announce tonight's repast. "Okay, Google, show the menu! *S'il vous plait!*" High above the center of the room, a giant four-sided hologram begins to animate tonight's fare. The decorative fonts are sparkling gold and cursive, as each dish is drawn one line at a time against a silver background. When the *carte du jour* is fully rendered, everyone applauds. Noël gushes with unrestrained pleasure and pride.

Le Grand Palindrome pour L'occasion

Salade du château en saison

Escargots à la façon chef Léon

Bisque de homard

Champignons farcis à l'oignon français

Cailles farcier aux champignons de la fôret Hanover

Coquilles avec crème d'échalote

Noisettes le venaison à la sauce chasseur

Granite aux petits fruits

Bolognaise de cerf aux pappardelles

Pétoncles frits

Caille garnie de fleurs sauvages de la forêt de Hanovre

Champignons à l'ail au fromage à la crème

Potage à la publicaine

Escargots sauce à l'ail

Salade Niçoise

Christopher stands up and walks over to the chef. You hear him say, "May I?" Noël nods vigorously, smiling at the boy. Christopher then calls out, "Okay, Google, translate to English."

The diners gasp as the change is instantaneously displayed on all four sides.

The Grand Palindrome for the occasion

Castle salad in season

Chef Léon's snails

Lobster bisque

French onion–stuffed mushrooms

Quail stuffed with mushrooms from the Hanover Forest

Gratinéed scallops

Hazelnut-crusted venison in hunter sauce

Berry granita

Venison Bolognese with Pappardelle

Deep-fried scallops

Quail garnished with wildflowers from the Hanover Forest

Cream cheese garlic mushrooms

Publican's French onion soup

Snails in garlic sauce

Niçoise salad

Returning to his seat, Christopher leans over to confide: "Noël included a soup dish from the pub, one of Bruce's specialties—a good sign, don't you think?"

You do. "It looks like he's not only got a palindromic assortment but he's also paying homage to Chef Emil," you say, pointing to the dishes containing mushrooms and wildflowers. "Hope they're not trippy dishes."

Christopher laughs, then informs you that after returning to his room, he looked up the word *palindrome*. Aside from the standard definition of a word or phrase or numerical sequence that reads the same backward or forward, he says he found a secondary meaning. "Here, have a look. I've jotted it down," he says, handing you the slip.

Palindrome: a segment of double-stranded DNA in which the nucleotide sequence of one strand reads in reverse order to that of the complementary strand.

"Just thought you'd like to know that," he says slyly.

"So what does it mean?" You don't get it.

"That every strand's connected, as I keep endeavoring to remind you."

"Is this another i21 thing?"

"Indeed. It might well signify that time can move forward and backward in a circular fashion," Christopher declares before turning away to request a lemonade from a nearby waiter.

Reggie and Mildred, Bruce and Savannah slip into their usual repartee. They also try to pry out of you details about your mysterious after-dinner event. You joke that you're going to conduct your own seminar on etiquette. "Because from what I've observed upstairs, boy do you people ever need it!"

The opening dishes from Noël's tour de force arrive, each one surpassing the last in visual splendor and taste.

Accompanied by Farnsworth, Adrienne comes over to offer her congratulations. You stand and clasp her hands, telling her how moved you were by her performance. In a burst of emotion, she hugs you. Then the couple withdraws radiantly, and you notice, disconsolately, that they still seem like a "couple."

As the dinner progresses, the other manor servants come to your table to be formally introduced. Several you recognize from the bar and the pub, but this is the first chance you've had to personally greet them and learn their names. They are mainly young people with fresh, eager faces—housekeepers, gardeners, mechanics, clerks, and spa employees. The cooks and waitstaff are busy tonight, but some manage to drop by with a quick hello or bonsoir. The men bow. The women curtsy. Everybody seems to be taking this seriously. It makes you feel somewhat self-conscious. Yet inwardly you chuckle, wondering how all of them will be feeling a few hours from now.

Suddenly and unexpectedly, the lights dim until the dining hall is enveloped in near darkness. The attendees stir, as no post-dinner event was previously announced. Yet clearly something is about to happen. And soon enough, the concierge again appears on the dais, illuminated by a single spotlight from the bank in the ceiling high above as she begins her narration:

"Good evening, one and all. Tonight we have a surprise, which I'm honored to present for the first time. As you know, for years, Hanover Manor has hosted periodic art exhibitions open to the public and free of charge, just as Lord Hanover wished. But what you don't know is the secret project he undertook in his latter days to utterly transform the manner in which we present these treasured works. Indeed, they say a picture is worth a thousand words, but for what you're about to see, I'm afraid there really are no words. Ladies and gentlemen, immerse yourselves in Claude Monet and sail away!"

Enya's "Orinoco Flow (Sail Away)" fills the room. Everyone gasps as a giant digital rendering of a single sailboat materializes in the middle of the hall just above the diners' heads, a three-dimensional image you reckon is two stories tall.

"We begin with Monet's *Voilier au Petit-Gennevilliers.*"

Sailboat at Le Petit-Gennevilliers. *Thanks, Storyteller. Did you enjoy the recital?* ***Immensely. Each and every time we attend it.*** *And the dinner?* ***Very funny.*** *Sorry, couldn't resist.* ***No worries. We've gotten used to you!***

Adrienne continues: "You can see it's a beautiful day for sailing. Notice the glossy reflection of the boat on the calm waters. The clouds are streaked and bold but give life to the cream-colored sky. The use of large strokes swirling the colors together to create the appearance of ripples makes it seem like a dream. Ah . . . but is it?"

You and the audience again gasp as the ripples in the painting begin to actually ripple. A wind gust billows the sail, and the boat begins to move slowly across the water. Enya's music fades away. A light spray momentarily envelops the room. It feels good on your face and further draws you and everyone else into the scene.

At the front, the concierge has returned to her piano and is now playing a sensual and melancholy piece. "'Moonlight'?" You recognize it from old movie soundtracks.

"'*Clair de lune,*'" whispers Christopher. "They taught us at school to always listen to Debussy when viewing Impressionist art."

"*Always*, Christopher, really? C'mon."

"Well, no. Sometimes Ravel," he says, grinning.

The mere mention of the composer takes you back to that climactic moment in the tub, watching Savannah gyrate just outside of it.

High above, you see the digital landscape has changed. It's now a scene crowded with boats. The concierge pauses her sonata, stands, and resumes narrating: "Now we are transported to *Régates à Argenteuil*, where many vessels have gathered. The central motif here is the water—how it glistens, displaying countless reflections. These are scenes Monet and his contemporary, Renoir, painted regularly under changing conditions in the sky and water."

All of the boats in the painting are drifting along with their reflections on this sunny day. After a moment, an artful digital transition changes the scene to the boats actually racing underneath a partly cloudy sky. Adrienne returns to her piano and proceeds to play—surprise!—the French national anthem!

"Christopher, isn't that— ?"

"*La Marseillaise*. Indeed, very apt of Ms. Van Scoy," he explains. "One often hears patriotic music at regattas, especially those on the Riviera."

What a fount of info, this kid, Storyteller! ***Fount, yes. Kid, not.***

Throughout the dining hall, you see several more Monet boat paintings bursting into view spectacularly. Several guests rise from their chairs and move from painting to painting, sometimes walking right through them to get a closer look. Slight sea breezes fill the room, accompanied by scents and sounds from the harborside dwellings. You marvel over how this show continues to assault all the senses.

In another moment, you see the displays throughout the hall change to water lilies floating in myriad ponds. A lovely citrus fragrance permeates the room carried now by warm, humid summer breezes. After a few moments, the watery scenes are replaced by vases—some filled with sunflowers, others with irises—that rotate slowly, enabling the viewer to see the three-dimensional bouquets from perspectives other than the original still life.

"Aha," blurts Christopher, "they've used AI to extrapolate the hidden viewpoints. Lovely."

Soon the flowers are everywhere in the room, flooding the floor, the ceiling, and the walls of the dining hall. You are astonished to find that you can examine the artist's individual brushstrokes. Onstage, the concierge is playing Bach.

"You know, Christopher," you say, "seeing all these sunflowers and irises reminds me that back home they did something like this with Van Gogh a long time ago. Impressive at the time, but it pales compared to this. This is just nonstop jaw dropping."

Christopher nods, turns, and sweeps a hand before the entire scene, saying, "I'm sure as soon as Uncle Artie learnt of the technology, he straightaway commissioned all this for the manor."

"Sounds like he was an early adopter all right," you observe. "We must be related!"

Christopher laughs, then says, "I could watch this all night, but shouldn't we, at some point, set up Three Families?"

You snap your fingers, exclaiming, "Oh, Christopher, you're so right. Let's see if we can slip away without notice. Don't want to appear rude, leaving my own gala early."

"Follow me," he replies, pulling out the real red remote. "We'll duck out through a supply closet in the service hallway to the kitchen the waiters use."

CHAPTER TWENTY-SIX

"Ladies and gentlemen, Master Christopher and I welcome you to tonight's gathering, which we sincerely hope you will enjoy and profit from."

You're on a dais, reading from a script to introduce the game. Everyone is seated in the first three rows.

"'Tis a simple exercise with a clear objective—to discover who among you shall be crowned King or Queen of the Occasion!" You hold up the crown from the game box. There are a few gasps; the replica, sparkling with what look like diamonds and studded with emeralds and rubies, is splendid and convincing.

"I beg you now to come forward and seat yourselves. Sit with whomever you like, but please make sure there are exactly eight members at your table."

It takes a few minutes for them to decide where to sit. There is the buzz of expectancy. The group probably assumed you were going to give some sort of formal address; they don't know what this is going to be, but you've certainly piqued their interest. You have their undivided attention as you call on Google to display the game's guiding principles.

The Wealthiest Pretender Shall Be King or Queen
All Others to Be Destitute
Allegiance to Family Is False
Play to Know Thy Fate

"The first: the wealthiest shall be crowned. Lords and ladies, tonight you are going to play a game in which you all begin as pretenders to a throne, yet in the end there can be only one victor—our new King or Queen of the Occasion!

"The second: all others are to be destitute. Lords and ladies, there is no runner-up, no exalted prince or princess, duke or duchess, nor lesser nobles in our imaginary realm. Tonight, to one victor alone belong the spoils. If you fail to become the reigning monarch, your title is revoked, your holdings seized, your entire fortune reversed.

"The third: family ties are false. Lords and ladies, each of you is seated at a table that represents the family into which you were born."

At this point, Christopher goes about placing a single card on each table.

The Paisleys of Abercorn
The Ogilvys of Airlie
The Frasers of Lovat

You notice that Thomas and Penelope are Paisleys; Reggie and Mildred, Bruce and Savannah are Ogilvys; while Noël, Farnsworth, and Adrienne are Frasers.

From the script you continue: "But marriage, shifting alliances, and other interventions of fate can change all that. In the course of our game, some of you may be transferred to another House or returned to the clan in which you started. Pay no heed to that, for these are only the vagaries of life. Whether from within or without, *all* are your rivals as you set your sights on the throne!

"And the fourth principle: play to know thy fate. Lords and ladies, though only one shall ultimately wear the crown, there is merit in the exercise for all. For this is a test of your ingenuity, powers of persuasion, knowledge of strategy and tactics, and your ability to work with—and against—others, for as little or as long as it suits *your* purposes."

Christopher distributes the choir robes, name holders, and badges, instructing players to clearly print Lord or Lady, followed by their own first name, followed by the name of the House. While he passes around pens and helps people find the right-sized robes, you unveil a new slide.

COINS OF THE REALM

FACE VALUE

Gold Sovereign = 50 pounds
Silver Crown = 30 pounds
Copper Shilling = 20 pounds
Nickel Pence = 10 pounds
Lead Penny = 5 pounds

NUMISMATICS

Five of a kind = 40 pounds
Four of a kind = 25 pounds
Three of a kind = 10 pounds

You explain: "Notice the monetary chart I have posted. You will be given pouches full of coins—this is your start in life, your initial stake. Your goal is to accumulate as much wealth as possible by every legal means. Whoever amasses the greatest fortune will be crowned king or queen. It is as simple as that."

The players exchange nods of comprehension.

You pause to let them study the Face Value portion of the chart. Satisfied that they get it, you continue. "Next, please note the Numismatic portion of the chart. Additional wealth can be accumulated by collecting coins of the same denomination. Here is a simple example: five lead pennies possess a face value of twenty-five pounds and a numismatic value of forty pounds, resulting in a total of sixty-five pounds. Again, does everyone understand? Any questions so far?"

There are none. You sense that already interest is running high and continue from the script. "My assistant shall now distribute the pouches. Listen well, my friends, to the first rule of this game. Never, under any circumstances, reveal the contents of your pouch—in other words, your wealth—to any other player." You pause to let this sink in.

"Any violation of this cardinal rule shall be punishable by a fine. The game master or his assistant, upon observing a transgression, shall call the offenders together and collect a coin from the person who revealed his or her wealth and from anyone who glimpsed it."

Reggie's got a question. "Can we say what coins we have—long as we don't show 'em?"

"Certainly," you tell him. You're glad he asked, for lying and dissembling are possible tactics players can employ. As you're sure some of them will.

Now you hear Noël calling out boisterously, *"Engage le jeu que je le gagne!"*

Ah! Your chef has summoned the perfect French palindrome for the occasion. *What does it mean?* ***Start the game so I can win!*** *Yes. Very apt for tonight.*

You gesture to Noël to acknowledge his clever outburst as you signal Christopher to begin distributing the pouches. Most peek furtively at their holdings. You see expressions ranging from satisfaction to disappointment to perplexity as they recheck the currency chart and calculate.

"And now, my friends, the way to increase your wealth. I will now explain the Rules of Engagement. Listen well." You watch them all lean forward, hanging on every word. "The path to the throne is a series of negotiations and trades among the contestants. In a few minutes, the first round of trading will commence—over there." You sweep your hand across the empty stage to indicate where the bartering will take place. "Now, regard the following."

RULES OF ENGAGEMENT

1. You may engage in trade, or not, as you wish.
2. Only traders may speak.
3. Only coins of different value may be exchanged.
4. Only one-for-one trades are permitted.
5. Once a trade is begun, only an exchange of coins can end it.
6. Once an exchange is agreed upon, a witness will be summoned.

"Allow me to provide a bit of dramatization with Christopher here."

Christopher steps forward with two coin pouches and hands one to you. From the script, you read, "To demonstrate rule number one: You may be satisfied with your holdings and have no wish to risk them. In such a case, simply do not engage in trade with anybody. Or perhaps there are certain individuals with whom you do not wish to negotiate, like Lord Reginald and Lord Bruce over there"—the group laughs—"because you found them conniving and suffered cruelly at their hands when last you bargained." There's more laughter. "Or maybe you just don't feel like trading at the moment but plan to resume later. In all of these cases, signify your unwillingness by folding your arms in front of you, as Christopher is doing now."

Christopher poses in the arms-folded position.

"But once having assumed this posture, you must remain silent. A violation of this rule will result in the loss of a coin from your pouch.

"Rule number two: you may only talk to the person you are trading with. If I wish to trade with you, for example, I extend my right hand. If you clasp my hand, it signifies you agree. Only when hands are joined may the two of you begin speaking. Please observe."

With your pouch in your left hand, you walk up to Christopher, extending your right. He keeps his arms folded in front of him; to underscore his refusal, he even turns his back on you.

"I indicated my willingness to trade but was refused. So that's the end of that. Now please observe this." Again, you approach Christopher with an outstretched hand, and now he takes it. You begin a simulation you rehearsed while setting up.

You: "I'll give you my silver coin for your gold."

Christopher: "Are you mad? How about a copper for your silver?"

You: "Surely you jest. Tell me, sir, are you collecting a particular type?"

Christopher: "Perhaps. And you?"

You: "I am. I desire more nickel pence."

Christopher: "Sorry, haven't got any of those."

You: "Say, you've got a copper? Well, then, perhaps you fancy more. Think about their numismatic value. And if it makes sense, give me a silver crown for my copper."

Christopher: "Agreed. But next time I shall expect the advantage."

You: "Agreed."

He looks at you with a twinkle in his eye and says, "We did the deed, now we're agreed!" The two of you release hands and pretend to summon a game master to witness the exchange.

You conclude, "Many more situations and rules will come up, all of which we shall expound on as they arise. But for the moment, let's get started with this first stage, shall we? Any final questions?"

There are none. Several players—notably Bruce, Reggie, Savannah, Noël, and Adrienne—are champing at the bit.

Trading is moderate. About half of the participants are either too shy or risk averse to engage at first. They seem to enjoy walking about with folded arms, stopping here and there to observe negotiations in progress. Perhaps they're also scouting for easy marks—or ones to avoid—in future transactions. But the twelve or so active traders keep you and Christopher busy.

Bruce and Reggie cause a stir when they join hands to conduct their first trade. The macho posturing, the one-upmanship, the put-downs, all the trickery and tomfoolery they try to foist on one another is hilarious. The pair is so entertaining that a sizable crowd draws around them to enjoy their staged histrionics. Finally, Bruce coughs up a nickel for a penny just to escape his best friend's grip.

Some players trade down because they are collecting a certain coin, aiming for the bonus. Others do so simply because an aggressive salesperson eventually wears them down—they just want to escape. A lot of promises are made and—after a transaction—broken, as victors fold their arms. Artful deceits unfold all over the room.

A smooth-talking gardener tricks Penelope into giving up a gold sovereign for a lead penny, claiming falsely that he's played this game before. "At the end of the round," he promises, "the leaders are going to invert the currency chart—lead and gold will flip-flop in value—just wait and see." You sigh inwardly, seeing her fall for it. Thomas uses his good looks and charm to prey on women and men who find him attractive. Mildred's one of the bystanders; she moves around and quietly observes as many trades as possible, smiling in her motherly way. You get the feeling that she's sizing people up, as is Farnsworth, and that they will become active later on.

Gradually, the momentum builds as once-shy participants unfold their arms and wander into the fray. Everybody appears to be disappointed when you call a halt to the proceedings after only twenty minutes.

"Aw, we was just getting started, mate," calls Bruce.

"Gimme just a minute more with this one," implores Reggie, who's in a negotiation with a timid spa employee.

You instruct all players to relinquish their hand holds. There will be many more trading rounds, you explain, but you want to tally holdings to see who's ahead. On your instructions, they return to their seats, drop their name badges inside their pouches, and give them to Christopher when he comes around to collect. While he tallies in another room, you'll describe a new activity to the group.

When everyone has rejoined their "families," you take three gold coins and place one in the center of each table. From your script, you read, "A bit of good fortune now shines, as represented by the gold sovereign you see before you. But what must be resolved is this: Who among the eight of you should receive it, solely? This matter is for each family to decide among itself. Thus, you have ten minutes to hold council. The value of the coin cannot be divided. The decision must be unanimous. Failure to reach it in time will result in no member receiving this reward. All right then, ten minutes. Please, by all means, discuss . . . negotiate . . . decide."

A babble ensues. Everybody feels entitled to the gold coin. You catch snatches of conversation. "I should have it because I didn't get a gold in my pouch." "I did poorly at trading; therefore, I deserve it." "I did well at trading; therefore, I deserve it."

Eventually, Farnsworth prevails among the Frasers by pulling rank. The butler uses his authority to practically order that the coin be awarded to him. Adrienne finally assents, but with a look that says, *Agreed, but next time, me.*

As the time limit draws near, at the Ogilvys, Bruce simply reaches across and snatches the sovereign—then defies anyone to dispute his claim. Reggie and Savannah back down, but not before they hurl a few looks of their own. The Paisleys award the prize to Thomas, who prevailed by simply smiling at everyone while looking wistful.

Christopher returns with a score sheet and newly assembled pouches. You instruct him to "add fifty pounds each to the tallies of Lord James Fraser of Lovat, Lord Bruce Ogilvy of Airlie, and Lord Thomas Paisley of Abercorn."

"Okay, Google, show the scores!" Christopher calls out. Similar to the rendering of tonight's menu, the scoreboard is displayed high above.

THE OGILVYS OF AIRLIE		THE PAISLEYS OF ABERCORN		THE FRASERS OF LOVAT	
Lord Bruce	185	Lord Thomas	105	Lord James	95
Lord Reginald	130	Lady Patricia	90	Lady Adrienne	90
Lady Savannah	125	Lady Felicia	85	Lord Noël	70
Lord Ian	125	Lord Byron	80	Lady Anne	55
Lady Yvette	115	Lord Jacques	70	Lady Lynn	50
Lady Mildred	115	Lord Timothy	70	Lord Peter	50
Lady Janice	90	Lady Jane	70	Lady Luck	45
Lord William	85	Lady Penelope	55	Foxy Lady	40

Those who didn't notice before laugh at the nicknames, Luck and Foxy, the two girls from the spa have added to their badges.

Consulting your script, you instruct Lords Thomas and James to come over to the Ogilvys and be seated. You want them to replace Lord William and Lady Janice, who should now join the Paisleys, as should Lady Adrienne. Finally, you want Ladies Jane and Penelope to transfer to the Frasers. They should exchange robes. Christopher makes the changes on the board while you distribute new badges to the affected players. After the family changes, Christopher quickly edits his grid on the tablet controller he's brought and presses REDRAW. The hologram switches the names in a short, pleasing animation.

THE OGILVYS OF AIRLIE		THE PAISLEYS OF ABERCORN		THE FRASERS OF LOVAT	
Lord Bruce	185	Lady Janice	90	Lady Jane	70
Lord Reginald	130	Lady Patricia	90	Lord Noël	70
Lady Savannah	125	Lady Adrienne	90	Lady Anne	55
Lord Ian	125	Lady Felicia	85	Lady Penelope	55
Lady Yvette	115	Lord William	85	Lady Lynn	50
Lady Mildred	115	Lord Byron	80	Lord Peter	50
Lord Thomas	105	Lord Jacques	70	Lady Luck	45
Lord James	95	Lord Timothy	70	Foxy Lady	40

Christopher returns the name badges and places eight pouches in the center of each table as you announce the beginning of a second trading round.

Now that everyone has an idea of how this works, the participants plunge into noisy negotiations. The din obliterates the music program being piped into the room. You and Christopher run from pair to pair to consummate transactions. Both of you are forced to levy some fines due to infractions. Lady Luck loses a coin because she cannot refrain from advising Foxy Lady during a trade with Lord Noël. Two gardeners try to break off their long negotiations without an exchange and are penalized. You're tickled observing the "counters"—contestants who compulsively recheck their pouch every few minutes. The "predators" are fun to watch too—aggressive traders who literally get in line to take their turn with the easy marks.

Lord Bruce is going after weaker men with brute force. He locks them in his iron grip and grins, squeezing until they give him what he wants. Lady Mildred is now actively trading. In her sweet maternal way, she finds young girls who need understanding and sympathy as they describe the merciless treatment they've just received at the hands of Lord or Lady so and so. In the end, they are happy to relinquish a better coin as a way of saying thanks for listening. Lady Mildred says "dearie" a lot and gradually gets rich. Ladies Savannah and Adrienne con all the men they can find, one using brazen sex appeal; the other, sophisticated charm. When you signal that time's up, no one is frustrated like before. They're exhilarated and exhausted—even those who fared poorly. An air of expectancy settles over each family when everyone's reseated. Christopher collects the pouches while you walk around and place two gold coins in the center of each table.

"Yes, lords and ladies, this time there are two. They can be divided between two people, or both retained by one, or awarded to no one. But this time, you've got only five minutes to decide!"

Pandemonium.

CHAPTER TWENTY-SEVEN

Just when you thought the decibels couldn't go any higher, they become deafening as the scenes at the three tables descend into pure chaos. By doubling the stakes and halving the time frame, you've induced panic, outrageous behavior, desperate measures, and ribaldry all at once. It shows many players will say and do anything for the gold.

In the Frasers, Lady Penelope is on her hands and knees begging for both coins so she can rejoin her beloved, Lord Thomas. But she's getting nowhere with her peers, many of whom have recently succumbed to the headwaiter's charms. You marvel at how open she is in declaring her unbridled affection for him—and what an actress!

At the Paisleys, one member has suggested a few quick rounds of Rock Paper Scissors to decide the awardees. Lady Adrienne tries to object but backs off when she senses the group is inclined to let chance decide. Fortunately for her, she emerges as one of the two winners.

"I rather think I should be the one called 'Lady Luck.'" She beams. The Paisleys, having amiably decided, turn their chairs to watch the others.

The Ogilvy clan, where the power players are grouped, is an intense scene. Lady Savannah bangs her fist on the table and states in no uncertain terms that this round's coins will "not go to a man." She is supported by Ladies Yvette and Mildred. Lord Reginald jumps up and says it's all right with him if Lords Bruce and James are excluded, but reserving *both* coins for women is going too far. Lord Thomas catches the drift of the Paisleys' Rock Paper Scissors solution and tries to offer it to his family. He is shouted down.

You start for the center of the room, intending to call time. You're spotted by numerous Frasers and Ogilvys, who alert their compatriots. At the last minute, Lady Savannah hurls a final offer: "One coin to Lady Mildred, the other to Lady Yvette—take it or leave it!" The men capitulate.

In the meantime, the lowly Frasers have gotten nowhere. All pleas were pitiful, but one after another tale of woe fell on deaf ears. Lord Noël's was particularly abject, but hardly anybody understood his tearful patois. You finally call time, sweeping the coins off their table. The House of Lovat has squandered its chance, which leaves them even more depressed.

While everyone waits in anticipation, you hear postmortems from two of the groups. The Paisleys agree that Rock Paper Scissors is an ideal permanent solution. They engage in a civil discussion of a proposed modification: that past winners be ineligible until all members have received at least one coin. The Ogilvys are also surprisingly restrained, considering their just-concluded ferocity. Although calm, the men are now telling the women in no uncertain terms that next time the coins must go to them. Lady Savannah says she might agree, but not if there are more than two at stake. The Frasers are downcast, silent, and wallowing in collective misery. Disparaging looks are directed at them. Looks that say *Losers*.

A hush falls over the crowd. Christopher's returned, ready to post results. You loudly inform him that "fifty pounds each should be added to the tallies of Ladies Mildred and Yvette Ogilvy, and to those of Lord Jacques and Lady Adrienne Paisley."

"And to whom among the Frasers of Lovat?" Christopher asks pointedly.

"The family has forfeited its reward," you solemnly announce.

You tell the group there will be some transfers. Soon Christopher's updated rendering reflects both the current totals and the new affiliations.

The contestants express surprise that only one change has occurred—Lady Adrienne is to switch places with Lord Ian. The concierge dons her purple vestment and joins the Ogilvys with a regal air. "It was only a matter of time," she announces.

When you start the bonus round, you again place two coins on each table. It's all over at the Ogilvys as soon as discussions begin. "Fair is fair, Lady Savannah. Last time you had your way, so now it's our turn." This is the gist of the argument used to award Lords Reginald and Thomas a gold apiece. Lady Mildred argues that Lady Savannah is the only member of the group not to have received a gold coin, despite her leadership role. Lady Yvette proposes that their colleague be rewarded next time. They are supported by Lords Thomas and Bruce. Lords Reginald and James and newcomer Lady Adrienne grudgingly agree—but "one coin only, no more."

The Paisleys again attempt to settle their disbursement with a Rock Paper Scissors tournament. All goes well until Lord William accuses Lord Byron of cheating, claiming that Byron tried to switch from rock to scissors after glimpsing William's paper. The furor subsides in time for the contest to conclude. You think this may be a sign of growing desperation in the House of Abercorn.

Lady Penelope again gives an impassioned plea to her fellow Frasers. But this time there's no sentimental fluff about wanting to join her beloved. She claims she's worked hard to pull herself up by her bootstraps, that she's just concluded a good round, despite starting with meager resources. She realizes that if the family awards her both coins, it probably means she'll be moving on, if not to the Ogilvys, at least to the Paisleys. But she swears she'll "never forget" them—and she'd certainly "never refuse to trade or associate" with them.

With time running out, Lord Noël leaps to his feet and makes a blatant offer of a bribe: award him at least one coin and the kitchen will deliver coffee and pastries to the entire table. "Both coins, à la mode!" Everybody laughs at the two novel approaches and agrees to give Lady Penelope and Lord Noël the sovereigns. The chef keeps his word and texts the kitchen for the refreshments. The updated standings reveal that Lord Noël and Lady Penelope have made it to the Paisleys, replacing Lords William and Byron. Thanks to a spectacular trading round and the bonus, they're at the top of the Abercorn heap, with the House of Airlie within range. But they both know there's likely to be room for only one of them to advance.

Christopher shoots you a questioning look, mouthing, "Think it's time?"

You do. From your script, you read, "Lords and ladies, I beg of you, lend me your ears, for I have an important announcement before commencing the next round of play. To enliven our proceedings, Master Christopher and I have decided upon the following revisions." You call out the changes to Google and the players.

AMENDING THE RULES

7. The Houses of Abercorn and Lovat may offer petitions.
8. Any current rule may be amended or rescinded.
9. The House of Airlie shall meet and confer on the petitions.
10. Petitions receiving at least five votes in the House of Airlie shall be adopted.

You explain that *any* of the game's rules may now be altered or thrown out altogether. New rules may be added. All changes, however, must be proposed by either the Frasers or the Paisleys to be decided solely by majority vote of the Ogilvys. The families may now freely deliberate on these topics. "Let your imaginations roam free. Let inventiveness abound," you conclude from your script.

Your new wrinkle is an immediate hit, prompting discussion at all three tables. The Ogilvys, although not allowed to propose themselves, entertain one another by predicting what proposals might come their way and how they will vote on them. Soon, Lord Ian Paisley of Abercorn is on his feet, seeking recognition. "We beg you, kind sirs and madams of the Ogilvys," he says with a flourish, getting into a parliamentary spirit, "to consider our humble petition." He clears his throat. "Be resolved: one, that negotiations no longer be required to finalize an exchange if either of the two parties desires to break them off; two, that contestants no longer be required to hold hands during the time they are bargaining; three, that contestants no longer be required to remain silent when they are not trading; four, that the bonus gold be awarded by simple plurality instead of requiring unanimous agreement; five, that contestants may show one another their coins during negotiations—this will help both parties find a satisfactory outcome more quickly. Thank you, dear lords and ladies."

Lord Ian takes his seat to hearty applause. The Ogilvys confer and quickly decide. Lord James is elected to speak for the family. "With regard to the first, that trades can be halted if mutually agreed upon, this is accepted. Regarding point two, the elimination of hand-holding, this is also accepted. Point three, regarding suspension of the rule of silence, this, too, is accepted—henceforth the ban on discourse shall be dropped. Point four, that only a plurality is required to disburse bonus coins, is denied. Point five, that the contents of the pouches be open to examination, is denied—*categorically* denied, I might add." Lord James then announces, "The chair now recognizes Lord Peter Fraser of Lovat."

"Esteemed lords and ladies . . . um . . . some of us were wondering about these pouches. It seems as though we Frasers rarely, if ever, receive gold and silver coins when first they are distributed. We'd like to propose that Master Christopher be required to place exactly the same amount—we thought one of each denomination would make for a fair contest—at the outset of every round. Thank you."

Lord Peter's proposal is supported by all Frasers and most Paisleys. Again, the Ogilvys confer, and again Lady Savannah is the lone voice pleading for fair play. She convinces Lord Thomas to support her view but none of the others budge, and the proposal is defeated six to two.

Lady Adrienne announces the decision. "We are certain that the current game best imitates life. All of us are here as a result of our hard work and skills—not as a birthright. The pouches arrive with differing amounts, but we believe the luck of the draw evens out in the end. Besides, Master Christopher places them in the center of each table, and they are selected at random. Therefore," she says emphatically, "motion denied."

The trading floor is lively, but more discussions center on rule changes than on actual barter. With the rule of silence lifted, people gather in small groups. Paisleys freely mix with Frasers to exchange ideas and form common cause. Lady Savannah, in particular, is sought out by the lesser nobility since she is known to be sympathetic. Lord Noël spends a lot of time frantically conferring with Lord James and Lady Adrienne and then rushing over to Lords William and Byron, members of his former family—and employees in his restaurant—and whispering in their ears. You wonder what they are up to.

Lord Thomas is now subsidizing Lady Penelope, but they are careful not to overdo it—lest her elevation comes at his expense. Lords Reginald and Bruce, secure of their position in the standings, swap bar stories and jokes.

A flurry of new proposals hits the Ogilvys. That more coins be added to the bonus round is denied; that more time be allotted to decide the bonus is denied; and that membership in the Ogilvys be increased is *categorically denied.*

When you see the session running out of steam, you call for the bonus award. The discussions are fascinating. Lord Noël convinces the Paisleys to drop their game of chance in favor of elevating the two highest-ranking members—Lady Penelope and himself—to the aristocracy. He promises they'll work for positive change. "We will reform every single thing. *Je jure à vous*!" The chef again sweetens the deal with the promise of coffee and dessert but keeps his voice low so that his former family doesn't overhear. Lady Penelope nods in agreement, oozes sincerity, and the two of them pull it off.

Among the Frasers, Lords William and Byron convince the others that only their tallies put them within reach of the leaders. They, too, promise reform. After receiving the coins, each wagers his in a best-of-three round of Rock Paper Scissors. The Frasers congratulate the winner, Lord Byron, and wish him well. They are proud of him and beg that he always remember them.

But now you must depart this touching scene, for your presence is required at the Ogilvys to adjudicate an unusual situation. Lady Savannah has informed the family that she wishes to renounce her peerage. She's flung her purple robe on the table. Moreover, she specifically requests to join the Frasers and distribute her wealth equally among them. Even if she did win, she states, "I'd never want to reign in the name of such a greedy, uncaring family."

Fortunately, your script has alerted you that this is one of the developments that might arise late in the scenario. You inform the group that if a majority agrees, you'll allow resignation and reassignment. The family is happy to see her go; after all, the woman obviously does not know her class. With Lady Savannah out of the picture, Lord James and Lady Adrienne sweep in for the bonus coins, arguing that they've never been awarded any—"as members of *this* family, that is."

Christopher is about to distribute new pouches when Lord Byron Paisley and Lord William Fraser rise. They have a special joint resolution they'd like to offer. Lord Byron speaks. "My fellow lords and ladies, Lord William and I wish to propose that the Ogilvy family join us in offering new rules and regulations." Immediately there are groans.

Lord William joins in support of his colleague. "They would not be where they are were it not for their wisdom and fortitude. All will benefit from their guidance. We trust them to be fair."

Lady Savannah leaps to her feet, shouting, "Outrageous—they'll ruin everything!" She is supported by cries of "Hear! Hear!" from many Paisleys and Frasers. At the Ogilvys' table, you see Lord James and Lady Adrienne speaking sotto voce to their colleagues, as if filling them in on something prearranged. It looks as though the fix is in. All eyes turn to you.

"Any rule may be changed, including this one," you inform the players.

The Ogilvys unanimously vote in favor of the motion. They now have the power to both propose new laws and approve them. The mood at the Houses of Abercorn and Lovat is all-encompassing dread. They are fearful of what the Ogilvys might legislate. Rumors abound. The recent relaxation of negotiating procedures will be tightened; the rule of silence will be reinstituted; currency will be revalued; some sort of taxation scheme will be imposed; or the bonus round will be altered to Frasers' collective disadvantage.

Lords Byron and William are shunned in their Houses. Both lower Houses now regret the loss of their champion, Lady Savannah, in the high council. Now they must place their trust in Lord Thomas, who, says one, "often takes our side and speaks on our behalf," and in Lord Noël and Lady Penelope, who, another says, "rose through the ranks and have promised to look after us." Lords Bruce, Reginald, and James are viewed as hopeless, as is Lady Adrienne. It now depends, conventional wisdom has it, on Lady Mildred, the swing vote.

Any hopes the Frasers and Paisleys might have had that they'd be treated decently are dashed when the kitchen staff finally arrives with coffee and desserts. Redirecting the waiters over to the Ogilvys, ex-Fraser-Paisley Lord Noël turns to Lady Adrienne and, in a voice meant to be overhead, asks, "Madam, let them eat cake?"

To which Lady Adrienne, herself an alumna of both Houses, replies, "Oh, Monsieur Noël, *I* should say."

CHAPTER TWENTY-EIGHT

While the Ogilvys enjoy their refreshments—with only Lord Thomas abstaining in protest—Lord James asks for permission to quickly dictate a new posting, after which he will elaborate to the gathering. You hand him the mike, and he calls out the text to be displayed.

AMENDED RULES OF ENGAGEMENT

11. The contents of a pouch may be shown.
12. Unequal amounts may be exchanged.
13. Reconstituted: once a negotiation is begun, an exchange must end it.
14. An unengaged player may not decline an offer to barter.
15. The bonus award shall be suspended.
16. Contestants shall remain with their kind.

After they are fully rendered, Lord James tries to sell the changes. "To begin, we're going to give you what you've always wanted—full and fair disclosure of the contents of the pouch. The family believes that point two—allowing multiple exchanges, in nonequivalent amounts, for example two-for-one or three-for-two coin exchanges—will deepen the complexity and broaden the appeal of the game. Thus, point three—we are reinstating this earlier rule in order to effectively implement the above.

"And to further make this a contest of wits—may the best one win—we shall henceforth require all to trade whenever they are unoccupied and invited. Regarding the bonus round—the Ogilvys see no reason to continue this practice. You Paisleys and Frasers often decide this valuable award by resorting to games of chance. We don't want luck to play any part in this critical matter of royal succession. May our next king or queen be decided through virtue and wit alone!

"And regarding the families—all this moving around takes too much time and divides loyalties. We'll all be much happier if henceforth we remain with our kind, for there is no greater devotion than filial, to the family in which one belongs."

Lord James sits down to applause from his fellow Ogilvys, but to silence sprinkled with hisses and catcalls from the others. Christopher has posted the scores and redistributed pouches. You signal that trading should resume.

Chaos erupts. As soon as the Ogilvys read the board and check their pouches, they leap from their seats and charge the others. Each Paisley and Fraser defends by finding a partner to be in technical compliance with the rules. They taunt the circling Ogilvys by talking about everything other than currency exchange while pointing derisively to the hologram, where it is immediately apparent that the new rule prohibiting transfers may have backfired.

Lords Byron and William, still shunned by their own, have joined hands. Over their shoulders they hurl epithets of *"Ami de cour!"* and "Traitor!" to Lord Noël. You get the feeling the triumvirate reneged on a promise to promote those two just before they slammed the door on any further admissions.

"C'est la guerre!" the chef fires back.

Panicked now, the Ogilvys reassemble in emergency session. As they deliberate the Frasers strike up a chant. "Hey, hey, ho, ho, the poorhouse, the gallows, all Ogilvys go!"

Above the tumult, turning aside dissents from Lord Thomas and Lady Penelope, and eventually from Lady Mildred, the family passes a targeted measure by a five to three vote. Lord Bruce rises to announce it. "Rule seven: if an Ogilvy wishes to trade, Frasers and Paisleys can't refuse."

Lady Savannah again leaps to her feet. "Hey, Reggie! Hey, Bruce! Why are you holding back? Go ahead and announce your final edicts. A bit shy, are we? Or maybe you're just cowards! So permit me to elucidate your points eight, nine, and God knows what else you'll come up with next."

Cries of "Hear! Hear!" fill the room.

"Point eight—all Paisleys and Frasers henceforth shall walk around with open pouches as the Ogilvys waddle up, peer inside, and remove whatever coins they fancy!"

There are guffaws of laughter, cheers of derision. Supporters stamp their feet.

"Point nine!" Savannah thunders. "Listen one and all to this point! Because after they ram it through, there is no further 'point.' Hear ye! Hear ye! Point nine—the next king or queen shall succeed from the House of Airlie—alone! An Ogilvy blue blood—solely! I, for one, am through with you scoundrels!"

Seeing Christopher coming with the pouches, Savannah snatches several, tears them open, and hurls coins at the Ogilvy conclave. She turns to you with furious eyes.

Before anyone can react, you announce that the game has ended. By a head-nod signal you and Christopher prearranged, the boy takes off.

"Aw, I thought I was to be crowned once and future king, mate," Lord Bruce protests.

You ask for silence and the group's attention as you consult your manual under the section titled To Be Announced—Following Act(s) of Defiance.

Lady Savannah's outburst met the game-ending criterion, you note. You plan to distill all these post-game discussion topics into a few cogent statements. But you want emotions to remain taut and are determined not to deflate the group by talking too long or explaining too much.

"Lords and ladies," you call, "allow me to congratulate one and all on a thrilling performance. I hope you got as much out of participating as Master Christopher and I did from hosting tonight's entertainment. As for Three Families, I'll leave it to each of you to draw your own conclusions as to its purpose."

"Ah, Lord Acton's persistent truth." Thomas sighs. "'All power corrupts; absolute power corrupts absolutely.'"

You turn to the House of Lovat. "In closing, dear Frasers, let me say this—you never really had much of a chance." Holding up your guide, you tell them, "Upon these instructions, Christopher made sure your pouches contained nary a silver or a gold—and only a smattering of copper."

Strong cries of "Nay, nay" and "Unfair! Unfair!" erupt.

"Whoever said life is fair or that this imitation of it would be?" is your scripted reply.

You turn to Abercorn. "To you, dear Paisleys, your lot was scarcely better. If you sat among this family for most of the evening, you probably noticed that not many sovereigns and crowns came your way. Yet valiantly you tried to make do with what little you had."

There's a few murmurs, but nobody calls out anything. The Paisleys seem ambivalent about these revelations.

"And to you, my esteemed Ogilvys, I'm sorry to say, Christopher always made sure the rich got richer. But surely, deep down, you *knew* that, didn't you? Sensed it each time you spied both a gold and silver in your fresh pouch while estimating the wealth of your neighbors. Though you are indeed a talented and resourceful lot—as many of you proved with your rapid rise to fortune—you did not arrive at your preeminent position solely through your own merits."

Though most Ogilvys remain glum, you think you see a few twinkles returning to the eyes of Bruce and Reggie and hints of bemusement crossing the faces of Adrienne and Mildred.

To all, you conclude, "And, given these disclosures, let us turn now to the question as to who should be crowned king or queen tonight. It may interest you to know that, actually, royal succession never occurs in this game. Three Families simply continues 'until revolution ensues.' So confident that this outcome will ultimately result every time, in every gathering, the creators—your historians, lords and ladies—have stated it right here in the manual, and once again you proved them right by enacting the very history they wrote in advance."

You set aside the script and spread your arms dramatically, like you often see your uncle do. "But no matter how you fared tonight, on behalf of Christopher and myself, we would just like to say there is one very important thing you all should attend to from this moment on."

The room is quiet. Faces mirror confusion while you start to walk away. But now the house lights dim as a muted, throbbing bass beat slowly rises to an explosion of synthesizers and blasting, insistent, falsetto vocals.

CHAPTER TWENTY-NINE

"'You Should Be Dancing.'"

The tug of the old Bee Gees hit sucks people out of their chairs and onto the floor. Tension evaporates as the room pounds with music. Frasers, Paisleys, and Ogilvys, friends and foes alike, move and groove to the pounding beat. The battlefield of moments ago has become a raging disco inferno! Complete with strobe lights and color wheels Christopher has somehow found and hooked up.

Then Christopher pulls out his mike and shouts into it, "Okay, Google, show the crests!"

High above the dance floor, where mirror balls would normally be, bursts three distinct family crests—one each for the houses of Airlie, Abercorn, and Lovat. The 3D crests display each house's decorative shields emblazoned with their respective coats of arms. They begin to slowly revolve. The crowd is dazzled, emitting loud shouts and cheers.

Doors fly open, and waiters bearing trays stream into the room. Pitchers of ale are placed on the tables along with decanters of red, white, and rosé wine. Champagne corks explode.

Dancers shimmy and groove over to the refreshments. The waiters are pulled onto the floor as one seventies disco classic segues into another.

A loud, cognizant cheer goes up when Sister Sledge intones "We Are Family" followed by "Dancing Queen," which inspires Foxy Lady and Lady Luck to seize the crown and gyrate on the tables, which in turn prompts Noël to shout, "ABBA! ABBA! *J'adore* ABBA!" Christopher then segues into "Take on Me," which triggers another cry from the now delirious chef. "A-ha! *C'est* A-ha! *J'adore* A-ha!"

In the center of the floor, several Paisleys are break-dancing. Your jaw drops when you get a load of James's and Adrienne's ballroom routine. He's spinning her like a ballerina. Oh, how you wish you could "unsee" them looking so blissful and perfectly in sync.

Noël is *Saturday Night Fever* incredible, as are his alternating partners Byron and William. Thomas is moonwalking while Penelope shrieks in admiration; Savannah's sultry moves, of course, trigger a titillating recollection of your bathroom encounter.

You can predict that Bruce's flailing about will never win any contests, but no one is more exuberant. Except maybe Reggie. He and Mildred have tapped into an inexhaustible supply of energy.

Your pub-party director and choreographer appears overhead. ***It's your turn, my lord.*** *Whoa, really?* ***I don't need to dictate anything. It's all inside you, ready for release.***

You feel a stirring inside. You stand erect, back arched. You flare your left hand flamboyantly in the air, place your right hand on your stomach. You hold the position for an exaggerated moment, then cut loose with furious footwork and swiveling hips—a collage of mambo, samba, cha-cha, tango steps, all in double time to a throbbing, flamenco, brassy beat.

Unreal, Storyteller, where did I get those moves? ***Muscle memory, my lord.***

The contestants are now joined on the dance floor by dozens of servants whose shifts have ended and who heard that a hot party had broken out. As a Blacker beat is overlaid on the Latin one, Christopher rushes over, yelling above the din, "How do you like my playlist?"

Your double thumbs-up signals, *Perfect!* Now the mix is coming into the eighties with Kool & the Gang, Michael Jackson, and The Gap Band taking over.

After a couple more mixes, Christopher signals he wants you to listen carefully to the opening lines of the Pet Shop Boys' next tune. He thinks they're especially appropriate for tonight. The duo is carrying on about buying and selling history, how whenever they need to facilitate a sale, they simply change the laws. "It's the Ogilvys' theme song!" he shouts, raising a clenched fist as nearby dancers cast knowing glances and thumbs-up.

You note that nineties rap has now given way to aughts and teens pop featuring Coldplay, Harry Styles, and Train. But then Christopher's mix does something unexpected—it makes a transition that drives many in the crowd wild.

The music has suddenly blossomed into a French-language mash-up of dance hits. As soon as the opening riffs strike the ears of Noël and his entourage, they collapse and shriek in paroxysms of joy. After a moment, Noël, Byron, and William recover, leap to their feet, and begin to swoon in the subdued yet highly sensual style you've often seen in French music videos. The vibe throughout the room and on the floor has totally changed; it's now infused with faint eroticism and simmering passion.

Of course Christopher has paid tribute because of all the French nationals on the manor staff. You've met some—and heard about the so-called brigands—but besides Noël, hadn't yet gotten to know any of them well.

Many now groove their way over to express their fervent appreciation. It's doubtful if ever again you'll have so many merci beaucoups tossed your way or your cheeks kissed as much. You try to tell them it's actually Christopher they should thank.

"But it was you who dreamed this all up, is it not true, monsieur?" one of them asks.

"No, I believe it was actually Lord Hanover who came up with the game—I just added on an after-party." You nudge Christopher and whisper, "So are these the infamous 'men from the kitchen who came in the night'?"

The boy merely laughs, adding, "No, they're neither *les 'snafflez'* nor *les saboteurs*."

Noël slides up, flushed with elation. *"J'adore musique de danse française! Demain, Monsieur Chris, je vous surprendrai avec mon cadeau de gratitude."*

A Storyteller translates, ***I love French dance music! Tomorrow, Master Chris, I will surprise you with my gift of gratitude.***

"Well, we've been to France," Christopher announces. "Anyone care to come along to Oz? We'll commence by going back a couple of decades."

As Kylie's "Can't Get You out of My Head" pounds forth, you survey the floor, locating Adrienne, Savannah, and Penelope all dancing together now. Oh, ladies! You can't get any of them out of your head, either.

Bruce and a few other Aussie employees rush over to offer acknowledgment and thanks. "She's still our number-one Straya songstress. Cheers, mate," he calls out. "Got any of Tame Impala's golden oldies?"

Christopher pauses then segues into "The Less I Know the Better." An apt song title for your entire stay, you muse. "Good on ya, mate," Bruce shouts as he tears back to the dance floor.

Savannah shimmies up and says to Christopher, "You're quite the deejay, young man. I'm big-time impressed."

"Oh, thank you, Ms. Reddy," he replies. "Lovely that you would say."

She turns to you with an enticing smile. "Say, if you'd like to tour the London clubs with me and my garage assists . . ."

"Sure, Savannah," you reply agreeably. "So who's in your outfit?"

"Oh, the *unusual* suspects—Noël, Byron, William. Plus some mechanics and landscapers you may not have gotten to know yet." She points to a trio of short-haired, mustached, muscular guys gyrating athletically on the floor, looking like a Village People redux.

She's then joined by Noël, Byron, and William, who have rushed up from behind after apparently overhearing her invite. "*Votre Excellence*, you must come out with us some night! You must, must, must. It'll be, *je vous assure*, too hot to hoot!"

Quickly, you fire back, "Your *top spot*, Noël? Promise?"

"*Oui monsieur*, Taco Cat!"

"Next time we go, Noël," Savannah interjects, "can we *puhleese* try a club with a female deejay for once? I hear they're quite good. And I want to support them."

Noël clasps his hands together. "*Oh, mon chéri*, at Taco Cat we may not have so many deejays who are the actual woman, but *je vous assure*, we have plenty of girls!" At that, Byron and William chortle insanely and dance around in circles. Christopher signals he thinks it's a funny line too.

Savannah sighs. "I see I walked right into that one."

You're exhausted but immensely satisfied and overflowing with giddy thoughts. You have not one, not two, but three major crushes going on all at once!

C'mon, Storyteller, tell me, which one—should I, did I, will I—go for? ***You know we can't do that. But continued inaction may make the choice for you, my friend.***

The dance floor gradually empties. Exhausted revelers gather at tables to enjoy the refreshments and reminisce on all the fun they had tonight.

When Arcade Fire's "Put Your Money on Me" begins, Lady Luck and Foxy Lady swivel their chairs, join hands, hold up imaginary pouches, and rock their bodies from side to side, rhythmically reenacting a "negotiation" from Three Families.

Their antics catch Christopher's eye, prompting him to remark, "Oh, the others have been coming up all evening long, clamoring, 'When can we play the game? When can we have a go?'"

What a sight! What superb performance art—dinner, game, dance, mime.

How magical this evening became, Storyteller! ***Immensely enjoyable for us too! We never grow weary of it. The game in particular.*** *Like watching your favorite movie over and over?* ***Indeed. Exactly.***

But now you really are completely wiped out and need to go. After bidding Christopher good night, you slip toward the exit, open the door, and step out into the hallway, where the transition to a rare, slightly danceable Penguin Cafe Orchestra tune somehow works.

You've never felt so high in your life. Now you understand how your uncle must have felt, staging fab games and springing big surprises around here. You hope everyone dances the night away—in Manor House, Hip-Hop, Dream-Pop, Neo-Psych Nation, somewhere in the British Empire, during the august Reign of King Bruce I, of the Australian Ogilvys from the House of Airlie!

You open your cottage door and walk slowly through your quarters, feeling your smile fall away as you do so. Your briefcase, your suitcase, your clothes, even your toiletries—gone.

CHAPTER THIRTY

Here we go again.

You pat your pockets and recheck the game box. Passport and other valuables are with you, so no need to panic. Let's see . . . what was in the briefcase? Legal documents, blue remote, trip diary, walkie-talkie, red remote. If Farnsworth got hold of the first two items, you suspect that'll be enough to set him off again. You sigh. It's back to the normal state of affairs at Manor House. Then a comforting thought wanders in. You were supposed to move to the royal suite. What if staff came by and simply transferred your belongings upstairs—like what might be expected in a competent household?

Nobody's around at reception, so you climb the stairs and find His Majesty's unlocked. Inside, you immediately spot a gold key with a purple jewel just like the one that unlocked this virtual room. You walk around, then enter a solid-marble bathroom. There they are—your toiletries, all nicely laid out. You walk back out and open a closet. There they are—your hanging items, all neatly arranged.

Across this magnificent chamber lies, of course, the door, the magical entrance to your heartthrob in the adjoining suite. But you wonder if she still resides there. You sigh and turn away. In a large closet, you find your gleaming Rimowa Cabin standing upright. Nearby, your briefcase. You snap it open. Everything's there, undisturbed. On a nightstand, someone's left an assortment of Godiva chocolates atop today's paper, which, due to all the activity this afternoon and evening, you haven't had a chance to read. You pick up *The Village Journal* and reach for a chocolate.

LOCAL WOMAN "ADDICTED TO CHOCOLATE" SUES MAJOR MANUFACTURERS

RECENT REPORTS about a brain lipid found in chocolate called anandamide, which apparently gives the sweet stuff addictive properties, have spurred a local woman, Doris Methwick of Nuttey Village, to file suit last Friday against a host of major manufacturers based in the UK and Europe.

Aha! This is the story TVTV has been previewing ever since I arrived. Finally!

You turn on the news and press 3DHolo, wondering if there's some synchronicity at play here.

Of course there is! This is your new home, your new life, where Christopher says everything's connected. On the news, it looks like Meredith is on location for this story. She's seated in a living room in the midst of a live interview with a very large woman who looks to be forty-something. At a coffee table, there are silver platters adorned with assortments of mouth-watering chocolates.

Meredith is introducing her subject: "Miss Methwick describes her medical diagnosis as 'phagomania,' claiming her weight of 325 pounds, massive dental bills, and £4,450 annual outlay for chocolate are all the result of her addiction."

"Oh, I've tried to quit, believe me," Methwick says plaintively. "But they've made it impossible, putting in all sorts of things that make you crave the stuff."

Meredith nods sympathetically, saying, "Miss Methwick, you've claimed that, up until Valentine's Day three years ago, you were an attractive single who the men in your life regarded as, in your words, 'svelte and sophisticated.'"

Methwick nods in affirmation and reaches for a chocolate, causing you to do likewise. "Won't you have one?" she asks her interviewer.

"No thank you," Meredith replies. "Not while I'm working. I might get a rush." Returning to the topic, Meredith says, "We understand on that unfortunate day, one of your suitors presented you with a Valentine's gift of *La Madeline au Truffle*, billed as the world's largest and most expensive chocolate. You say your addiction began when you consumed the giant truffle in a single sitting. Is that correct?"

"From the first bite, I knew I was instantly and hopelessly in love," Methwick sobs while reaching for another truffle. You indulge as well, noticing that the chocolates are quite delicious but also taste a little bit odd.

Meredith reaches out and brushes the woman's shoulder to offer comfort. "Miss Methwick, do you have any idea of precisely what was in that truffle that triggered your instant addiction?"

"Oh, I'm certain it was the Perigord mushroom at its center. Here, have a look." Methwick hands Meredith an empty gold box stamped with the name Chocopologie from the House of Knipschildt.

"Fascinating," Meredith says after scanning the description. "Do you mind if I share this with our viewers?"

"Go ahead, though just hearing it might reignite my cravings unbearably for another *La Madeline*. It's been so long," says Methwick.

Meredith reads from the box while Methwick plugs her ears. "*La Madeline au Truffle* starts with a seventy percent dark chocolate, heavy cream, sugar, truffle oil, and vanilla as the base. A rare French Perigord truffle is then surrounded by this rich ganache; it is enrobed in Valrhona dark chocolate and then rolled in fine cocoa powder." Hearing this causes you to join Doris Methwick in reaching for yet another chocolaty morsel.

The scene switches back to the studio, where Michael is reporting on the story's legal ramifications: "Methwick has been meeting with her solicitor, James Prance, to continue preparations for the case, which is expected to be heard sometime this month in Coventry. She is seeking £500,000 in punitive damages from Godiva, Cadbury, and others, charging that her 'chocoholism' has made her so bloated and addicted she now stands no chance of having a rewarding career or nurturing relationships in life."

The screen fills with the clip you must have seen a dozen times. Seeing it again, this time with commentary, indeed calls for another truffle!

Explains Michael, "To dramatize her plight, Methwick has taken the extraordinary step of posing nude atop a diminutive white horse and prancing around her Nuttey courtyard. She's distributed glossy photographs to tabloids, in addition to posting video clips online."

You can see that Michael is having great difficulty preventing himself from laughing aloud. He struggles to regain his composure and is finally able to wrap up the story: "When shown, the Lady Godiva attorneys refused comment beyond branding her charge as the naked untruth aimed solely at massive publicity."

Storyteller, you're right—everything's connected. ***Simple for us. And you're learning fast.***

Still, you can't get to sleep. So, might as well see if the party's still raging or what else might be going on in the wee hours. You get dressed and pick up the blue remote before setting out.

At the chef's office, Noël and his assistants are discussing tomorrow's menus. Farnsworth briefly enters the scene, nodding and smiling, apparently en route to the kitchen once again. At the whisky bar, you see Thomas, Penelope, and several others talking about an outdoor show they plan to stage when the weather clears. Down at the Falstaff, Bruce and Savannah, Reggie and Mildred are singing karaoke—and, surprisingly, Adrienne has joined in too. Your last stop, outside the butler's office, yields a big surprise. Farnsworth is there talking on his phone in a language you don't recognize at first.

Storyteller? ***He's speaking Japanese.***

Farnsworth is listening intently. Finally, he slaps his head in exasperation and speaks rapid-fire Japanese, which a Storyteller immediately translates.

Kobayashi-san, how many times do I have to tell you: I can't right now. I'm still on duty! A short pause, then, ***Couldn't this have waited until our usual meeting?*** He listens briefly then signs off with, ***Midnight or thereabouts. And again, I must insist, never call me when it's going on. Defeats my concentration. And for God's sake, don't ever come inside when I'm working.***

You quickly depart, fearing that Farnsworth may soon decide to leave his office. Walking back, you're quite puzzled. Farnsworth speaking Japanese to a Japanese guy? Who's this Kobayashi-san? Is he somewhere around here? You wonder if this is another part of Farnsworth's secret life. A new liaison perhaps? What might Noël or Adrienne think if either knew? How were these people getting "inside" Manor House? Plus, now that you think back on it, Farnsworth said earlier the three designers taught him simple Japanese expressions, but just now he sounded fluent in the language.

Storyteller, what's going on? ***Sorry, but for now, the less you know the better. Wait and see.***

Back in your suite, you're still not sleepy so you switch on the TV. There's not much this time of night, so you settle on whatever's on Netflix. Ah yes, those instantly recognizable piano chords, that eerie background hum and whistle—once again, the opening bars of the *X-Files* theme.

Remember those notes. *Yes, I will, you told me before.*

It's an alien organ-taker episode, complete with crop circles, frightened cattle, and abducted sheep. Reminds you of the crazy commotion at the dairy farmer's ranch you watched back home. You lie back contentedly, now noticing a tingling feeling circulating throughout your body while the show's theme song replays and another episode begins.

But your reverie is interrupted by a soft knocking sound. Rubbing your eyes, you sit up and discern that they are not coming from your entrance; they are emanating from the connecting door, from Her Majesty's! Which most likely means they are from the suite's last known occupant. From—dare you think it?—the object of your desires, the woman of your dreams, the incomparable Adrienne Lynn Van Scoy! You scramble out of bed, toss on your Hanover Manor–monogrammed robe, and scurry to the door while brushing your hair back in place as best you can.

"Yes, yes, who's there?" you call, panting, hardly able to suppress your excitement.

From the other side comes soft coquettish laughter. "It's me, Adrienne, silly." Then, in a singsong voice, she says, "I seek admission to your quarters."

"Come in, come in, by all means," you beckon. Looking down, you see that the door is unlocked. A long, curved platinum handle gradually rises up, and the solid wood door is slowly pushed open. But you're not at all prepared for what you next see. Standing before you is a towering, green-eyed, brunette goddess in a lime satin negligee.

"I also seek admission," the concierge purrs, "to you."

With that, Adrienne steps forward, brushing both of her hands outward to motion you back into bed. Compliant, you climb back in and sit up straight against the tufted headboard. Adrienne has indicated she's in charge here, which is more than okay with you. "I have much to show but little to say." She reaches behind her back and unfastens her garment. It slides over her curvaceous form and settles quietly onto the thick rug below.

Your jaw literally drops. Adrienne's body is voluptuous to perfection.

Now she continues, "Yes, I seek admission, and I am the only one here you should choose."

"Sure, Adrienne," you call to her, "I'm all yours."

But she has more. "Penelope, who you've undoubtedly regarded, went to finishing school, studied all forms of etiquette, and is prim and proper. Savannah, who you've undoubtedly contemplated as well, studied philosophy and played sports at university, and stands rough but ready. I, on the other hand, was schooled in but one discipline—the *Kama Sutra*. Allow me to present my dissertation."

With that, your goddess extends her hands above her head, bringing her palms together. She proclaims, "I am your time piece, and it is now midnight." A clock from somewhere unknown chimes out twelve musical notes, after which chamber music begins playing softly in the background. An enticing fragrance fills your nostrils.

"A che ora vorresti adesso?" she sings in Italian over the warm sustaining sounds of a solitary cello. "What time would you like now?"

"I don't know," you stammer. "How about three, um, three in the afternoon, or morning, does it even matter?" You're highly aroused but also completely flabbergasted.

Adrienne merely smiles, then in mime fashion, rigidly pivots ninety degrees, her arms assuming the requested position, her "clock hands" punctuated with long, lavender nails, pointing at twelve and three, respectively.

"Quelle heure voundriez-vous maintenant?" The same question, sung this time in French.

After a moment, you call out eagerly, "Oh gosh, I don't know, how about half past six?" You relish this exotic foreplay, set to music, while certain that never before have you felt this turned on. Or so steadfastly erect.

Again, robotically, Adrienne drops her hands and pivots another ninety degrees, bending over while keeping her legs perfectly straight. She brings her palms together and places her fingertips lightly atop the stone floor. It's six thirty on the dot all right. Unbelievable—she's even a contortionist, of all things.

"¿Le gustaría ver una rotación?" Adrienne calls out operatically. Your high school Spanish makes understanding this next variation easy. You nod as Adrienne prepares to rotate. She slowly straightens, stiffens, elevates both arms high above her head, rises to her tiptoes, and performs a 180-degree turn just as a ballerina might. Again she bends over, placing her palms on the floor. Now you are thrilled at the sight of her in the reversed, half-past-six position.

Via cantabiles to accompany the featured violin or viola, cello, contrabass or harpsichord, she continues to elicit repositioning requests—in Dutch, in German, in Russian, in Japanese. You think she's literally poetry in motion, with each new pose exceeding the previous in pure eroticism and wonderment.

You dare now to glimpse a possible future together. Adrienne is indeed a spellbinding temptress while at the same time a multilingual woman of the world. And now, you muse, if all goes well, she'll become a permanent presence and partner here with you. A realization hits. It's no longer lust. You think you may be falling in love.

But suddenly, after her full-frontal nine fifteen, Adrienne relinquishes her pose and persona, drops her hands to her side, and abruptly announces, "Sorry, but my time is up." With that, she gathers up her negligee and quickly flees the room.

But you can't let this end, will not let her go. Not after all these days of yearning. Not after this incredible seduction. You leap out of bed, rush to the door, and tap repeatedly.

No answer. You try to turn the handle. Locked. You continue tapping, now more urgently. At last comes a rustling sound accompanied by a sleepy female voice.

"Yes, what is it? You must know, it's terribly late."

"Adrienne, why did you leave so suddenly?"

"Leave? Sorry, I haven't a clue as to what you mean."

"Here, Adrienne, sweetheart, here. You were here, just now, performing a kind of clock dance."

"Clock dance? No idea about that," she says resolutely. "And the way you've addressed me just now is, well, a bit disconcerting, I must say." She pauses, then continues, "Look, I think you were having some sort of intense dream. I do hope it wasn't frightening. But now, at this particular moment, I really must say good night. I will be vacating these quarters first thing tomorrow."

Silence. Pressed against the door, you hear the faint sound of receding footsteps. You sigh in frustration and return to your bed, sliding disconsolately beneath the covers, feeling abandoned and awash in total confusion. "Locked out of Heaven" replays in your head.

CHAPTER THIRTY-ONE

In the morning, or what could be morning, you wake feeling refreshed but still highly confused about last night. You find that a breakfast tray has arrived. And someone has left a stack of notes and cards. Pouring your usual cup of tea, you start sifting through the messages. They're thank-yous—all heaping praise on last night's festivities. It looks like there's a note from every attendee. Some have signed with their game names—"Lynn Fraser, Countess of Lovat" or "Jacques Paisley, First Earl of Abercorn." They go on and on. It seems you scored a hit with your new circle, whose membership has been greatly enlarged, from the looks of things.

Your message light is blinking too. Frantically, it almost seems. The first is from Bruce, who says, "Your game last night really was the greatest thing since split scones, mate. Cheers." In the next, Reggie's eager face appears. "What will tonight's game be all about? Millie and I can hardly wait." This is followed by Mildred herself, gushing, "Oh, thank you. Thank you. Thank you, dearie. Last evening was so magical, and I'm so proud of Christopher!" Noël appears, smiling broadly. He's reading from a note card. "Your excellency, are you aware you are now your excellency?" Farnsworth's message is next. "Your Three Families was absolutely smashing, great rollicking fun. And it has led to my achieving some insights into the current state of affairs. We look forward to seeing you this morning when you are ready." The last is from Adrienne, who looks and sounds completely normal, as if last night's disturbance never happened. Adopting her usual professional demeanor, she says, "That was an extraordinary simulation last night. The Village literary society meets monthly at the manor. With your permission, and perhaps Christopher's assistance, I'd like to stage the game for them. I think they'd get a big kick out of playing it, then probing its not-so-hidden allegories."

The manor's atmosphere has changed as well. Light seventies disco is currently playing on the PA, perhaps as a paean to last night's dance party? Lady Marmalade is wondering in French if you'd like to sleep with her tonight. You smile, wondering which manor lovely has become a naughty deejay this very morning.

Now fully awake, you are confronted by a much more serious thought—the remaining excerpts of your uncle's diary. You finish breakfast and call the butler's office. Farnsworth answers, reporting that Christopher has the virtual manor up and running and that some new items have shown up. He's anxious for you to join them. You dress, thinking he sounds sincere.

But has he found a virtual blue remote? If so, has he got it working? If he has, what happens when he points it at a painting—would it pan an empty room, show conversations, or both? If it does, what's your story going to be should Farnsworth ask about a real blue remote? Full disclosure in keeping with all the good vibes this morning? Nah—you probably won't go that far.

An Aussie Storyteller appears and chimes in. ***Wise decision, mate.*** *But he sure sounded sincere just now, don't you think?* ***Yes, he*** **sounded** ***sincere.***

Farnsworth is seated at the computer. He and Christopher have found the blue remote, and the butler says he's glad you've arrived because "we need some additional bandwidth to figure out what it does." They've also found another DVD in the assembly hall where you were last night. "That dance party was great fun but exhausting!" he adds. The concierge opens her door, calling out a cheery good morning. She asks the butler if he could step into her office for a moment to go over the payroll.

Christopher uses his absence to whisper, "Soon as I walked in, he apologized for yesterday."

"Sound sincere?"

"I guess. But wouldn't bet a sum on it."

"Did he ask if Lord Hanover was my father?"

"Nope."

"Christopher, what's our story on the real blue remote, if it comes up?"

"We play dumb unless he works it out on his own," he replies. "After that, we play it by ear." You nod—fine with you. Nearly everything this fourteen-year-old mastermind comes up with sounds right.

Farnsworth returns, asking if Van Scoy can join. You gesture welcomingly. She looks completely normal and relaxed. The butler fills her in on what was found yesterday, asking Christopher to replay the four previous excerpts, which serve as a useful review of Lord Hanover's strange disclosures. The concierge gasps when she sees virtual Arthur Hanover for the first time—seated on-screen in the very chair she's now occupying. As she watches the clips, you deduce that she's putting all of this together with what she's been experiencing herself and undoubtedly hearing from Farnsworth.

"And to the publications I mentioned yesterday," she announces, "we can, as of this morning, add *The Times of London*, *Der Spiegel*, *L'observatoire*, *The New York Times*, and *Time* magazine to the list. Something's definitely going on. I started to think as much yesterday when the Royal Society called. If we were not in the midst of the longest unbroken storm in the history of northern England, I'm sure the manor would be crawling with reporters."

"Shall we have a look at the item we found a minute ago?" Farnsworth asks. Everyone nods as he inserts the virtual disc.

Lord Hanover looks at the camera and says, "Oh, good morning, Ms. Van Scoy. I see you're here too."

Farnsworth pauses the clip, exclaiming, "It knows who's here?"

"Voice, facial recognition," says Christopher. "I've heard it's coming to AI-driven games, but this is my first time seeing an implementation. Kudos, Uncle Artie!"

Lord Hanover puts on his glasses and reads: "A partial but puzzling success today after the electrophoresis—there was a match with the new me, all right, but it 'proved' I am the subject's father or brother, not the uncle. Perhaps removing a few determiners might work a treat—lightening the recipe, so to speak. Hmm, I wonder if some deceased family member from my subject's tree can call out a solution from the grave. No matter what happens, their descendants will inherit millions, so perhaps they have a vested interest."

"I think," says Farnsworth, "we're starting to get a definite idea of what Arthur was up to. But we don't know the why of these endeavors."

You're wary, even though you think you perceive a 180-degree change in the butler's attitude. Yesterday, with each new revelation, he became more suspicious and resentful—as if you were somehow your uncle's co-conspirator. Today, though, he's open and affable, seems just normally curious, like the rest of you. Maybe last night's gala really did do the trick. But then again, there was that strange—and a bit unnerving—conversation he had with that Japanese guy you eavesdropped on. He's definitely hiding something.

A few minutes later, as Christopher passes through the virtual lobby, he clicks on *The Village Journal*. Not surprisingly, the stories have once again changed, as if a new edition had been delivered to virtual Hanover Manor. Included is the article about Noël's palindromic luncheon. Then Christopher navigates over to the reception area and soon finds the vehicle list.

"Aha, so that's how you got in." Adrienne sounds good-natured about it.

Having the virtual red remote available is a time-saver. Even on the computer, it was becoming tiresome to "walk" those lengthy hallways from one distant location to another. This reminds you that you've been so busy you haven't had a chance to try out the real one. You pull it out of your briefcase.

Christopher sees the device, gets the look of someone who's just had a bright idea, and turns to the butler, requesting, "Mr. Farnsworth, would you mind showing me how that one works?" The kid is skillfully matter-of-fact. When the butler says he'd be glad for the chance to stretch his legs and walk around to demonstrate the device, Christopher suggests that Ms. Van Scoy come along with them. She's pleased to do so.

Departing, he looks at you and suggests, "Why don't you stay here and see if you can get the blue remote working? We've been stumped all morning."

What a smooth operator.

The three of them leave by way of the bookcase. As soon as it shuts, you push the mouse and head for the nearest wired painting—which at the moment requires a long trip down "Impressionist Row."

Arriving at the fruit bowl, you rotate the panorama to align with the painting and then click the blue orb. The painting dissolves and . . . oh, wow . . . there's a pan of the chef's office. This is shocking, but not nearly as shocking as a moment later when you are able to bring up the image grid on your virtual living room wall and play enough of the clips to determine that, while compressed to fit the screen, they are identical to the ones in your real room.

Next, you find the mantel button and rotate the fireplace. There, in the narrow space between the rooms, stands a graphical representation of your briefcase. Astonished, you glance down at your real one, noting how perfectly it has been duplicated on-screen. You click the virtual one. It opens, and inside is Lord Hanover's correspondence, plus all the notes, cards, and invitations you previously received. One by one you enlarge them.

Unbelievable! Right, Storyteller? ***Correct. And wait till you find out how it was done.***

Fearing the others may return soon, you close the briefcase and hurriedly click your way to the second floor. With bated breath, you try the painting outside His Majesty's, which produces a pan of the empty suite.

"Spot on!" exclaims Christopher, startling you by coming up from behind.

"Oh, marvelous!" Farnsworth exclaims. "Tell us, have you divined its purpose?"

"I don't know, aside from being able to see inside rooms." You're stammering, hoping no one appears in the clips.

"I think I understand what it does," offers Adrienne. "Look." You turn back to the screen but see only the empty room. "Hang on," she says. "Wait until it comes back round. There! I say, can you stop this thing?" You press the blue orb to freeze the image. "Can you zoom in, please?" she asks. You hold down the Shift key. The panorama's focal length remains unchanged, but the small scene inside the painting enlarges to reveal a black case behind a photograph on a table. "There!" she exclaims.

"Well, do we go inside and pick it up?" asks Christopher.

You unlock the virtual door and retrieve the case. It's apparent that—with only an edge exposed—it would be unnoticed by anyone inside the room. "Fine work!" exudes Farnsworth. "I say, don't we make quite a team!"

You return to the office for the next installment. There's regret in Uncle's voice as he reads: "Will have to postpone further tests with the restriction enzymes until after the golf tournament. Kohlberg has issued his usual double-or-nothing challenge. Not as foolish a bet as it once was, considering my condition. Must play a practice round early tomorrow. Must also consider deeply where and when to take that final pill. Imagine—a sip, a swallow, and *voilà*! A counterfeit person."

"This must be the experiment he's about to perform on himself, the one Professor Gatsby mentioned yesterday," the concierge surmises.

You could use a break, so you switch places with Farnsworth, who can't wait to get started.

Christopher and you could save everyone a lot of time by telling him which paintings will work—but of course you don't. Besides, it could be different here. You hold your breath every time the camera starts to pan a scene, and then silently sigh in relief when no private conversations or licentious encounters are replayed.

At the portal outside the billiards room, the concierge spots another DVD. Once again, it's positioned in such a way that it would have been nearly impossible to spot from inside. When Farnsworth uses the red remote, it's a virtual hop, skip, and jump back to the butler's office.

Then a realization hits, and you direct the butler to save the file before playing this latest clip. He raises the curtain. "We've never tried that LIVE button," you say, pointing to it. "Look, it's always been set to SCREEN." Farnsworth clicks it. Nothing happens.

But now Christopher's on his feet. "I think I've got it! Hang on—be back in a flash." He snatches the real red remote and darts through the bookcase.

Christopher soon returns holding a real black case. Inside, a real disc. "It was in the bar, right where the virtual one was," he reports breathlessly. Handing the disc to you, he says, "Let's see what this does."

What it does is totally unexpected. As soon as it's inserted, a large piano keyboard materializes in the center of the screen. Below it, an oblong box containing ten small circles followed by a small square with a musical note icon inscribed. Unseen, Lord Hanover speaks: "LIVE is a protected mode. You have been recognized. You must now enter the pass notes."

Oh good lord, what now? You turn to the group, exasperated. "I have no idea which keys to click. I don't even play piano."

"Just click some in randomly," says Christopher. "Let's see how this works."

As you tap in a sequence, the circles fill in black. You click the MUSIC icon to play it, which causes the notes to sound cacophonously. The fill color in the boxes turns to red, and after a moment, they clear.

"I'm sorry," Lord Hanover intones. "Please try again. You are granted two more attempts." Adrienne offers to take your place. But as soon as she does, the virtual keyboard disappears.

"Looks like it's got to be you," Christopher surmises. "Awesome. Facial recognition capability here. First Ms. Van Scoy, now you."

You reseat yourself, impatiently tapping your fingers on the desk. You have no idea what to do next. Says Christopher, "Don't you remember those sound puzzles in *Myst*? Where you had to key in a certain sound effect to progress in the game?"

You nod, vaguely recalling dings, clunks, hisses, and chirps you had to enter in the right order—sequences that unlocked doors or transported you elsewhere. "Back then, I thought they were the most unique puzzles in the game. And the hardest to solve," you tell him.

"Me too," Christopher says. "Looks like Uncle Artie has put a musical one in virtual Manor House . . . Figures."

The butler's and concierge's blank expressions suggest they don't have a clue. Christopher goes on, "Okay, Uncle Artie expects you to come up with this. Can you think of a song, a jingle, a ditty you've heard lately? Any tunes in your head?"

"Well, those Japanese girls had a theme for their mushroom skin-care ads," you reply. "I must have heard it a dozen times." You try to hum it.

"I've just this morning seen the adverts," Adrienne says. "I think I can play the opening measures. May I?"

"Sure," you tell her. She stands behind your chair, leans in, and places her two index fingers on the touch-screen keyboard. Her scent is luscious, her breath warm—you're back in heaven. And now it's unlocked.

She plays the chords. In a near whisper, she asks, "Does that sound right?" It does, but nothing happens. The red dots reappear, then clear.

Once more, Lord Hanover speaks. "I'm sorry, please try again," he says stoically. "You are granted one final attempt."

Farnsworth looks agitated, as if this is crucially important. "Oh dear, what song could it be? Think, Masa, think!" His statement draws quick reproachful looks from both Adrienne and Christopher.

"Excuse me, Mr. Farnsworth, what did you call me just now?" you ask.

Nervously, the butler replies, "Sorry, I was thinking of something else and misspoke, a slip of the tongue. Please ignore. Again, very sorry."

Storyteller, who's Masa? ***Someone you know.*** *I don't know any Masa.* ***Before you did and again you shall.*** *What do you mean "before"—before when?* ***Before you met us.***

Christopher rises to interject. "I'm sure you can figure this out. Remember how you reached down deep and came up with April Fools'?"

Adrienne walks over and places a caressing hand on your shoulder, reminding you once again of last night—that glorious intrusion. "Think back. Think back. Think back," she purrs hypnotically.

So you try to think back—as hard as you can—back to just before you heard that lovely knock on your bedroom door . . . and *voilà*! The notes sound clearly in your head. "Adrienne," you ask, "do you happen to know the *X-Files* theme?" She shakes her head no.

"Hang on!" Christopher shouts. "I've got it in my ringtone collection." He pulls out his phone and finds and plays the measures. Adrienne listens only once, leans over, taps in the chords, and clicks the icon. The notes play; the lights flash green. A loud whoosh sound fills the room accompanied by a dense silver cloud, which soon achieves clarity.

Farnsworth gasps. "My God, Arthur." Adrienne emits a small shriek. Christopher shouts, "Hooray, Uncle Artie!" You nearly fall off your chair.

Arthur Hanover, life-sized and holding his diary, is sitting in his chair, preparing to put on his glasses. Visually, it is every bit as convincing as the servant holograms you saw on the ride up. Everybody soon recovers and laughs admiringly as Lord Hanover greets, "Mr. Farnsworth, Ms. Van Scoy, Master Chris, my beloved heir. I'm heartened to see you all here, but I'm afraid I bear ill tidings." He opens his diary and reads his next entry:

"After all these decades of despairing that the Hanover line would end with me because of this abominable affliction, salvation. At a high price, yes, but one I'm prepared to pay. Still, swapping my life for the chance to edit the genetic code means I'll not see the results. Pity, that." He shimmers out of view. Silence and sadness fill the room.

"Did Uncle, do you think he—" Christopher is shifting around in discomfort.

Adrienne looks distressed at the implication, now so openly expressed, while Farnsworth performs an unexpected gesture by touching Christopher's shoulder and speaking to him with sympathetic understanding. "We don't know, Master Chris, not for certain. Arthur was a very sick man, lad, that we now know. Perhaps he meant to do something especially meaningful with his life . . . just as the end drew near." Adrienne reaches over to stroke the boy's hair. You've seen many sides of this pair. This is the side you like best—but is it genuine? Or are they acting?

Christopher straightens up, saying he's okay. If the butler doesn't mind, he'd like to take over for a while. They trade places, and soon the lad is off and running, exploring the Manor House portals with the blue remote.

In the virtual library, he finds another case. Before playing the disc, he switches from Live back to Screen, saying he has no intention of running upstairs for a real one just yet. Everybody concurs. Continuing to see Arthur Hanover life-sized seems a little too much right now. His next revelation is more thought-provoking than emotional:

"The ethical implications of this genetic switch do give one pause. After all, if the criminal and terrorist elements recognize the chameleonlike potential of this technology, the world will be in a sorry state soon enough. Must think long and hard about this. After all's said and done, it may be better to destroy my lab notes and apparatus. Can any possible good for humankind come of this? Perhaps not, but the world must know it can be done."

Adrienne's cell chimes. "Yes, I see," she tells the caller. "No, you don't need to bring it. I'll come up and get copies straightaway . . . Right . . . Thank you for letting us know." She signs off and turns to everyone, her expression serious. "That was Penelope. The afternoon paper's come. She thinks we should see it right away."

Turning in your direction, she adds, "Especially you."

CHAPTER THIRTY-TWO

Adrienne returns and distributes copies to everyone.

SPECULATION RIFE OVER IDENTITY OF HANOVER HEIR

NEW FACES turned up at nearly every corner yesterday as representatives of the press and various scientific groups and genealogical societies poured into the village to join the ranks of the merely curious. All were clamoring loudly for the answer to the question of the hour: Who is Arthur Hanover's newly certified heir?

You pause reading because of several knocks sounding at the door that connects to reception. "You may enter," Farnsworth calls.

Penelope bursts into the room, breathless. "It's now all over the tele. You should see!" Adrienne flips on the remote and quickly switches from a gay musical to the local channel. She casts a quick look of consternation in the butler's direction as she presses 3DHolo to fill the room with the report. On-screen, Michael, the coanchor, is in midsentence. Adrienne pushes the button to start the program from the beginning. After a brief rewind, Michael begins the segment from behind the news desk.

"Lack of access to the estate and any clarification from the manor combined to keep everyone in the dark and guessing for another day. A chartered helicopter had to be turned back because of high winds and the threat of lightning strikes. Though facts were in short supply, there was no shortage of theories from local residents and visitors alike about the origins of the late Lord Hanover's presumed offspring."

Meredith is shown listening through her earpiece. She looks up and says, "We go now live to The Village Television reporter Malcolm Dupont, who is in the square asking villagers who they think may have brought forth Lord Hanover's heir."

The camera shows a tall man with a friendly face swathed in rain gear. "Good afternoon, Meredith. There's been a bit of a break in the storm, so we are taking the opportunity to speak with those delighted to be out and about for the first time in days. Standing beside me is local travel agent Harold Donnelly. Good day, Mr. Donnelly. Tell us, what is your theory concerning this mysterious heir that has set all tongues wagging around here?"

Donnelly is a well-tanned, jaunty fellow who looks to be in his fifties. "Unquestionably, the inheritor is of non-British descent," he says in a thick Irish accent. "When he wasn't working, Lord Hanover spent most of his time abroad. This son or daughter is no doubt the result of some dalliance in a foreign land. Be good to have some fresh blood in the line, I say."

Malcolm turns to another man standing beside the agent. "Donnelly's pub mate, dairyman Cowan Cowherd, couldn't agree less," says Malcolm.

The shot moves to Cowherd, a short fellow who looks to be about the same age as his friend. He is equally as confident in expressing his opposing view. "Certain to be a local—would bet my last farthing on it. Lord Hanover was always entertaining and such up at the manor. Probably got carried away with a village lass on an occasion. Had to keep it all hushed up until he passed. Now he's gone and done the right thing, as expected."

A middle-aged woman standing nearby has overheard and steps into the scene, strongly asserting, "Oh, I've no doubt it's a peer, possibly a royal." She looks highborn and wealthy.

"And, madam, you are?" Malcolm inquires in a friendly tone.

"I am Mrs. Harriet Hickinbottom, from London." She steps in closer. "Lord Hanover knew his station and responsibility to his class. And he was such an honorable man—he would never allow any of this to surface in his lifetime. After all the royal family has put us through, I'm sure this will prove to be nothing so scandalous. And, at the end of the day, the estate and the line will be in good hands, I'm certain."

Malcolm thanks her and moves into the center of the square, where he encounters a brightly dressed thirty-something woman who carries a slight bohemian air. "Hello there!" he hails her. "May I ask your name?"

She brightens. "Katherine Kingsley, at your service!"

Malcolm pauses, apparently getting a message through his earpiece. After a moment, he says, "Ah, nice to meet you, Ms. Kingsley. I've just been told you're head of the Village Players, whose productions we all so enjoy. What do you suppose about the source of Lord Hanover's heir?"

Without hesitation, she replies, "Surely an artist or a musician. Everyone knew how much he adored the theater and the symphony, the ballet and the opera. Probably grew enamored of one of the great performers therein. Any prior revelation would have harmed or shortened a career. Perfectly understandable."

"Thank you, Ms. Kingsley," says Malcolm.

"Oh please, call me Katherine or Kathy or Katy or simply Kat, if you like!" she says.

"Okay, Kat, mind if we inquire about your friend?" The shot turns to Kingsley's companion, an intellectual-looking young man.

"Certainly," she replies. "This is my dear friend Jason Jacoby. He's a guest lecturer at a Middlesex private school and enjoys acting in our plays from time to time. Jason, please tell Malcolm what your best guess is."

Jacoby steps forward, adopting a dramatic tone. "How could it be anyone other than another scholar or scientist? Only a fellow traveler in the lofty realm of ideas could have provided the stimulation and sustenance the great man required. Why, the Hanover line has probably gained a new Einstein in the bargain, the progeny of two geniuses."

"Hard to argue with that, eh?" Malcolm says gaily to the studio anchors.

The shot briefly returns to the news desk, where Michael says, "Hard to dispute any of their reasonings, actually. The marquis was truly a man for all seasons."

Meredith nods and simply says, "Yes, quite."

The scene shifts back to the village square, where Malcolm is standing by a distinguished-looking elderly gentleman. "Michael, Meredith," he says, "this is Professor Garfield Gatsby of the Royal Society, whom I've just pressed to please state which of the foregoing suppositions he thinks might be most plausible."

Gatsby's face is shown smiling timidly in close-up. "None of the above, I'm afraid."

Malcolm's expression registers surprise as he gestures to the camera. "Okay, Michael and Meredith, back to you!"

The shot returns to the studio, where Meredith is addressing her colleague. "Hmmm, 'None of the above.' It sounds like the professor knows much more than he's disclosing."

"He probably does, Meredith," Michael replies. "The Royal Society is not prone to idle conjecture."

Meredith turns to the camera and says, "There is so much more to learn here. We'll be back shortly." With that, the broadcast goes to commercials.

The humor and irony in the report come as a welcome relief. "I was intrigued," says Farnsworth, "by the way everybody adjusts a personal lens to view the situation."

"And how might you have guessed, James?" the concierge asks with a faint smile.

"Had I been interviewed," Farnsworth replies, "without, of course, knowing what I do now, I would have guessed the heir to be the offspring of a manor servant."

The concierge starts to reply but is cut off by Christopher rushing in with two more black cases. Even before he plays them, you get the feeling that the moment of truth has arrived and the big revelation will be forthcoming. Adrienne collapses the holographic scene and mutes the sound on the office TV.

Lord Hanover's diary is open, but instead of reading from it, he glances at the passage, removes his spectacles, and addresses the butler, "Dear faithful James, I'm certain you were counting on being named in my will." He sighs. "But I beg you to understand that unless I bequeath to a total stranger, one originally selected at random and documented as such, the world will never grasp the point of my life's work."

Before anyone can react, Christopher plays the second segment. Again, Uncle Artie is pensive, staring vaguely into the distance, again preparing to speak extemporaneously.

"Off to Switzerland on Friday. Special gear already packed and ready, and unobtrusive enough to escape notice. Damned hard to smile at everyone, knowing I'll likely not be back. If my hour does come, however, I'm ready with the pill just beforehand—but will it work? Will I, at the very moment of my passing, become an uncle to an unknown person, a spontaneous new branch in a stranger's family tree?"

A prolonged silence follows. You know Farnsworth is embarrassed to have been directly named by his longtime employer. To be told that he was deliberately excluded must be tough; that all of this was bequeathed to a total stranger, tougher still.

Finally, the butler, his eyes downcast, says gamely, "Well, then, I think we have it. Our explanation."

Penelope points to the TV. "Oh, dear me, look!" she calls breathlessly. "Can we please have the enlarged scene and the sound on again?" The screen caption reads:

LORDS HANOVER, ROLLINSBY
RUMOURED FOR POSTHUMOUS AWARDS

Michael appears highly charged, as he seems to realize this is no typical story recounting daily village life—this is big, breaking, international news. The backdrop is an enlargement of the foundation's logo, featuring Alfred Bernhard Nobel in relief at the center of a disk resembling a gold coin.

Michael leads with, "The late Lord Arthur Hanover, well-known British inventor, scientist, and lifelong local resident, was the center of intense speculation today as various Nobel committees readied nominations for the next round of awards. At the same time, similar rumors swirled around one of Hanover's colleagues and fellow countrymen, Lord Dennis Rollinsby, whose disappearance last year has recently prompted a British court to rule him 'missing and presumed dead' at the request of his family. Authorities refused further comment and did not rule out foul play."

The camera switches to Meredith, who continues the narrative. "Several independent sources confirmed that Hanover may be up for an unprecedented posthumous prize in the physiology and medicine category if additional confirmation of his research in genetic-code transference can be garnered in time. At present, Nobel foundation bylaws strictly prohibit the awarding of any prizes to nonliving persons. Sources throughout the scientific community, however, said that the extraordinary nature of Hanover's research may cause an exception to be granted."

Now, at the center of the news desk, between the two anchors, sits the same scholarly individual who appeared at the end of the earlier segment. In front of him a placard reads, PROFESSOR GARFIELD GATSBY, UK ACADEMY OF SCIENCE. Nodding to him, Meredith says, "Professor, why do you believe the foundation may make an exception in these two cases?"

The professor is steadfast. "Oh, they'll have no choice other than to revise the charter since Lord Hanover utilized his own terminal illness and death to prove his daring hypothesis—that one's genetic fingerprint can be edited."

"And Sir Dennis?" asks Meredith.

"As for Lord Rollinsby," says the professor, "his achievement is so monumental, the committee must make an exception in his case as well."

Meredith explains: "Sir Dennis Rollinsby, who has been long missing and presumed dead, is likewise being considered in physics if reports of his breakthroughs in matter transference can be verified." Meredith turns back to her guest. "Professor, anything else to add?"

Gatsby recapitulates, "Though their work is unrelated, Hanover's research repudiates most of what has been supposed about the uniqueness of an individual's DNA, while Rollinsby's work simply transports the whole of that individual to another place."

Michael now reappears. "If chosen, Lord Rollinsby's two adult children, Roland and Cynthia, would presumably attend the ceremony and acknowledge the award in his stead. Lord Hanover reportedly has a single living relative who we've been speculating about all day. This individual is as yet unidentified but rumored to be currently in residence at Hanover Manor, and thus it is not known whether this person would acknowledge the prize on behalf of his or her kin."

Michael turns to Meredith. “The weather is soon expected to clear. We’ll be able to transport up there. Then, at last, we’ll know.”

She nods and says, “And so we shall. And that concludes our morning broadcast for April sixth. See you back at one.” Meredith waves as “The Village News at 11” closing signage spins into view.

“Well, it’s patently obvious,” Farnsworth says. “Some sort of verification is required by these organizations.” He turns to you. “What are you going to do?”

“I have no idea,” you tell him. You honestly don’t. Despite these revelations, you’re not certain you know the whole story. But you have learned one important thing—“Uncle Artie” did not really commit suicide; he was sick, about to die anyway, when he performed these dramatic experiments. This is what you try to impress upon Christopher, who acknowledges that he fully realizes this.

“Anyway, thanks,” he says, “but I’d wager there’s more. Look at the stage.” You see what he means. The arrangement of keys, DVD cases, and devices scattered about appears haphazard. Taken as a whole, they form a kind of mosaic, but with a pronounced space in the center that indicates a missing piece. Otherwise, you’re sure that the objects would have been arranged with more space between them. That i21 crew does everything artistically and precisely.

Adrienne, who has checked her office devices, returns to report that her video mailbox is full. Scientific organizations and press from all over the world are calling. Texts, faxes, and emails are pouring in. “Care to read any of them?” she asks you.

“Not yet,” you reply. “I agree with Christopher that there’s more.”

“Should I start on a draft of a statement, incorporating the facts as we now know them?” she asks.

“Yes, good idea. But don’t release anything just yet,” you tell her.

“Of course,” she says. “Also, people from the Nobel organization itself have left messages. They want to know if you’re available to travel to Stockholm soon.”

You shrug. “Sure, why not? I dropped everything and flew to England. May as well go on to Sweden. Jeez, Uncle Artie, what’s next?”

Farnsworth laughs. “I’m also convinced Master Christopher is right and there’s more,” he says, studying the stage. “I say we order lunch and press on.”

Noël personally delivers lunch, a mouthwatering mushroom and cheese soufflé. He departs, chattering about the great time he had last night and informing you that he has souvenir menus if you'd like. This reminds Adrienne that she has a recording of her recital she'd like to give you. You tell her that will be lovely and to please drop it off anytime, chucking inwardly that maybe then you'll get another chance to ask her for "the time of day."

Yay! Go for it! calls out one of the resident teens. ***Don't listen to her***, replies an elderly female. ***Romancing servants is simply not done here at the manor.***

After lunch, you need to stretch, take a walk, and clear your head. Wandering through the hallways, munching on some gelatin squares you brought from your room, you hear the music get interrupted. "Good afternoon, everybody. This is Penelope speaking, and I've got wonderful news. There'll be clear skies and sunshine later today. And now, a special announcement from Thomas."

A calliope sounds. "Lords and ladies of the realm, masters and mistresses, children of all ages! Don't miss the fabulous Thomas and Penelope Magic Show this very night on the steps of Manor House. See amazing feats, hilarious stunts, and much, much more at this incredible, unbelievable, unforgettable manor extravaganza! Come one and all and be dazzled tonight!" Thomas obviously went to the effort of prerecording his announcement and mixing it with a stirring fanfare.

A giggling Penelope comes back on the air. "Thank you, Thomas. Today's musical program is as bright and cheerful as we hope the weather will soon be. Have a lovely day, everyone."

You stop off at your suite and sit down for a moment to reflect while devouring a few more squares. Just before he died, you muse, your "uncle" really did manage to alter his entire DNA profile to link it to yours. Or at least that is how it appears, since the experiment was obviously successful. So here you are as the sole undisputed legal heir to everything he owned. It seems that he has proved to the world, in dramatic fashion, that it is possible to change genetic fingerprints—in this case, his. Arthur Hanover may have appropriated your identity, but he paid you a fortune for doing so.

So how come, you wonder, you don't feel so great? Is this what they call an embarrassment of riches? What are you going to say to dozens of reporters? To all those scientists? The genealogical societies? So, Mr. Ivorsby, you fantasize, what's my entry in the next *Burton's Peerage* going to say? . . . Oh, at a complete loss, are we? Then you'd better get cracking on inventing a life for me—replete with marvelous deeds I've done—to go with my precious title.

Your phone chimes. Farnsworth looks breathless. "Glad we finally caught up with you. We think you should come back straightaway."

"You found something?"

"Oh, yes indeed."

You walk back in and immediately spot it in the center of the stage, slotted in the last remaining space—a cream-colored remote, exactly like the other two, but with a green orb. Stacked up beside the monitor are the black cases Christopher retrieved from their real locations in the manor. "You won't believe what it does," enthuses Farnsworth, who is seated before the monitor.

CHAPTER THIRTY-THREE

Farnsworth clicks on the on-screen green sphere. A faint beep-beep is heard as the orb lights up. "This works anywhere." He is clearly enthralled. You soon grasp why. As the current scene dissolves, the music changes. The classical track is replaced by a New Age composition, spacey and haunting. The manor scene is disappearing into pure points of light and color.

"Oh, that music," whispers Christopher. "Isn't it lovely?" Now a recognizable image comes into view as the music reaches a crescendo. An art gallery of individual Manor House scenes has become the new panorama, a kind of magical array. The floor of the gallery is identical to the stage. There's no ceiling, only night skies and stars overhead.

Rotating the image presents a collection of paintings of every room—the Falstaff, His and Hers, the library, the cottage rooms, the grand dining hall, and all the rest float by in their gilded frames—a gleaming panorama of panoramas. The presentation reminds you of those dance-party scenes you previewed in your room before they even happened. This place keeps getting trippier!

Farnsworth points to the screen, gesturing for you to select a destination. "Okay, there," you say, pointing to the lobby.

He starts to click inside the lobby painting, but Christopher motions for him to wait. "Oh, please show the other new feature," he requests. Farnsworth nods and mouses up to the curtain fold to reveal the control panel, changing the buttons by the ear icon from OFF to ON.

"Just *tell* it where you want to go," Christopher instructs.

You hunch toward the monitor. "Okay . . . go to the lobby." The gallery disappears as a powering-down sound effect plays, and you are left standing in the middle of the lobby listening, once again, to light classical music. The transition momentarily takes your breath away.

"If only we'd found this remote first," marvels Farnsworth, "we could have saved hours."

"Yes, and if only we'd turned that silly button on," Christopher adds, "we could have saved a great deal of wrist wear and tear."

You, however, are on a completely different wavelength as you recall all the messages from that frantic Rollinsby tandem. You thought them foolish, talking of dire consequences from harmless objects when at first they didn't even have the color right.

Christopher and you exchange apprehensive glances. You know what he's thinking. Exactly what you're thinking—there's no tool or object in this virtual manor that doesn't exist in real life.

Jeez, Storyteller, and what was it the news said about Rollinsby and his rumored prize for physics? ***Suggest you find the real one before certain others do.***

Hearing this causes you to snatch the red remote and thrust it at Farnsworth, asking, "Have you ever seen a device around here just like this one, only with a green orb? Seriously, Mr. Farnsworth, I need to know."

"No . . . I assure you . . . I have not. But I see what you're driving at." The butler rises and knocks on the concierge's door. When she enters, Christopher shows her how the gallery works. She immediately gets it. Everybody now seems nervous.

"Hey, everyone, look!" Christopher was node-hopping on "Military Row" when his mouse cursor disappeared, which always signals an event is about to take place. The panorama rotates and zooms to the face of a nobleman in a painting. It's the painting depicted on the one remaining spot on the cottage grid that up to now hasn't triggered anything. The face slowly morphs into that of Lord Hanover.

"Greetings, heir. I note that you have located only one of the discs I prepared for you." He pauses, as if waiting for a reply.

You shrug, saying to no one in particular, "I have no idea."

The image blinks, then says questioningly, "Indeed? . . . Frankly, I, too, am at a loss as to the whereabouts of the second volume. But I ask you to find it as soon as possible, inspect its contents if you like, and then forward it to the scientific organization I have listed on the case." Again, he pauses.

"Okay, okay," you stammer, "I'll do my best."

Lord Hanover nods. "Good. Also, I posted my last letter for you to Miss Stratton some time ago. In my note to her I suggested she place it in a safe location until you asked her for it. Make sure you obtain this letter, because it will no doubt clear up any remaining questions you may have." Again he pauses, awaiting your reply.

"Sure, I will, I promise," you tell him.

"Excellent!" he calls out. "Oh, and not to worry, there's much more excitement to come." His eyes twinkle. He smiles warmly. "Good day."

The painting is restored to its original state. The red ruffled theater curtain falls, covering the entire panorama. After a moment it begins to again rise, revealing the now-empty lobby as the changed scene. Flushed with excitement, Christopher says he's going to do a Save As so that hopefully the scene can be triggered again after a restart. "Let's see how good their AI is," he instructs. "This time say gibberish whenever Uncle pauses."

But when the program is restarted and the old file reopened, all cases, keys, and devices are gone from the stage, except one—the green remote. And when you return to the painting, nothing happens, except now the music from the virtual program is identical to that currently playing over the manor PA.

"Wow—5D." Christopher whistles. "It folded time and caught up." Then—shockingly—Christopher, Farnsworth, and Adrienne all appear in the virtual program, walking about the stage, perfectly composited into the scene wearing *the identical outfits* they're wearing now.

Whoa. Whoa. Whoa. You can't believe your eyes. Adrienne inches forward to closely inspect and sighs nervously. "Well, I really don't know how much more of this I can take." Again you catch her alluring scent. Her dark-brown hair lightly bushes against your face. Your heart starts skipping a beat—you don't know how much more you can take either.

"We need to locate Miss Stratton," Farnsworth states emphatically. The concierge opens the connecting door to the lobby reception area and calls for her but receives no reply. Adrienne says she'll check down at the pool where the receptionist often trains; Farnsworth says he'll head down to the kitchen and dining hall; Christopher says he'll go up to the pub and bar; you say you're off to the library via the real red remote.

Penelope's not in the library. It's deserted.

In addition to Uncle's letter, you wonder if the missing DVD is also hidden inside one of the books. But where to begin? The place is huge; the shelves contain thousands of titles—it could take hours. Nevertheless, you search section after section, opening and examining the volumes you find at eye level while noting several titles you plan to delve into when things settle down. It makes you realize you're thinking in terms of a long future, as if you've unconsciously decided to permanently remain.

In one corner, a ladder has been left standing in front of one of the bookcases. Could it be? You don't suppose Penelope would go to all that trouble to shelve a special book up high and then leave the ladder just standing in a telltale location—do you? But, knowing her, that's exactly what she might have done. If you're lucky, nobody else has moved it since. It's certainly been your lucky day so far. You climb the ladder.

On the top shelf lie twelve black books with gold-and-peach trim. One by one, you examine them. The eighth in line appears slightly different; it's bulkier.

Eureka! It's not a book but rather a hollow leather case fashioned from the original book cover and secured by a gold band that extends from the front around the spine to the back. Embedded in the band are three recessed squares with black digits and tiny dials. At present it is set to 000. When you turn the dials to that "time and pace," the volume pops open. Inside, you find a letter and some typewritten sheets but no disc.

You start to remove the contents when you hear a gasp. Standing below is Penelope. "I was just instructed to fetch that for you, but I see you've found it—and *opened* it as well!" she exclaims. "My, but you *are* clever. I'd forgotten where the book was and the combination I'd used."

You smile. "Guess it's just our lucky day, Penelope."

"Oh, that reminds me," she says, "there was also a disc of some kind for you. But I . . . uh, sorry . . . accidentally posted it to the Royal Society, which was where it was supposed to go next. And those other papers—now where did I set them?"

You pull the typed sheets from the case, asking, "These?"

Penelope brightens. "Yes, yes! Oh, terribly sorry about all my dreadful mistakes. Thank goodness you're so resourceful . . . Right. I'm off to practice for tonight's show. I'm better at that sort of thing, you'll see." Penelope, embarrassed, departs in a hurry. As you watch her gracefully dash away, you can't help but think she is indeed a sight to behold.

Again, must you always initially regard women as objects? You are so annoying at times. Yikes! It's that scolding female again. *Okay, okay, I'm sorry. I'll try to do better.*

Feeling capricious yet anxious to read Uncle Arthur's letter, you climb down, intending to return to your suite. But once again, you're starting to feel a tingling sense of excitement building inside.

As soon as you reach the floor and turn around, you are greeted by a most astonishing sight: somehow the library has been transformed into a dining scene and is now packed with patrons wining and dining, along with waitstaff scurrying about—pouring wine, placing cocktails, setting entrées, and, here and there, tossing salads or attending to flambés. The air is filled with the hum of conviviality, joyous conversation, and occasional bursts of loud laughter. Another holographic show? You lean forward, squinting hard. Are these real people out there? You can't quite tell.

You hear a "Good evening" from behind you, causing you to wheel around. "May I show you to your table?" Shock! A transformed Penelope is standing before you, outfitted in a stunning silver bandage dress that takes your breath away. Her one-piece is so tight it appears as though she's been poured into a second skin. She's smiling broadly, with a charming mix of shyness and confidence. Which leaves you utterly speechless.

"I'm auditioning for maître d' at Thomas's new establishment. Please follow me," she calls out saucily. But you cannot move. It seems as though the bar game from a few nights ago has burst into real life, for floating high above the gathering is a giant neon sign brightly proclaiming BEERS & REARS.

You soon see why Penelope will likely get the job. Cradling what appears to be a large menu, she strides ahead like a parading contestant in a beauty pageant. Her long raven hair tosses seductively while her see-through dress presents the full catalog of her charms. Nearby diners are also riveted. Intermittently, she turns slowly and enticingly and beckons you forward. But still you cannot move. This is too much. Can this be real?

It isn't. From behind, the library door opens, and a blast of outside air seems to obliterate the dining scene. You turn and see Christopher bounding into the restored library, asking if the receptionist has found you. You take a deep breath and point to the book safe, managing to say, "Good that I did, because she'd completely forgotten."

"Are you okay?" Christopher asks. "Your face is completely flushed."

"I'm fine," you fib.

No way, Storyteller, am I going to talk about what just happened—if it even did. ***What do you think happened?*** *The library was suddenly full of people wining and dining.* ***Didn't see anything of the sort.*** *You didn't see Penelope greeting me?* ***No, sorry.***

You take several deep breaths, hoping to slow your pulse and collect your wits. Finally you do. "Well, shall we?" you ask, waving the pages. Christopher nods enthusiastically. You mention that the book safe was locked but the numbers on the pool timer unlocked it. The two of you bump fists—another puzzle solved!

Lord Hanover's letter appears to run several pages. But as you look at the stack, you see that the top page is blank. You pick it up to examine more closely. The page flashes, and the text appears. As soon as you begin reading, you realize that at long last, this is going to explain everything.

CHAPTER THIRTY-FOUR

My beloved child,

If all goes well, you will receive this letter from Miss Stratton after the inheritance matters have been well and truly settled. But no matter what has transpired to date, the time for final revelations is at hand. You are entitled to a full disclosure as to the nature of our relationship, and you shall have it.

In spirit, I have always been your uncle. But that which makes men kin—the connection of blood—did not exist until I was near death. And it was I who fashioned the link, through a method of DNA manipulation I devised. Demonstrating that this was possible has been my life's greatest work, and now you stand as living proof.

A frightful thing, eh? But then nothing was ever done to you, although I was forced to have someone "appropriate" your medical records so I could alter mine accordingly. The result is that we are now related by blood, genes, and everything considered necessary by the courts and even the genealogical societies.

Well, no doubt you are wondering why I did this. The answer lies in the distant past. I learnt I had a genetic disease, one I had no desire to pass on to another generation. I will not go into details here; suffice it to say that my affliction kept me from siring an heir of my own.

I had been blessed with the relative freedom wealth brings, the joys of science, and good friends. I was determined to squeeze everything I could out of life. But even while still relatively young, I foresaw that with my passing, the Hanover estate would almost certainly be parceled out to the highest bidder. That I could not abide. There is something noble about the continuity of a great house; like a living being, massive yet delicate, it draws vitality from its master or mistress.

As you finish each page, you pass it to Christopher. At one point, however, you accidentally pass two to him. When he tries to read the second, the page remains blank.

"Well, I'll be," he says, returning the page to you. When you bring it eye level, the small flash occurs and the text materializes. Christopher, though, immediately gets it. "Looks like Uncle Artie embedded some sort of facial recognition tech in the document, just like in the game. And apparently it requires your face at first. Astounding!" He holds the page up to the light in hopes of detecting some microcircuitry but finds nothing.

"You know what this means, right?" you ask.

"I do," Christopher confidently replies. "It means they were never able to actually read your correspondence from Uncle Artie whenever they intercepted it. Heh heh. Must have driven them barmy." The two of you again bump fists and continue reading.

At some point, then, I began actively searching for a cure for my illness. I never found it. Instead, I discovered an alternative path, the one I currently follow. My diary and lab notes, which you should possess by now, detail my efforts to match my identity with yours. Other than a few select colleagues scattered round the world, no one knew of this line of research. Put simply, I set out to demonstrate that any individual's unique molecular identity could be altered to match anyone else's. For this, a random subject was required.

To avoid the spectre of connivance, I rejected as candidates anyone I knew. And so, during my travels, I began searching for the perfect stranger who could become my heir. I discovered you, among several others. Thereafter, as unobtrusively as possible, I shadowed your life.

When I extrapolated my own demise from the genetic makeover, I thought, "So be it." I was near the end of my span anyway. And although I would dearly love to be recognized as more than a talented dabbler in the field of biotechnology, I am wary of the potential of my discovery. It could cause a paradigm shift of massive proportions. Yes, the gene switching is fatal, but given enough time, I believe I could have solved that as well—as could others less scrupulous. The world must decide what to do with this knowledge, which could do great good if used intelligently.

My last and boldest experiment will take place shortly after I finish this missive, when I take the capsule that triggers the transformation. I have already arranged for an autopsy and exhaustive postmortem tests to be performed, and for the results to be forwarded to the relevant courts, various scientific and medical associations, and genealogical societies. If you've received enquiries from representatives of these esteemed bodies, I am certain they've accepted my new genetic makeup.

Soon enough, of course, the scientific community will know about my experiments, and our counterfeit kinship will be postulated. But the terms of my final will and testament are irrevocable; with no caveats, everything I own is yours. If I may make one final request, though, it is that you keep and cherish my servants as I did.

Ah, the spirit lingers, and in such odd ways. Fare thee well, my beloved child.

Affectionately,
Arthur Hanover
Lucerne, Switzerland

Without comment, Christopher sets aside the last page, his expression sober. “Well,” he says at last, “now we have our explanation.”

You speak briskly, hoping to change the somber mood. “By the way, Penelope told me she accidentally mailed Uncle Artie’s second DVD directly to the Royal Society. Leave it to her—now we won’t have a chance to examine it.”

“No wonder they keep calling to ask if you exist,” Christopher says with a trace of his usual humor returning. You pick up the sheaf of typewritten pages. “Aha, Christopher—it’s the full story behind Rollinsby’s research.” Like Lord Hanover’s letter, each sheet initially requires your face to be recognized. But unlike it, the text on each page disappears whenever you hand it to Christopher.

“For your eyes only.” The boy laughs. He gazes upward. “Uncle Artie, you are truly astonishing.” Then he says to you, “Perhaps in addition to serving in the House of Lords, you’ll also be required to assist MI6.” He’s clearly enjoying this.

You laugh, saying, “Even if it’s ‘top secret’—I’m going to share it since we’ve come this far together.”

“Right. Let’s hear it,” says Christopher. You read a few paragraphs silently, then decide to summarize them. “Okay, Uncle Artie begins by stating that his lifelong associate, Dennis Rollinsby, did the lion’s share of work on the matter-transfer project. He explains that he gave his old friend the funds to continue the research since Rollinsby’s own estate had been bankrupted by the effort.”

You read further, silently, and after a moment, say, “Okay, Christopher, says here that, about two years ago, Rollinsby became convinced that the security forces of several foreign nations were plotting to abduct him—or worse. Fearing this was imminent, he arranged for all his notes and prototypes to go to Uncle.” You snap your fingers. “Wait. The news we all saw in Farnsworth’s office said Rollinsby was missing and presumed dead. But when I was watching TVTV at home, they ran a story about UFOs, and the newscaster said Rollinsby would appear on the next broadcast to comment on it. Plus, I’m reasonably sure the chauffeur who drove me up here was Rollinsby in disguise . . . so I don’t get this.”

“Oh I caught that broadcast,” says Christopher. “At the beginning, the newscaster apologized because Sir Dennis was a no-show. She said he’d reportedly returned to the dairy farm but hadn’t been seen or heard from since. They don’t know if another intelligence service, or maybe even actual aliens, got him. Or if he chose to vanish by himself.”

You laugh. “Maybe he simply teleported himself away from the clutches of secret agents.”

Christopher laughs too, saying, “Maybe. Hope so.”

You continue summarizing Uncle Artie’s lab notes. “Since this was around the time he began renovating the manor, he had the engineers install the transfer base stations according to Rollinsby’s specifications in various rooms, without explaining their purpose.”

“Aha, those Germans and Japanese,” says Christopher, “so that’s what they were up to.”

You recount all you’d heard about them from Thomas, then go on with your summary: “Uncle says here that whenever he had the time and the inclination, he continued his friend’s research. The prototypes of the system were already quite advanced, he says, although Rollinsby had successfully transported only inorganic matter.”

“Transported?” Christopher interjects. “This is starting to sound pretty sci-fi.”

You nod in agreement. “It says here that he went further but refused to transfer any life-form more complex than a few insects. Until, one fateful day about six months ago, Uncle took the leap and tried out the system on himself.”

“Blimey!” Christopher blurts. “That took nerve.”

You nod, holding up the sheet and pointing to a passage. “He states right here that he had to summon courage to stand in the staging area and press that red button on the metal box.”

“What happened?” Christopher’s riveted.

You tell him the account says it resulted in the projection of a 3D image of the Manor House floor plan on a nearby wall. A red tracer beam pointed to a room at the far end of the manor. When he pressed the button a second time, the beam and the image both vanished.

“So he didn’t go anywhere?” Christopher looks puzzled.

"Right," you tell him. "So he switched it back on, directed the beam at the room next door, and again pressed the button."

"And?"

"Uncle says that he felt slightly disoriented and tingly as a shimmering veil seemed to surround him. When his vision cleared, everything was normal except he was now standing in the middle of that other room."

"Well, beam me up, Scotty!" Christopher shouts, wearing an incredulous expression. "How did it actually feel? Does he say?"

You read further, then say, "Yes, I found it. He says he felt fine once on the other side but had no memory of the actual transfer. I'll read you what he said exactly. 'Quite understandable, considering my molecules had been disassembled and then reassembled all in a span of time so infinitesimal it can only be expressed in negative powers of ten.'"

You pause to reflect on the enormity of this disclosure. Had the impossible come to pass? Did somebody finally invent the real-world equivalent of the *Star Trek* transporter? Were those somebodies Dennis Rollinsby and your ersatz uncle? You look up at the boy. "Christopher, did you ever suspect that he might be working on something like this?"

"No, it must have been when I was away at academy," he says.

You read further, then summarize: "After a few more tries, he learned the device would transport him only between rooms on the left side of the mansion. It shut off if the beam was focused on the right."

"So what did he do?" Christopher is excited, now hanging on every word.

You scan for the answer and, several pages later, find it. "Aha! It meant that while the transfer base stations were all working, the system as a whole was underpowered. He gave the specifications to the engineers, ordering that the capability be quadrupled. They did so without knowing about the system they were upgrading."

"Those German and Japanese engineers, right?" Christopher asks.

"Right. Oh, and this part's funny," you tell him. "Says here that as a final touch, he asked the two teams to design an infrared remote to replace Rollinsby's cumbersome metal box, devices identical to the ones geared for the surveillance system and the passageways. The only difference was that the new one would have a green orb. A competition was held, and the German team won."

"That's just like Uncle Artie," Christopher reminisces. "He so loved contests and games."

You read further, then summarize: "Uncle says that, after experimenting with the juiced-up system and the new remote, he felt confident enough to resume using the device on himself—"

"Does it say where he went?"

You quickly rescan the current page, then shake your head. "No, not that I can see, but he vowed that as long as he was alive, he would never reveal its existence to anyone, since, and I quote, 'the mere mention of such a device would cause listeners to have me carted off to the loony bin. To actually demonstrate it might bring all manner of secret agents swooping down.'"

"He's right," Christopher observes. "Not only M16, CIA, FSB, and others but also actual aliens themselves . . . in search of alien technology!"

You chuckle, then return to the memo. "Okay, I'm almost at the end here. Uncle concludes by stating he would never allow anyone but me, his heir, to use it—and only if *I* chose to do so after becoming fully informed. Which is why he simulated the mechanism in the virtual program."

"That was the coolest bit in that game," Christopher recalls, shaking his wrist. "Though I do wish we'd found it earlier!"

"Right . . . Okay, so the last thing he says is that this is a potentially disruptive technology. He's not sure the world is ready for it but has decided to let me make the call."

Christopher picks up one of the sheets, which immediately goes blank, and speaks directly to it. "Terrific, Uncle Artie. Just one minor detail—where did you hide the controller?"

"Where was the green remote in the virtual manor?" you ask.

The boy shrugs. "I don't know. I was out of the room when Mr. Farnsworth found it." You shudder at the thought of the butler having the device in his possession. You still don't really trust him. Especially after eavesdropping on his phone call with the Japanese guy.

The two of you leave the library, neither with any idea of where to begin looking. Christopher's dying to know if you're going to try it if it's found.

"Are you kidding? How could I resist?" you tell him. But in truth, you don't know. You'll cross that bridge when you get to it—literally.

You return to the butler's office, but both Farnsworth and Van Scoy are gone. There's no answer when you knock on her door. Christopher opens the door to the lobby and calls back that no one's at reception or the main entrance. He tells you to wait here while he makes a quick reconnaissance of the first and second floors. You pick up the remote and turn on the local news. The screen caption reads:

CRUNCH IS TEAM'S NEW MASCOT AS 'NAPPERS PREVAIL IN SUIT

Wow! You never saw that coming.

Michael opens with, "Crunch, the recently dognaped rottweiler, has evidently adopted his former abductors. It remains unclear how the missing rottie was reunited with Runaway Dogs team members Tug and Timothy Skaddle. Crunch reportedly sought out the brothers last evening and made his desire to remain with them strongly felt."

The broadcast cuts to a prerecorded video clip of the Skaddle brothers inside their refurbished cottage, along with Crunch, who is calmly seated between them, looking happy and panting loudly. Timothy leans over to pet him and is heard saying repeatedly, "Good Crunchy, good doggo."

Tug Skaddle steps forward to explain. "Crunch sat outside our bedroom window all night, howling and whimpering as if he was the most miserable soul on earth. We'd no choice but to take him in."

The shot returns to the news desk, where Meredith makes an observation: "It is well-known in human psychiatric circles that kidnapping victims sometimes bond with their abductors. Apparently, this can also happen with canines."

Michael has a related development. "Crunch has also been named official mascot of Runaway Dogs Rugby Club, according to James Prance, a local solicitor who represents both the Skaddles and the team, and who now joins us in studio this afternoon."

The scene widens to show Prance now seated between the two anchors. Says Michael, "Mr. Prance, tell us about Crunch's new role as mascot."

Prance, attired in a purple jumpsuit over long yellow sleeves and sporting a purple ball cap with the letters *RD* embroidered in gold on it, smiles broadly and seems eager to respond. "Right, Crunch, our new standard bearer. If anyone can help turn our disastrous season round, Crunch can."

"How so?" Michael asks.

"Well, as you know," replies Prance, "Crunch is quite ill-tempered. For now, he must remain on leash, but we plan to train him to roam the sidelines, threatening to bite opponents whenever they threaten to score."

Meredith has a question. "Counselor, does the team have any plans to produce Crunch-themed merchandise? You must know that the pooch already has quite a following throughout the tri-county area. He's actually quite beloved in some quarters."

"Indeed," Prance replies. "I thought as much from the moment you first broke the story, which prompted me to quickly get in touch with the principals."

Says Meredith, "Our ratings have skyrocketed since we began reporting on all of Crunch's misadventures."

Prance nods amiably and says, "Glad to be of service."

Michael continues with another development. "Meanwhile, the Skaddles have prevailed in their lawsuit against former owner Nigel Wanton. This morning, Magistrate Winston McConnell awarded the plaintiffs custody of the dog and five times the sum of £2,000 they'd petitioned, terming Crunch's upbringing and recent conduct reprehensible. 'Owners must take responsibility,' McConnell wrote in his official judgment."

Meredith wraps up the story on a melancholy note. "Nigel Wanton, bereft over abandonment by his ten-year-old pet, stated he may be forced to sell his Flogway farm as a result of the verdict. We now go live to Wanton's residence."

Wanton, looking defeated, is standing on his front porch. Says Meredith, "Nigel, we're so sorry. But don't you rather think this is a case of poetic *injustice*?"

Wanton sighs. "I don't know. I just hope this ends it."

Adopting a sympathetic tone, Meredith consoles with, "You never know, Nigel. One fine day, Crunch might decide to return." She turns to the camera. "And if and when he does, we'll be there to cover it."

Christopher's back. He gazes up at the screen. "Ah, yes, Crunch. How did he fare?"

"He suddenly moved out to start a new life," you inform him.

"Sort of like you," he quips. He then snaps his fingers in remembrance. "Of course! How could I forget? Follow me."

CHAPTER THIRTY-FIVE

At long last, the front entrance is unlocked. You swing one of the massive doors open and step outside into glorious late-afternoon sunshine. The grounds are teeming with activity. Live fiddle music is interspersed with the hum of people congregating. You cross the driveway, and from the base of the Shakespeare monument, you spy the manor gang assembled in front of the spa annex.

From the other direction is the sound of a dog barking somewhere near the rear of the dining hall, which causes Christopher to tear off in that direction. Something sure smells good, and you hear Bruce's voice calling, "Hey, Noël, mind givin' me a hand? Toss some more prawns on."

"*Oui, Monsieur Bruce*. But I do not know *la préparation spéciale* for this dish," the chef cries in consternation.

"Ah, no worries, mate," Bruce reassures. "Just baste and toss 'em on."

"Hey, Noël," you call out teasingly. "Loved your repast last night—guess there's just no cure for ailihphilia! You really outdid yourself."

The chef beams appreciatively. "I did, did I?"

A Storyteller pipes up with a suggested reply, which you quickly call out. "Is it crazy how saying sentences backward creates backward sentences saying how crazy it is?"

Noël furrows his brow, deliberates intently for a moment or two, then jumps and claps his hands repeatedly, exclaiming, *"Ah, un palindrome symétrique des mots. J'adore!"*

Immediately a Storyteller translates: ***Ah, a word-symmetric palindrome. I love it!***

You decide to walk down to the main gate. Looking around, you marvel at the ridges of the hills and valleys beyond. For a moment there, your imagination plays tricks, as you think you see snow-capped mountains in the distance.

From behind, a woman sighs. You turn around and see James Lowell Farnsworth and Adrienne Lynn Van Scoy holding hands and looking blissful. "We've something to tell you," Adrienne says. "We're engaged! We're about to announce our intentions to be married in the spring. We don't know your plans, but we'd be honored if you could attend our wedding."

Damn, looks like you've lost out. Perhaps for the best, though, given your station here. "Of course I'll come," you tell them. "And congratulations! I wish you both the very best."

Hastily, the butler adds, "And if you'd agree to keep us on, we'd be absolutely delighted. Do think about it, won't you?" It's clear he'd like to leave it at that as they hurriedly walk away.

"Oh, James," you call out, "where did you find the green remote in the game?"

"In the armory," Farnsworth calls back.

"Bon voyage," Adrienne shouts playfully.

You rush back inside to retrieve the remote, which, for the time being, you plan to hide somewhere in your quarters. But the armory remains locked. You start to turn away but are startled to hear muffled voices coming from inside the room. There aren't any nearby wall hangings that might be a portal, so you press your ear to the door, hoping to gain a sense of who might be in there. From inside come the hoarse sounds of two men grunting and cackling. You thought everybody was outside, but apparently not.

Storyteller, what's going on? ***Those two shouldn't be here***, a young Storyteller above informs you, looking concerned. *Who are they?* ***The butler's friends.*** *What are they snickering about?* ***How they shouldn't be here, but they don't care.*** *Did they find the green remote?* ***No. At least not yet.***

Now, you think you hear one of the men speaking. *Is that the guy Farnsworth was talking to last night?* ***Yes.*** *Is he dangerous?* ***Yes, they both are.*** *So is Farnsworth dangerous as well?* ***Not when he's on duty.*** *"On duty"—what's* *that supposed to mean?* No answer, instead he assumes a commanding tone. ***Leave now! They're about to come out.***

You hurry down the hallway and out the main entrance, perplexed by the Storyteller's enigmatic last reply, which seemed to imply that Farnsworth might be dangerous after all.

And I thought everything was going to be okay, Storyteller. ***Always assume that it will be. And most of the time it will.*** *Okay, I've just told myself everything's okay. Okay?*

Returning to the barbecue, you help yourself to marinated sautéed mushrooms and a glass of chardonnay. As you are enjoying the appetizer, Thomas and Penelope stroll up. "Miss Stratton and I thought we'd take the Land Rover—that is, if you don't mind—and see if we can get down to The Village," Thomas says.

"We need to pick up a few items for tonight," Penelope adds, while looking adoringly at Thomas.

"Sure, go right ahead." You're half tempted to tag along but quickly think better of it, particularly since you now notice Penelope's hands lovingly massaging the back of Thomas's neck. The headwaiter's expression is blissful.

"If we do manage to get down there," Thomas manages to say, "I hope we won't be besieged by hordes wanting to hitch a ride back with us. Everybody wants to see you in the flesh."

"We'll say, 'No way,'" Penelope promises. "We don't want to share you with all the gossipmongers and paparazzi." You're now sure those two lovebirds won't be sharing one another with anyone else, either! They take off for the garage, calling out that they'll see you tonight at the show.

Next, you're joined by Bruce and Savannah. "G'day, mate. We're just off for a spin on the Harley. This one's been promising me for ages, and now it's time to deliver."

"Just hope you live to tell the tale, Sherlock." Savannah turns her back on him, winks at you, and whispers devilishly, "It won't take long to get this out of his system." Your pulse quickens.

Storyteller, now that Adrienne's unobtainable, should I reconsider Savannah? ***Go for it!*** a young teen calls out. ***Resist the temptation***, counsels an older voice.

You tell the barkeep that as your first official act you are considering rescinding your uncle's decree barring Farnsworth from the pub. "Honestly, Bruce, what do you think?" you ask him.

"Me and Reg already beat you to it, mate," he replies. "Got on with 'Lord James' so well during the game, we had him and his lady in for a nightcap after."

"You should have been there," Savannah moans, shaking her head in mock disgust, "and listened to the three tyrants go on and on about how had they only done this or only done that they could have ended up with everyone's money. Mildred and I were appalled."

Then, quite unexpectedly, Savannah throws her arms around Bruce, pulls him close, and plants a giant kiss on the landlord's lips. With a feigned Aussie accent, she tells him, "No worries, mate. I'll be your special sheila one of these cold and lonely nights." She caps it off with a French wink. At that, they laugh uproariously and bid farewell. Soon, you hear the roar of a motorcycle revving up, followed by cries for help and outbursts of trepidation from Bruce.

Looks like you've struck out with her as well.

Hat trick! Right, Storyteller? ***Well, I think not.*** *Why not?* ***You certainly didn't score once, let alone thrice.*** *No, it's baseball slang, not soccer.* ***Ah yes, forgot about that one. Indeed, you struck out thrice.***

Shouts of "Help! Help!" pouring forth across the lawn first alarm then amuse you. It's Mildred, running like the wind with Reggie in hot pursuit. The doorman catches up to her and throws an arm around her waist. They're both barefoot. Breathlessly, Mildred blurts out, "Thank goodness you've come along. Rescue me from this impossible man. I'm too old for all this cavorting."

"Ah, Millie," Reggie says fondly, "I've never seen a woman in such fine shape. And so light on your feet as well."

"Seen Christopher?" Mildred asks. "Lad's in seventh heaven. Noël dashed out early, made it down to a neighboring farm, and bought the dear boy that 'present' he's prayed for every night. I hope you'll let him keep it."

Reggie squints at you. "Ah, I can see that you'd never say no to the lad." Taking her hand, Reggie pulls Mildred away. "C'mon, Millie, there's many more to be danced this fine day."

You head off in the direction of a dog barking. On a grassy knoll behind the dining hall, you find Christopher and his new puppy, an English bulldog. Their backs are to you, and it seems like they haven't heard your approach. The boy hugs the dog, who snuggles closer and wags its stub of a tail. When he finally notices you, Christopher turns and performs an introduction of sorts. "Look, Artie, look who's come." Grinning from ear to ear, he looks at the dog, then shouts, "Let's go for a run, Artie!"

And they're off. A young boy and his new pup, a beautiful sight to behold. If you could stop time, this would be the moment.

Continuing your trek while fancifully "mending" your thrice broken heart, you recall your recent surveillance of the chef and think that your hunch about Noël's intentions was correct; in a complete change of character, he'd certainly been "up to some good" bright and early this morning. But you're still puzzled by that zany encounter where the chef challenged you to a "duel" while speaking in palindromes. Crazy? Yes. Comical? Yes. But the more you think about it—concerning.

What do you think, Storyteller? ***Don't overthink it. Noël's just a fun, funny guy.*** *But what about his directing his guys to intercept Savannah two days ago?* ***Somehow we missed that. We'll revisit that episode and let you know.***

Your olfactory sensors are now registering maximum on the appetizing scale. Cheeseburgers are being charbroiled. You're almost stuffed but can't resist. Bruce and Reggie join you, their plates piled high with sliders—some smothered in chili, others in sautéed mushrooms, still others entirely plant-based—on steamed brioche mini-buns. Bruce says you can travel the world over and never find anything to compare with a juicy burger with proper trimmings. Reggie nods, his mouth too full to speak.

"Incroyable! Jamais rien goûté de tel avant!" shouts Noël, raving that never in his life has he tasted a cheeseburger, and he thinks they are sensational. The French language, he asserts, does not contain enough superlatives to describe this peasant triumph. He says he plans to visit the Falstaff often if this is an example of what can be found on its menu.

Farnsworth and Adrienne come back by, accompanied by Mildred, who is now hearing about their engagement. The housekeeper looks thrilled and hugs them both. Bruce and Reggie pound James's back in congratulations.

The butler turns to you, beaming in approval at your mushroom burger. "Indeed, the gourmet's top choice," he proclaims.

A short distance away, people are taking turns making friends with Artie the pup. You've never seen Christopher look so happy.

You look around. Sunset is long past, and darkness has fallen on the manor. The stars are out, and a breeze is stirring, but the temperature is mild. Guests from neighboring farms who've walked onto the grounds mill about chatting with servants they already know or enjoying the congeniality of new acquaintances.

Camelot, eh, Storyteller? ***Indeed it is. A magical place. Where Time stands still.***

Suddenly, conversations are stilled by the blare of trumpets. The audience lightly applauds and cheers, then hushes in anticipation.

Thomas, dressed in his headwaiter's tuxedo, has added a black top hat to his ensemble. He is smiling confidently at Reggie, who stands near him. To the audience, he says. "Now that night has fallen, the atmosphere has become distinctly more magical. However, before we begin, I'm afraid I must point out that Master McCabe has been putting on a bit of weight. So much that his buttons are in great danger of popping off. Behold!"

With this, he gestures in Reggie's direction, and the doorman's jacket buttons fly off and into Thomas's outstretched top hat. Everyone applauds, and Reggie cries out, "Now, see here, Thomas!"

The headwaiter scoops out the buttons and replies, "Not to worry, my good friend." With another wave of his other hand, the buttons fly back and reattach themselves. "There they are, back in place. No telling how long they'll remain, though, if you don't take more exercise!"

Laughter. More applause. Now a spotlight from a nearby maypole shines on Penelope, who wears a cone-shaped hat with a star on top and holds a wand that sparkles. She directs it at Reggie, and his coat changes from cardinal red to royal blue. With repeated swoops, her magic wand cycles through the doorman's entire collection. The audience gasps.

Then with all the assurance of a professional actress, Penelope calls out, "Observe poor Shakespeare over yonder, sitting in the moonlight, toiling over his sonnets and plays. Do we not suppose he tires of eternal confinement?

William, hear me. I grant thee a brief respite." Penelope points her wand in the direction of the statue.

The Bard rises from his seat, groans audibly, stretches his arms to the sky, and recites, "If thou rememb'rest not the slightest folly that ever love did make thee run into, thou hast not loved. Love is a spirit all compact of fire—the course of true love never did run smooth. Love sought is good, but given unsought, is better. Love's best habit is a soothing tongue. Love looks not with the eyes, but with the mind; and therefore is winged Cupid painted blind."

Shakespeare retakes his seat, again frozen in his deliberations. Suddenly, the stone lions stand, toss their mighty manes, and roar.

A spotlight illuminates Thomas, who has exchanged his top hat for a chef's toque. "My friends," he begins, "Penelope and I would like to present our impressions of Manor notables. Let me begin." And with a shift in posture, he becomes Noël. Employing an exaggerated French accent, he exhorts, "*Non, non, monsieur*, we cannot possibly play *le karaoke* in *le grand* dining hall! Eet would disturb too much *l'ambiance* I have created."

The spot returns to Penelope, who has removed her hat. She regards her audience with disdain. In a faultless imitation of the concierge's PA singsong, she states, "Good evening. The butler has asked me to announce that he has completed his tour and finds everything in an appalling state. All staff are dismissed—permanently. Don't carry on—and do *not* have a nice day."

Adrienne feigns cries of protest before she laughs with good humor and joins in the applause.

Now the spotlight is back on Thomas, who has switched to a morning coat and tails, obviously readying an impression of Farnsworth. He is clutching silverware in both hands as he adopts a cultured tone. "Good evening. I am Professor Knives and Forks of the Tableware Institute with tonight's lecture. When preparing a formal setting, be sure to place all the cutlery on the right side, not on the wrong side. Put the pronged utensils on the outside, not sticking up inside cups where they might poke diners in the arms. Or on chairs where they might poke diners in the rears." While instructing, à la Farnsworth, Thomas fumbles with knives and forks, which intermittently fly out of his hands and crash loudly on the stone driveway. The audience guffaws. "Place the soup-gathering instruments where they are supposed to go and not where you only suppose they are supposed to go. Any questions?" Fumbling ever more madly, he drops all the remaining items.

Huge applause and laughter. The loudest from Farnsworth himself.

Penelope has now assumed the distinctive pose of Savannah Reddy. With hands perched on her hips and an amused expression, she says in a genuine American accent, "Bruce Sherlock? Never heard of him. Says he's from Australia. Where's that? Do they even know how to drive down there? I'd never hook up with this Sherlock rube. Sooner go out with a kangaroo." There are sympathetic groans for Bruce from the audience interspersed with chuckles over Penelope's impersonation.

The spot moves to Thomas, who, as Bruce, offers the landlord's rejoinder. "Savannah Reddy, you say? Now why do you reckon I'd waste time with a sheila like her? She's got grease splattered on her face and calls it makeup. Bet she goes around in coveralls—and thinks it's fashion. Zero interest in that one, mate."

The audience responds with a chorus of disbelieving murmurs and applause.

From out of the shadows, Christopher appears. With a look of mischief, he thrusts an oversized remote controller into your hands. Then as suddenly as he appeared, he darts away. What in the world?

Now Thomas removes his top hat with a flourish and calls in the manner of a ringmaster, "Ladies and gentlemen! Boys and girls! Children of all ages! Arthur Reynold Hanover, in association with imagine two-one productions, is proud to present the one, the only, Zodiac Circus! The greatest show . . . *off* earth!" He turns to you and frantically gestures that you get things started. You figure you should press the power button on the remote Christopher just handed you. So you press it.

From speakers mounted high, John Philip Sousa's "Stars and Stripes Forever" blasts across the lawn. All eyes turn in your direction. Dumbfounded, you stare at the remote, which has twelve buttons. Now, which one to press? Then you spot one at the bottom labeled PLAY ALL. You push it.

High in the sky tromps a dazzling assemblage of brass players, performers, acrobats, clowns, contortionists, costumed showgirls, and circus animals tromping, prancing, marching, somersaulting, and riding round the cheering panorama.

The audience is transfixed.

The stars overhead, the crystal-clear images in the sky, and the full quadraphonic audio send viewers dizzyingly around in circles as they strain their eyes and crane their necks to take it all in.

It overwhelms.

You're among the first to collapse on the lawn to witness this divine spectacle flat on your back. Within seconds, most of the audience is also lying supine on the grass. Struck by amusement, you laugh out loud, thinking that the manor green must resemble a battlefield of ecstatic casualties.

High above, marchers at the head of the parade disappear one by one as the skies gradually darken. But there must be more, much more to see, you're sure. Giddily, you roll over on your side to look down at the buttons, which you now observe are imprinted with astrological symbols. Aries through Pisces; you press them all.

In turn, the constellations light up in colossal stills—each panel frozen at the climactic moment of a separate big-top act. When the cosmic band is filled in, you again press PLAY ALL, which instantly produces more concentrated light, more color, sound, action, and magic than you would have ever imagined.

In Aries, a throng of strongmen, sword swallowers, fire-eaters, snake charmers, nail walkers, and others perform astonishing feats. Beside them, a trainer points a wand, and massive mastodons fall back on their haunches, raising their front legs while curling their trunks.

Your gaze shifts to Gemini, where twist-tied twin contortionists handstand, clasping both feet around their necks as a circular dais beneath them slowly revolves. Nearby, trapeze artists triple somersault and land in the outstretched hands of their catchers.

In Leo, a dashing costumed tamer barks a command, and seven lions bound from stool to stool. Beside them, a beautiful young woman whistles shrilly, and seven tigers obediently roll over one after the other. Which prompts you to roll over to behold the other end of the sky, where, in Pisces, a riot of colorful clowns, in mad dashes or wacky walkabouts, are assailing one and all with weapons of water, flowers, and confetti.

Delirious, you roll back in time to catch a bare-chested motorcycle daredevil burst through a Sagittarian ring of fire.

To the left, a Libran family of twelve balances a pyramid of chairs, stools, bicycles, and humans. Next to them, a lone high-wire walker tilts . . . teeters . . . wobbles, then inches to safety.

To your right, bareback riders fly and stunt around Capricorn atop and underneath galloping horses. Then from Aquarius, a man shot from the mouth of a monstrous cannon streaks across the heavens into a target net—suspended just above the lion act in Leo.

The clips are set to loop endlessly as a separate soundtrack enables a circus medley to play on, unfettered.

Suddenly, there's a *boom*! *Boom*! *Boom*! High above the circus panorama, a barrage of fireworks explodes. After more spectacular pyrotechnics, Penelope appears in the spotlight. She holds a remote identical to the one in your hand. She pauses, looks up at the sky, and says in the housekeeper's brogue, "Enough said—and done, dears." She points her remote and panel-by-panel powers down the heavens.

Applause and cheers and shouts for an encore fill the air. But overriding the calls is the sound of hearty laughter coming from far away. You instinctively look skyward to the spot where Lord Hanover appeared on opening night. This time, there are no thunderclaps or flashes of lightning, but the stirring orchestral music returns as Uncle Arthur's gigantic, beaming face bursts into view. The vision intones, "My beloved children, oh my, what a fine evening's entertainment that was. I haven't laughed so hard in ages. Ah, at last you are a whole family again. Believe me, it fills my heart with such immense joy to see you all together on this truly magical night. And I am further gladdened, for I now know that my final experiment has succeeded, and my life's work will be verified. Farewell, my children, as I go at long last to rest in peace."

Lord Arthur Hanover—noble, scientist, showman, nonpareil—fades slowly into the night sky. Handkerchiefs are out; some wiping away tears, some waving in fond farewell. But clearly the gathering is not astonished by his spectacular departure. You figure they've witnessed occurrences like this before. Well, if Lord Hanover prepared this one in advance, then so be it—they are moved by yet another touching reminder of what a wonderful man he was. Of how much he loved and cherished them all. His family.

Now yours.

Storyteller, this seems like a perfect ending. Is my story over?

Your original apparition, the old man with the flowing white beard, reappears. ***Do you know your own name?*** *Um, no, not the one I came with.* ***Then it is by no means finished.*** *Can't I just christen myself with a new one and attach it to Hanover?* ***You may, but your story does not end until you can recall the original.*** *Any previews of coming attractions, like before?* ***Sorry, not now, old chap.*** *Well, I don't see how whatever's next can possibly top all this.* ***Indeed, but perhaps, like the old refrain says, "Just when you least expect it . . ."*** *Right! I know. It's "just what you least expect!" I can't wait!*

You really can't.

PART THREE

THE RETURN

CHAPTER THIRTY-SIX

Deliriously happy, your head exploding with questions, you are dying to find Thomas and Penelope to congratulate them on their fabulous show and get an explanation of their "heavenly" laser system. How was that twelve-ring circus projected, and how did Uncle Artie arrange to have his dramatic farewell broadcast on high? Christopher once promised to show you the lions and the statue tricks; maybe he or someone can fill you in on Uncle's departure as well. And Reggie's magic coat and that button trick. They definitely flew into Thomas's outstretched hand and back again to reattach to the doorman's coat, which then repeatedly changed colors. The skits moved so quickly you scarcely had time to absorb all the effects.

Still, there's a lot of activity—fiddles playing, glasses clinking, laughter, and enchantment lingering in the air. Some revelers have lit sparklers and are parading around the lawn.

Then, without warning, there's an intrusion.

Sounds of cars at the main gate. Headlights one after another sweeping into the cul-de-sac. Horns blaring. Doors slamming. Now flashlights are on the lawn, obliterating sparklers. Muffled shouts—the spell is broken. From above, a helicopter rattles and shakes into view. The chopper performs a wide, deafening turnabout over the center lawn, exposing its side.

"Oh, look!" somebody yells. Printed clearly are the letters BBC. A man with a bullhorn leans out, bellowing that they intend to land, alerting all below to move to safety. The outside world has arrived.

You have no idea what to say to it.

Seeking the sanctuary of Manor House, you make a mad dash to the entrance. Nobody's in the lobby when the entry door closes, stifling the commotion outside. The candlelight, the soft classical sounds, the perfect stillness . . . it feels like home.

"I *knew* I'd find you here! *Do not* try to escape. You *cannot*!" Good God! It's Farnsworth, bellowing, rushing toward you from the far hallway. He crosses the lobby, now waving a pistol wildly overhead. He draws closer, his face contorted in rage. Your heart is pounding. Searing fear courses through your entire body.

"You incompetent fool! You—you—you actually thought you could *manage* all this?" he stammers. "Never!" Farnsworth turns and points the pistol directly at you. Reflexively, you dive to the floor. Gunshots. Rapid fire. The pungent smell of gunpowder fills your nostrils . . . Silence. Relief. Not hit.

Storytellers, another hallucination? Or was it real this time?

No answer from above.

You plant your shaking palms to the floor and push slowly upward until you can at least squat. Your heart is still pounding, but gradually the fear recedes. Slowly, you rise to your feet and look around. Farnsworth is nowhere to be seen. The stillness, the soft notes have returned, as if the tranquil scene was never disturbed. Was it because Farnsworth was never there? Did this never happen?

Finally, an elderly Storyteller appears. ***It happened as far as you're concerned. But we cannot tell whether it was real or imagined.*** *Why can't you?* ***Possibly it was a plant-projected hallucination. We're not able to directly witness those.*** *But I heard shots, smelled gunpowder.* ***Both auditory and olfactory hallucinations can occur.*** *Where is Farnsworth now?* ***In his quarters.*** *So he was really here?* **Oh yes, that much we can say.** *Did he find the green remote?* **No, he did not.**

Plant guides, can you read me?

The familiar peyote cactus flower appears overhead, warbling, ***Yes, we're here in your system.*** *Was that a hallucination just now?* **Not from us.** *Then it really happened?* **Sorry, we're not able to discern events we did not project.**

This convinces you it really happened. You think back to your last exchange with the butler just a short while ago. He and Adrienne were so friendly and warm as they shared their wedding plans. You thought this battle of succession was over, that you were all going to live happily ever after here in "Camelot" . . . Fat chance.

You'd like to sink into the nearby sofa, calm down, and try to sort this out, but a telephone rings. The source is the antique at reception. You walk over and lift the receiver.

"Good evening, this is Dennis Rollinsby speaking. If you know who I am, I beg you not to be alarmed. Your Uncle Arthur condones this call. In keeping with the spirit of tonight's magic show, I have arranged to make that device you have fully operational now—that is, if you're interested in having a go. If all that Arthur says about you is true, then I'm certain you are curious about experiencing, shall we say, a new mode of transport. As to its safety, we're reasonably sure you'll experience no ill effects, but one can never be certain, so of course the final decision is yours. I'll look in on you shortly."

What's he talking about? You don't have any green remote. Before you can ask, however, the line goes dead. You have no idea how to get inside the armory. But if you could get your hands on it, maybe you'd just go ahead, press that button, and whoosh—escape all those reporters and photographers who any moment now will burst through the door hurling questions, demanding explanations.

Well, there's no remote to spirit you away.

So, Storyteller, where to hide? ***The laboratory?*** *Of course. Thanks.*

As far as you know, the only way in there is through the cottage's fireplace. Should be quite a while before your pursuers figure that out. Farnsworth may not even know about it. Holing up for a spell will give you time to think, get over the shock. Eventually you'll have to face the press, but Adrienne should be able to handle them for the time being. But does she know about Farnsworth's attack? Was she in on it?

The cottage door is unlocked. Gasp—sitting on the nightstand is the green remote. You pick it up at the narrow end so as to not accidentally switch it on. You'll decide what to do after you're settled in the lab. If the BBC barges in broadcasting live, their viewers will get more than they bargained for when they catch your vanishing act, ha ha.

Uh-oh. Sensing someone has entered the cottage, you slowly turn. Standing there, smiling warmly, is none other than Lord Dennis Rollinsby himself.

"Lord Rollinsby, you're here! In the flesh!" you exclaim.

"Indeed I am, but please call me Dennis," he says. "Or Stephen if you like."

You chuckle, replying, "I knew you weren't just a chauffeur. You seemed to know everything about everything in tech."

But what does he know about me, Storyteller? Does he know my name? ***He does. But don't bother asking at this point.*** *When can I know?* ***When the Time comes.***

Rollinsby, who's dressed in a formal black tuxedo with white tie and tails, is brimming with excitement. "Well, my lord, have you decided what you'll wear to the ceremony?"

You're mystified. "Ceremony? What ceremony?"

"Surely you've seen the news," Rollinsby replies. "I'm referring to the upcoming Nobel gathering." With that, Rollinsby switches on TVTV. It's the news hour, which tonight is broadcasting live from Stockholm. The screen caption reads:

LORDS HANOVER, ROLLINSBY TO RECEIVE UNPRECEDENTED POSTHUMOUS NOBELS

He mutes the volume and says, "I rather think we should make a surprise appearance, don't you? Add high drama to the proceedings."

This makes no sense. "But how would we even get there?" you ask. "Just getting down to either of the London airports would take—"

Rollinsby interrupts with a dismissive wave, saying, "My lord, please regard what you're holding."

Your jaw drops. "With *this*? You're saying this actually *works*? Over distance? . . . Uncle's lab notes said he could only transport himself from one room to another."

Rollinsby smiles, saying, "Oh, I can assure you there have been quantum leaps since those early days. Let's see for ourselves, shall we?"

"All right," you reply tentatively. "I guess I should go change."

Says Rollinsby, "If possible, you should prepare a short eulogy of sorts. You can get dressed, stand in front of your mirror, and rehearse it!"

Entering your bedroom, you project a question: *Storyteller, whoever's on duty, this is important. Does his transporter really work?* The reply is sweet and grandmotherly. ***No spoilers, my child. You must find out for yourself.*** *So, just go with the flow, then?* ***Of molecules? Why, yes! How clever of you to***

phrase it that way! By all means you should "flow" into Sweden for the ceremony. It was such a grand occasion. *Was?* ***Was, is, will be. In Time, your mind will become more attuned. And you'll be able to relive cherished moments Time and again.***

Her phrase "grand occasion" sparks an idea about what to wear. Back home, you shelled out several thousand on evening wear, hoping at manor soirees you'd get a chance to "turn out" in these stylish threads. You especially looked forward to donning your blue tuxedo ensemble on some grand occasion. Sounds like this should be it.

"Do you want to *really* turn out?" you recall the tailor asking. "Sure, why not?" had been your eager reply. "Then may I suggest . . ." He then presented a stunning midnight-blue paisley tuxedo jacket and navy striped pants. For you, it was love at first sight, especially when he brought out the powder-blue, French-cuffed shirt and burgundy bow tie embedded with sparkling crystals. And he didn't stop there.

"Of course you can wear the traditional black or navy shoes, but why not push the envelope a bit further with these?" he proposed while opening a box and pulling out a gleaming powder-blue velvet tuxedo shoe and raising it up so that you could see how it glistened in the light. "Oh my, yes!" you had exclaimed but then wondered if it would be too much for formal occasions with members of the nobility in attendance.

A Storyteller quickly intervened: ***The conventional follow. The bold lead. These garments epitomize haute couture. Express who you intend to be: Lord of the Manor. Earliest adopter. Trendsetter extraordinaire.***

Hearing this sealed the deal. And now, the grandest of occasions, the Nobel Awards Ceremony, is at hand! "Stylin'!" you call to the Storyteller above and to yourself in the mirror as you adjust your glittering bow tie. ***Oh, honey, you look divine.*** *Storyteller, I was just advised to prepare a brief statement but have no idea what to say, how to even start.* ***We can assist with that if you like.*** *Oh, please do. You folks are so good at speechmaking.* ***Stand in front of the mirror, smile broadly, and repeat what I say.*** *Okay. Tell me.*

"Your Majesty, Your Royal Highnesses, Mr. President of the Nobel Committee, Excellencies, honorees, ladies and gentlemen. I am deeply honored tonight to acknowledge the award you have bestowed upon my genetic uncle. I must apologize, though, for I am not yet well versed in the details of his research, and thus cannot deliver the traditional scientific lecture in his stead. But permit me to briefly pay tribute to Lord Arthur Reynold Hanover, the man."

Pause. Now turn slowly to the side and look up. Good . . . Now continue.

"Thank you, kind sir, for everything. You have blessed me with a new home, a devoted family, and friends enough for a lifetime. Thank you, too, for allowing me to become an integral part of your legacy."

Pause. Now turn back slowly and look straight ahead . . . And continue.

"Ladies and gentlemen, I know my uncle would want to share this moment with the staff at Hanover Manor, whose decades of devoted service enabled him to pursue his great and varied interests unfettered by the ordinary demands of life. Tonight, let us acknowledge him for all that he was—a brilliant scientist, a patron of the arts, a true Renaissance man. Most importantly, though, he was a devoted friend and colleague, a generous benefactor of many causes, a loving head of household. Farewell, dear Uncle Artie!"

Short, sweet, and sincere. Well done!

Returning to the drawing room, you see Rollinsby nod approvingly while observing, "Their dress code is very strict, but they'll have to make an exception in your case. Come along, we'll depart from the dining hall."

Storyteller, this is really unbelievable. **Believe it!**

Upon entering the near-pitch-black, empty hall, you can see that Rollinsby has set up his "transport station," or whatever he calls it, on the dais where Adrienne performed her recital and emceed the digital art show. Rollinsby has stepped up and onto the dais and motions you to join him. The platform's floor has four circular white lights embedded and spaced evenly apart. Above, a canopy ceiling holds the same lights in their corresponding positions. To you, it looks just like the transport stations from a dozen old *Star Trek* movies.

"Well, shall we be off, then?" Rollinsby beams with a roguish expression. All you can manage is a faint nod. Rollinsby extends the remote and presses its green orb.

Immediately a loud hum ensues. The orb flashes light and dark, and a thick fog envelops the room. "You should probably shut your eyes tight during the teleport," he advises. You comply, and after several seconds, the hum fades to silence.

"We've arrived . . . my lord! Behold!"

You blink repeatedly because you cannot believe what you are seeing now. Except for the dais on which you're still standing, the entire venue has been transformed into an ebullient gathering of dozens of men and women clad in formal evening wear and seated in semicircular fashion on a royal-blue stage. Above them, on an extended balcony, more dignitaries are gathering.

"Look! There's a large letter *N* in the center of the stage," you whisper to Rollinsby. "Are we really where I think we are?"

He leans in, whispering, "We are indeed. Are you well?"

You're fine, didn't feel a thing. "Can they see us way back here?"

"Not yet," he replies. "We've not yet fully materialized into their field of vision." You wonder if this is all a hallucination and pinch yourself. You also note that this fantastic occurrence has completely overwhelmed the harrowing experience you had earlier.

A tall, distinguished elderly man approaches the podium. He's holding a short stack of what appears to be leather-bound diplomas. "Who is that?" you ask.

"The king of Sweden," says Rollinsby, "a really fine fellow. I'm sure you'd get on splendidly with him and the queen . . . Say, why not invite them to the manor sometime?"

You're amused by Rollinsby's matter-of-factness. "Right, I'll just pal around the manor with the king and queen of Sweden." You roll your eyes.

"Of course you should, my lord." Rollinsby remains plainspoken. "You can tour the grounds in your new hovercraft."

Thinking back to that very first TVTV report, you ask, "Is it like the one the sheep farmer spooked the cattle with?"

"Yes. I can procure one for you if—" Rollinsby pauses and checks his stopwatch. "We'll be coming into view momentarily."

All of a sudden, shouts and gasps erupt from the attendees, many rising from their chairs, straining to get a better look at the sparkly twosome now slowly materializing before their very eyes. "Look! It's Lord Rollinsby!" you hear several calling. "Who's that—Lord Hanover's heir?" others are clamoring. The king steps to the microphone and requests that everyone return to their seats, as he will now present the next award, which strikes you as perfect timing. As if the two of you have arrived on cue.

"The Nobel Prize for Physics," the king intones, "is awarded to Lord Dennis Rollinsby of the United Kingdom." A thunderous hurrah erupts. You realize that the attendees already knew who would be named, but you marvel at how shocked they must be to see that Lord Rollinsby is not dead after all. Not only that but the sensational manner in which he arrived is an irrefutable demonstration of his momentous breakthrough.

Rollinsby, beaming, waves with both hands to the gathering, then leans in slightly and whispers, "You're next."

Your heart skips a beat. "What do I do? Do I have to go down there?" you whisper.

"No, no," is Rollinsby's hushed reply. "When introduced, just smile and wave with great enthusiasm, like I did."

"I've got that speech ready," you tell him.

"I know," he says. He then hurriedly explains that he can now see it won't be possible to deliver it from this far away. "But I can have the recording released to the media if you'll permit." Your thumbs-up signals it's more than okay with you. You do want the world to know how much you revere the uncle you never met but have come to know so well. Besides, you're dying to see yourself on TV in that outfit!

The king now returns to the podium and informs the audience, "Lord Rollinsby's Nobel lecture was prerecorded earlier and will be available online at the conclusion of this ceremony. It will explain in detail his findings in matter transference."

He then announces, "For the first time in the history of these awards, we shall grant a prize posthumously. The committee has made this exception because of the heroic gesture the recipient made in order to prove his stunning hypothesis. Therefore, it is my great honor to announce that the Nobel Prize for Physiology and Medicine is awarded to the late Lord Arthur Hanover of the United Kingdom."

Another round of loud exclamations and prolonged applause. The king continues, "Here tonight, to acknowledge the award on behalf of the deceased, is Lord Hanover's genetic nephew and heir apparent, an individual who was chosen at random as proof of the scientist's revolutionary advances."

Rollinsby gives you a gentle nudge. "You should now step forward," he says softly.

You stand erect, move to the outer edge of the dais, smile broadly, and wave your hands high above your head to deafening shouts and applause that equal the clamorous reception given to Rollinsby.

When the commotion subsides, Rollinsby motions you to step back. "Time to return," he whispers as suddenly the hum and the fog return and your view of the ceremony disintegrates. In a few seconds, the hum recedes. The fog lifts. You blink a few times. You're back in the cavernous but empty dining hall.

"Well, it worked!" exclaims Rollinsby gleefully. "I knew it would, but there's nothing like finding solid proof in the pudding!"

You're incredulous, asking, "You mean this is the first time you went that far?"

Rollinsby's face beams in merriment. "Well . . . yes and no," he replies. "I've oft traveled between here and my hideout down south. But this was the first time teleporting across a great distance, across an ocean, from one land mass to another. Which reminds me, I'd best be off and back into hiding before the intelligence goons once again get hot on my trail! You do realize, these days I'm their most-sought-after mad scientist!"

His laughter indicates he's not really all that worried—and given his newfound disappearing trick, it comes as no surprise.

Offering your hand for a farewell shake, you say, "Stephen, Mark, Dennis, Lord Rollinsby, whoever you really are, they'll never catch you. Your transport gadget is just too double-oh-seven! But thank you so much for everything on my journey thus far."

Rollinsby smiles. "Oh, the pleasure was all mine, my lord. Here, this is now yours." He hands you the remote. "I've got another one I can use to get home."

You stare at the device, asking, "Will this take me back to Sweden?"

Rollinsby shakes his head no. "I've just reprogrammed it to do something entirely different—safe and right here in the manor! As your uncle was fond of saying, 'Life is discovery. And discovery life!'" And with that, he departs.

You stare intently at Rollinsby's magical device. As thrilling as the ceremony was, you're not sure it really happened. So much of your manor experience to date has been surreal, hallucinatory, or flat-out insane. Was this some kind of theme-park attraction executed on a grand scale? You wouldn't put it past those two.

"But wait. Hey, Storyteller," you call aloud, "if it really did happen, it should be all over the news, right?" ***Right, kiddo. Got to be the lead story!*** Your fashion consultant seems excited.

Well, if that's true, it means that, going forward, there's no turning back to anonymity. You are the living proof of concept. Your appearance at the Nobel ceremony has instantly accorded you international stature.

"Not many people can say that, eh, Storyteller!" ***Could count them on one hand, sweetheart. That is, if we had hands!***

Laughing, you quickly return to your quarters, anxious to see if, when, and how this will be reported. It isn't a long wait. You gasp as your smiling countenance and dazzling outfit fill the screen just as the top-of-the-hour newscast begins. You press 3DHOLO and immerse yourself in the scene. The screen caption reads:

ROLLINSBY, STILL-UNNAMED HANOVER HEIR SHOCK NOBEL AWARDS

Hey, Storyteller, you still around? How do I look? ***Smashing, my dear lord.*** *This is really neat.* ***Certain to be a highlight of your trip.***

Michael and Meredith are seated in their usual places. The backdrop is a giant photo of you and Rollinsby smiling and waving enthusiastically to the Nobel audience. The camera brings Meredith into close-up as she begins:

"Every year people around the globe—and especially those in academia, the sciences, and the arts—express a keen interest in the Nobel Prize ceremonies. But this year's gathering, I think it's safe to say, was one for the ages. To begin, I'm certain no recipients ever arrived in quite the scintillating fashion Lord Dennis Rollinsby and his mysterious companion did this evening. Just take a look."

A video insert shows you and Rollinsby slowly materializing on the elevated dais far across the venue. The camera then pans the wildly cheering audience, most of whom are standing in the center of Stockholm Concert Hall. Seeing this on live television makes you start to believe it really happened after all. Especially when close-ups of you are shown. The video ends, and the camera turns to Michael, who continues:

"The audience was stupefied not only by the duo's teleported entrance but also by the fact that Lord Dennis Rollinsby, long presumed dead, was here, very much alive, and delighted to accept the award for Physics in person. Which he did with great fanfare." The backdrop image switches to a close-up of a smiling Lord Rollinsby waving to the audience.

Adds Meredith, "And if that weren't enough of a shock, Lord Rollinsby's companion turned out to be none other than Lord Arthur Hanover's genetic nephew, who remains at this hour unidentified, but is now reported to be an American, possibly in his forties or fifties, and in residence. We are on-site and hope to be able to find and interview this individual shortly. At the ceremony, the Hanover heir apparent acknowledged Lord Hanover's posthumous award of the Physiology and Medicine prize."

Following, your entire speech is replayed.

"Wow, that was really good. Nice job, Coach Storyteller!" ***My pleasure, my lord.***

Michael concludes on a lighter note as the last frame is frozen on-screen: "Well, Meredith, while next to nothing is known about the Hanover heir—not even his name—there is quite a bit of buzz tonight in Stockholm, London, and elsewhere about him. Whoever he is, the new marquis has utterly smashed the time-honored Nobel tradition of a formal tux with tails for gentlemen.

"As you can see, he showed up in a dazzling tuxedo ensemble complete with glistening velvet shoes and a bow tie embedded with crystals that literally sparkled. While no one reportedly has taken offense, there's speculation as to whether this is a harbinger of sorts—a sign that the new Lord Hanover intends to be every bit the eccentric his pseudo-uncle once was. Oh dear, let us all hope so!"

Meredith agrees. "Indeed, Michael, that would be wondrous. Perhaps, too, the ascendant lord can find a way to install teleportation stations around the grounds to thrill the hordes of visitors who will soon descend on the manor in search of yet another dazzling attraction. Really give Disney, Universal, and the others a run for their money!"

A loud knock sounds at your door. You stand, stretch, mute the TV, and quickly make your way toward the entrance, calling out, "Who's there?"

There's no answer. Just the sound of someone jiggling the lock.

Oh no, is Farnsworth back? You pray it isn't so, but you brace yourself for the worst.

CHAPTER THIRTY-SEVEN

Finally, from the hallway comes a familiar voice. "It's me. Christopher." You sigh deeply and open the door. "Sorry, couldn't answer you at first," Christopher says, still panting heavily while holding his sketch-pad. "Was all out of breath from dashing all about. Had no idea you'd come back inside."

"Sorry, Christopher, had so much on my mind since reading Uncle's last letter. Just had to get away. And I wasn't ready to field questions I have no idea how to answer."

Storyteller, should I tell him about Farnsworth's attack? ***No, don't frighten the lad.*** *What about the trip to Stockholm?* ***Oh, by all means. He'll be delighted to hear about that.***

"Oh, I do understand." Christopher chuckles. "Uncle's last letter was a tome all right. Well, since they couldn't locate you, they've been interviewing everybody under the sun and moon *about* you."

You're dying to know. "What did they ask? And what did people say?"

Replies Christopher, "Oh, Reggie, Bruce, and others went on and on about your pub performances, Three Families, and the dance party." The boy laughs. "Chef Noël gesticulated wildly and uttered a French patois nobody understood—but one gets the impression he's now your number-one fan . . . On balance, you got rave reviews. Which made the horde even more mad about meeting you."

"How about Farnsworth?" you ask.

"Funny about him," Christopher replies. "He seems to have completely disappeared for some reason. Odd, because Ms. Van Scoy was there chattering amiably with the press."

Storyteller, where is Farnsworth now? ***Back in his quarters, stewing in his juices.*** *I don't get it. He seemed so happy earlier. Does he still think I have designs on Adrienne?* ***No, it's not that.*** *Is he still bitter about the inheritance?* ***Not that, either.*** *Then what on earth is it?* ***You'll find out soon enough.*** *When my story comes to it, right?* ***Yes, precisely.***

Christopher now spies the green remote on your desk and cries out, "Egad! You found it!" His eyes widen. "Should we see what it does?" he asks.

"Go ahead," you tell him. "Let's see where it takes us this time."

Christopher's jaw drops. "'*This time*'? You've already had a go?"

"I'm not sure, Christopher. Maybe I did. Maybe I only dreamed it. I'm not sure of anything anymore."

The boy presses. "Where did you go—or think you went?"

"Stockholm. With Lord Rollinsby."

Christopher's jaw again drops. "The Nobels—you actually attended the ceremony?"

You're still not certain but tell him, "I just saw it on the news, so I must have. And no ill effects from the journey. So I guess I'm all in on seeing what it does if you are."

"Am I ever! Hell yes!" Christopher shouts.

"Lord Rollinsby said this controller is programmed to do something here in the manor. So I guess we won't be going anywhere this time."

"May I?" the boy requests.

You nod. "Sure, go ahead."

He presses the orb. Immediately, the hum sounds and the orb begins flashing. Total darkness envelops the room, and you can no longer see anything, not even your hand you raise in front of your face.

Now comes the sound of minor chords on a guitar followed by sharp staccato hits on a snare drum, which provide a reentry point for hypnotic major chords that evoke eerie feelings of a psychedelic adventure about to unfold. You think you know this song—the drums are playing a bolero underneath just like the night Savannah burst into your bathroom. Or you thought she did.

After thirty seconds or so, a commanding female voice, drenched in echo, rising and falling with precision, sings about one pill making you larger while another makes you small. Now you recognize the Jefferson Airplane classic and take a deep breath to enjoy Grace Slick's powerful, spine-tingling vocals about ingesting mushrooms and seeking Alice's counsel about their effects. The vocals continue to build toward the inevitable climax, which, when reached, causes the room to explode in a dazzling white light.

After a few seconds, your eyes adjust, and the scene achieves clarity. Across the room, there's no longer any wall that separates the cottages, or the kitchen that would be behind it. You're looking at a phantasmagoria of holographic humans and animated characters seated on one side of a long, rectangular table covered by a white linen cloth strewn with white roses and a multicolored assortment of wildflowers and topped with flower-patterned teapots and baskets of blueberry scones. The holograms, silent and motionless, are staring out at you with an air of expectancy.

"Christopher," you call out, "are you there? Are you okay? You seeing what I'm seeing?"

The boy waves and calls from across the room, "I'm here, and I'm fine, and this is fantastic!" He says he doesn't quite know what happened but believes the two of you have been granted a preview of "Uncle Artie's latest theme-park attraction." He motions you to his side. "Looks inviting. Let's go in, go for a ride, enjoy whatever it does."

You take a few steps forward, then pause to take the scene in. Behind the seated characters stands the white stalk of a giant mushroom—red with white warts dotting its cap that forms a canopy over the table. The walls are painted with forest scenes displaying perfectly formed trees and clusters of oversized wildflowers beneath them. Apparently, the roof in this part of the cottage has somehow been retracted, and thus a clear night sky full of twinkling stars is visible overhead. Floating slightly above the arc are several pinkish cotton-candy clouds.

Christopher looks blown away. He turns to you, gesturing excitedly toward the seated characters, asking, "Recognize them?"

You inch closer. On the far left is a bespeckled white rabbit outfitted in a red tuxedo jacket with an enormous pocket watch attached. Beside the rabbit sit identical twins dressed in schoolboy uniforms with blue bow ties and red propeller hats. Next to them, a grinning red-and-gold striped Cheshire cat.

"Yes I do," you call out. "I certainly do recognize them! Of course, given that song intro, who else could be here!"

You step into the scene and lock eyes with a smiling young man adorned with white pancake makeup, red lipstick, and red shading beneath his hazel-green eyes. His red curly hair bursts out the sides of a large top hat with a pale-orange sash. You point to him, saying to Christopher, "Now that's one wild and crazy-looking guy."

"Of course he is!" Christopher exclaims. "It's the Mad Hatter." He pauses. "Oh my goodness, just look at her." He places his right hand over his heart and takes a deep breath. The boy is clearly smitten. It's Alice herself sitting frozen in the centermost position of the long bench. Her expression is pert and lively. She's wearing her signature costume: blue dress, white pinafore, black headband with bow atop her long blonde hair. You think she looks incredibly lifelike. To her right sits another rabbit, this one bucktoothed and decked out in an auburn tailcoat and gleaming gold silk bow tie.

"Christopher, I forget that one's name," you say, pointing to the brown rabbit.

"The delirious one?" he asks. "That's the March Hare. Oh look, beside him, the whisps of smoke rising. Nice touch, Uncle Artie!"

Christopher has drawn your attention to a large cyan caterpillar holding a tube connected to a large hookah. Its expression is languid. "That caterpillar looks stoned," you observe.

"You would be too," Christopher replies with a cuckoo face, "if your life only required lounging around smoking a hookah." He then adds, seriously, "The creators of all this got every detail. I'm truly gobsmacked. And I don't use that term often or lightly."

Next to the wormlike creature sits a very large and imposing woman in a white gown patterned with red hearts. She's wearing a gold crown and holding a long, black-stemmed scepter topped with an enameled red pommel. Her expression is fearsome. Pointing at her, you say, "So, if memory serves, that's one of the meanies."

"Indeed," Christopher replies. "She's an angry old tyrant, that Queen of Hearts."

It's enchanting all right, but you don't get this—any of it. You point to the elaborate set, saying, "All these characters just frozen there? Is something supposed to happen? Another Uncle Artie spectacle? Are we now supposed to say or do something?"

The boy merely shrugs, so you continue, "Christopher, I thought the game was over. Thought we'd solved every puzzle. Got the will and the deed. United the household. Didn't we just witness Uncle in the sky bidding one and all a fond farewell?"

"I haven't a clue what's supposed to happen here," Christopher replies. "Be smashing, though, if they'd all come to life."

Which is exactly what happens next—the scene bursts to life. From the looks of things, it's a tea party in full swing. The gathering is loud and raucous, with heads bobbing back and forth, arms flailing up and down, everybody jabbering at once, not a single word intelligible. You follow Christopher as he moves forward to try and interact with the characters. "Hullo, I'm Christopher," he attempts to introduce himself, "and you are . . ."

"I'm late, I'm late! For a very important date," cries the White Rabbit, consulting his oversized pocket watch. "No time to say hello, goodbye. I'm late. I'm late. I'm late!" With that, his image freezes.

You point to the twins. "Who are those two? I forget their names."

Christopher nods, indicating he knows. "Tweedledum and Tweedledee." He gestures to them, hoping they'll say something.

They do, in unison. "How do ya do! State your name and business."

"I'm Christopher," he says to the pair. "And standing beside me is the new lord of this manor. So mind your manners!" he informs them with mock sternness.

"That's manners!" cry the twins, after which they, too, freeze in place.

"This is a crazy place!" you call out. "Just like Alice described it in the book. Now I remember."

Your outburst prompts the Cheshire cat to widen its grin and state, "I am not crazy; my reality is just different from yours."

To which you quickly reply, "Mr. Cat, you've no idea of how crazy *my* reality is at this point." No answer, just that plastered grin.

Christopher turns to the Mad Hatter. "So what's the occasion here?"

With great fanfare he replies, "We're having an unbirthday party."

To which the March Hare leans over and calls out, "They don't know what an unbirthday is."

Christopher turns to him, saying, "Oh, but we do. As your story says, it's a celebration for everyone who's not celebrating a birthday this day. Mine's not today. And neither is his. So are we not invited?" But once again, both characters simply freeze.

Seeing the caterpillar exhaling smoke, you wonder if there are any olfactory accents present and decide to "sniff" it out. As you draw closer, the creature removes the tube from its mouth and loudly demands, "Who are you? Explain yourself!"

Good question. You wish you knew. Not getting any answer, the caterpillar puts the tube back in his mouth, inhales deeply for a long moment, then releases a plume of smoke that smells oddly like undercooked brownies.

Christopher grins, dazzled. "A hologram with a scent!" he exclaims. "Only Uncle could dream that up!"

In a sleepy tone, the caterpillar nods toward the red cap and says, "One side will make you grow taller, and the other side will make you grow shorter." He freezes, but amazingly, smoke from the hookah still lingers.

"Christopher, are there mushrooms like these around the manor?"

He nods in affirmation. "The fly agaric? Oh my, yes, they are at times all over the grounds. Grampy said they are hallucinogenic but extremely poisonous and I shouldn't sample them."

"Did he ever?" you ask.

Christopher's sure he did. "Grampy said he had some procedure for detoxifying them. I know he intended to show me, but . . ." His voice saddens, then trails off.

"What's the caterpillar supposed to be smoking?" you inquire. "I couldn't place it. But it didn't smell at all like tobacco, weed, or hash."

Christopher raises an eyebrow and teases, "Oh, you're an authority on those scents?"

Smirking, you reply, "In my youth, I attended a few concerts. But seriously, Christopher, any idea?"

The boy sniffs and studies the hookah intently as recognition slowly dawns on his face. He explains that the creators of the attraction are simulating burning opium, an inference he believes they took from Alice's tale. Here on the estate, he says, in addition to psychotropic mushrooms and peyote cactus, opium poppies grow on the grounds and in nearby forests.

"Red poppies. Red mushrooms. Whew, what did your grandfather have to say about the poppies?"

"That one should only take them if one is in severe pain from injury or illness," Christopher replies. "He forbade me."

Your exchange is cut off by cries of rage from the end of the table. The Queen of Hearts is bellowing, "Off with their heads! Off with their heads!"

At last, Alice herself speaks. "Nonsense!" she calls to the queen in a commanding tone, silencing the fuming monarch. Then, to the two of you, she announces, "Wait, I'm coming to welcome you."

Now it's your turn to freeze. Astonishingly, Alice actually rises from the bench, walks to the edge of the table, turns, and approaches. Gradually it dawns on you: This is no hologram or CGI creation. This is a live human being, in the flesh, walking up to Christopher with palms extended.

CHAPTER THIRTY-EIGHT

"Oh, hullo, Christopher. You're finally here! Won't you have some tea?" Alice, her blue eyes sparkling, has placed both her hands in his and is smiling ever so winsomely.

The boy nods and nods but momentarily cannot speak. Finally he manages to say, "Tea. Of course!"

Alice releases Christopher, turns to you, and curtseys. "Welcome, my lord. 'Tis an honor indeed." Motioning toward the tea table, she lowers her voice to a near whisper. "I do hope you're more agreeable than the king and queen of this place."

You're thoroughly charmed by this lively girl and whisper back, "Don't worry! I don't bite or behead." Christopher and Alice laugh with delight. You feel as though a magic spell has been cast over the scene, as well as a palpable spark of attraction between the two youths.

Alice returns to the bench and motions the two of you to sit facing her. "I've just finished my very first tea party, and now I shall commence with my second!" she announces. She picks up a remote and addresses her guests on both sides. "Thank you one and all so very much for coming this fine day. You'll be going now." She begins pressing buttons, and one by one, her cast of characters disappears. She retrieves two nearby teapots and places them in front of you and Christopher along with baskets containing the scones. "Don't worry, they did not consume any of these."

"Of course they didn't," you tell her. "They're holograms—that would be impossible!"

Alice is quick to correct. "In Wonderland, there are few impossible things."

You play along. "How do you get to Wonderland?"

Alice twitches her nose, then responds, quoting her own story, "Some say over the hill or under land or just behind the tree, but I say through the door with the golden key."

Finally, Christopher has regained his composure. "Alice," he says, "I loved your stories when I was younger. And I love this Wonderland re-creation."

She pauses thoughtfully, then asks, "But don't you find it rather odd?"

Christopher gestures toward the lab exit. "No," he says, "as we come from an even odder place."

Alice exclaims, "Really? What's in there? I've never been."

You can hardly believe your ears. Is she telling the truth or remaining in character while following some script? You strongly suspect the latter but decide to continue playing along. "Alice, is it true what the caterpillar said about those mushrooms—that they can make you taller or smaller?"

She's eager to explain. "Oh my, yes, one can grow and shrink here. What is big and small is determined by what potion you've currently ingested. You could very well have to make friends with insects if you found you were as small as one."

"And when you're ten feet tall," asks Christopher, "what's that like?"

Alice laughs. "Oh, in such a case, I can speak rudely to the queen, the duchess, the hatter, the hare, or whomever I please!"

Christopher opens his sketchbook and lays it on the tea table. "Would you like to see?" Alice nods eagerly as Christopher shows her his latest additions: the penguin trio wearing sunglasses, Mr. and Mrs. Magic Mushroom, Miss Wildflower, and Sir Peyote Button.

"Christopher," you say to him, "you told me you were going to sketch them, but I hadn't seen them until now. They're quite good. I see you're now doing them in color, too."

Alice rotates the pad so she can get a better look at the characters. Placing her elbows on the table, she cups her chin and studies them intently. "They're amazing!" she shouts. "You must think impossible things too!"

Christopher's face flushes bright red. He looks both embarrassed and ecstatic. Flustered, he glances around the table. "White roses? Aren't they supposed to be red?" he asks. "The queen insists on red, does she not?"

"Shhh," Alice whispers, motioning to the far end of the table.

"Okay," Christopher whispers back, "my lips are sealed." You place a hand over your lips to indicate yours are too. Alice continues to marvel at the sketches. She is particularly drawn to Miss Wildflower, who is depicted as a bright-yellow daffodil with a burnt-orange eye.

Alice looks up and says, "It's such a beautiful result. Yes, sometimes I do fancy becoming a flower."

Observes Christopher, "But you might have to grow in harsh conditions. Would you really be willing to withstand all that cold and rain?"

Alice's expression turns dreamy as she lowers her voice. "Yes, especially the rain. How could I appreciate the sunlight without having felt the rain? Or the sun itself without having felt the cold?"

Christopher leans in. "Alice, have you ever tasted wildflowers?"

Alice shakes her head no, seemingly surprised by the question. "Should I?"

"Well, it's up to you," he says. "But flowers and other plants have much to teach."

Alice's voice trembles with excitement. "Do they now? Can you recite one of their lessons?"

Christopher nods, explaining, "They tell you what the bees in the bushes are buzzing on, what the birds in the trees are chirping about, and what the beasts in the forest have to say. They also teach you how to relive a past time or glimpse a future time."

"Aha!" Alice cries. "At my first tea party, that Mad Hatter said to me, 'I daresay you've never even spoke to Time.' Can plants teach me that trick?"

Christopher smiles warmly at her. "If you like, Alice," he assures her. "They certainly can."

Alice claps her hands gleefully. "Oh jolly, how much I have learnt at only my second tea party!" she shouts. "Curiouser and curiouser!"

Ah yes, you know that quote well. You think their sentiments are sweet to be sure. But these two sound like they're reciting lines, not conversing naturally. Notwithstanding, Christopher's unbridled attraction to the girl and hers to him is, you're certain, completely authentic. Alice is now staring at her pocket watch. She gets up and starts putting the teapots away.

Startled, Christopher says, "Oh! Is the party over?"

"It's been over for a long time. I'll be going now." She begins to walk away.

Christopher jumps up. "Wait! Where are you going?"

Replies Alice coyly, "Nowhere, of course." Their silent gazes lock for a long moment. Suddenly they both burst out laughing as if they have completed a private joke.

"Nowhere is one of my favorite places!" Christopher enthuses. "But today I must go somewhere. Trust me, I'd much prefer to go nowhere with you, but we have our own party to get back to. And, regrettably, it's not nowhere. It's somewhere."

Alice looks enthralled, asking, "Another tea party? How wondrous!"

Christopher shakes his head. "No, Alice, nothing like that. But won't you come along and see somewhere for yourself?"

Alice steps forward, offering Christopher her hand. "I'm curious to see where somewhere is and what a party without tea looks like. Yes! I'll join you. Are we going to play or be in one?"

Christopher looks as if he may soon burst with joy. "I'm not sure, but Alice, you're going to love my new dog! His name is Artie!"

"Won't you come too, my lord?" Alice turns and asks politely.

"Oh, no thank you, Alice. I have many impossible thoughts I must now recollect," you say, trying, just for the fun of it, to sound like her. "But I'll see you both out." The three of you pass through the living room and out into the hallway. The place looks deserted. You stroll to the lobby and bid them farewell, musing on how great this is for Christopher, to have a new friend his age, and with so much, it seems, in common. You have a feeling those two are really going to click. Seeing them reach the exit doors, still holding hands, makes you smile.

One thing—well, apart from the enigma of your forgotten name—bothers you: you're now certain that Alice was scripted. Both of them, actually. It seems as though Christopher's in on something here that for some unknown reason you're not.

You glance across the room and find the intervening wall has been restored. Wonderland is no more. Also, a package has been delivered while you were away. Inside, there's a letter affixed to a brand-new copy of *Burton's Peerage and Baronetage*. You open the letter and begin reading.

My beloved colleague,

My name is not Arthur Hanover, and what I am about to tell you may come as rather a shock. I am not a member of the nobility, nor are you. Most importantly, you are not named in my will as the inheritor of my estate, title, and wealth, because none of these things exist. There is no ancestral home of mine. No new life awaits you there.

In order to secure a full explanation, however, there are some documents that you must read and absorb, stories you must listen to, and others you must meet.

Why not a full disclosure as quickly as possible? You may be in such a state of utter confusion at this moment that I would not be surprised if you demanded it and then desired to leave as quickly as possible.

But please allow me to reveal this in my own time and at my own pace. We have important work to accomplish. What awaits you besides full remembrance is this: a complete explanation of your relationship to me and, most importantly, your relationship to you. Curiosity, I am certain, is what propels gifted people like you through time.

Finally, as a reassurance that I am not who I once said, I've included a copy of Burton's Peerage.

Yours faithfully,
Stuart Arthur, a.k.a. "Arthur Hanover"

You remove the shrink wrapping from the book and thumb through the familiar volume. There is no entry for Arthur Reynold Hanover.

My God, Storyteller, have I lost my mind? From above, a dapper-looking young man replies, ***Well, yes, but you've known that for some time, right?*** *Very funny.* ***Sorry, couldn't resist. But don't fret, your story is coming to the really good parts.***

Now sounds a familiar ping you haven't heard for days—your cell phone! "Hello, world! Yes!" you shout before scanning the text you've just received. "Please make your way to the laboratory. All will be revealed."

You reach up under the mantel to rotate the fireplace and then make your way into the pitch-dark laboratory. Searching for a light switch, you're comforted by the familiar click-click of the units revolving and closing behind you. For the moment, you feel safe. But now, in a far corner, a computer monitor switches on, and you see the silhouette of someone seated in front of it. "Don't be alarmed," a voice calls to you. "Please, over here, if you don't mind. Take a seat beside me." The voice is soothing. "Everything is going to be fine, I assure you."

You make your way over. The aisle is narrow; you have to maneuver carefully to avoid bumping into all the worktables and chairs. An elderly man is seated with his back to you, staring at a document on-screen. His hand beckons you to take a chair near him. He swivels around slowly to face you.

A giant shock. An unbelievable sight. You gasp. Heart beating rapidly, you clutch your chest. It is not Rollinsby nor the chauffeur who called himself Stephen. Nor any real person you've met so far.

You're face-to-face with Arthur Hanover.

"Good evening," he says quietly. It's dark, but you can see the warmth in his eyes in the glow from the screen. He's dressed in his familiar ensemble of charcoal slacks, white shirt, ascot, and blue blazer. He's chuckling. *"Otsukari sama deshita."* You can't speak, shaking your head to indicate you do not understand. Lord Hanover quickly explains: "It's Japanese. Translates as 'you must be tired,' but think of it more as a standard acknowledgment among colleagues. 'Well, it's been a long day, but we finished our tasks.'" Lord Hanover rubs his hands. "How about a beer? I've got your favorite kind." He produces glasses and two bottles labeled YEBISU, clearly an Asian brand but of no significance to you. He pours and toasts, *"Kampai! Taihen otsukari sama deshita."*

An Asian-looking Storyteller speaking with an accent appears and translates: ***Cheers! You must be really tired.*** Lord Hanover continues speaking. "I know how little sleep you've had." You take a sip. It's very cold, especially smooth; it tastes great and somewhat familiar. "This place is secure. We shan't be disturbed," Hanover says.

You're aware that you've been with this person for several minutes yet haven't uttered a word. You're still shocked but reasonably comfortable. The beer hits the spot. For the moment, you'll go with the flow. Besides, what choice do you have? He hands you a printed sheet, obviously a recording script. From his own copy he reads excerpts.

[Act One—audio only; will synch to statue animation—Shakespearean, highly dramatic, theatrical]

"As my good fellow Puck would say, 'If we shadows have offended, think but this and all is mended.'"

[Act One—video and audio; film against blue screen—Shakespearean]

"My beloved child, at long last you have come. I am your uncle, Arthur Hanover."

The printout lists several more utterances from Lord Hanover you recall hearing throughout your stay. Then your companion issues another surprise: "My real name is Stuart Arthur, and I am a professional actor. My life has always been the theater. Lately, I mainly appear in yours."

You're numb. You should say something—but what? Finally, you manage to speak. "Should I ask questions? And what should I ask?"

This pleases Stuart. He hands you a business card. "Ask me about this."

Somehow, you're not surprised to see another imagine21 card. This one reads "Masa Ginza" and "untitled-1." Like the others, it is bilingual. The name means nothing to you. "Who is this?" you ask.

Stuart takes a deep breath. "You."

Hold on. Storyteller, I remember Farnsworth addressing me with that name just yesterday. ***A slip of the tongue perhaps?*** *What about the night I arrived when he burst into my bedroom calling me by that name?* ***Sorry, but we witnessed no such occurrence.***

Then Stuart chuckles. "It's one of several aliases. But 'Masa' is what all of us around here have always called you. I, myself, am untitled-2." He hands you one of his own cards.

"Why are they called 'untitled'?"

"In this company, we thumb our noses at job titles, especially pretentious ones," Stuart replies.

You're totally confused. "And my next question is . . . ?"

"Ask me if you really traveled to Stockholm"—Stuart chuckles—"to attend a Nobel ceremony on my behalf."

You've now gathered you didn't—along with not inheriting untold riches. You extend the green remote. "So how about this?"

Again Stuart laughs. "Only in *Star Trek* episodes, I'm afraid." He takes the remote and demonstrates that all it does is light up and issue a humming sound. "Nor did I crack the genetic code to manipulate my own DNA. But now, Masa, we need to discuss your game experiences while they're fresh. Afterward, you'll fully remember everything about your actual life."

Hearing this causes you to exclaim, "So the butler shooting at me a while back—was that part of this so-called theater you say you and I are starring in?"

Stuart winces. "Masa, nobody shot at you. If you think someone did, then you must have experienced some sort of hallucination. Perhaps resulting from sleep deprivation."

You're not buying this. "Stuart, can we check the video feeds for the lobby?"

He shakes his head no, replying, "Sorry, they're turned off after the game finishes—after everyone's outside."

Your agitation increases. "So, have I flipped my lid? I'm certain I was shot at. I could even smell the gunpowder."

Stuart leans forward, clasping your shoulders. "No, no. That could not have possibly happened. Listen, Masa, you are not mentally incapacitated. It's just that everything is, well, a bit 'in between' at the moment." He seems sincere.

You venture another guess. "So was all of this some kind of reality TV show?"

Stuart is quick to reply. "I daresay it was not. On reality TV, while they don't always know what might happen next, they are always cognizant of being participants in an entertainment spectacle. They always know it's not real." He pauses to take another sip. "This is much different indeed."

Yes, you see that. By now, you've gathered that the others—Christopher, Farnsworth, Van Scoy, the servants—are actors as well. "So can we talk about the others?" you ask.

"Certainly." Stuart seems pleased to be back on his timetable. "They're professional actors and contract employees of the manor or i-two-one." He spreads his palms. "Their characters are all your creations, my friend. You're their 'historian,' as you're fond of saying. By the way, from behind the scenes, it looked as though you were having quite a time in there."

"Absolutely," you tell him with high enthusiasm, "it was the most powerful, gratifying, 'life-changing experience' I've ever had. Great people, fabulous accommodations, extraordinary technology. The food was out of this world. Not to mention those pub meet-ups every night. And that outdoor sky spectacular awhile ago? I was thrilled beyond imagining."

Stuart smiles and says, "So glad to hear it—and you will be too."

"But Stuart, I must ask, what in the world was the purpose of the *Alice in Wonderland* spectacle Christopher and I saw just before you called me in here? It was weird and enjoyable, but we thought the game was over by then."

"It had no purpose in this particular trial," he states, "but we're planning to weave it into future scenarios. This time around, we wanted to check the mechanics, the effects, the Wonderland characters, the interaction between Christopher and Alice, and, of course, the protagonist's reaction to everything and your willingness to be drawn in. By the way, the boy and the girl were in separate script readings. They'd never met before in real life."

"So, same with the Nobel ceremony? Gotta admit, I bought into it for a while. Especially after seeing it on the news."

Stuart chuckles. "We're banking on the assumption that most players will be like you—forgetting, for example, that the Nobels are awarded in December!"

"I see, yeah, that was the last thing on my mind," you admit. "Well, it was all fantastic. The whole time I was there, I felt like my life had turned surreal."

And was even quite smitten for a spell! With three lovely ladies, no less. Right, Storyteller? ***Indeed, but several were surprised you never acted on your desires.***

"Now don't bridle that enthusiasm," Stuart counsels. "Believe me, you'll need it when you're back on the job having to cross swords with *les saboteurs*, Messrs. Kobayashi and Watanabe."

You tell Stuart you've heard that term before, pointing to the lab exit. "In there. So who are these guys? And why the nickname?"

"They are your fellow i21 board members," Stuart replies, "and, like you and I, active in the day-to-day running of the business. Kobayashi's director of sales; Watanabe, of marketing." Stuart sighs. "We don't get on with them, to put it mildly. Fortunately, we've always had the support of the chairman and the president."

Now you're even more confused. "What kind of business?"

"Our little 'life-changing' enterprise"—Stuart chuckles—"to employ your phrase." He explains that the manor is one of the world's cutting-edge entertainment venues for those with enough money, time, and the desire for psychic adventure. He points to your card. "Your 'untitled' title could actually read 'scenarist.'"

You sip more beer, not sure what to say. Finally you ask, "So, Artie, oh sorry, Stuart, what's actually going on here?"

"We've been testing *Manor House*," he replies. "It's a working title for a new live scenario game we're hoping to add to our playbill—it's already a big hit with the cast. My word, you even sprang a surprise dance party on them." He raises his glass as a toast. "Well done!"

You stand up to stretch, feeling the need to recapitulate. "So, Stuart, let me see if I've got this so far. A Japanese-owned company . . . based in England . . . offering futuristic psychic entertainment to rich people . . . and you and I are the creative force behind all this?"

Stuart holds up three fingers, replying, "Out of four, my friend." He claps his hands. "We're nowhere near the UK."

CHAPTER THIRTY-NINE

Japan? Storytellers, Stuart says we're in Japan! ***Not "we." You're in Japan. We're everywhere, my good fellow***, an elderly gentleman replies, then quickly disappears.

"But, Stuart," you protest, "I flew to London. A chauffeur met me at Heathrow. Drove for hours on the motorway. On the left."

Beyond saying, "Japan does as well," Stuart offers no explanation. He simply hands you a full-color brochure and excuses himself, again insisting that the two of you need to discuss the production in detail when he returns, in order to get all your impressions while they're fresh. "It's critically important," he says, "because when you fully 'return,' so to speak, you won't remember that you played."

A serious-looking, bespeckled Storyteller appears. He speaks with an American accent. ***The authentic you may not remember us, either. But we're not sure about that. Just have to wait and see.***

The brochure runs twenty or so pages in eight languages. It describes a mammoth theme park and resort called Camelot, located in an area called Nagano, near a town called Shirakawa, in Fukushima prefecture, a three-hour drive northwest from Tokyo. Thumbing through, you find that Camelot is a re-creation of an English country estate and adjoining township. In effect, it's an Anglo equivalent of Disneyland's Main Street, USA—a hodgepodge of period buildings and environments always in sparkling condition. Nearby bungalows offer luxurious guest accommodations. Guests can choose from a variety of outdoor activities—tennis, golf, croquet, horseback riding—in addition to dozens of theme attractions and rides scattered around the park.

There are gift shops, pubs, restaurants, tearooms, and coffee shops. The brochure invites you and your family to enjoy an unforgettable holiday totally immersed in an authentic British setting—in Japan.

At certain times of year, an insert reads, Camelot becomes "Hanover Manor," home to a variety of "scenarios" for individuals or groups. "Visit imagine21.jp for details," it urges.

Then you turn to the inside back cover and see that your eyes weren't deceiving you earlier. The surroundings are mountainous—dramatic, towering, snow-capped. The page is blanketed with photos of skiers flying down powdered slopes and listings of the tour packages that Camelot, Japan Railways, and Japan Tourist Bureau offer in winter.

Now Stuart is back. "The relationship is quite symbiotic," he says. "Camelot is owned by the same corporation that owns i21, so we're tasked with the challenge of developing special events for the park."

You recall that you were never told exactly where in the Lake District Hanover Manor was. How the newspaper was simply entitled *The Village Journal*. How the surrounding towns had crazy names. How the "storm" always prevented you from going out and about during your stay. "Stuart," you say, "Wi-Fi was never available, at least for me, and my cell phone never worked."

"Oh, everything works swimmingly up here," he replies. "We just made sure none of your devices did. It certainly wouldn't do for you to have contact with the outside world in this scenario."

Yes, you can see this. It makes sense. "So this *Manor House* scenario and the eccentric character of Lord Hanover were tailored to this place?"

"Precisely," Stuart replies. "Watch." Using a giant HDTV monitor, he divides the screen into twelve windows and streams separate videos into each of them. It is a phenomenal experience, seeing scenes from the past six days played back on a massive video wall and learning how you were secretly and expertly filmed—and fooled.

Stuart hands you a remote that enables any window to be individually controlled and its audio activated. You start to worry that there might be clips of those highly risqué encounters with Savannah, Adrienne, and Penelope, but, thankfully, none appear. Your newfound "colleague" takes detailed notes as you review scenes and recall your thoughts and feelings at key junctures.

Later, he lets you in on the Shakespeare trick. "An identical frame-frozen image first cloaks the statue as it is lowered underground, leaving the holographic Shakespeare to stand, stretch, recite, and reseat himself in the original position, after which the real statue is raised and the hologram shut off."

"Same with the lions?"

"Yes," Stuart replies. Then he explains Reggie's magic coat. "The doorman and the headwaiter were operating a hidden electromagnetic device that sent the buttons flying back and forth, after which a holographic fan projector rapidly switched the coats as Reggie stood perfectly still."

You ask about the circus extravaganza and the immersive art exhibit.

"All made here on workstations, modeled after live footage taken from circus highlight reels," Stuart explains. "In the case of the paintings," he says, "they were digitized, then special effects were applied so that flowers could sway gently in the breeze or sailboats could move ever so slightly in a harbor. But it's not always a circus or Impressionist paintings. There's a sizable collection we've licensed—musicals, sports, sci-fi, abstract art—that will depend on the player's tastes."

As you suspected, there was never a six-day storm, although the small amount of rain that fell on the first night did happen. Yes, they can simulate thunder and lightning convincingly. And, yes, they control everything from back here. Or, Stuart says, it's embedded in the virtual MH source code.

Stuart explains that the compressed clips you saw on the computer are for a device version of *Manor House*. "You were, in effect, testing both the live production and the digital game, with its artificial-intelligence framework."

"Doesn't the code have to be continually updated?" you ask.

"It does, and that's part of your role as software architect for the program," Stuart replies. "Plus, there's a team of remote developers who are constantly sending revisions round the clock."

"Okay, back to the live production—how will that work?"

Says Stuart, "For those willing to pay—and you might be surprised how many there are nowadays—we'll edit their adventure down to a feature-length film. Our subjects will become stars of their own movie." Intriguing. Already, you'd like to grab some popcorn and watch yours.

"Stuart, what's the story on the manor staff?"

"Them? Most are British expats with extensive stage experience like myself. A few, like Savannah, an American model you recruited in Roppongi, are your basic world-traveler types."

You're shocked. "I *know* her?"

Stuart nods. "Oh my goodness, yes—you two go back a very long way indeed, all the way back to when she went by Savoy Reddy, who, by the way, had parts in our early scenarios." Stuart pauses to recollect. "Savoy-then-Savannah, she's young, but an old hand around here—simply the best."

You think back on the chauffeur's persona and some ambiguous comments she made; somehow this revelation seems not so far-fetched. "Wait!" you exclaim, snapping your fingers in remembrance. "Savannah told me in the pub that she played on the men's soccer team back in college."

Stuart smiles, saying, "Indeed, Savoy was quite the striker, I'm told. Could occasionally blast them in from thirty meters out."

Gosh, Storyteller, will wonders ever cease in this place? ***Oh, believe me, they're just getting started with wonders***, says an American-accented female.

"Now, let's see . . ." Stuart resumes. "Ah yes, Farnsworth. Before he became an actor, James Farnsworth—his real name, by the way—really was a professional butler, a graduate of Ivor Spencer's, in fact." He sighs. "Unfortunately, in real life, he's in cahoots with *les saboteurs*." You'd like to pursue this, but Stuart's rattling on. He says that Noël is a real chef and quite a celebrity in Tokyo's posh gay restaurant and nightclub scene.

Now you're giggling. "So, is Noël Elle Léon his real name?"

Stuart shakes his head no, saying, "It's Stefan and he's French Canadian. He speaks native English, but as you've seen, he does broken English convincingly."

"He certainly does. Plus, he speaks fluent palindrome."

Stuart laughs. You can see he's happy that you're starting to relax more as you voice your next question: "What about that steamy scene with Farnsworth?"

Again, Stuart laughs. "Oh, we just staged that to spice up the drama, make you wonder." Well, it worked. You wondered a lot. You'd so hoped James and Noël had found true love!

"Let's see," Stuart continues, "regrettably, we're saying sayonara to 'Adrienne.' Her real name's Serena, and she's heading back to England to be married."

Whoa. Getting married in real life as well! Looks like you never had a shot with her—in or out of the game . . . Oh well.

But hearing this makes you decide to be a little more forthcoming. "Stuart, I have a small confession. The whole time I was in there, I had quite a crush on the concierge."

Stuart's expression registers complete surprise. "Oh? No one here had any inkling."

You decide to become even more forthcoming. "Seriously, Stuart, one night she came to my room, in a negligee no less. Like, was that a planned part of the scenario?"

Stuart looks genuinely shocked. "You must have imagined it."

Undeterred, you press on. "Then, the night before, Savannah showed up and barged in while I was soaking in the tub! Honest."

Again Stuart is incredulous. "Do you really think that happened as well? I can assure you it's not scripted in any fashion. And I cannot, for the life of me, imagine either of them doing it on their own. And had they done so, their comings and goings would have been caught by our cameras."

Storyteller, you saw them, right? ***We did not. On either occasion as we've said before.***

Come to think of it, when you knocked on Adrienne's door afterward, she acted like she didn't know what you were talking about.

"Stuart, then what about another scene where Penelope auditioned for maître d' at Thomas's fantasy restaurant? A completely transformed Penelope, I might add. Her dress was skintight and see-through."

Again, Stuart shakes his head. "No idea about that, either. Sorry, it's not part of our production guide. Nor something we would ever do in any case. Again, nothing of the sort was picked up by our cameras."

Storytellers, help me out here. ***Possibly you experienced powerful illusions involving those women, which, unfortunately, we are not able to witness ourselves.***

Stuart resumes his rundown on the cast. "And there's Bruce Sherlock, actually Barry Sherwood, who's one of your close friends. You said we should cast him because 'nobody parties like Sherwood.'" You smile, recalling the ever-exuberant barkeep. Stuart goes on to explain that "Reg and Millie" are professional actors, married in real life, who, along with the actors who played Thomas and Penelope, were referred by a troupe called Tokyo on Stage, which is where i21 gets most of its talent. "That reminds me," he says, "Malcolm is positively dying to see you."

"Who's Malcolm, and why's he dying to see me?"

"Our director and chief talent scout," Stuart informs. He says that Malcolm's head of Tokyo on Stage and untitled-3 in the company. He also does TV and movie bit parts—whenever those samurai dramas call for a Western missionary or a seaman, that sort of role. "Malcolm will also want your impressions while they're fresh."

The director needn't worry. As far as you're concerned, all the performers were completely convincing. That reminds you—"Stuart, you forgot Christopher."

"Oh, him. That's Timothy Lovett. Lad's nineteen, just looks younger, and really did attend boarding school in France. We like to draw on real backgrounds wherever possible."

Again, you're stunned. "He's an incredible talent. I really thought he was fourteen or thereabouts . . . Oh, and how about Alice?"

"Yes, indeed," says Stuart. "She's seventeen. Real name's Alicia. Attends the British School in Tokyo. Her father's a diplomat, and her mum's with the British Council. We're well connected in the expatriate community."

"So, 'Uncle Artie,' what's my next question?"

"Ask me about the history of i-two-one, or allow some of your closest colleagues to come in and say hello." You opt for the latter. Stuart reaches inside his blazer pocket and pulls out a walkie-talkie. Suddenly he's speaking rapid-fire Japanese: *"Moshi-moshi . . . Ah! Rei-chan, Ima modotta . . . Hai, so desu . . . Geimu-wa owatta . . . Genki mitai . . . Chigaimasu, mada, demo daijobu . . . Malcolm-san iru? . . . Mada . . . Hai, wakarimashita . . . Ja mata."*

After he hangs up, you tell him, "I don't speak Japanese, but didn't you just tell someone named Rei-chan that I'm here and seem to be fine and the scenario's finished, plus you found out that Malcolm's not arrived yet?" Stuart confirms you got it all.

Thank you, Storyteller. ***Delighted to be of service.***

At the rear of the laboratory, a light flicks on. You hear chirping sounds that could be birds approaching—feminine Japanese speech, actually, very high pitched and melodious.

When they come into view, you're stunned. It's the mushroom serum trio! "Hi, Masa," one of them calls to you.

"Masa-san genki?" greets another.

"Konban-wa, Ma-chan," sings the third. The young women look joyous, as if they've just been reunited with a family member. But they're also nervous, constantly giggling among themselves while raising their palms to shield their mouths.

One of them shyly ventures, "Masa-san, don't you remember us?"

Sure you do. "I remember meeting you in New York and seeing you in London and here on TV a lot."

"Oh, it was so fun," says the one you remember as Megumi. The ladies have brought an assortment of Japanese snacks, which they set down on a table while you regard their graceful movements with admiration. They're all short, slender, with long, silky black hair, and smartly dressed in business attire. Not the ultra-casual getup you normally associate with techies.

"Hai, o-sembei, dozo," one of them invites you. Then, with radiant smiles and elegant bows, they depart, chattering excitedly. *"Sugoi! . . . Ah yokataz . . . genki so . . . anshin-shimashita!"*

"Stuart, they're yakking about how happy they arc, how good I look, how they're so relieved." You note that a Storyteller is now not always needed to translate. You're starting to get it all on your own. A good sign?

Stuart nods and pours more beer, saying he'll give you an abridged history of the company while you two wait for Malcolm. "To begin with," he says, "you work closely with those—"

"Yes," you interrupt, "I heard about them from Farnsworth and Adrienne in the scenario. Only I didn't know I actually worked with them, obviously. But, Stuart, those Fountain of Youth commercials—what did that have to do with anything?"

"Oh, aside from antiaging potions being a subject near and dear to you," Stuart replies, "Namiko, Reiko, and Megumi, especially Megumi, just wanted to somehow be in this. They pestered Malcolm incessantly. Finally, he created those skin-care adverts, possibly because they look and act so youthful. We really haven't figured out if and how we'd actually use them in a real production. But since this was a trial run, you wanted us to experiment with all sorts of added characters, devices, scenes, and plot twists."

"I see," you tell him, as you think you're starting to grasp more of this production. Stuart picks up a remote and replays some of their ads. The girls really do seem to enjoy singing and jumping around. You hadn't noticed when you were in the game, but now you find the lyrics to their ad jingles to be somewhat hilarious: "Oh joy, sweetie pie me / Forever young with mushy cream I'll be."

"Stuart, that reminds me. Can you explain TVTV?"

Stuart replays the soccer match clip. "Oh, that and the newspaper were utilized to embed clues, provide comic relief, and flesh out the servants by disclosing parts of their private lives away from work. By the way, did you notice that the anchors—"

"Michael and Meredith?" you interrupt. "I thought they were quite good and very professional. Always looked forward to the newscasts. Especially the Crunch stories."

Stuart shakes his head. "No, Masa, what I meant was, did you notice that no matter the hour, those two were always on the air?"

You're floored. Somehow that clear anomaly never registered. "Wow, 24/7 news with 24/7 newscasters! I completely missed it. How come you did that?"

"Budgetary considerations largely," Stuart replies. "Since this was a trial, you wanted to save some yen wherever possible. But now we'll have to ask Malcolm to find more anchors or possibly create some AI holographic ones . . . Oh, and by the way, several additional Crunch installments were filmed but did not make it out of postproduction in time for your trial. Would you like to see one now?"

"Oh, absolutely! Could not get enough of that saga!" Besides, you could use a break.

CHAPTER FORTY

YODELING CRUNCH RETURNS TO ORIGINAL OWNER

Michael leads with: "Crunch, the recently dognaped rottweiler, who chose to remain with his abductors after a lengthy court proceeding that gripped the tri-county area, has evidently had another change of heart. The ten-year-old, half-blind, three-legged pooch turned up early this morning at the residence of his original owner in Flogway Down. Our correspondent, Mark Stephen, is there with Nigel Wanton. Mark, this is a stunning development. What have you learned?"

"Please pause it," you call out. "The correspondent! That's my chauffeur Stephen and Lord Rollinsby."

"Indeed," says Stuart. "Stephen is quite versatile." You laugh and motion him to resume.

The clip cuts live to Wanton, standing alongside Crunch, who is resting on his haunches, his face nestled against his former owner's waist. Both wear blissful expressions. Mark asks, "Nigel, what in the world happened?"

He extends his mike to Wanton, who recounts his startling wake-up call. "About four a.m., I heard loud scratching at the door. As I approached, I could hear yodeling."

"Yodeling!" exclaims Mark. "I didn't know dogs yodeled."

"Crunch does, but only when stricken with sadness or palpitating with extreme joy. This morning, as I opened the door, Crunch's remaining eye was welled up. As presently were mine." Wanton then leans down to rub behind Crunch's ears, which causes the rottie to rise up and wag his tail nonstop while slobbering all over his former master's face. Then suddenly, the dog jerks his head and yodels, "Ay-ee-oooo," several times in rapid succession.

Meredith now appears in a small window superimposed on the scene. She wipes a small tear from her eye. "This is quite touching. But since Nigel Wanton is no longer the dog's legal owner, one wonders how Tug and Timothy Skaddle, who were recently awarded custody, will react to this homecoming of sorts."

In the scene, the camera whirls to show a police car pulling up in Wanton's driveway. "Meredith," Mark says excitedly, "you may soon have your answer. I think we have actual, live breaking news here."

From the car, two uniformed constables emerge. They stride quickly up to Wanton and hand him a printed document. One constable says, "Mr. Wanton, we're here to retrieve this pooch and return it to its rightful owners."

"Oh, officers, please don't," Wanton pleads. "I don't think either of us can bear another separation."

"Sorry," the constable says, "we're only attending to duties. We're not keen ourselves on having to do this."

His partner steps forward with a leash, and Crunch emits a low growl, as if daring the deputy to take one more step. Which, foolishly, he does. A riotous scene unfolds. Crunch chases the deputy round and round in mad circles, barking and snapping at his trousers, as if trying to yank them down. Somehow, the officer manages to jerk open a backseat passenger door and dive inside to safety. The other officer is frozen in place.

Crunch slowly walks toward him before coming to a silent halt about ten meters in front of the deputy. The camera switches back and forth between their faces—the dog's with bared teeth and the deputy's fear-stricken countenance. Suddenly, the opening bars of *The Good, the Bad and the Ugly* begin to play.

"What the—" you exclaim.

Stuart pauses the playback. "Oh drat! Wrong version. Sorry."

"Well, Stuart," you tell him, "it fit perfectly, but this story was supposed to be live and breaking."

Stuart nods, explaining, "Indeed, our rambunctious sound engineer, Megumi, sometimes gets carried away in postproduction and does her own thing, not fully understanding the requirements of the scene, or in this case, the constraints. But sometimes she does come up with audio effects that I daresay nobody else in the universe would have dreamt of . . . Let me see if I can find the correct clip, the one we'll use."

"That's okay," you tell him. "Let's just finish this one. Actually, I love that theme music." The clip resumes with a prolonged stare down between Crunch and the constable scored by Ennio Morricone. Finally, the deputy raises both hands, as if surrendering at gunpoint, and backsteps slowly toward his vehicle. Crunch emits a sustained low-toned growl as he lets him go.

As the constables drive away, Michael appears in the screen window. "Well, that certainly was one of the most dramatic scenes we've covered live. We'll be right back after adverts. Mark, stay with us." The reporter gestures with a salute that he's standing by.

Stuart pauses the video. "We haven't yet decided where in the scenario to place these episodes, but I'm highly encouraged that you enjoy them so much. The authentic you will surely like them too," he surmises, "since he wrote them."

The "authentic" me. Sheesh! Wonder what he's like. Any idea, Storyteller? ***A hail fellow well met, perhaps?*** *Seriously, do you know the other me?* ***Not at all. The other you lacks bicameral endowments. We can't connect.*** *But when I return—wake up, snap out of it, whatever it's called—do you stay with me?* ***Good question. We'll just have to wait and see.***

"By the way," you ask Stuart, "how did I get my nickname? To me, it sounds so weird."

"Oh, your moniker, 'Masa Ginza.' You adopted it because it always makes the people you meet over here laugh."

"What's so funny about 'Masa Ginza'?"

Stuart grins, relishing this. He wants you to picture this in a Western context. "Say you're a businessperson visiting a fancy corporation for the first time," he explains. "You hand over your name card without comment. It's on heavy stock with a smartly designed logo and creative typography. But the name card identifies you as, say, 'Joe Las Vegas' and lists your title as 'Con Artist.'"

"Risky in a business setting," you counter. "But, yeah, definitely kooky."

"Well," he explains, "that would be the rough equivalent of springing 'Masa Ginza, untitled-1' on Japanese people."

"I pull stunts like that?"

"All the time." He laughs, then elaborates, "If Japanese businesspeople get a card before meeting you in person, then it's even better. At first glance, they're confused. You could be male or female—for the name can conjure up a goofball yakuza or a glitzy *mama-san*."

"Really, Stuart, *really*?"

"Oh my, yes," he gushes. "And to have no official title in a *kabushiki geisha*, a registered Japanese corporation? Unfathomable in this culture. And you must understand that a *meishi* is considered as almost a sacred relic by Japanese."

"Oh I do understand. When I first met the mushroom trio and they gave me their cards, the ritual seemed so familiar. But I couldn't remember why."

Stuart continues. "Then eventually, you stroll in, quite obviously a Westerner and everyone gets it and laughs—especially younger, hipper tech execs."

"All right, then," you ask, "what about these other directors, these guys you say we quarrel with? And what's with Farnsworth?"

Stuart grimaces. "Right, the infamous *saboteurs*, Kobayashi and Watanabe. Yes, they are quite our nemeses." He proceeds to fill you in by relating how after i-two-one was reorganized as a Japanese corporation and started to develop scenarios, the chairman forcibly transferred the two Japanese over from Camelot corporate to allow you more time to create, unencumbered by sales-marketing responsibilities.

"I gather it didn't work so well," you venture.

"That's an understatement," Stuart replies. He explains that *les saboteurs* despise scenarios and the presence of foreigners in upper management. They want Camelot to remain the traditional British theme park it always was.

"And Farnsworth?" you ask.

Stuart scowls, then replies, "James is an entirely different story." He says the butler was with Camelot from the very beginning and was always in charge of entertainment.

"So, Stuart," you surmise, "I take it what we're now doing came as rather a shock."

"Indeed," he replies. "When the chairman announced he was going to invest heavily in psychic entertainment, Farnsworth assumed he was the heir apparent to the top job. But then, from out of the blue, the chairman brought you in, which substantially reduced his role."

"He got demoted."

"Yes, he's no longer head of our little family here. You are."

"Highly ironic, Stuart," you observe, "considering my just-completed contest with the butler in the game."

"Ironic, yes, but here, in real life—unpredictable. Deep down, James is seething. We can all see that."

"Do you consider him potentially dangerous? I mean, should I?"

Stuart takes a long pause, then says, "Masa, I honestly don't know how far he'd go."

"Still think he shot at me earlier." You remain steadfast in that belief.

Stuart's expression seems troubled, as if he's now considering that a potentially lethal altercation with Farnsworth may have actually happened. "Masa, I don't know what to tell you. Maybe he—"

His cell phone rings. He glances at the caller ID and mutters, "Speak of the devil" as he clicks to answer.

Farnsworth speaks in hushed tones, "Stuart, can you talk now?"

Stuart motions for you to shush and puts the phone on speaker. "Yes, James, what is it?"

"Is he any better? I mean, has he come to, come back, whatever you term it?"

"No, there's been no change."

"Is there any way I can join in and assist?"

"James, you know full well that we do not allow actors from the live scenario to be present when we're helping the player return to their normal state."

"Yes, I know, but if there's anything . . . I'm so concerned."

Stuart grimaces. "Yes, James, you are. I'll let you know as soon as there's any signs of progress. Good night." Stuart clicks off and asks no one in particular, "Have you ever heard such an outpouring of insincerity?"

Storyteller, where is Farnsworth now? ***In the underground passageway.*** *Is he alone?* ***No, he's with two Japanese colleagues.*** *The bad guys?* ***I'm afraid so.***

"Okay, then," you ask, "what's the specific problem with these Japanese guys?"

Stuart's expression turns cold. "Nary a thing," he says, "beyond their deliberately setting out to wreck this production. Ruthless blokes who will absolutely stop at nothing." He finishes his beer. You reflexively refill his glass. "Like this latest scenario," he continues, "you're going to have a bruising battle royale getting final approval, no matter how well you think—we all think—it went."

"Why?" You're perplexed.

"Well, as I've stated," Stuart tries to explain, "those two are dead set against all modern scenarios. But the chairman has forced them to work with us."

"So what do they want?" you ask.

Stuart says they just want to stick with the tried and true. As does Farnsworth. They don't want to stray from the market-proven productions—like Agatha Christie mysteries inside the manor, *Downton Abbey* knockoffs, Sherlock Holmes mystery theater, quests for the Holy Grail on the grounds, that sort of thing. "Adaptations, not originals. Short time frames, not extended ones."

"Previous productions here?" you ask.

"Yes," Stuart replies. "The precursors of scenarios. Doubtless they'll report to the chairman that this new trial was all flop and fiasco."

"It certainly was not!" you shout indignantly. "What can we do?" All you know is that you loved it—even if it was only a brief fantasy life. You bet other players will too.

Storyteller, should I tell them everything about my time in there? A trio of countenances appear. ***You mean your connection to us?*** one of them asks. *Yes. Should I?* ***We think it would serve no useful purpose at this juncture***, says another. *Okay. I'll hold off. But might he already know?* ***He has no idea. None of them do. Your game identity was preprogrammed, but your connection to us was completely unforeseen***, says the third.

Stuart reaches into his briefcase, pulls out his tablet, and hands it to you. "Had a reviewer in. Afraid it's not one hundred percent glowing as we'd have preferred, but the chap was decent enough to email an advance copy. Heard Kobayashi and Watanabe got hold of it too. They're probably gleefully translating it for the chairman as we speak, while cutting out the positive bits."

The letterhead says INNER SPACE with an Amsterdam URL. "I think he said he was going to vid blog it as well," says Stuart. "Let me check if it's up." You hand him back his tablet.

After a moment, he finds that it's posted. On-screen, a very young, red-haired Dutchman is offering his take. "A fourteen-year-old who freely quotes Samuel Beckett and expounds on Jungian synchronicity and plant intelligence? C'mon, i-two-one scenarists, give us a break here. Very few, if any, central characters are going to buy this kid."

"What are you talking about?" you shout to the screen. "I totally bought this kid."

His review is mixed, praising some aspects of *Manor House* while panning others. He concludes with, "While the performances and special effects kick the central character's overall experience to the level of a decent theme-park production, the addition of several mind-numbing puzzles, on the order of CD-game-era predecessors *Myst* and *Riven*, may keep *Manor House* from being the compelling mystery it really should be."

You again voice strong disagreement. "No, Stuart, the balance between what I was told and what I had to figure out was about right, I think. Besides, all that puzzle-solving with Christopher was fun and gratifying."

"Glad to hear this," says Stuart. "The puzzles were everybody's—especially yours—key concern when you wrote the scenario and is what, in this critical debriefing, you the playwright particularly want to learn from you the player." But Stuart does concur with the reviewer's first gripe. "I do think we should either tone down the boy intellectually or script the character older."

You're not sure. "Maybe," you reply. "But at most times, Christopher, although admittedly very bright, still seemed credibly boyish to me."

Stuart's walkie-talkie rings. *"Moshi-moshi, Reiko-san desu-ka? . . . Malcolm-san kimasuka? . . . Hai, onegaishimasu."*

Stuart waits a moment for Malcolm to come on the line. "Hi, Malcolm. Yes, I think we're ready for you . . . Masa seems fine . . . No, not yet . . . Right, we're back by the workstations . . . Oh, and bring a glass. Cheers."

A moment later, Malcolm appears. This time it's no big surprise as you greet him with, "Malcolm! I just saw you earlier, down in the square interviewing villagers!"

CHAPTER FORTY-ONE

Malcolm smiles and says, "Indeed, sometimes I cast myself in a bit part or two, just to keep a hand in." Now that you see him in person without rain gear, Malcolm Dupont looks to be in his early forties. Tall, blond, and ruggedly handsome, he seems well suited for those Westerner roles in Japanese films. He shakes your hand vigorously along with a few solid pats on the back. "Marvelous performance, absolutely splendid. Thought everyone—everything—was brilliant."

Stuart pours him a beer, asking, "Think we have a winner? Seriously?"

Malcolm drains his glass. "I do," he says, holding it out for a refill. "I most sincerely do." Then, pointing to the tablet illuminating the Dutch reviewer's comments, he says, "Despite that."

Malcolm summarizes his impressions. "First, Three Families went better than I could have imagined. Second, Masa, your not asserting yourself early on and demanding to be told exactly what was going on was a mild surprise."

"For most of the time," you interject, "I felt cool and collected in there. Like I should just go with the flow. Like I'm doing in here since it's all so surreal."

Malcolm nods understandingly, then continues: "Third, your not being overtly smitten with any of the characters was also a little surprising."

"Well, Malcolm, you're wrong on that count," you tell him. "I just never got up the nerve to make a genuine move."

Don't say we didn't try, cry familiar teenage voices. *Yes, you youngsters were quite persistent in that regard.* ***Oh, you oldsters were so no fun!***

"Malcolm," Stuart interjects, "Masa disclosed earlier that he was infatuated with Serena's character from the get-go, even though she was plotting against him."

"Intriguing," says Malcolm. "Van Scoy as femme fatale. We'll definitely want to discuss this possibility with you when you return." He has more on the romance aspect. Though their roles have been fully conceived, they've yet to cast any of the Roland and Cynthia Rollinsby tandems.

You're intrigued. "How will that work?"

Replies Malcolm, "An ensemble will be utilized for those parts. Which pair is selected for a particular performance will depend largely on the central character's age."

"But regardless," adds Stuart, "the Rollinsby pair is always attractive and available. They show up late on day two, braving the storm to assist you. One or the other will act openly infatuated almost at first sight. Which one will depend, naturally, on the player's identity and orientation."

"If romance happens, how far do we let it go?" you ask.

Of that prospect, Stuart stresses caution. "Up to now, we've been strictly G-rated. And I think we should remain that way. The Rollinsby characters should be instructed to keep their mutual focus on helping the player solve the mysteries at hand."

"But if there are genuine mutual sparks," Malcolm says, "some scenarios could get pretty steamy." Recalling yours, you smile inwardly. *"Les saboteurs,"* he adds ruefully, "if they had their way, no doubt there'd be call girls galore and plenty of corpses scattered about."

"Well, gentlemen," you tell them, "I'm not going to worry about people I've never even met. I've got more important things on my mind—like its whereabouts."

"We'll get to that soon. I promise," says Stuart, his eyes filled with merriment.

Malcolm's phone pings. After scanning a message, he says, "Reiko's just texted that she's got the next Crunch uploaded if we'd like to see."

"Of course!" you answer, swiveling your chair toward the monitor.

"ATTACK DOG" LITIGATOR TAKES UP CRUNCH CUSTODY CASE

Michael is listening through his earpiece. The scene at Wanton's farm is still being broadcast live. Michael looks into the camera and says, "Our reporter on the scene says there are new developments."

Mark steps forward and reports, "Michael, there are. We've just received word that an important visitor from London will soon be arriving at Flogway Down, and with that, more news may be breaking."

The camera whirls to find a stately, chauffeur-driven Rolls-Royce pulling into the driveway. A serious-looking woman in black professional attire gets out. She strolls up to the befuddled farmer, handing him a business card and announcing, "Mr. Wanton. My name is Jamie Prance. I'm a solicitor. My view is that you'll soon be needing representation. May we go inside and confer in private?"

Wanton is speechless, but Crunch is smiling, panting, and wagging his tail, signaling strong approval of the woman. The farmer, looking confused but hopeful, turns to the reporter and says, "I'm sorry, but if you'll excuse us," as he beckons the solicitor and Crunch indoors.

"Of course," Mark replies, "and best of luck to you, sir." With that, he signals his report is over.

The shot returns to the news desk where the countenances of Wanton and Crunch, James and Jamie Prance, Tug and Timothy Skaddle fill the backdrop. Meredith speaks to the camera:

"As those following this story undoubtedly know, the Skaddle brothers, who are currently the legal owners of Crunch, are represented by James Prance, a local barrister who also represents the Runaway Dogs Rugby Club for which Crunch serves as team mascot. TVTV has learned that Jamie Prance is the estranged twin sister of James Prance and that the two of them haven't spoken in years. Ms. Prance, her conference with her new client just concluded, now joins us from her car.

"Good evening, Ms. Prance. Thank you for joining our Zoom. Tell us, what has brought a high-powered solicitor from a prestigious London firm here to The Village to contest a local case of canine ownership?"

"We seek justice and settlement for Mr. Wanton. And we shall gain it," the solicitor replies forcefully.

Stuart pauses the video and observes, "Ms. Prance has the demeanor of a person who has never in her life smiled."

You nod in agreement, stating, "She's very good."

Stuart says he and Malcolm have got her pegged for other roles as well. He resumes the video.

"What do you mean by settlement?" Meredith inquires.

"As you may know, Ms. Lane," says the solicitor, "Crunch merchandise has become enormously popular in this region. Now the fad is spreading to London and other cities—both online and in stores. We're talking about substantial revenues this pooch has generated." She elevates her tone to near oratory. "And what has the dog's original owner, the man who raised Crunch as a pup, who nursed him through all of his trials and tribulations—the loss of a leg and half of his eyesight—what has this man gained? Nothing. Not a farthing. Nothing, beyond the loss of his life savings, and possibly his farm, and most egregiously, the loss of his beloved pet."

She pauses, lowering and softening her tone. "Now that Crunch has returned and made his true feelings known, we are bound and determined to rectify matters."

Says Meredith, "But your firm could have sent anyone to litigate this. Yet here *you* are. Forgive me, Ms. Prance, but I must ask, is there something personal here?"

"You mean with my brother, James?"

"Yes."

"Ms. Lane, this matter is intensely personal," Jamie replies.

"Oh my, such candor." Meredith is genuinely taken aback. "Unusual in your profession, I must say."

"James has spent his entire career preying on others' misfortunes," the litigator asserts. "It's high time to put a stop to it once and for all. We shall file a countersuit that will exhaust his resources and drain those of his clients in this matter."

"I see," Meredith replies. "Counselor, I have one last question before we let you go. You're known in legal circles as an 'attack dog' litigator. Is that a fair characterization?"

"It is," Prance assents. "Perhaps Crunch knew the moment he sniffed me."

"Nice deadpan," you call out enthusiastically. "Nice."

The camera shifts to Michael. "What a gauntlet our guest has thrown down! Don't go away. We'll be back after these messages." The screen goes black.

"So, is there another? Dying for more here."

Malcolm shoots a quick text and almost immediately gets a reply. "She says she should have the next one finished soon," he reports.

"Okay, then," you announce. "I'm still brimming with questions about the game. For example, what happens if I don't figure something out, or fail to take a certain course of action?"

"To begin," Malcolm explains, "there's no fixed plotline. If you can't solve a puzzle, the Christopher character or another ally will."

Now that you think about it, you tell them, Christopher sure prompted you a lot. And it was at his urging that you got the nerve to break into the butler's office.

"Or maybe someone else just shows up and imparts key information or leaves telling DVDs in your quarters," Malcolm says. "Or maybe we film 'Uncle Arthur' here and rush him into a painting, a mirror, the swimming pool, or project him as a floating apparition somewhere else. If your scenario had led you to the music room, you would have seen busts of famous composers mounted on pedestals all around."

Stuart plays a clip of famous composers making funny faces and babbling. "Via holograms," he explains, "they come to life and speak to you. That's another method of imparting key information in a mystic fashion."

"I take it if I never break into the butler's office, I never experience virtual *Manor House*," you tell them.

"Correct," says Stuart. "You're either led to those real DVDs or get the explanation from my last letter. And if you can't locate that," he says, grinning, "then I'll burst into a mirror or float through a room and spell it all out for you, you numbskull."

Everyone laughs. Malcolm goes on to explain how they're always tweaking the drama in real time. "We're constantly pulling cast members backstage and outlining a new course of action their character should take—but within the bounds of the current plotline and time frame. Do you remember when Serena's character confronted the chef over an affair she believed he was having with the butler?"

"Of course. It was my first inkling that the concierge might be including me in her future plans!" you say, recalling how hopeful you were at the time.

"Well," says Malcolm, "when you told the Christopher character you were going to the spa, we pulled the trigger on a live scene we'd previously rehearsed with Serena and Stefan, and sent them in."

Adds Stuart, "But they perform it only if you duck out of sight, which you did."

"And if I don't?"

"They act like they don't see you, turn around, and go back out."

"But," Malcolm says, "Stefan did have a lapse in that scene with Serena. He dropped his Quebec accent. Nerves, I guess. We've already brought it to his attention."

"I did notice that at the time," you tell them. "Even mentioned it to Christopher."

"We know. Discussed it with the boy backstage. Told him to keep ignoring questions about it," Malcolm explains.

"I suppose you set that up to pair with the earlier bedroom scene involving the butler and the chef, right?" You feel like you're really catching on to the production's strategy.

"Correct," Malcolm affirms. He now wants to discuss the simulation game and the dance party. "I'm ecstatic that you found the Three Families game box and elected to stage it. And then dreamed up that dance party on your own. Incredible."

"What happens if I don't find the box—oh, wait, let me guess, Christopher brings it to me," you venture.

"Yes, or some other ally you've made," says Malcolm.

"What happens if the game isn't staged? Is there some alternate event?"

"There is indeed," Malcolm replies. "Farnsworth gathers everybody in the assembly hall and shows an IMAX-style tour of the estate along with humorous commentary, and holds a gala affair afterward. It's designed to endear Van Scoy and him to you. Hopefully make you think they're not such bad sorts after all."

"Might they even throw a 'surprise' dance party afterward?" you ask.

"Maybe," replies Stuart. "We can discuss after you've returned and watched your bash from the standpoint of a first-time observer."

"I see," you tell them. "Mind-bending to think one me will see it one way while the other might see it differently."

Malcolm has something else to show you. He gives you a binder containing the galleys and proofs of a volume entitled *Manor House—Production Guide*. It contains the full scenario. "Be sure to check the Alternate Scenarios section," he says.

Thumbing through, you inform them, "I'm now looking at events that did not occur in venues I never got to—like the armory and servants' quarters, the music room and chapel. This is really wild."

"I'm certain you can appreciate how we have to be prepared backstage for almost any contingency," Stuart says.

"I certainly can," you tell him, shaking your head in wonderment. "So many paths I didn't take, choices I didn't make, so many ways the scenario can veer at critical stages I can now see. Wow! Just wow." You close the guide, saying, "Well, considering the various outcomes, I think I played a pretty decent game."

"Oh, by all means," Malcolm enthuses. "Indeed, a 'winner' would be a central character able to reconcile warring factions and reunite the family, as you did. At least that's how the scenario was conceived. Romantic entanglements, solving puzzles, locating documents, unearthing genetic mysteries—all secondary. I gather you probably read how we plan to have the green remote simulate teleportation in the actual production."

"Well, I think I got a taste of it at the Nobel ceremony," you tell him. "I really couldn't tell at first if we'd traveled to Stockholm or if it was all smoke and mirrors. Rollinsby and I were standing quite far away from the gathering. Eventually, I figured out no way did we teleport, but it was a fantastic ride anyway."

With that, you clap your hands and announce, "Gentlemen, I hate to say this, but I now find myself in partial agreement with what's-their-names."

"Kobayashi and Watanabe?" they exclaim in disbelieving unison.

"Right. No way we can make any money on this. To start with, our *customers* are offered a fifty-thousand-dollar enticement just to come here—a sum they may elect to simply cash in, then not show up at all. I sure thought long and hard about that option—especially since I was nearly broke and out of a job."

Stuart clears his throat. "I think Malcolm and I are quite satisfied with this debriefing."

"Now, Masa," says Malcolm, "we want to know, while it's still fresh, is there anything else—major impressions, bottom-line judgments—you feel you should share with us?"

"Well, I've still got a million minor questions but believe all my main impressions have been noted."

Stuart leans forward, once again measuring his words. "Masa . . . nobody sent you any money. You didn't fly anywhere. Almost everything you thought happened before you arrived never happened at all. They are false memories. Implants."

He pauses to take a deep breath. "Your present reality began when the drugs fully kicked in. The actual scenario began outside, when Raemond Starr's overture struck, the lions roared, and William Shakespeare stood."

CHAPTER FORTY-TWO

You're absolutely confounded by this latest disclosure. You need details, explanations, insights. You need them now. But again, Stuart's walkie-talkie rings. After another conversation in Japanese, he turns to you, asking, "Well?"

You tell him, "'Nami-chan' called because she and the girls are dying to get back in here—if Malcolm gets to join, why can't they? So, Stuart, you finally relented. Especially when they offered to bring in a platter of sashimi and homemade sushi rolls. But they have to be 'quiet as mice.'"

Stuart claps and says, "Brilliant!"

"No problem with those three," Malcolm assures him. "After they settle down, they're always quiet as mice. And *negitoro temaki* sounds fabulous."

The crew returns, bearing platters of raw fish, jars of sake, and cups. Says Megumi, "Uncle Stu-Stu, can we work?"

Malcolm leans over and whispers, "Work. That's what they're dying to do."

The trio flit around the lab, flipping on monitor switches and lighting up the area, transforming it into a multimedia wonderland. You're dazzled. The thirty or so workstations, they tell you, have actually been on all the while, rendering.

"Ma-chan, would you like a tour?" asks Reiko. You would. Strolling around and looking at screens, you're given explanations of how all of this is put together.

"Reiko, this is fantastic," you tell her. "It's what I'd imagine Pixar or Disney would look like with one of their animation features in development." Some workstations are smoothing complex wire-frame models into textured images. Others are rendering manor artwork into transitions. Still others are "stitching," as the girls say, source photography into nodes and compositing live video into them.

There are dolls and toys and TV memorabilia perched atop monitors and scattered around on worktables. And storyboards are nearby with hand-drawn panels for various sky spectaculars. In one corner, there's a huge video console where raw footage from cameras throughout the manor streams in for capture when a game is on. In another, a recording booth, where musical scores are being transformed into orchestral works.

And yes, they confirm, there is a library of prerecorded Shakespeare quotes. But most impressive is their demonstration of the game's voice-recognition and AI capabilities. Video characters will pause in midsentence, awaiting your response, and then reply in a completely appropriate fashion, or simply state they didn't understand what you just said. Sometimes, they ask follow-up questions or even initiate new topics on their own. Reiko says, when completed, the entire interface will be voice-driven in an AI framework. Right now, you can see that they are expanding the character interaction at Alice's tea party.

"So next time," Reiko says, "you'll be able to go back and forth with the Mad Hatter and the others for as long as you like."

You shake your head, marveling at the possibilities for theme-park attractions with this tech when fully developed.

The young designers hop from one screen to the next, alternately smiling in satisfaction or frowning in dismay, depending on the results observed. Any sound or music that might accompany these creations is muted—although Namiko now has a headset on and is obviously listening to a musical composition while following an on-screen MIDI score.

Malcolm's right—the three are very quiet, and soon the room is ablaze with their creations, albeit silent for now. From a nearby table, you pick up a memo you'd apparently written pregame. It reads:

> **To:** Nami-chan
> **From:** Masa G
> **Re:** Stuff you must make me do as soon as I return
>
> Accept no excuses. No matter what, make me attend to the following ASAP after rehearsal. If I procrastinate, punish me,

unmercifully if you must—serve instant coffee, disconnect the satellite during MLB, threaten to quit, whatever it takes.

* What should replace Three Families when it's worn out? Devise a new simulation? Or bring in a new unaware cast of players each time?
* Discuss with staff whether we should bring AI-enhanced holographic characters into the scenario. Could be a huge cost saver.
* Best answer to the *Journal*'s "What day would it be?" contest:

Weekday = MOD (Julian Date + 2, 7) If it returns a zero, that's a Sunday. From there, cycle through the week to six, Saturday.

Huh? You don't recall seeing that puzzle. Maybe another omission or glitch?

Your memo now gets technical, enumerating several high-end computer products you recommend your group should test or upgrade for "RenderRama," the apparent nickname for this lab and its deployment of servers. But, like that formula, it's all way over your head in your current state.

"Whoa, it's Crunch!" you shout excitedly, pointing to a nearby monitor showing the notorious rottie cavorting about on Nigel Wanton's farm.

"That's installment nine. I just finished editing it," says Reiko. "There's one more, the final one, but we haven't filmed it yet. Anyway, would you like to watch this one from the beginning?" You nod eagerly. Reiko rewinds and soon you see:

SIBLING RIVALS; PRANCE V. PRANCE IN CRUNCH CUSTODY FIGHT

Meredith, who's seated at the news desk, leads with, "Crunch, the well-known rottie mascot for the Runaway Dogs rugby team is currently at the center of an intense custody battle between his current and former owners. At stake is whether Nigel Wanton, the Flogway Down farmer who raised the pooch from birth, or Tug and Timothy Skaddle, the Witless brothers who are the dog's current legal owners, will retain ownership of the ten-year-old, half-blind, three-legged pooch, who, its infirmities notwithstanding, has become a national celebrity and a marketing sensation. However, earlier this week, Crunch found his way back to his first home in what was apparently a tearful reunion between him and his original owner. Wanton has refused to surrender the pet to authorities even though he no longer legally owns Crunch."

The camera turns to Michael, who continues: "Adding spice and intrigue to this confrontation is the fact that the warring parties are represented by an estranged brother and sister who reportedly can't stand the sight of one another and haven't spoken in years. Earlier today, our correspondent caught up with James Prance, who represents the Skaddle brothers and the Runaway Dogs Rugby Club." The scene changes to the field where the team can be seen practicing in the background.

You pause the video and call out, "Malcolm, again I see you're the correspondent in this one. Another cost-cutting measure?" Malcolm nods yes and comes over to join you. "Am I really that tightfisted?" you ask with a slight frown.

"Indeed you are," Malcolm replies. "Always trying to cut corners. Having me and others pull double, triple duty with bit parts."

"But this was just a trial run, right?"

Reiko overhears this and says, "Right, and *Kaicho* knows Masa's always trying to save money. That's one of the things he likes about him."

"Really?" You're pleased to hear this. "The chairman said that about me?"

"Oh no, not directly," interjects Malcolm. "The ladies here have a secret friend in the chairman's office. As for his or her identity, it's on a need-to-know basis." Malcolm laughs. "And I'm afraid none of us *gaijin* qualify, eh ladies?" Reiko merely smiles and nods as you resume playback.

On-screen, Malcolm is shown standing beside James Prance, who is dressed in a lavender sports coat, a white ruffled shirt, charcoal slacks, and an orange polka dot bow tie. Asks Malcolm, "Mr. Prance, how is the side faring now that Crunch has made his way back to Flogway Down?"

Malcolm extends his microphone to Prance, who looks flustered as he speaks. "Oh, Malcolm, it's been pure disaster. The team's lost all its matches since Crunch ran away. Attendance is down because it's really the dog and his antics the fans come to see. Sales of merchandise has fallen off. We'd planned to film Crunch yodeling, but that went kaput. The pooch is legally ours, and we must have him back."

Malcolm continues. "How are the Skaddle lads themselves taking this?"

Prance uses an embroidered purple handkerchief to wipe his brow, then replies, "Very hard, very hard indeed, Malcolm." He begins to sniffle. "Both lads are seriously off their game as well."

He pauses, now holding back tears. "Just when those dear boys thought they'd forged a heartfelt bond with Crunch, he left them." Prance uses his hanky to wipe the tears now flowing down both cheeks. "Left the team, left the fans, left all of us, Crunch did." The barrister again pauses to regain his composure. When he's able to resume, his tone becomes strident, angry. "And when my clients traveled to Wanton's farm hoping only for a short visit, the Witch wouldn't let them on the property, much less near the pooch."

"The 'Witch'?" Malcolm asks.

"It's Jamie, my sister." Prance's tear-stained eyes are blazing.

Malcolm is now shown listening intently in his earpiece. After a moment, he turns to Prance with a request. "Mr. Prance, I do hope you stay with us. I've just been told your sister Jamie is in fact in studio. After we hear from her, we'd like to get back to you for your reaction." Prance nods his assent silently while maintaining his infuriated expression.

Again, you pause the playback. "Wow, real tears, then convincing anger. The actor playing Prance is quite good. Why does he dress and act so flamboyantly?"

"Your idea, actually," replies Malcolm. "You recently told us that an over-the-top character like Prance will really stand out. That zany Noël alone is not enough. You're now thinking of creating a major servant role for Prance."

You're curious. "What kind of role?"

"You've been thinking that Bruce need not manage both the Falstaff pub and the whisky bar," Malcolm explains. "That Prance could take over the latter and emerge as a colorful character who is outrageous in dress, speech, and mannerisms."

You smile and shake your head resignedly. "Malcolm, you've no idea what it's like to hear you tell me what I've been thinking when this me has no recollection of thinking it!"

"Indeed, it must feel strange," Malcolm agrees.

"Well," you tell the group, "I do like the other me's idea on this! Let's create a permanent role for our Mr. Prance—the surname's perfect by the way." You resume playing back the scene.

Michael and Meredith are seated at their news desk with a fierce-looking woman in formal business attire—accented by a single black rose attached to her lapel—seated between them. A chyron identifies her as "Jamie Prance, London, Solicitor."

"Her brother was right," you say to Malcolm in hushed tones. "She does look like the Wicked Witch of the West—great casting!"

Meredith greets their guest: "Good evening, Ms. Prance. This contest over Crunch has intensified since we last spoke. Tell us, why are you not allowing the Skaddle brothers to even lay eyes on the pet they dearly love and legally own?"

Jamie Prance clasps her hands and speaks directly into the camera: "We all witnessed where Crunch's true loyalties and affections lie when the heroic pooch braved heavy traffic and inclement weather to make his way back to his true home and master."

"But, Counselor," Michael interrupts, "Crunch came home in the wee hours. There was no traffic. And on a clear night. There were no storms."

The woman glares and points her index finger at the anchor. "You have your facts. I have mine." She then sweeps her arm in dismissal. "Anyway, it matters not in this case."

Says Meredith, "What, then, does matter, Counselor?"

Prance does not hesitate. "Money. Money is what matters here." Both anchors lean forward in anticipation as Prance sets out her case: "As I told you both last time I was on, my client now realizes the immense revenues Crunch merchandise has generated during these past few weeks—growling and snapping dog dolls, yodeling bobbleheads, T-shirts, hoodies, all manner of charms and trinkets, even paw prints and logoed eye patches. People who don't even follow rugby, much less Crunch's affiliations, are snapping up the items right along with die-hard fans."

"Why do you suppose that is, Counselor?" asks Michael as the backdrop displays an enlarged still image of the rottie surrounded by an array of Crunch paraphernalia from the Runaway Dogs gift shop.

"Well," Jaime Prance replies, "I'm no psychologist but I'd venture to say that Crunch, being the antithesis of cute and cuddly, has somehow captured the public's imagination as some sort of canine antihero. The Darth Vader of dogs, perhaps."

She turns and gestures at the collection of merchandise. "And how much of those proceeds is my client receiving at present?" Her clenched fist comes crashing down on the news desk as she thunders, "Zero! Aught! Nil!"

Startled, Michael looks momentarily frightened but manages to say, "So, how are you and your client going to rectify matters?"

"Nothing. It's my ne'er-do-well brother's move," she quickly and confidently replies. "It's up to James to hand my client a major share of Crunch's NILV earnings to date. And revenues going forward."

Meredith signals she has a question. "Ms. Prance, precisely what is 'NILV'? Some in our audience may not have heard the term."

"Name, image, likeness, voice—especially the last," Prance explains. "Crunch's yodeling is a sight and sound to behold. We've heard there's a music video in the works."

"I see," says Meredith. "So, the ball's in your brother's court, then?"

"Precisely," the solicitor replies. "We're prepared to be reasonable. But until the team negotiates a settlement and pays up, we do nothing. Crunch does nothing. No photo-ops with the press, no reunions with the Skaddles, no roaming the sidelines at matches, no yodeling on the radio or telly. We sit here. We wait. We do nothing. Time's on our side. My brother can always go back to chasing ambulances or bamboozling distraught 'Lady Godivas' into suing chocolatiers if he so chooses. Up to him."

Meredith leans forward. "But surely you realize that the county court ruled—"

"That ruling was premature." Prance then snaps, "We've already filed with the Court of Appeal Civil Division, who says they will hear the case. We're confident they will see things our way and overturn the unjust lower ruling that took Crunch away from his loving, rightful owner in the first place."

The solicitor now spreads her open palms and addresses the anchor: "Ms. Lane, I'm certain you know the old adage, 'Possession is nine-tenths of the law.' Well, in this case it's ten-tenths. We are in possession of the animal. My brother is not. And when we do go to court, Crunch will show one and all with whom he wishes to belong."

Says Meredith, "Thank you, Ms. Prance. We plan to cover the proceedings live as soon as they begin."

Again you pause the playback, saying, "Jamie's incredible. I'm still trembling."

Malcolm palms his chest. "Every time I see her, I get the heebie-jeebies. And I've watched her takes a dozen times."

"So, any ideas on how we plan to cast her going forward?" you ask.

"Actually, Masa," Malcolm replies, "even before this test run, you'd been saying that we need an overtly scary character and she'd be perfect for it. You pointed out that most real manors have a full-time nurse, and she'd be ideal in that role."

You freeze a close-up of her face. "Yes, I can picture this," you state. "A kind of Nurse Ratched character."

"Precisely. A bit terrifying," says Malcolm.

You tap to resume the broadcast, musing softly, "If this is my job, oh, how I do love my job!" The scene shifts back to the rugby pitch, where Malcolm and James Prance have just watched Jamie Prance's interview. The two anchors are in separate windows in the upper corners of the screen.

Michael begins. "Mr. Prance, now that you've heard what your sister is demanding, what is your reaction?"

James Prance looks pale, his voice trembling as he says, "To tell the truth, Michael, I'm terrified. I can just imagine what the Witch is doing with that poor animal, how she's training him."

"My goodness," says Meredith, "whatever do you mean, Counselor?"

Prance looks deeply troubled. "I'm certain she's teaching the dog to bare its teeth and growl menacingly, maybe even snap and bite on command. They'll come into court, and, with a mere nod or slight gesture, she'll indicate my clients, prompting Crunch to exhibit his fierce disdain for them."

Says Michael, "Sounds darkly Pavlovian and truly sinister—are you serious? What makes you think she'd resort to such tactics?"

Prance shudders, seeming to recall a bad memory. "Because that's what she always did to me as we were growing up." He begins to sob. "She turned all our pets against me. She even, at times, bared her own teeth at me!"

Apparently, Jamie Prance has remained in studio and is still seated between the anchors. The shot returns to the news desk. Meredith turns to the solicitor, saying, "Ms. Prance, your brother has just made an extraordinary, and frankly macabre, prediction concerning your likely courtroom behavior. Care to comment?"

The solicitor leans forward, saying, "Ms. Lane, you must know that anyone in my profession, anyone who's any good that is, never telegraphs their cuffs and clouts in advance. Tell me, though, is my brother still present, still able to view the broadcast?"

"He is. Would you like to address him directly?"

"I certainly would."

"Please make it brief, though," Meredith requests. "I've just been signaled that it's almost time for adverts."

The camera goes to an extreme close-up of the solicitor drawing her quivering lower lip between her teeth. In a snarling tone, she commands her fraternal twin: "James, *look* at me! James, *listen* to me! I will *see you* in court! Until then . . ." You're astonished at the next sight. Jamie Prance, her eyes bulging, thrusts her face forward, opens her mouth wide, bares her enormous teeth—and freezes her expression.

After a moment, the scene switches back to the rugby pitch, where James Prance has fainted dead away. The segment ends. The screen goes black. It takes a moment or two for you to recover. Finally, you turn to Malcolm and say, "Whew, you went full horror with that ending. Never saw it coming."

"Think perhaps it's too much?" Malcolm looks concerned. "We can always cut it if you think we should. The other you had not seen this either. This ending came at the suggestion from both Prances—they were simply dying to do it. The girls here all voted yay." He motions toward Stuart, laughing. "Even stodgy old Uncle Artie reluctantly gave his assent."

"Spooky Kabuki," yells Megumi, who's been following the conversation from her workstation.

"So, Malcolm, was I the cat who was away while all of you were the mice at play?" you ask.

"Yes," Malcolm replies sheepishly. "Something along those lines."

"I don't know," you reply with genuine uncertainty. "That ending was certainly powerful. My creator mindset loved the entire saga. But I'm not sure how I would have reacted as a player to this going so dark, so suddenly, and so over-the-top. Too bad we couldn't get all the episodes into this trial. Then I might have a ready answer based on actually experiencing it."

"Yes," Malcolm sighs. "All the earlier episodes you viewed as a player. But these last few, as a creator. The lenses and POVs are completely different, I'd imagine."

You nod in agreement. "I guess the critical questions are: Does *Manor House* really need an element of horror? And how might a real protagonist react? As shocking as those exaggerated bared teeth are, do they fit the scenario's overall milieu? I'm going to venture a guess here that the other me would not think it fits, would not support its inclusion."

"Indeed, Masa," Malcolm says, "we must all deliberate on this when you return."

"Would someone mind rewinding the clip to just before Jamie directly addresses James?" The clip plays, and just after Jamie says, "I'll *see you* in court!" you signal Malcolm to pause the playback. "I'd end it right there. That's impactful enough, scary enough. Now that I've seen it again, I'm certain. And I bet the other me will agree."

"That's where the script you wrote ends," says Reiko.

"Ha!" you exclaim. "Great mindsets think alike."

"I guess we all kinda added on," Namiko confesses. "And got carried away."

"Oh, Masa, you sound like you're going to be no fun when you come back to boss us around," Megumi grouses with a mock pouty expression.

"Megumi, I already feel like I'm kind of back on the job." Turning back to the director, you say, "In the meantime, Malcolm, this was the penultimate episode, right? What's in store for the finale?"

Namiko signals that she has scripts and storyboards.

"For now," you ask the group, trying to stifle a yawn, "can someone please just summarize? I'm so exhausted right now that reading scripts or squinting at storyboards would immediately conk me out, I'm sure."

"Oh, let me tell the story," Megumi implores, waving her hand in the air. "Let me! Let me! Please! Please!"

"All right, Megu-chan," Malcolm assents. He turns to you and says with a wink, "This ought to be good."

Megumi begins. "This whole scene is in a courtroom, and it is very funny. Tuggy and Timmy—OMG! They're *so cute*!—surprise everybody. They bring in a girl French poodle to try and charm Crunch with a special smell they put on her. It works! Pooches have a great time smelling each other's *chin-chins* and walking in circles sniffing the back ends like doggies love to do. Crunch is too old for sex probably, but in court, he never growls at anybody, which makes the lady lawyer upset but the guy lawyer happy. The judge listens to both sides and decides they have to share the dog. 'Joint something,' he says. Tuggy and Timmy get to keep him on game days and evenings. The farmer guy, the rest of the time. Oh, and they have to share all the money fifty-fifty. It's kind of a happy ending for everybody. The guy lawyer, who is crying at the end, wants to give the lady lawyer a big hug, but she won't let him. Instead, they just shake hands, and she smiles a little bit. All while Crunchy yodels and yodels away so happy, and the poodle looks so happy too. The end."

Megumi receives a hearty round of applause.

"Megumi, that was terrific," you tell her. "Joint custody, eh? Malcolm, did I come up with that ending?"

"You certainly did, Masa. It's so you—reconcile the warring parties, bring peace to the household."

"Like *Kaicho* wants you to do in here too," adds Reiko.

"One thing, though," Stuart informs you, "we have to figure out how to work Crunch into the game. That's what you told us would be a priority once all the installments were filmed."

"Yes, I can see that," you reply, rubbing your chin. "Let me give that some thought because there are so many possibilities. For sure, though, *Crunch* should be a keyword in a puzzle solution, don't you think?"

Of course, everyone signals.

CHAPTER FORTY-THREE

"So this is what I do for a living?" you mumble to no one in particular.

"Not entirely," replies Stuart, brightening a little. "Often your contribution, as you've grasped, stems not from what you know but rather from your extraordinary ability to *forget* what you know." Malcolm chuckles, nodding his agreement.

Storyteller, are they finally about to explain? ***We believe they are.***

You need answers and decide to push hard for them. You rise to address the group. "Listen, everyone, though I've apparently lost my mind, somehow this no longer seems frightening. However, there is one not-so-minor problem here—the new aristocratic life I thought I had vanished a short while ago. My real one, the creator role you're describing now, I've no recollection of. And the chemical one I brought into this manor six days ago has no confluence with this scene. In fact, you told me a short time ago that all those memories are fake." You pause and exhale. "Stuart, why don't you start by explaining 'turn' and 'return'?"

The debriefing now concluded, Stuart is happy to do so. "Remember, Masa, how you entered this room. You had to revolve the fireplace, right? From either the cottage living room or the drawing room, right?"

"Right, right."

"Now picture one room—let's say the living room—as your normal state of consciousness, the one in which you would immediately recognize all of us," says Stuart.

You slowly shake your head no, mumbling, "Not sure I follow."

Stuart is undeterred. "Now picture the drawing room as an altered state, the one you're in now, the one where you don't recognize us but must be convinced by now that we know who you are."

You nod more confidently. "All right, I can at least understand that."

"Now envision the fireplace revolved to its open state when you used to go back and forth in the game," Stuart says. "If you went, say, from your normal state through the opening to your altered state, from the living to the drawing room, that would be 'turning.' Follow me?"

"Yes."

"And if you came back, from the drawing to the living room, that would be '*re*turning.' Follow?"

"Follow."

"Right. So we're all sitting in here drinking beer and sake, eating sushi, watching clips, getting your firsthand impressions of the game, follow?"

"Yes—and hiding from dastardly foes," you laugh, "two of whom I've never even met. Seriously, I'm still 'turned,' as you say."

Stuart lightly taps your head. "Mentally you're still in the drawing room. But we're 'describing' the other room, your living room, where all of your authentic memories, like furnishings, are stored. Get it?"

"Got it."

"Lovely." Stuart stands and walks a short distance, then continues, "Now let's say we're in the drawing room near its fireplace. What are we *really* doing?"

It doesn't take long to get it. "We're feeling around the mantel—for the button, so to speak, right?"

"Precisely. Why?"

"You want to open the passage so I can rejoin all of you in your living room."

"No, Masa, in *your* living room," he corrects. "We're already quite comfortably ensconced in ours."

"Yeah, okay, I think I can even take it a step further." The group draws forward in anticipation. "If I'm in my 'drawing room' and meet the cast, I know them as Christopher, Bruce, Savannah, et cetera, having no memory of creating the game, their roles, or knowing any of them in real life." You pause momentarily. "But if I'm in my 'living room,' I won't remember actually playing. I'd have to read some account or have you all tell me about it."

"Or you'd watch that," Namiko says, pointing to the video wall.

"Of course," you reply. "Thus, in my so-called living room are the actors we work with every day—I'm guessing here—and maybe relax with in the pub on some evenings? And that's why none of them came backstage tonight because I'm now, as you said earlier, 'in between.'"

"Exactly," Stuart says. "It could be counterproductive, further confuse you. And we, you included, didn't want you returning too soon, before we'd thoroughly dissected the play."

Adds Malcolm, "So having accomplished that, we're now free to search for that 'button,' so to speak. Have no fear, Masa, we'll find it. We always do."

Hey, Storyteller, just had a thought. Do you think our connection is somehow preventing my return to normal? ***Great question. But in all honesty, we don't know.***

You stand up to stretch. "Oh, I rather think you'd better sit down for the next bit," Stuart advises. "So," he begins, "all that you thought happened before you arrived are actually 'pseudo-events,' artificial memories that were 'downloaded' beforehand—in a specially created apartment located in staff quarters, but not where you actually reside here. There, while in a deep waking trance, you were fed your new identity and background while potent drugs were administered under strict medical supervision."

"You mean at first somebody hypnotized, then drugged me?"

"Not exactly. You are easily able to enter these altered states yourself, have been for most of your adult life."

This is bizarre. "How?"

Stuart laughs. "Don't fall off the chair." He takes a deep breath and exhales slowly. "Intense fantasizing. Aided and abetted by prolonged self-hypnosis and, on some occasions, by psychotropic substances, my good friend."

Holy moly, Storyteller. ***Just go with the flow.*** *Yeah, like I have a choice.*

"But," says Stuart, "I hasten to add, that was *not* how you turned on this occasion. This time we tried something new, something much more powerful and longer lasting, something the chairman arranged." In technical terms, he explains, this all results from temporarily reprogramming your NR2B gene cluster by means of NMDA protein blockers and substitutes delivered via "extraordinary concoctions you ingested at the outset of your adventure."

You vaguely remember drinking something from a vial just before that courier arrived with the parcel from England. "So, Stuart, any psychedelics while I was in there?" you ask.

"None whatsoever," he replies. "They are specifically excluded from this regimen."

Storyteller, this doesn't sound right. I remember mushrooms and cacti communicating with me. ***Sorry, we're not cognizant of communications from the plant kingdom.***

Stuart continues: "These brand-new drugs enhance recently acquired memories and can selectively dim or suppress others." He switches to his Lord Hanover voice. "Imagine—a sip, a swallow, and *voilà*! A tabula rasa." Somehow, you recall hearing that before.

Storyteller, should I now tell them about you people? ***Not yet. Wait until you learn more.***

You're curious. "Where do these drugs come from? How did we get them?"

Stuart explains they were obtained from another company the chairman owns, a Swedish firm that's developing what they call "biological software routines" for memory and consciousness.

Hearing this, you say, "So, Stuart, about my pregame preparation, please tell me what actually happened."

"Picture a novelist deeply immersed in their story," he says. "Or an actor intensely getting into character. Your preparation had elements of both. The one big difference being that, by the end of it, you thought it was for real."

You nod in full agreement. "I always thought all of it was for real. Even the parts like flying on an airplane, you now say weren't. There's no difference in my memories of them."

"That's what we were told by the pharmaceutical scientists—that both false and true memories would seem the same," Stuart says, then explains that after you "acquired" a new background and personal identity, a packet was actually delivered to your halfway house. You became absorbed in Lord Hanover's correspondence and video message. "You really did read fake magazine stories, actually watched a fake BBC documentary, and downloaded information and digital clips from simulated sites," he says.

"I thought I did all these things, still do in fact, but you say I didn't. So tell me, what did I really do, and not do, before I came?"

Stuart quickly itemizes all the things that never happened. He says you never got fired from any job or talked on the phone to individuals you believed worked for British Airways and Browns Chauffeur Hire. And you never went to a bank or a library, visited any professor, stopped over in New York, or drove around London. "You were simply provided with vivid memories of having done so."

"So I never even went shopping?"

"Correct. The clothes were purchased for you and a pseudo-memory implanted."

"What about seeing the girls in New York and again the next day in London—more fake memories?"

"Again correct," says Malcolm. "The girls wanted to be part of that too. So they dressed up in kimonos and we narrated a couple of 'memories' to you under hypnosis in conjunction with the drugs."

Megumi chimes in. "That was big fun. We love to dress up fancy."

"How come they spoke English in New York but couldn't in London?" you ask.

"Oh," Megumi replies, "we also like to play tricks on Masa's mind."

You laugh, then inquire about that long drive up. "That actually took place," says Stuart. "In an actual Bentley from the manor garage as Stephen drove you around at night, largely to imprint characters, create expectations of a forthcoming manor mystery."

"Those holograms certainly did the trick."

Stuart nods. "Nifty tech, eh?"

"Yeah, but when he stopped for gas, the station's sign was printed in Japanese. I wondered about that for a long while," you tell them.

"Right, we saw that too," Malcolm interjects. "It's one of many glitches we need to address. There are plenty of petrol stations whose signs are in Romaji."

Stuart goes on. "Stephen really did park the limo and escort you up to the entrance. That short walk, by the way, was the crucial final transition from your in-between state to the full-fledged scenario, which, you may recall, started off with quite a bang."

"In other words, prior to that," you observe, "I was literally stoned out of my real mind?"

Stuart pauses. "Well, yes, in a manner of speaking, but relatively safely—and legally. Once inside, you weren't served any additional drugs, in case you're wondering."

"But, Stuart, I *am* wondering. I often felt like I was on something in there. I felt mentally sharp, aglow, and tingly inside."

"There are no known physical side effects of these drugs," Stuart says. "In fact, small dosages were administered to you before this lengthy trial. You never had any problems turning or returning previously. Or reported any hallucinations. Or physical changes."

Storyteller, should I still keep mum about the plants? ***Yes, for now. We'll tell you when we think it's time.*** *Plant pals—what do you think?* ***Up to you.***

But again, Stuart's cell chimes, and again, he signals while putting his phone on speaker that it's Farnsworth. "Stuart, listen, I'm getting intense pressure from Kobayashi and Watanabe. They're demanding that I and they be allowed in to try to snap him out of it."

"James, that's a terrible idea," Stuart replies coldly. "Extremely dangerous, and you should well know it."

"They say it's what the president wants them to do. I think we have no choice here."

"I don't believe that, James. Not one iota."

"Well, that's what they said. You must understand how determined they are to see him."

"James, the lab must remain shut. No one's allowed in or out. Now just be patient and wait for my word—that he's returned, safe and sound." Stuart ends the call, grumbling something unintelligible under his breath.

"Stuart, I'm sure more than ever that Farnsworth fired a gun at me. So I just have to ask, do you think those other two may be armed?"

"I can't imagine it in this company, or in this country for that matter," he replies. "Ordinary people don't carry armaments in everyday life."

Storyteller, are they armed? ***No, not at present. But they're attempting to procure pistols.*** *From where?* ***Do you know "yakuza"?*** *Yeah, Japanese gangsters.* ***From them.***

"Okay, Stuart, we'll just put that aside for now. Now, can we go on to something I consider most important—*re*turning. Whosever life is mine, I'd like it back, please."

Everybody laughs a little, slightly easing the tension in the room.

"Returning, Masa, is a different matter," says Stuart. "No drugs are involved, though it's much trickier, akin to suddenly snapping out from hypnosis. In fact, it's what you had to prove to the chairman and the president you could consistently do in short sessions before they would let you take these chemicals for a prolonged duration."

"Well, I'm glad they were concerned for my safety and well-being," you observe. "Sounds like they're okay guys."

Namiko overhears and speaks up. "They are, Masa, spooky at times, but nice."

Megumi calls out, "Spooky Kabuki!"

Stuart smiles and continues: "Masa, since this is your maiden voyage, nobody's entirely sure what to expect on this, the return flight. In the past, we've always gotten you back—usually in less than an hour—by showing you scrapbooks and photo albums, diaries and video clips. Or by telling you your own stories until something clicks."

"This sounds like quite a procedure," you tell him.

"Indeed," Stuart replies. "We never know in advance, however, your arrival gate, so to speak, for the method requires free associations and random occurrences or it simply won't work."

"Stuart, you're starting to sound like the Christopher character."

"He's your creation, Masa. Anyway, you're particularly likely to return if some truly elegant synchronicity occurs—two or more seemingly unconnected events that happen simultaneously, or nearly so—what most people would term coincidences, but which in an altered state are most certainly not."

You snap your fingers. "So is this why I had the Christopher character so into Jung?"

"Yes, in your scenario," Malcolm replies. "Not necessarily in others. But we'll see."

Stuart goes on. "These synchronicities can somehow switch you from one mindset, with all its stored memories, instantly to another with its cache. If everything works, you'll suddenly break in, often in midsentence, conveying information only the authentic you would know."

"In other words, returned," says Namiko.

This is mind-blowing stuff all right. But after the events of the past week, you could almost believe anything. Again, you decide to take a stroll to clear your head. You start to get up, but without warning, a commotion erupts at the lab entrance.

Malcolm is yelling at a couple of unexpected visitors to get out. Stuart rushes away to join him. Again, you start to rise, but Namiko motions for you to stay put. A spate of angry Japanese. Whoever has come is demanding to see you. Stuart and Malcolm are refusing. Then it becomes clear that the intruders are the infamous *saboteurs*, as you hear "Kobayashi-san" and "Watanabe-san" frequently addressed.

You hear that they're also demanding the recordings, so they can see for themselves what a disaster they're certain this has been. Even as their speech grows angrier and their threats more imminent, Malcolm and Stuart continue to adamantly rebuff them. For a moment, you think a fistfight might even break out.

Then suddenly they appear—middle-aged, dressed in blue suits; one tall and slender, the other short and pudgy; two sets of beady eyes.

"Ah, good evening, Ginza-san," the short one says softly behind a controlled smile and a polite bow. You nod tentatively.

"Since you are feeling better," the tall one says silkily, "we request a meeting. Would you please come with us now?"

A teen Storyteller pops up, practically screaming, ***Don't go!***

For several seconds, you say nothing, feeling their hot collective stare. Finally, you murmur, "Not tonight—maybe some other time." Their faces redden with suppressed rage.

"We are waiting for you, Ginza-san," the tall one hisses. They again bow, then depart with an air of authority. Malcolm follows them out. The lab door slams as he walks back in, flushed with anger. He summons Namiko into a corner for a conference.

Reiko has draped a protective arm around Megumi, who is trembling and muttering, *"Kobayashi to Watanabe, sukebe, sukebe, sukebe. Daikirai."*

Whoa, Storyteller. She really despises those two, called them perverts. ***Be very careful. They are seriously bad dudes***, the teen warns grimly.

Yes, you totally get that now. But at least they didn't flash any weapons.

CHAPTER FORTY-FOUR

You're pacing around, trying to think of something, anything that could trigger a recollection when an Australian-sounding Storyteller offers a suggestion: ***Why don't you visit your quarters here at the manor? See if familiar digs does the trick, mate.*** *Right! Great idea. Can't hurt. Certainly worth a try. Thanks.*

Your train of thought, though, is sidetracked by the chime of Stuart's cell, further delayed when you realize it's Farnsworth on the phone, then completely derailed by a buzzer at the lab entrance.

Malcolm goes to see who has arrived while Stuart fills you in on the call. "Farnsworth, again," Stuart says. "Now he's saying he might ask the president about having you committed to a psychiatric hospital." He pauses to reflect. "But he'll slit his own throat if he tries that."

"Why?" you ask, surprised.

"Because on the organizational chart, I'm his superior, as you are mine," Stuart explains. "If there were a problem and you were incapacitated, it would be my place to see the president."

Adds Namiko, "The one thing we never ever do in a Japanese company is to go over the head of our supervisor. Even if the sky's falling down."

All of this is confusing and prompts another question. "Stuart, why in the world do we have to work so closely with people we despise and who despise us?"

"It's the chairman's way. His samurai view of business," he replies.

Not the answer I was expecting, Storyteller. ***Indeed there are cultural disparities at play here.***

Stuart goes on. "We came with you from i-two-one. But you inherited

Farnsworth and others." He pauses, then adds, "Another handicap—you can't fire anybody. Only the president can—and he almost never does."

"How can I handle them?" you ask.

Stuart explains that the chairman and the president think that you, as managing director, should find a way to resolve all these conflicts and achieve what they term *wa*—in English, "group harmony"—the ultimate value in this culture's workplace. "But the sad truth," he says, "is that they're rich old men who love sitting back watching corporate blood feuds."

"Told ya," Megumi calls out. "We're all trapped inside *Kaicho*'s *kabuki-za*."

"Doesn't sound like a viable structure for any company to me," you tell them.

Everyone nods in agreement. "You were so hoping," Stuart continues, "that the object of the *Manor House* game—uniting warring factions, achieving *wa* throughout the household—would please them."

Your curiosity is piqued. "So, Stuart, what do they think of our work?"

"Who knows?" he replies, throwing his hands up in exasperation. "They've never set foot in here. Never watched a recording. Nor read a single scenario. Frankly, I don't think they're all that interested." He pauses, then says, "Except the bottom line monetarily and what the outside world thinks."

"But they always know what's going on in here," Namiko reminds him. "Even though they pretend not to."

"Are we making money, Namiko? Stuart?" you ask.

"Not yet," Stuart replies. "But, since our earlier scenarios have been successful, we're close to breaking even." Stuart taps the production guide. "We have high hopes for *Manor House*. Could be make-or-break, though. What the chairman giveth, he's often been known to snatch away."

Somehow this strikes you as familiar, causing you to ask, "Without, I take it, any warning?"

"Right, Masa. The Japanese way: Take forever to start something new. But when ending, instantly pull the plug."

Stuart's phone chimes. Apparently seeking privacy, he walks to a far corner.

When he returns, Malcolm asks, "Farnsworth again?"

Stuart shakes his head. "No, this was much worse."

He explains that it was the chairman's secretary reporting that *Kaicho* is troubled over the translated review he's just read. But most of all he was confused. "Why in the world," he'd asked the secretary to ask Stuart and Malcolm, "would we publish these excerpts on our own site? For all the world to see."

Stuart sighs. "Obviously, *les saboteurs* and Farnsworth. They're setting fires everywhere."

You hear approaching voices. Malcolm is escorting a short, slender, curly-haired man who looks from a distance to be late twenties or early thirties. From his exuberant expression, you suppose you're about to be reunited with yet another colleague or close friend you've never seen before in your life.

Wrong. In walks Raemond, who was both *The Hollywood Reporter* guy and Jake the sports reporter who you well remember from stories on TVTV. You figure, like Malcolm, he's an integral part of this i21 crew and was just doing cameos for the production. "Let me guess, 'untitled-4,'" you venture.

Stuart nods and says, "Say hello to Rae Starr."

Hearing his name, you recall the concierge's PA announcements introducing his classical repertoire, and thus realize he's i21's composer in addition to bit-part actor. Rae is high-strung. He bursts into your corner, charging the atmosphere, energizing everyone. You get a déjà vu feeling about this guy but can't place him beyond his TVTV appearances.

"Our resident genius here composed all the original music in the production," Malcolm informs you. "The symphonic overtures, the dining hall's violin and piano concertos, the Spa's saxophone and piano jazz programs."

"Rae, I had no idea it was one person, and, yes, I'm mightily impressed with your versatility. Loved all the music."

Rae beams. "I'm very pleased, Masa, to hear this since, as I hope you'll soon recollect, you're my boss!"

"Well," you laugh, "remind me to give you a raise if I ever remember how to do so."

"Hey, everybody," Rae says excitedly. "I've got some big news."

But you interrupt with a request. "Rae, do you mind holding off for a moment and tell me how the two of us met? I get the strong feeling we've met before. And I want to follow this premonition in case it can help me make some connections here."

"Sure, Masa. It all started one night while you were on vacation in Sofia, Bulgaria, where you happened to be seated next to an elderly Japanese couple in a hotel restaurant. You struck up a conversation with these total strangers—like you almost always do."

"I'll say." Malcolm nods in agreement, then adds, "'Always talk to strangers,' seems to be your credo."

Rae continues, "You mentioned to the couple that you were currently searching for a composer back in Japan. The man turned out to be my *shacho*—the president—of Tokyo Music College, where I teach part time. *Shacho* told you how I compose in a variety of genres, that the school where I teach is actually in your Kishibojin neighborhood, that you probably walk by it often. Maybe you just never noticed the small sign out front."

Kishibojin sounds familiar, but you can't quite place it. Rae continues, "I said, 'What a coincidence!' But, Masa, you claimed there are no coincidences and I should study Carl Jung. We immediately hit it off."

So you tell him, "If I never talk to that guy, we never meet. And you never compose all this music for us. Got it—always talk to strangers!" You then tell Rae to go ahead and report his news.

Rae takes a deep breath. "Sony-Epic wants to add 'Music from *Manor House*' to their international catalog."

Megumi screams, jumps from her seat, and breaks into an impromptu dance. Malcolm and Stuart pound on Rae's shoulders while Reiko and Namiko exchange hugs. "The music aside," Malcolm turns and explains to you, "what this really means is that this corporate giant has faith in the production and wants to make an early deal."

"It also means," Stuart says to you, "that you'll have something impressive to pull out of your briefcase at the next board meeting, to offset that review and whatever other dirty tricks *les saboteurs* and Farnsworth have up their sleeves."

Something about all this shoptalk, along with that expensive production guide, bothers you. So you ask, "Until the AI game comes out, which Stuart said would be much later, only a very few people would ever directly experience this *Manor House* scenario. So why would its music be marketed on a grand scale? For that matter, why would a magazine review a production that the vast majority of its readership would never directly experience either?"

Silence. They're clearly puzzling over how best to explain this. At last, Stuart answers. "I know this will sound odd right now. But do understand that shortly after we have enough sessions with real players, we'll publish documents, teasers, and podcasts that fully describe the scenario."

To you, that makes even less sense. "Why would anybody want to *read* a game scenario? Wouldn't that spoil it for them?"

Stuart realizes that he hasn't made himself clear enough. He explains that the book, along with certain productions that are serialized through streaming services, will recount the experiences of celebrity players. This has been, in the past, the main revenue stream, one that far exceeds the income from a few individuals who actually come and act it out. "Some of whom, I should add, we *pay* to play," he says.

"Who, for example?"

"Movie stars, sports heroes, TV personalities," says Rae. You nod. Now you get it.

Pretty cool enterprise, eh, Storyteller? ***Oh, it's a celebrity trip all right.***

Malcolm relates that about an eighth of a percent of the world's population in developed countries is using these same drugs in one form or another. Most are people in therapy to dim—or erase altogether—acutely painful memories that are still harming them. Post-trauma disorders, that sort of thing. But lately, increasing numbers are using them purely for recreational purposes. "The other you knows all about this," he says.

"So, do the recreational users have this much trouble getting their real memories back?" you ask. Stuart assures you that most people have no difficulty when reintroduced to familiar acquaintances, scenes, and mementos.

You're encouraged by hearing this and totally preoccupied now with "returning" to your true self. You mentally cast about for a new approach, which soon leads to a simple request, one that one of the Aussie Storytellers suggested earlier before you got sidetracked by the disturbances. "By the way, Stuart, can I visit my actual residence here at Camelot? Maybe familiar surroundings will spark a remembrance or something."

"By all means," Stuart says. "You'll like it. It's, shall we say, eighties, nineties, aughties retro." Rae bolts from his chair to speak quietly to Stuart, who nods in assent, and the composer hurries out of the lab.

"He wants to dash ahead and power everything on," Stuart explains. "Your bungalow is packed with special effects, and he wants you to get the full impact upon arrival. Thinks it might spark something, help in some way."

“Anything that might help, I’m open to,” you say agreeably.

“Better brace yourself,” Stuart warns, his eyes brimming with mirth.

“Hi, I’m Masa Ginza’s Fun House!” shrieks Megumi, evidently describing your abode.

“Rae told me he needed a quarter hour or so and that he’d wait for you,” Stuart says as he hands you a map of underground passages to the staff bungalows.

“Think going out there will be safe?” you ask.

“I do,” he replies. “I think *les saboteurs* were just trying to intimidate you when they were in here.”

Storyteller, will I be okay? ***No worries this Time around, mate***, says the Aussie who suggested you go in the first place.

Stuart says he’ll use this interval to try to get to the bottom of the review mess—“excerpts of which are now being posted at dozens of sites,” he grouses while perusing search results on his tablet.

Apparently, there’s a war going on out there.

CHAPTER FORTY-FIVE

Namiko escorts you out the lab's main entrance and down the inner hallways. Once outside, she points you toward the correct passageway and quips, "Masa, I'll see you when you *return*. Or if not"—she giggles—"I'll see you anyway."

As you walk along, you see nothing but concrete and white slab wall. You encounter no one in the long, winding passageway.

Then, you're overcome with uneasiness, a premonition. And now, as you approach a roundabout where your map indicates five passageways converge and you spot the spoke you should take at two o'clock, you hear voices. Instinctively, you want to avoid being seen. You slip back into the roundabout and flatten against the pillar in the center. Out of the corner of your eye you see Farnsworth, Kobayashi, and Watanabe nearing the intersection. You inch back. Now they're close enough for you to discern speech.

They're all speaking Japanese, but you find you have no trouble translating it without assistance from above. Says Kobayashi, "A lot of time has passed. James-san, are you sure?"

"I can't be absolutely certain," replies Farnsworth. "But I was careful to select several of every variety I could find. And I always prepared the tea strictly according to recipe. And made sure the laced gelatin and chocolates were available whenever I got the chance."

"I forget, what was the tea supposed to do?" asks Watanabe.

"Not entirely sure," Farnsworth replies. "But the chairman's pharma reps told everyone that it's extremely dangerous to mix psychoactive drugs with memory suppressants, so naturally . . ." He pauses and laughs menacingly. "I thought we should stir them in as well."

After a pause, Kobayashi continues, "I see. Did you try to see the president about hospitalizing Ginza-san?"

"Still thinking about it. I want to, but it's risky to not go through channels," Farnsworth replies. He again emits a cruel laugh and muses, "Well, we can always hope that lingering side effects or the admixture or an overdose will cause something permanent. I mean, if one can't remember how to do one's job, then what earthly good is one any longer?" There's silence, as one or more of them have apparently lit cigarettes. The pungent smell of tobacco fills the air.

After a moment, their conversation resumes. You can only hear bits and pieces of what Watanabe is saying. "We'll have to think of something else. Maybe we could . . . Oh, by the way . . . not sure yet . . . a recording contract . . . find out tomorrow . . . our friends."

"Heh heh," Kobayashi grunts. "Maybe they can take care of our problem once and for all, like on *Hissatsu Shigotonin*!"

Now you're really frightened as you fight hard to suppress a cough. *Storyteller, what's he referring to, some movie?* ***It's the name of a popular TV series,*** **Murder Is My Job.** ***Been on for decades.*** *Are they serious?* ***Afraid so.***

Watanabe resumes talking. "Or, James-san, you can try again to do it yourself. Our friends have procured this for you."

"The last one must have misfired," says Farnsworth.

"They swear this one works perfectly," Watanabe assures him.

There's a prolonged silence, except for occasional clicking and snapping sounds. You sense Farnsworth is examining the pistol but can't risk sticking your head out to check. Finally, he speaks. His tone is again sinister. "It shouldn't have come to this, but it can't be helped."

"You'll place the gun in his hands after?" asks Watanabe.

"Yes, I will, then burn my gloves," Farnsworth replies. "They'll think those memory drugs drove him mad, made him do it."

Their voices and footsteps recede. You quickly enter your passageway, spooked to the max over all you just overheard. You stop and wipe the sweat from your brow, your heart still pounding. This is simply too much. That last utterance from Farnsworth was especially chilling. Damn, Farnsworth and his cohorts have been attempting foul play all along. This confirms it—his attack in the lobby was real, not any hallucination.

Storyteller, I knew I hadn't imagined it. Why didn't you warn me? ***Sorry, but you should know by now we can't risk disrupting the timeline of your story's key events.***

Okay, you get it. A profound insight hits. You realize that the psychedelics, your fake memories, the theme-park illusions—all resulted in a mad, psychic mash-up, further intensified by the Storytellers and the plant presences.

Whew! Finally, I'm getting it, Storytellers. ***Indeed you are. So are we. Remember, this phenomena is as new to us as it is to you.*** *A story even you guys hadn't heard before!*

You continue walking and projecting. *So these are all side effects the drug makers didn't know about?* ***Yes, precisely.*** You stop and gaze up at the old man. *But why don't you know?* ***Those who have pioneered this aren't dead yet.*** Aha! *So they can't impart their knowledge right now . . . I see.* ***Yes, 'tis a pity.***

Another realization hits. You now recall seeing Farnsworth on several occasions furtively passing through the chef's office on his way to the kitchen. You didn't make much of it at the time because so much else was going on.

So that's what he was up to, Storyteller. Lacing snacks with acid, substituting mushrooms in recipes, spiking the tea. ***Correct.*** *Lucky to still be sane.* ***And alive.***

But then, as if on cue, the techno voice sounds, as if audio effects have been applied. One of the plant beings has returned.

Above, it displays as a slowly rotating red-capped mushroom, and it warbles soothingly: ***Don't worry. You shan't fall ill. There were no nasty ones amongst us.*** *Magic shrooms?* ***Yes, we were mixed in throughout your stay. We do hope you enjoyed us!*** *Yeah, well, I certainly enjoyed the encounters with those women.* ***Ah yes, courtesy of our lysergic friends. You thought it was real?*** *Never was sure. But I'm really worried now, having just overheard Farnsworth and his cronies talking about doing me in.*

The rotating mushroom appears to emit a glow while again warbling: ***Don't fret over those scoundrels. We will soon present an insane inspiration to foil them.***

The reassurances cause your fear to subside. In fact, now you almost feel relaxed—and intensely curious. You spot a nearby exit and step outside for some fresh air. The clamor on the main lawn can be heard in the far distance, but no one's outside on this side of the building in your vicinity. A nearby bench looks inviting.

As soon as you're seated, a black-bearded Storyteller appears with an invitation: ***Say, how would you like to meet others here of some renown who have been following your adventure with great interest?*** *Of course.* ***Kind spirits, please introduce yourselves.***

Suddenly, there's a booming voice.

Hello! I'm Carlos Castaneda. My fervent wish is for you to realize that you have everything needed for the extravagant journey that is your life.

You're stunned. Not only are you hearing him, but, like the Storytellers, there's a three-dimensional headshot of the author, who you quickly recognize, floating above. Since no one's around, you decide to speak aloud to the apparition. You've found it's easier than having to concentrate and structure each thought to transmit telepathically. But the mode requires privacy, which you now have in this particular location.

"Great. Thank you, Carlos. Good advice. I look forward to resuming my life as soon as I can find it! Now, Carlos, please tell me, what went on in there with all the hallucinogens?"

You sipped a lot of pink tea. More mescaline than Don Juan ever consumed.

"That sounds scary. Will I be okay?"

Castaneda doesn't reply but instead departs. A serious-looking female countenance appears and answers. ***Nothing in life is to be feared; it is only to be understood.***

"Hey, I think I recognize you from history books."

Je suis Marie Curie.

"Ah yes, Madam Curie. So nice of you to stop by. Trying, as Carlos suggested, to retrieve my life's purpose. Got any advice?"

You must believe you are gifted for something and that the thing must be attained.

Another female face, young looking, appears beside Curie, who says, ***May I present Ada Lovelace, who I trust a man of your profession would be especially keen to meet.***

"Why do you say that?"

Countess Lovelace was the world's first computer programmer.

"Really? Wow! Fun fact! Did not know that before. I work in IT. So I'm honored to meet its founder."

Madam Curie continues, ***You should also know that Lord Byron, the great English poet, was her father.***

"Wow. Impressed to the max. Countess, do you understand my predicament here? Any solutions?"

I never am really satisfied that I understand anything.

Then suddenly, an exuberant-sounding male image pops into the space above, replacing the two scientists.

Peace, love. Hey, Timothy Leary here. Always remember, there are three side effects of acid: enhanced long-term memory, decreased short-term memory, and I forget the third.

"Ha ha, I could use a laugh. Timothy, you are one funny guy. Did I trip a lot in there?"

A whole lot. Those women dancing around. The butler's and the chef's antics. So funny.

Next, there's a trill that sounds exactly like Stephen Hawking's familiar voice generator. ***Life would be tragic if it weren't funny. Stephen Hawking, at your service.***

"Oh, hello! I'm so honored. Say, I loved your book about time."

Did you actually read it?

"I did! Even finished it."

Congratulations! You're among the very few.

"I also loved your cameos in the Big Bang sitcom when I was younger. Stephen, you are one funny fellow! You really practiced what you preached, that life is funny."

Dance first. Think later, chimes a new voice. ***It's the natural order.***

"Hey! I know you—the *Waiting for Godot* guy! Christopher quoted your sayings throughout."

Words are all we have.

You can't resist. "So, Samuel, did Godot ever show?"

Beckett sighs. ***Nothing happens, nobody comes, nobody goes, it's awful.***

"Gosh, all that waiting. Sorry."

A new headshot flashes into view. ***Ah, I see a portion of your bicameral mind has begun to function. Good evening, I'm Julian Jaynes, and I do hope you realize by now that consciousness is a much smaller part of your***

mental life than you are conscious of, because you cannot be conscious of what you are not conscious of.

"Oh my, Professor Jaynes, but aren't you one clever man! I do enjoy bending thoughts and twisty sentences. And most of all, I adore palindromes."

Tattarrattat. Tattarrattat.

"Who's there?"

James Joyce here with a knock-knock joke. Fancy to hear?

"Sure, love jokes."

Smashing, you start.

"Knock. Knock."

Who's there?

Prolonged silence. You don't know how to answer because you don't know who you are or where "there" is. But finally, you get that the joke's on you.

"James, you got me. You're one funny guy too. Your novels are sure hard to grasp, though."

Shut your eyes and see.

Smiling, you stand and stretch, marveling at the night sky. As soon as you see the next arrival, you realize the forthcoming salutation will be from Christopher's favorite psychoanalyst.

Greetings. My name is Carl Jung, and first I must say, you are what you do, not what you say you'll do! Whether you know who and where you are—or not!

"Thank you, Dr. Jung. Say, is there any way I can get your autograph?"

No way, they're all dead, interjects a boyish Storyteller with a giggle.

"Yes, of course. My apologies. Now, what was I thinking? Where was I?"

Says Jung, ***You were wondering what you were thinking and where you are.***

"Very funny. But I do have a serious question, if I may."

Do tell us, please. But wouldn't you first like to recline on our couch? Tell us about your childhood, perhaps?

"LOL! Christopher told me a lot about synchronicities in the game and in life, and Stuart and others expounded further backstage. Can you help me 'return' to my normal mindset?"

I'm "a freud" not, old soul. You must trigger the synchronicities yourself. There are signs and symbols everywhere. Look, listen for them each waking moment and also while dreaming, right Sigmund?

Right! exclaims Freud, who now joins Jung above. ***And may I add that dreams are often most profound when they seem the craziest.***

"Yeah, figured as much. Docs, if I may say so, you two seem like wild and crazy, fun guys."

We are! Have fun—always! they call out in unison with strong German accents.

"See you guys later!"

Or you could have said, "See you Time and again." Hello, I'm Albert Einstein, past, present, and future. I loved the song your pub mates sang about space-time.

"Professor Einstein, this is such an unexpected honor. I don't have the words."

I very rarely think in words. A thought comes, and I may try to express it in words afterward.

"Or before?"

Very good.

Now you're seized by a new question: "Storytellers, what about the discovery of NMDA receptors? All that memory encoding Stuart has been trying to help me understand. Are any of them around to explain?"

An elderly Storyteller appears and is quick to respond: ***I'm afraid not. You see, they're all still alive. When they're no longer with you, they'll be with us, and you can speak to them then. Or, obviously, when your Time comes and you seek admission here, you can commiserate.***

The scene grows quiet. It seems like the stream of historical personages has ended.

But a familiar face suddenly reappears—one you instantly recognize as Lil' Teller, the high-spirited teen who previewed your dance party. ***Yo! Masa, my main man and fav space case, wassupity up! Say, why not give the "James Gang" a big ol' surprise? Pay 'em back big time. C'mon, let's have us some wild times tonight. Wanna see what's gonna drop?***

Sure you do. And instantly, you're able to preview it. A brand-new scenario unveils. Scene by scene, it explodes in orbiting panels above you, illuminating the night sky. Your eyes are bulging as you stand and literally stumble around in circles, contemplating the riotous activities about to unfold—each projected in separate panels floating by in a captivating panorama. Just like before the dance party.

One panel shows Farnsworth shielding his eyes while fleeing the cluster of Native American paintings who are now animating wildly. Another shows Watanabe running around in circles, covering his ears. Still another shows Kobayashi with a panicked expression slumped in a corner. The final one shows the old man in the painting manically winking and grinning. It's like Disney's Haunted Mansion ride on steroids.

Now, far from feeling paranoid, you're laughing out loud. The "James Gang" will absolutely fall for this. They'll walk right in. Those amateurs think they can drug you up and blow your mind? Ha! Wait till they see what happens to theirs!

Above, a young Storyteller appears, looking excited. ***Yes, it was, is, shall always be, exhilarating.*** *So, from now on, I have nothing to fear?* ***Relax, enjoy the ride.***

Ah, yes, now you fully understand. *Plant intelligence—herbal friends and allies, vegetal dreams and schemes. Just love all you—guys? Gals? Seeds? Buds? Secretions?—whatever, whoever you—my brainy companions, my psychic guardians—are. And this wondrous gathering from the collective unconscious! Might you all be collectively watching over me?* ***Always!*** call out tonight's voices in unison. And once again, the song plays longingly and lovingly inside your head.

CHAPTER FORTY-SIX

Standing before the cottage entrance, you take a deep breath. *So, Storyteller, this is where I live . . . my actual life.* ***Welcome home.***

The door is ajar. Pushing it open, you cast a quick glance inside while calling out for Rae. But there's no reply. Then, overpowering brightness, overwhelming anxiety. A powerful whoosh rings in your ears. You take a deep breath. You're nauseated, dizzy, cold, and filled with dread. Again and again, you deeply inhale and slowly exhale. Little by little, the brightness and noise recede. You feel calmer, warmer. Fear gradually subsides. Furnishings slowly materialize.

There are scents—powerfully familiar scents. The scene achieves clarity, becomes audible, comfortably warm. But you're struck by an anomaly: the place looks different than it did just moments ago—rearranged somehow. You don't feel as though you're remembering; it's more immediate—like reliving. Now, suddenly, your thoughts rush into the maelstrom of a different mindset. Streams of thought collide, disintegrate, reassemble, and reemerge in a different now.

What did the NHK jingle just say? News at 21:00?

Jeez, it's already nine p.m. You're running late. Rae is arriving shortly. You are *stressed*, nothing is ready. The bar is stocked, arrays of sushi and yakitori laid out, but details of the stomach do not concern you. What does concern you is of greater importance. Which background visuals should flicker on the periphery tonight? What sounds? What lights? What special effects to relax and unwind your guest?

You need to create a milieu to stimulate a full awareness of a startling new medium so one Raemond Starr can tell you how all this should *sound*—before, during, and after the live production. But there's no more time to deliberate. You'll fire up the full arsenal. Anything worth doing is well worth overdoing!

A quick spin around the apartment, and you load a succession of animation classics now rendered as 3D holograms: *The Best of Max Headroom* and Pixar's *Onward*, *Cars*, *Soul*, *Inside Out*, and several of the early *Toy Story* films. Interspersed throughout the space is a familiar collection of Japanese manga characters. The clips project soundlessly in midair as video guests float and mingle throughout the rooms.

Hurry now. Only a short time remains. Switch on the refrigerator's special effect—a neon waitress blinks into existence. Flip on overhead pastel spotlights—Yamagata's *Circus in the Square* flashes onto the dining room wall while Picasso illuminates in the living room and Matisse glimmers in the hall. *Hurry, hurry.* You position talking dolls and undulating plants, cuckoo clocks and infrared wireless marionettes, musical chimes and kaleidoscopic viewfinders. Switch on the glow globes and liquid light displays.

Almost there. A tape is popped into the deck to record tonight's session. Glancing out the window, you see your guest alight from a taxi in the snowy street below. Your fingers fly across the multitude of remote controllers, and suddenly the place is packed with more guests—a frenetic strobe-lit Pee-wee Herman is mincing along the wall; an oversized Groucho is mouthing silent jokes; Disney and *Zelda* characters galore are milling about.

There. The rooms blaze with the sparkle, color, and clarity of high-tech "Jamerica." All that's missing is sound; the apartment is enveloped in a golden silence that you want Raemond Starr, musician, composer, arranger, and job candidate, to fill. So whatever musical future he's tromping up the stairs with right now, you guess you're as ready as you'll ever be to offer a high-tech, high-touch, holographic "howdy" to him and it.

Doorbell. Greetings. Pleasantries. Rae is a bounder, the type of guy who explodes onto scenes, into rooms—beaming, bowing, scurrying about. Now he's pummeling you with questions about these wild special effects.

Chimes. Cuckoos. Dinner.

You settle in for hours of fantasizing, eating, and drinking, but mainly listening to the broadest spectrum of music you've ever heard from a single composer—classical, jazz, folk, pop, rock, New Age, neo-psych—just about everything required to score the scenarios. Eventually, though, you see by the cartoon Swatch on the wall that this party's over; it's time to let him go—before the trains stop and the taxis quit. You tell him he's hired, but you both know that was a foregone conclusion. Rae ejects himself from the couch and propels to the door.

Thank-yous. Good nights. Powering down.

Video guests likewise depart. You make a mental attempt to sum up your dinner guest. Musically, artistically, he's the real deal, a great guy, a fabulous hire. You're sure glad you struck up that conversation with that Japanese guy in Sofia.

As always, whenever you have strong impressions, you reach for your diary to dictate into. The blank page you're staring at begins to blur. You put the book down and drift into the darkness and quiet but sense light and noise from farther away. Someone's calling you.

"Masa, you okay?" It's Rae's voice.

You blink. You're back, standing in the entry hall once again. "Why don't you come in? Check out your digs," Rae calls out.

Storyteller, what's going on? ***You stepped outside Time for a spell. Now you're back inside.***

You struggle to calm down while taking tentative steps inside. The cottage is silent, the temperature comfortable. The furnishings are the same, but everything is rearranged, different from moments ago. Rae is again asking if you're okay. You blink—now he's standing before you. A few more blinks and your eyes and mind sync—it's the oddest sensation. Now you're here, too, speaking to him. "How long was I standing out here?"

"I don't know," says Rae. "I was lying on the *tatami*, listening to music on headsets. Didn't even know you were here until you called out just now." He gestures at all the special effects. "Did seeing all of this ring any bells?"

Your memory of having been present just now for a past event remains clear. "Rae, tell me, when and where did we first meet—like, face-to-face?"

"Let's see," Rae furrows his brow. "It was a few winters back, an evening I'll never forget. You'd invited me to your condo in Tokyo. I remember there'd been a snowstorm. Nearly impossible to get a taxi."

"So, what happened that night?"

"Oh, we had a great time, mainly listening to music. Best 'job interview' I ever had," he replies.

"Was all this stuff there back then?"

Rae nods affirmatively. "I felt like I'd walked into a Fellini film. I'm more used to the sensory and kitsch overload now."

"Okay, I've seen it. Let's head back," you tell him while powering down the effects. You give Rae a hearty slap on the back. Feels natural to do so, like he's an old friend.

Rae's wide-eyed. "Did you, like, turn back?"

"Yes. Relived most of that evening. I understand our friendship, how we got started working together."

The rooms are now dark. You step outside. Rae looks at you intently for a moment, then asks, "What's it like . . . coming and going . . . at the exact moment?"

"It's the strangest sensation," you tell him. "It's like I'm there but not there. Like I'm completely aware of the room but at the same time oblivious to it. Just now, Rae, you were there, but not there, simultaneously."

"Whoa."

"I know it sounds nuts—my eyes were seeing you. But my mind was seeing another you. They couldn't agree if you were really there or, shall I say, *which* of you was there. Then, after a moment, my perception of you 'not there' was gone. Leaving only you . . . here."

"Masa, did you feel like you were outside your body?"

"No, not at all. How to put this? It felt like I was outside time."

"Whoa. Now I get it," says Rae. "Actually, the other you told me how that all works."

You clap your hands in remembrance. "Guess who I ran into on the way over?"

Rae is again wide-eyed. "Who?"

"The James Gang."

Hearing this, Rae bursts out in laughter. "Ha! Good nickname. Farnsworth and the 'sabotagers,' right?"

You nod. "Yeah. Guess what else?"

"What?"

"They know about your record deal, pal."

"Bummer."

You fix on his gaze. Your tone is resolute as you grin and wildly gesticulate jujitsu moves, declaring, "The James Gang is trying to get me, you, all of us. We've got to take them out! Muhahaha!"

Rae jumps high in the air, then lands and fist-bumps you.

And so, you begin outlining your plan as sparked by Lil' 'Teller's preview. The more Rae hears, the more hysterical he becomes. "Sucks that there won't be time to write an original score," he says. "But it's okay. Already the perfect music to accompany your high jinks is playing in my head."

As the two of you continue along the passage, you describe how those scenes were projected in space so that you could actually preview the near future while also finding reassurance, obviously, that you are no longer in immediate danger.

But you're surprised when Rae acts not the least bit surprised. "Those voices you hear and scenes you see are from the collective unconscious," he informs you. "It may mean your mind has become temporarily bicameral."

"Bicameral?" That's a term you've heard repeatedly from the Storytellers and a short time ago, when Professor Jaynes uttered it.

"This is funny, Masa," Rae muses. "I'm now telling you all the stuff the other you is always telling me."

"That is funny, Rae, but tell me—does the other me know how it works?"

Rae is quick to reply. "Yes. The other you said he'd never experienced it directly but from what he'd read, there's no special trick to turning on the voices. If one is bicameral, they're just always present. They can coach you, warn you of danger, translate the foreign speech you hear."

Storyteller, should I tell him? ***Go ahead.***

"Rae, that's what they've been doing ever since I arrived."

Rae laughs and says, "So now that you know this firsthand, you should inform the other you the next time you meet."

"Rae, let's just keep this between you and me for now, okay? I don't want to alarm the others. Especially since the James Gang is trying to have me committed. They might think I really have gone berserk-o."

Rae says his lips are sealed, and after a moment, he again turns from clown to professor. "Okay. I'll be the other you giving one of your spiels," he begins. "How about . . . sometimes light travels like a particle, sometimes a wave—two properties, right? But only one thing, and at a constant speed."

"So?"

"So, Masa, the other you once told me that I gotta look at Time in two ways. Time, like space, is curved—hey, just ask any physicist. It's only *timekeeping* that proceeds in a straight line." Rae pauses to let that sink in. Then he continues holding forth à la you. "In the collective unconscious, all events exist simultaneously. Like those looping circus performances in our sky panoramas."

You snap your fingers. "That's *exactly* how they depicted our battle plan."

"Time was speaking to you, Masa, wouldn't you say?"

"Maybe, Rae, maybe. That's a good way to look at it, you old Mad Hatter, you!"

Now reaching the roundabout, you point to the exit door. "Right out there, in fact. All laid out, illuminated—I could see everything that's going to happen. Man, I got so dizzy turning round and round gaping at it."

"See, you just said 'turning'—that's how you say Time is." Now Rae's really wound up. "So, ideally, Masa, you have one hemisphere synced to time's passage—for example, us right here, right now—while the other is synced to time's eternalness—like us back there, back then, or us in the near future. Like what you say you just previewed. That make sense?"

It does. "We've got minds that can switch back and forth?" you ask him.

Ray taps his skull. "AM and FM, baby."

"Wow. Prove that one, Rae, and you'll win a Nobel!" you exclaim.

"Ha! I could sure use the money!"

"So, Professor Starr, any idea of how I switched back there and relived a past event?"

Rae's not sure but thinks maybe entering your apartment here triggered the "turning synchronicity"—because those special effects, when first encountered, can be overwhelming.

"Yes, they are," you tell him. "But I wasn't overwhelmed at all. I felt used to them."

"Your old place was outfitted the same, and we were present in both instances," he conjectures.

"Yes, we were." You laugh. "I was just there and here!"

“I think at the conclusion of the original evening,” Rae theorizes, “you might have picked up your diary. Then, tonight, when you opened it again in real time, those events melded into the ‘returning’ sync.”

“But I haven’t ‘returned,’” you remind him. “I’m not in possession of my real memories. I don’t know who I am, only who you and others say I am.”

“Make that ‘turned back,’” he amends. “To where you were just before you stepped inside your apartment but outside time.”

“I can picture this, Rae, but only abstractly.”

He grins and reaches up to lightly tap your skull, instructing, “In that case, stay tuned.”

CHAPTER FORTY-SEVEN

"Oh, you people are gonna *love* this," Rae prefaces, wild-eyed.

You stand and summarize what will be needed—a few quick scripts generated and voice recordings made, some audio samples from a collection of pop and classical recordings you assume they have, stock footage of certain rooms you know they have because the girls showed you the video library earlier, a short filming session against the blue screen, and whatever postproduction is required.

"Sorry I can't help much. Got no idea how to actually do all this," you say, sweeping your hand before the vast array of equipment. "Did I ever?"

Rae brightens and declares, "Masa, you're already back on the job. Imagining is what you do. Assets are what we do."

"Oh gummy good drops!" yells Megumi. "More fun than a barrel of Montys."

"It's 'monkeys,' Megumi," you say, trying to correct her.

"No, she's talking about your dog," says Rae. "You've got this killer-cute Westie, which by the way I've been taking care of this week. His name is Monty."

"Oh." *But Storyteller, would my Monty recognize me, since I wouldn't know him right now?* ***Good doggies never forget their true humans. Remember Crunch?***

Namiko signals she has a question. "Masa, do you now recognize the old man with the white beard on the second floor?" She brings the cluster up on a nearby monitor. "Look closely, and tell us who you see in the center."

"Gosh, is it supposed to be a future me?" you venture. "I swear, every time I walk by, I ask myself that." You'd been meaning to bring that up and are glad she did, obviously trying a different tack to snap you back.

"No, my friend," says Stuart. "Does look somewhat like an aged you, but it's not." He pauses, taking a deep breath before informing, "That's your father, your real father. Namiko thinks it's time to tell you."

You're surprised and puzzled. "So why is his portrait hanging at the manor?"

"In that location, we will always hang something belonging to the current player," Namiko explains. "A favorite painting, a family photo, or some other cherished item."

"As such, it will likely always fail to fit the decor," says Stuart.

Adds Malcolm, "Serves as a kind of reality check." He explains that throughout the scenario, continuous lack of recognition will let him know the player remains successfully turned. However, should recognition occur early on, then it's back to the halfway house for more preparation.

"You passed with flying colors," says Stuart, "by never once mentioning one of your most precious mementos, your father's self-portrait."

"Oh, is he an artist?" you ask.

"Yes," Malcolm replies. "He also painted all the Indians in the cluster."

"Had no idea," you tell them. "Good for the game, I suppose, but not so good for me trying to get back to the actual me." And once again the strong doubts creep in, causing you to wonder if you'll ever find a way back. "There has to be a way," you tell them, with no small amount of desperation seeping into your voice. "Gotta admit, people, I'm starting to get the real jitters over this."

"There is a way, and we're certain to suss it out," Stuart reassures. "Look at this." He directs your attention to a science site he's pulled up on his laptop.

FALSE MEMORIES OF LIFE EVENTS CAN BE PLANTED, THEN REVERSED, NEW STUDY FINDS

You scan the article, learning of several techniques that purportedly correct false recollections without damaging true memories. "Sounds encouraging," you say. "Thanks for showing me." Your high anxiety momentarily subsides.

"We'll sample them all"—Stuart brightens—"and find the one that works a treat!"

You smile and say, "Mind if I ask one more small question?" Stuart gestures to go ahead. "What's my name?"

Stuart places a reassuring hand on your shoulder. "Masa, we can't tell you yet."

"On the drug scientists' explicit instructions," Malcolm hastens to add. "You're not to be addressed by your real name until you've 'fully returned.' They said it could be dangerous, could snap you out of your turned state prematurely. Under no circumstances, they told us during the hypnosis phase, should any name be embedded in your alternate mindset."

You clap your hands. "Hey, I just now realize that nobody in there ever addressed me by name. It was always 'm'lord,' 'dearie,' 'mate,' or something else."

Malcolm nods. "The entire cast was informed, and reminded over and over backstage, not to address you by name."

Says Stuart, "Masa, if I may ask, what happens now, right at this moment, when you try to recall your name?"

You furrow your brow, press your fingertips against your temples, try to intensely concentrate—but to no avail. "Nothing," you say. "I draw a complete blank. I recall that happening throughout my stay in there. It's the same way you feel whenever the name of someone or something simply escapes you. You try your hardest, but you just can't recall it. Then later, without even trying, the missing name or word just pops back in. Not uncommon, right?" Everybody nods in agreement. "Well, for me, my name never does," you say glumly. "But for now, I'll stop trying."

CHAPTER FORTY-EIGHT

You were actually able to contribute. Writing those short scripts with Stuart was great fun. You wish it hadn't been so rushed, though, so they could have been more original. Now that the scripts are finished, they've told you to relax.

You've had time to think. There are a few nagging game questions that you want to bring up. You pick up the production guide and open it to the first edition of *The Village Journal*. "Stuart," you ask, "this Ice Age story was supposed to be my 'rebirthday' reminder, right?" Stuart nods. "It's an awfully tough clue," you observe, "for something as critical as divining a password."

"Yes. By the way, that actually happened," Stuart says, opening your scrapbook to an old clipping from *The Japan Times*. There, you see the identical story, this one penned by a "Gene Guy."

"Who's this?" you ask, pointing to the byline.

"You! You, again!" Stuart calls out. Your stupefied expression causes everyone to laugh out loud. You had no idea—naturally. But beyond writing a clever hoax, you tell them, which apparently was recycled into this game, you still don't get it. Stuart picks up the scrapbook and adopts his newscaster voice. "For the first and only time in Japanese history, an April blizzard struck Tokyo early that Sunday morning. When the city woke up to the article, it was paralyzed, buried in snow."

Malcolm takes up the tale. "Many panicked citizens, frantic for details, didn't take the time to even glance at your giveaway photo before calling the newspaper, the police, the national defense agency, or anybody else they could think of."

Malcolm and Stuart are both laughing. As long-term expatriate residents, they remember reading about the incident and its aftermath. "It was reminiscent," Malcolm says, "of Orson Welles's *War of the Worlds* that caused a panic in the US in the nineteen thirties."

"Oh, I remember reading about that," you tell them. "People listening to a Halloween radio drama thought the Martians had actually invaded."

"I'm into their archive." Malcolm has pulled up a front-page story penned by the paper's then managing editor himself. He summarizes aloud: "This follow-up story describes the series of misunderstandings that resulted from your prank. Among them: immediate visitations by the Tokyo police and Japanese Self-Defense Forces demanding access to the journalist and all source materials related to the story."

"Really?" you exclaim. "The cops raided the paper? You gotta be kidding."

"No, Masa, they actually did. Says here they relented only when shown the globe, the Lego satellite, and the twine used to suspend it. But when the Japanese press picked it up and translated the article, they hadn't included the photo."

"This is wild," you tell them.

"Oh, it gets much wilder, I can assure you." Malcolm gulps some sake before continuing. "It says here that there were panicked entreaties from National Panasonic, Mitsui, and other manufacturers of refrigeration equipment for more information."

"Room air-cons in the Ice Age—tough sell," quips Rae, shaking his head in mock despair.

Malcolm continues, "The paper got dozens of calls from embassies and hundreds more from ordinary citizens in hysteria. There was even an international call to the editor from the Japanese prime minister, who had heard the report secondhand while abroad."

"It's hilarious, all right," you tell them, "but to me, this just sounds like a freak snowstorm that turned out to be marvelously coincidental with the spoof."

"When you return, my friend," Stuart informs, "you'll resume preaching mercilessly about the curvature of Time, its properties, and the causality of events. You'll proclaim, self-righteously, if you hadn't written the story, it wouldn't have snowed."

"I take it I often rant in pubs?" you ask sheepishly.

Again, Malcolm is amused. "We all do. It's how we unwind after work. There's not all that much to do up here."

Adds Rae with a fiendish grin, "It's all grist for our scenario mill."

"Great story," you tell them gloomily. "But, sorry, doesn't ring any bell." You check your scrapbook for more articles by "Gene Guy." There are two pieces, the first being a retrospective on *The Japan Times* itself, published in an anniversary edition. Apparently, as an editor's introductory note explains, the paper had you search its archives and recount offbeat stories they'd run in the distant past.

One of them is really bizarre. After World War II ended, your introduction explains, the merchants of Tokyo's Ginza desperately wanted to welcome the cash-laden American occupying army. Not knowing a single Westerner, they tried to give themselves a crash course on Christianity and holiday gift-giving.

You'd written:

> At ten o'clock, on that long-awaited December morning in 1946, at the most famous intersection in Japan, the curtains parted on Mitsukoshi department store's main display window. And there it stood—a life-sized Santa Claus nailed to an eight-foot cross.

Nearby, Megumi signals she's aware of the story. "Sorry, Santy-san!" she calls. You continue reading.

> The sizable crowd out front marveled at the display, at what exotic spiritual beliefs their conquerors must hold. For hours, not a single merchant or passerby had any idea that anything was wrong. Not until the first GIs arrived. The Americans, immediately sensing a colossal cultural misunderstanding but with no harm intended, tried to explain the true meaning of Christmas to the mystified shopkeepers, who with sincerest apologies, took Santa down from the cross.

You chuckle, holding up the pages with the story and announcing, "Well, I guess there was no way to stick that one in the game."

Everyone nods in agreement.

"But does it help you remember yourself, Ma-chan?" Reiko asks.

"I wish it did, but it doesn't. It's just another weird, funny yarn I hadn't heard before and have no memory of writing it."

The other "Gene Guy" piece is also odd but in a different way.

"Disneyland!" you exclaim, glancing at the headline photo that accompanied the story. "But where is everybody?"

Stuart chuckles. "You like to call it your 'Emperor's New Clothes' story."

Malcolm offers a quick summary: "It tells how Tokyo Disneyland was virtually empty the first few days after it opened—because Japanese people, due to all the preopening publicity, had collectively assumed that no tickets would be available for days, maybe weeks. As you know, they often group think en masse."

"No, I don't *know*, Malcolm," you tell him. "How would I?"

"Sorry, I misspoke," he replies. "I forgot. Assuredly, the other you certainly knows."

You examine the photo more closely. "Whoa. The caption says it was taken on a Friday afternoon in spring. I can see sunny skies above this totally empty park."

"Talk about overhype backfiring!" Rae throws both hands up and pantomimes an explosion.

"So what happened?" you ask.

"After your story broke on the front page of the paper," says Malcolm, "the Japanese-language dailies and Asian wire services picked it up. Attendance at the park soared virtually overnight."

"Ah, a perfect Disney happy ending," you muse.

"Like your April Fools' spoof, this story had quite an aftermath as well," says Stuart.

"Okay, Stuart, do tell." This session keeps getting funnier—and stranger—even though it produces no memory jogs.

"For days," Stuart says, "the Japanese press ran with a rumor that Tokyo Disneyland's American marketing manager had secretly put you up to this 'exposé' to boost attendance, because, they speculated, you're a fellow American and the manager figured you'd be willing to help."

"Was this true? Was I in cahoots with Disney?"

"Most certainly not, you told us when we first heard about this years later."

"So I thought to do this all on my own?"

"You said Disneyland had been open for a week but you didn't know a single soul who'd actually been there, it was a slow news day, and that a voice in your head suggested you 'cruise on out to the park.'"

Was that you, Storyteller? ***Nope. You hadn't connected with us yet.*** *Plant folks?* ***It was! Fun times.*** *But how—was I under some influence that day?* ***Yes, us.*** *Goodness gracious!*

Malcolm signals that he's found the follow-up. "Oh yes, the press conference where the Japanese media confronted the Disney guy on the rumor that they'd invented some phony journalist named Gene Guy and either planted the story themselves or persuaded some *gaijin* reporter to do so."

Rae whispers, "Masa Gene, *gaijin* means 'alien' in English."

You tap your skull, mouthing, "I know, I heard." Then you say to the group, "So that's what inspired my pen name?"

"Yes," Malcolm acknowledges, then continues summarizing. He says the Disney guy said no, they didn't put any reporter up to it. And no, they didn't write the story themselves, asserting that they are not that smart . . . and not that stupid."

"By the way, when did Tokyo Disneyland open?" You vaguely sense some connectivity here but can't get it to crystallize into an authentic memory.

"April fifteenth, 1983," Malcolm says. He chuckles. "Your story ran a week later. We thought you'd never ask."

"Didn't you notice the year on your April Fools' spoof?" Stuart adds. "It was 1984."

No, you hadn't noticed and now you're flabbergasted. "All this Gene Guy stuff is clearly not from my lifetime. So I'm totally not getting this."

"Oh, but it is from your life, Masa Ginza-Gene-Guy-san." Reiko laughs. "You don't know how old you really are?"

Your spine tingles and chills. All of a sudden this has become unnerving. "Um, I can't even remember my name, let alone my age."

"Look in the mirror. Take a guess, *ojii-san*," says a giggling Megumi as she pulls out a compact from her purse.

Asks Rae, "What's *ojii-san*?"

"Grandfather," Stuart replies.

Rae winks at you, improvising, "Mirror, mirror, in my hand. Please tell me how old I am."

"Oh, I don't know," you mumble, peering into the glass while moving it back and forth, side to side, examining your countenance from every angle. "Midforties, maybe early fifties?"

Lingering silence. Everyone looks blankly at one another seemingly wondering which one is going to break the news.

Finally, Stuart does. "Try . . . midseventies."

"Stuart!" you cry out. "Wha-wha-what are you saying? No way. Not possible. This is nuts."

"Mushroom magic," declares Malcolm. "Best natural antiaging remedy on the planet, so you claim. Told us that while the multitudes are spending fortunes on all these new regenerative therapies, you've been using the serum your entire adult life. It works quite nicely on most people—just look at those youthful female faces gathered round us. But it really works incredibly, almost miraculously, on you . . . We don't know why."

A shiny brownish-red mushroom brightens overhead, warbling: ***We know.*** *Tell me, tell me, plant pal. How in the world?* ***Most users apply but never ingest us.*** *Or the other way around?* ***Yes, but both regimens are required.*** *To do what?* ***Seriously slow aging.*** *That's all there is to it? You shrooms are the fountain of youth? Really?*

The mushroom pauses its revolution and lowers its cap, appearing to nod yes. ***Plus diet and exercise, of course!***

You glance around at the trio, asking, "So, Namiko, just how old are you three?"

"Midthirties," she replies. "All of us . . . Surprised?"

Absolutely. If you were running a bar, you'd ask for IDs. "So, do you gals eat healthy, work out? . . . Do I?"

"Oh, they certainly do," says Rae. "And you too, religiously."

"Masa Gene-san," says Reiko, "you've got a yummy diet—mainly vegan, sometimes vegetarian, but with lots of sashimi, of course!"

"Well, if that's true," you tell her, pointing to the lab exit, "I certainly fell way off it in there."

Malcolm nods, adding, "Oh, you forsake it on special occasions. But here in the manor environs, you say the surrounding forest is chock full of nutrients, and that we should all forage out there ourselves for health and happiness."

You give him a slight smile, not knowing what else to say or ask concerning these mind-boggling revelations.

So I'm actually an old guy, Storytellers? An old hippie-type with flowers in his flowing gray locks fades in, advising, ***Hey, man, just go with the flow. Like enjoy yourself!*** *Been flow-going ever since I got here. No other choice.* ***You know, friend, being an oldster but looking like a youngster ain't so bad. Think about it.*** *Hey, dude, I am. So far, no downside . . . Yeah, a hundred percent, I could get used to this.* **Far out, man.**

You take a deep breath, letting go of all your previous disquiet, refocus on your colleagues, and simply return to the topic at hand.

"So, people, all these Gene Guy anecdotes must have occurred before we started working together, correct?"

"Oh yes," Stuart replies. "Long before any of us knew you."

"Or were even born," adds Rae, gesturing at himself, Malcolm, and the girls.

Reiko leans over, saying she's ready for you on the blue screen.

"Time to prepare for righteous skirmishing!" calls Rae. *"En garde! Saboteurs!"*

CHAPTER FORTY-NINE

Reiko's got cameras and lights set up the way she wants to minimize shadows. But after peering through the lens, she steps back and says, "Sorry, Masa, your shirt has too much blue."

"The idea," Rae says, "is to remove all the blue and composite the left-over image—you—into the target scene."

"Is this okay, Masa G?" Megumi has retrieved a white sweatshirt from a nearby garment closet. She also produces an orange ball cap with an embroidered MASA G emblem and a plastic propeller on top. "You like to wear it at work," she says while placing the cap and giving the propeller a spin.

"Oh, that'll do nicely," you tell her.

Rae plays the song you two have chosen. You sing along a few times, trying to sync with the artist. When you think you've got it, Reiko films several takes.

While you were filming, Megumi retrieved an item she thought you'd like to see—a full-size rendering of the Hanover coat of arms. "Namiko-san showed me some books to get ideas," she explains, "but I didn't like the pictures so much. So I just put in things *I* liked!" Her brow furrows. "But oops, I thought Manor House meant M-a-n-n-e-r House."

"Hilarious!" you call out. "No wonder that professor didn't know what to make of all the flying tableware."

But Namiko catches your comment and reminds you, "Another false memory, Masa-san. There wasn't any visit to a professor. That never happened."

Except you know you've heard that "M-a-n-n-e-r House" quote before.

Storyteller, can you help out here? One quickly appears and replies, ***You did. But it was an accidental leak during hypnosis into one of your false memory imprints.***

Memory leaks? Into false memories at that! How can you possibly have a clear recollection about things that never happened to begin with?

The lab has become a beehive. Stuart has finished his multiple voice recordings. Megumi and Rae are editing, adjusting pitch and tempo, and adding vocal effects. Namiko and Reiko are editing you out of the blue background and into manor locales. They've even got you plugged in to the occasional odd job. At last, the time comes for RenderRama to take over and process all the audio, musical, and video data. Everybody reassembles.

"By the way, ladies, your English is quite good. Where did you all learn it?" you ask.

Namiko is first to reply. "In Japan, we study English grammar at school, but I first learned to speak it a little from watching TV commercials that had English slogans in them."

"Me too," says Reiko, "plus I learned a lot from repeating over and over the English I found on fancy stationery and shopping bags."

Megumi is eager to share how she practiced English back in the day. "Back in junior high, every Sunday, I went down to all the T-shirt shops in Harajuku. I studied all the English on them, then bought the ones I liked best. At home, I'd put them on, look in the mirror, and say them out loud every day."

"Interesting," you tell them. "I'm trying to imagine a vocabulary principally derived from T-shirts, shopping bags, and TV commercials."

But it's hard to follow any longer—you're so exhausted. Been up for nearly twenty-four hours now, you figure. Your head is heavy; finally it droops down and you fall silent.

But not for long. T-shirts, shopping bags, stationery, TV commercials. Feels like you're turning, gradually entering some kind of waking dream.

You find yourself outside, under the glare of hot lights, sitting at a table labeled JUDGES in what looks like the largest, most glittering TV quiz set ever constructed. High above, a giant neon sign proclaims EIGO J-POP TEEN IDOL FINALS.

Onstage, television cameras are being positioned while a technical crew scurries about. All around you is the loud murmur of youthful excitement.

Stuart is seated on one side of you, Rae on the other. "Look," says Stuart, pointing upward, "there are at least ten thousand middle school kids up there!" You lift your gaze and turn your head in all directions, blown away by the multitudes of riveted, expectant Japanese youth in black school uniforms packing the stands. Then you regard your colleagues more closely—both look quite a few years younger! Those Japanese makeup artists you hired are simply incredible. You wonder how you look.

Now you remember! *Storytellers,* you *previewed this the night I got the first letter.* ***Indeed, we did.*** *So what is this?* ***Apparently, you're now reliving a real event that occurred here just last week.*** *Really! And we can also communicate inside these flashbacks?* ***Of course! Just like inside real Time.***

"Well, Masa," exudes Rae, "at last, the finals. This is *it*. Tonight, one of our lucky girls will be crowned Team Heavenly's J-Pop Princess of Pout!"

You turn sideways and look over at the finalists, one of whom you'll be crowning later this evening. It's Namiko, Reiko, and Megumi, all outfitted in pastel spaghetti-strapped party dresses. You're absolutely floored—every day at work, they are thirty-somethings; tonight they look like teenagers.

You look around for a mirror or some reflective surface to see if you look younger too. You finally find one. Unlike Stuart and Rae, nary a single year has been peeled back from your face, it seems. You look exactly the same.

Storyteller, can you explain? ***Their makeup artists are nonpareil. And of course, mushroom serum, when properly applied, immediately takes five years away.*** *But why not me?* ***Already applied, old chap. You couldn't possibly look any younger.***

You see that each contestant holds a microphone in one hand while clutching a small stuffed animal with the other. They all look on the verge of tears.

Because you only have a bit part and were too busy to attend prior rehearsals, Rae leans over to fill you in. "Since they are all equally petite, bubbly, and cute, the upcoming interviews and, later, the song competition, will decide the winner." He then explains the rules: "Masa, every answer they give—every song they sing—has to consist of English catchphrases that originated in Japan. Either printed on a product or excerpted from a broadcast."

Now, striding onto the stage is fabulously handsome, now thirty-something Malcolm, tonight's master of ceremonies. He greets the audience with the great gusto of a proud impresario. "Please, boys and girls, tonight, let's enjoyment without thinking disgusting things. Become a superhero of Team In. Because when our hearts are free and young, fashion is the way of the world!" The CGI crowd cheers, claps, and stomps its strong approval.

You nudge Rae. "What's all that gibberish from Malcolm?"

Rae explains, "His script has him speaking totally authentic shopping-bag English, same as the contestants—isn't he great?"

"Contestant number one, Reiko-chan," booms Malcolm, his resonant voice filling the starlit stadium. "Can you name your truest desire for happy life in Club Heavenly?"

"Oh! Easy peasy," gushes Rei-chan. "A ¥300 million wedding at My New Otani!"

"Oh really?" Malcolm gasps, then lowers his voice roguishly. "That would mean a super My Championship Honeymoon with an eeeeeeeenormous sumo star, now, wouldn't it?"

Stunned, Reiko drops her fluffy rabbit and shrieks, *"Yaaaaaadaaaaaa,"* in three octaves as her hand shoots upward to cover her mouth.

Stuart leans over to quickly explain that this is part of the compulsories—judges must pay very close attention to holding all the notes in a *yada*. They expect good hand-to-mouth coordination throughout, and the same scrutiny applies whenever a contestant whines out an *uso*, or simply stands and pouts with tears welling up.

Rei-chan continues: "Being cool isn't the only thing in life. It is life!" She shrills, squinting her eyes, clenching her fists, and running in place, "So don't let some hotshot ruffle your feathers."

The crowd leaps to its feet and chants, "Fight on! Fight on! Fight on!"

Malcolm returns, flashing a wide Ryan Seacrestian smile. His impossibly white teeth actually sparkle, like in manga anime, when the overhead lights hit them in a certain way.

"Here's contestant number two, Nami-chan. Sooooooo, young lady, what's your super idea for life in Team Paradise?"

"Be individually basic, sweet, nice, and really sugary," she admonishes one and all.

The throng yells, "Keep charging!" for a full thirty seconds.

Stuart leans in and whispers, "Good, but her answer really needed more elaboration."

"So you're going to mark her down?" you ask.

He nods. "I'm afraid so."

Now it's Megumi's turn. With no hesitation she begins. "Be a sing-a-song writer-singer, meet Mr. Guy, idol of girls, and go artificial surf-making!"

The crowd roars its approval, and Megu-chan jumps up and down, waving her stuffed kangaroo, shouting at the top of her lungs. "Be a true-to-your-school winner and keep challenging fashion's spirits!" she implores the crowd, which responds with a prolonged standing ovation.

You glance over at Stuart. "Well?"

He gives a thumbs-up.

Malcolm returns to center stage, smiling at the contestants and complimenting them effusively. The girls in the audience shriek their adoration of their newfound idol, Emcee Malcolm. "And now," he shouts, "our Super Sing-a-Song Fest. Contestants, you are the new-wave generator, forever living the famous songs and favorite fashions from the fifties. Sooooooooo, girls, let's Hai Teen Boogie!"

"Right on! Right on! Right on!" chants the throng in the stands.

First up is Namiko. Rae leans over and gives you a quick rundown on her earlier sessions. "I swear, Masa, throughout the prelims, her *uso* and *yada* intonations were flawless, her hand-to-mouth technique exceptional, her pouty expressions classic. You should've been there."

"Wish I'd had the time," you tell him. "But I'm completely absorbed in preparing for our test run right now."

"Feel like you're ready?"

You nod. "As I'll ever be."

"When do you take all the memory drugs?"

"Will start in a day or so—the plan is to have me arrive here on April first."

It's so weird, Storyteller. It's like I can pause this playback anytime and talk to you. ***We're outside the event's timeline. Shall we "go back in," and allow Time's flow to resume?*** *Sure, but I still can't believe how cool Time is.*

Onstage, Nami-chan presses her toy squirrel to her heart, closes her eyes, and begins swaying softly as she intones: "Oh I'm a happy preppie from

Mississippi, here for beautiful human life. Let's take enjoymently in fashion and sports."

The crowd oohs and ahhs.

"California dreamin' in Long Beach, a healthy day in the life of me. Neat and now feeling in Super City—let's squash! Now, with a joy in my heart, I say gay togs is the super idol of girls. It's so neat. Fine. Gimme chocolate!"

Rae, whose eyes are tearing up, leans in and whispers, "Masa, what more could any girl say?"

You nod in agreement, saying, "Hard to see how either of the remaining two can possibly top Nami-chan."

But Rei-chan almost immediately does. Her "Boogie Woogie Puppy Love / Yum, Yum, Follow the Sun" song-and-dance routine is an absolute showstopper. Now the whole stadium's out of their seats and rocking. Even Stuart and Rae are up, stomping and clapping to the pulsating sounds and zany lyrics. It looks like, as judges, they've cast aside any pretense of neutrality.

The commotion eventually subsides. And now, once again, Megumi steps forward. Her confident expression seems to indicate she already knows she's going to win.

Megu-chan's "I love cookies / Hot me" medley starts off as a riotous mix of J-Pop, K-Pop, and rap that once again gets the entire stadium up and jumping around with wild abandon. Now she's spinning and spinning like a disco top, each time tossing her stuffed toy high in the air and catching it, sometimes even behind her back. You wonder how long she had to practice that one. At least ten tosses. Not a single dropped kangaroo.

Unexpectedly, and dramatically, her vocals slow and segue into a heart-rending ballad, the soulful lyrics pouring forth with an irresistible poignancy. "The twilight kittens' soft, peaceful, paprika symphony dances to the beat of flickering stars."

Weeping tears of joyous admiration, Rae makes no attempt to hide his emotions. "Oh, Masa, how I wish I could compose like that," he sobs. "And that look will haunt me forever, I'm certain."

"Rae, you cannot possibly be serious."

"Well, no"—he laughs—"but I like acting, too. This skit is so much fun."

But as the stage lights dim, the sweet music fades, and Megumi manages to hold her wounded countenance for what seems like eternity, you unexpectedly snap out of it.

Storyteller, that was nuts. What a show! ***It was. We rarely witness scenes like that.***

Now you feel you've turned back to the present. You're back in the lab, hearing Rae speaking in his normal voice. "Masa, you okay?" It's the normal Rae, not the younger-looking version who a moment ago was excitedly judging a teen pageant.

"Rae, that was so incredible," you mumble, still a bit dazed. "Hey, which one won?"

"Aha! Masa, you must have turned to the song contest!" Rae exclaims. "We just finished filming last week. The other you loved it—said afterward we'll definitely try to use it with Japanese players someday."

Now you remember. "Yeah, earlier I think Stuart said they were going to show me the video of the skit, but apparently I've just now relived it, or part of it. I was at the judge's table. A presenter or something."

"Right. All you had to do was crown the princess at the end," Rae says, "which you did with great fanfare."

Glancing over, you see Stuart and Malcolm sitting nearby, looking normal. You also spy the trio—in their usual attire looking like their usual selves—scurrying about RenderRama like they've been doing all evening. You call out to them. "Ladies, I just turned to the craziest scene starring the three of you."

"Were we cute?" Megumi calls back from far across the lab.

"I'll say, you all were so . . ." *What's the word I'm trying to think of here?* ***Kawaii***, replies a young Japanese-sounding Storyteller. *Arigato.*

"Right, girls, you were the quintessence of *kawaii*!"

"So what were we doing?" asks Reiko.

"Singing songs. In a contest."

Namiko looks amused. "So you turned back to last week's princess pageant?"

"You know I won! Woo hoo!" Megumi calls out.

"I didn't know," you call back. "My turn-back ended before the winner was announced."

Megumi walks over to you and says, "At the end, you crowned me Eigo J-Pop Princess! Hee-hee."

"Well, you three were highly entertaining and ultra . . . mega . . . uber . . . *kawaii*!"

"When God created Japanese females," Rae pipes up, "he omitted the bitch chromosome. Substituted an extra *kawaii* one instead."

"Oh, shut you up, Rae-san!" Megumi shouts.

"For example," Rae laughs, pointing to Megumi, "when we took that one to America last year—"

"Yamate kudasai. Hazukashii." Megumi's professing embarrassment, but your internal read assures you that actually she's dying for Rae to spill it.

"We're, like, in a taxi," Rae explains, "going from the San Francisco airport to Novato for a meeting with Broderbund about *Manor House*. So I ask Megumi what her very first impression of America was." Rae gestures to her to please reprise her classic line.

"Sugoi! Shinjararenai! America-niwa Makudonarudo made aru yo!" she yells.

"Wow! Unbelievable! They've even got McDonald's in America!" Rae yells in translation.

"She was perfectly genuine," Rae assures you. Then to her, he says, "Megumi, why don't you tell Masa your GOAT story."

"Oh, Rae-san, are you going to make me?"

Reiko leans over to whisper, "She means, 'Rae-san, make me tell it, please.'"

You turn, smile, and mouth, "I know."

"Megu-chan." Rae wags a finger. "Masa's your boss, and he has ordered you to tell your 'Greatest of All Time' legendary tale. So spill it, Miss Mega Cute."

"But Rae-san, I have to say bad words. Is it okay?"

"It's okay," Rae assures her. "Masa's a big boy."

Megumi stands, adopts an impish expression, clears her throat, and begins. "When I started working here, my English was not so good. It was my first time to work with foreigners. So I'd often see Masa clap his hands and say to his computer, 'Oh, I'm so fucking smart!' And Rae too. He would listen to some music and say out loud to his keyboard, 'Rae, you are fucking brilliant!' And Masa would say, 'Rae, you're a fucking genius,' and Rae would say the same thing back." You can see that everyone watching is highly amused—even though they've probably heard this yarn before.

Megumi continues: "So I asked myself, what does *fucking* mean? I'd never heard this word before. We didn't study it at school. And I couldn't find it in my dictionary I'd had since junior high. It wasn't printed on any of my T-shirts."

You look around and spot anticipatory smiles on every face as Megumi goes on. "I listened to Masa and Rae more. I figured out that *fucking* must mean *quite* or *very*, and that it's probably some cool word native speakers use. Maybe it's a classy saying I should remember." She pauses, then motions to Rae. "Okay, you can tell them what happened."

Rae is snickering, almost uncontrollably, but eventually is able to pick up the story. "So the chairman gets our entire crew invited to a big embassy party in Tokyo. We all dress up in tuxes and gowns. He has us flown down there and then chauffeured to the venue. We walk into the biggest home I've ever seen in this country. The place is packed. Ambassadors and diplomats and other VIPs from everywhere. Standing and talking and sipping champagne and cocktails. I thought maybe I was overhearing every language in the world."

Rae pauses and takes a deep breath. "So, we walk up in pairs to be introduced to the host and hostess. Masa's with Namiko. I'm with Megumi, behind him. Finally, we reach the couple. They greet us warmly. The hostess clasps Megumi's hands and tells her she knows we'd come all the way down from Camelot and how happy she is to meet us."

Rae stops and says, "Megu-chan, it's back to you. Tell Masa what you said to the hostess, quite loudly I should add."

Megumi steps forward. "Ma'am, you have a fucking beautiful house!"

Rae continues, "Total shocked silence in the room. Only the faint clinking of glasses could be heard. For thirty seconds or so, everybody stopped talking. Gradually, the hum resumed, as if nothing untoward had happened."

Megumi wraps it up. "Masa and Rae hurried me off to a corner and told me to please never, ever say that word in public again. Especially on a formal occasion."

You're still laughing but manage to say, "Megumi, I must apologize, on behalf of the other me, for setting such a bad example. But that's about as funny a story as I think I've ever heard."

Megumi's face is flushed. "Rae says it was 'Megumi's Big My-Bad.'" *Makudonarudo.* Big My-Bad—*kawaii* stories, all right, the kinds you bet are recounted endlessly in the pub after work.

You look around. So much creative energy, so many screens aglow with digital countermeasures in the making. Your gaze shifts to the video wall, with its twelve separate scenario scenes endlessly looping.

Idly, you pick up the HDTV remote. In the bottommost right window you see a relaxed scene after sunset—Bruce, Reggie, Noël, and you are standing around on the lawn munching sliders, discussing something. Now what was all that about? Curious, you enlarge the window to full screen, then bring the audio up.

Bruce and Reggie are offering their advice on finding secret restaurants, which is soon followed by Noël's passionate praise of cheeseburgers, this "peasant triumph." The conversation is interrupted by the appearance of James and Adrienne, eager to announce their engagement. You can now see your attention was diverted as you greeted them and strolled away for a few moments. Thus, you never heard then what you're watching Reggie ask Bruce now. "So where is the absolute best, melt-in-your-mouth cheeseburger you've found?"

Bruce chugs his beer before replying. But already, in your mind, blooms the answer he's about to give. Of this, you're certain. You sense a floodgate of memories about to break.

Now Namiko walks over, her gaze captured by the enormous starry night above Reggie and Bruce, prompting her to break into song about big, bright stars. You mouth what you unquestionably know the landlord will say next—"deep in the heart of Texas"—at exactly the same moment Bruce is replying on-screen, "Lone Star, deep in the heart of Texas, mate. Ever been?"

Great! Because you know—absolutely know—that you've been. Many times, in fact. And he's right about their chili cheeseburgers—they just melt. But there's one more thing—actually, a major caveat—Reggie needs to know. "Tell him, Barry, tell him," you call to the screen.

"Tell Barry what?" Namiko is bursting with excitement, as you've just addressed Bruce by his real name.

"Watch!" you call to her.

On-screen, the barkeep snaps his fingers. "But be sure to go on a Saturday, Reg. Because—"

"They only serve the chili ones on Saturdays!" you shout just as Barry echoes, "They're off menu, and you can only get them on Saturday special, mate."

"Kris's coming back!" Namiko calls triumphantly.

Shouts. Hoorays. Yahoos. The whole gang rushes over, relief evident on their faces.

Returned?

CHAPTER FIFTY

Not quite. But you're getting there, you sense, as disparate thoughts from both mindsets are bouncing around in your brain.

"So, Namiko," you begin, trying to put yourself in the frame of mind of authoring that memo you found earlier—something about a single-line formula that determines the day of the week for any given date, "did we neglect to put that puzzle in the game?"

"No," she replies. "Just before we finalized the scenario defaults, you texted us and said not to use it after all because it was too difficult."

"Where was I?"

"In the States. Dallas, Texas, I believe."

Upon hearing "Dallas," a detailed memory from the authentic you pops on like a light. Your consciousness shifts. You spot the rest of your crew and greet them heartily, feeling like you've just returned from your Texas trip and it's your first day back at work.

"Hey, Rae! As we say down at the Hawaiian ice cream parlor—whadda scoop, bra? . . . Yo, Malcolm-Director-Man, lights, camera, action! . . . Oh, Unk Stu, you're here too! . . . Ah, ladies! Nice to see me again. Charmed, you're sure."

There are puzzled looks all around. You start spinning a just-remembered yarn: "Okay, right, so I'm only in Dallas for the day. Have just finished a Saturday lunch at Lone Star and am now cruising around, killing time before this meeting I've got to attend. Then, because I hadn't been in the city for, like, thirty-some-odd years, a thought registered: Gee, wonder whatever became of my old dance partner, Candace Berry. We sure had some rip-roaring times in those Big D and Cow Town clubs."

"We haven't heard this one, Kris," says Namiko.

You leap forward. The gang rolls their chairs back, giving you a wide berth. They know the usual you tends to flail around when you're really wound up and retelling tall tales. It can be dangerous to sit too close.

"So, gang, at that very moment, right there on the tollway, I'm musing over Candy's possible whereabouts when what should appear?"

Blank stares. No guesses.

"Ha! It was a giant billboard proclaiming, 'Nordstrom presents the incomparable fashions of renowned designer Candace Berry,' or some such verbiage. Didn't matter, though. The sign definitely spelled out her name in giant letters."

You see that Stuart has turned to Malcolm, saying under his breath, "Ordinary consciousness can't trigger the synchronicity that transposes the thought and spotting the sign."

You flash him a quick thumbs-up.

"You mean, an ordinary person might happen to catch the billboard and so naturally be reminded—but not the other way around?" Malcolm asks.

"Exactly," you interject. "It's that odd way a powerful synchronicity can curl Time to answer your thought question. It also means coincidence no longer plays a part."

Nods in agreement all around. You continue, "Blown away, I exit the freeway and zoom into this mall with the Nordstrom store. Inside, I spy the Featured Designer space, scope out all the merchandise, and spot Candy's photos all around. I google her company and get their number in Beverly Hills. I call, introduce myself to her business partner, who tells me Candy's on a flight to Houston to do a store promotion, but she'll give her my message next time she checks in."

"Hold on. Were you in Dallas or Houston?" asks Reiko. "I'm confused."

"Dallas, Rei-chan . . . So I buy some presents for you gals and split. Five minutes later, I'm driving along, just thrilled over these neat gifts and the amazing synchronicity that unearthed them—when my cell rings."

"Wait!" Megumi interrupts. "Where are our presents?"

You start to tell her that you'll be handing them out soon, but, unexpectedly, you turn and mentally suspend the present scene. Someone is calling from far away, "Kris, Masa, Gene, don't go! You just got here."

It's scary at first, but there's this mental signpost flashing over and over, as if pointing to a safe space where your mindsets can coexist. You calm down, thinking perhaps these are residual effects of memory regulators coupled with psychedelics. You collapse in a chair—just in time to buckle your psychic seat belt. There's intense brightness for a moment, then it slowly dims, revealing a partial new scene. In a heartbeat, you've shot from telling your tale to smack-dab inside the story itself. You're *there*, behind the wheel of a rented Lexus, now parked on a side street in Dallas, Texas, preparing to FaceTime with your old gal pal.

Yet when you gaze outward, you still see the lab on the periphery, as well as your colleagues gathered round wearing incredulous expressions. The whole scene seems like some weird picture-in-picture on live television. But not at all scary.

You hear Rae confiding to Malcolm, "Here she comes, right on schedule."

"Too bad she wasn't going to Dallas that day, right?" Malcolm replies.

Says Rae, "Don't be so sure."

Then she appears on your phone. "Hi, it's Candace. I'm at D/FW. Just got your message."

"Wow, Candy, you look great! You're actually *here*?"

"Right. Changing planes."

"Me too, in a manner of speaking."

"But I can talk a little. I mean, it's been like thirty years. This is a *trip*!"

"Yes! And, Candy, big congrats. Just saw all your creations at Nordstrom's—can certainly see you've done very well."

"Thanks . . . so tell me, Kris, did you ever wonder what became of me?"

You're sure this has never happened before—turning unexpectedly while retaining an acute awareness of your physical whereabouts and of present events transpiring. It seems, too, like your mindsets have merged—scenario you and normal you.

You hear chimes from throughout RenderRama signaling that their processing is finished. It's time to launch the counterattack. But it looks like your squadron doesn't know what to do.

"Should we wait for Masa to snap out of it or fire away now?" you hear Rae asking the team.

Silent, uncertain looks all around. "Time is running out," Stuart says impatiently.

Somehow, you find you can mentally pause your session, enabling you to call out, "Go for it, gang!"

Rae salutes and replies, "Aye, aye, Captain! Launching phase one!"

Stuart picks up his walkie-talkie, puts it on speaker, and calls Farnsworth. "James," he says, his voice grave, "it looks as though our leader has permanently flipped out—it's been hours, and we haven't succeeded in bringing him back."

"I'm deeply concerned," Farnsworth says. "Has he made any progress at all since we last spoke?"

"None whatsoever," Stuart replies. "In fact, his condition seems to worsen as time passes." As he speaks, Stuart casts an occasional glance your way. You reckon your facial expressions, hand gestures, and propeller cap probably make it easier for Stuart to fabricate your mental breakdown.

"James, I think I'm ready to see the president after all," Stuart confides.

"Yes, Stuart," Farnsworth replies. "Regrettably, I, too, believe the time has come. We must try to help him in any way we can."

You see collective eyeballs roll at Farnsworth's attempt to feign concern and suppress joy.

"How about you and I and Malcolm go in together in the morning?" Stuart proposes.

"Of course," replies Farnsworth with enthusiasm. "I think it's a grand idea, the proper thing to do under the circumstances."

"James, are you free this evening? Malcolm and I would enjoy having a nightcap with you," Stuart then adds nonchalantly. "We could go over how to present this and how to reorganize the creative side if worse comes to worst."

Stuart gives you a wink. You smile and flash back a quick loco gesture with your index finger.

"Of course. When?" Farnsworth replies eagerly.

"Would right now be convenient?"

"Dining, pub, or bar?" Farnsworth is nearly breathless.

"Pub," Stuart replies.

"On my way," Farnsworth says, and quickly disconnects.

"Ready torpedo one," Rae whispers, and the girls load the clips.

CHAPTER FIFTY-ONE

You mentally refocus on the call with Candy, who is now asking, "So, Kris, what are you up to these days? What's your latest scenario?"

"Well, Candy, since our 'last dance,' I've been around some blocks. Met some cool folks. Fell into some great gigs."

"Bet you did. You always do. Always talking to complete strangers. I so remember that about you."

"Speaking of scenarios, that's what I'm actually doing these days. I'm creating them for Camelot, in fact. Heard of it?"

"Really? How in the world? Of course I've *heard* of Camelot. How'd you land that one?"

"Just lucky, I guess."

"So tell me, how do players reinvent themselves? Isn't that what playing these new psychic adventures requires? Forget who you are and become someone else? How do they—"

"They're called NMDA blockers, enhancers, and substitutes. I've now got a galaxy of tabs and potions to regulate the old hippocampus. But when I test our next production, it'll be my first time actually using them. Before, it was just hypnosis and psychedelics."

"You'll test by becoming the main character yourself?"

"Yes, that's the plan . . . Hey, can you hold on a sec?"

You can see that Namiko has switched the wall over to the feed from cameras on the second floor. Farnsworth is on the staircase and is about to set foot on the library side of the rotunda.

"Rei-chan, get ready," Malcolm calls, while studying Farnsworth's progress toward the wired wood carving. "Okay, now!"

On-screen, Farnsworth appears to be riveted by the wood carving, which is dissolving into a rising theater curtain. You see him seeing you in close-up, inside the panoramic outdoors revolving slowly in the background. Farnsworth clutches his chest, stumbles backward. Now you're singing to him. But it's not your voice. It's the original Police version of "Every Breath You Take," from the album *Synchronicity*, with Sting supplying lead vocals, now perfectly synced to your lip movements—lyrics that promise the butler that you'll be watching every move he makes from this moment on.

"Fantastic!" you call out. "You synced it perfectly." The curtain falls and the scene is restored. Farnsworth rubs his eyes and hurries across the rotunda, slipping several times on the gleaming hardwood floor.

"Get ready at the cluster," Malcolm calls. Farnsworth, peering over his shoulder and looking distraught, is striding down the hallway. "Now!"

As he passes the Indian cluster, a shrill whistle stops him cold. His head snaps around. He edges closer to the frame, his eyes bulging. Your dad is winking at him! Then, accompanied by maniacal laughter, the old man's face morphs into yours and back again—aging then youthening in an endless loop. The Indians, in the meantime, are dissolving, distorting, and switching around from frame to frame within the star layout. Their faces look like reflections in fun house mirrors. It's a kaleidoscope of utter madness. Finally, Farnsworth grabs his head and rushes away.

"Get ready at His Majesty's," roars Malcolm, sounding like a swashbuckling sea captain in one of his Japanese movies. The landscape painting dissolves, and there's you, standing in the middle of His Majesty's suite, again reminding Farnsworth in song that you're watching every move he makes as Sting's vocals pour through the speakers. You once again praise the team's efforts by silently clapping.

Seeking refuge, Farnsworth dashes into the pub. Right where Malcolm wants him. He presses a button that remotely locks both exits. The video feed switches to the Falstaff's interior. The room is pitch black. You and your crew can barely make out Farnsworth, who is propped against the bar and struggling to keep his balance.

Suddenly, the karaoke machine fires up, and surrounding stage lights blaze on. A full holographic image of you shimmers into view. You glow eerily in the dark while belting out the same song. But this time, it's your version, sung a cappella and horribly off-key.

"Dude, you never were any good at karaoke," quips Rae, throwing you a sidelong glance. Seeing your pitiful performance, you vow to never again set foot on a song stage.

Malcolm throws a switch that fully illuminates the entire pub. "Let's see how he likes the finale." Your crooning hologram is replaced by a young Bruno Mars. Malcolm hopes that, to Farnsworth, it looks like you instantly "turned into" the singer as the, hopefully, soon-to-be ex-butler slowly sinks to the floor. After a rousing performance of Mars's classic "Uptown Funk," Malcolm shuts off the music, dissolves the holo, and unlocks the pub. He signals to Namiko to get the music room ready.

"Candy, sorry to keep you waiting. There's a lot going on at work that I have to keep tabs on. I'll be right back."

Says Candy, "Oh, you're on two lines?"

You smile and say, "Definitely."

Candy assures you she doesn't mind these brief interruptions as you turn back to the battle.

Stuart picks up a house phone and calls Farnsworth's room. In a remarkable impersonation of the Camelot president, Stuart speaks in accented English as he leaves an urgent message. "Mr. Farnsworth, the chairman and I have received disturbing reports from our sales and marketing managers. We now wish to receive a detailed memorandum summarizing the current crisis, namely your assessment of our managing director's sanity and the competence of his closest associates. I trust you'll attend to this forthwith."

Stuart places his next call to Watanabe, as he impersonates Farnsworth speaking Japanese.

Namiko summarizes the call for Rae. "He told Watanabe-san to meet him in the music room in five minutes. He said that he had discovered something in there that he's sure would get Masa fired. Watanabe-san was very excited."

While waiting for the next bombshell, you reconnect with Candy, who's now saying, "Listen, they've delayed the boarding but only for a short time. Quickly, tell me about your latest production."

"Sure. So, we've got this nearly finished scenario called *Manor House*, which we're planning to test as soon as I get back. Goes like this: the central character is tricked into believing they've got a long-lost uncle who's a British nobleman. Guy's about to die. Tells the protagonist, me in this case, that I'm the sole heir to everything he owns."

"Mysterious relative leaves you a fortune. How quaint. Kris, how'd you come up with that?"

"Well, Candy, it's all loosely based on something that actually happened to me many years ago. When a law firm contacted me out of the blue and announced that this British nobleman was my uncle."

"Whoa, did he leave you his fortune?"

"Hardly. The guy was broke, selling off his titles. That's the only reason they contacted me. Would I care to purchase them?"

"So what did you do?"

"Flew to London. Looked him up. Turned out he was a stage actor down on his luck. We immediately hit it off. I didn't buy his titles but did offer him a job. He relocated to Japan, and Uncle Stuart and I have been conjuring up park scenarios ever since."

"Wow, Kris—so how'd this guy get to be your uncle, if you don't mind my asking?"

"By the time I was contacted, my parents and grandparents had all passed. So I had it authenticated with a DNA sample. Told Uncle Stuart I didn't need to know any lurid details from the past."

"Amazing. So you really do have a long-lost uncle."

"Um. Hold on again, Candy. Be right back."

On the wall, you see Watanabe pacing around the music room, repeatedly looking at his watch. The girls are still blown away by Stuart's ability to mimic Farnsworth's speech so convincingly. Reiko voices their admiration: "Stu-chan, we know you do voices for your job, but we had no idea you could do *Kansai-ben* just like a foreigner would sound."

"What's *Kansai-ben*?" asks Rae.

"It's the dialect of that region," Malcolm informs him. "Farnsworth first learned Japanese when he lived in Osaka, so he speaks with that accent."

"*Le petit saboteur* is in the house!" Rae announces, pointing to the monitor. He begs Malcolm to be the one to click the buttons this time. He is allowed.

The music room doors lock. "Bombs away!" he yells, pressing another button.

"See ya! Wouldn't wanna be ya!" hollers Megumi. She then turns to the group, announcing, "Now, everybody, listen to what I recorded for Rae's and Masa's tricks."

All eyes fasten on the video wall, which erupts in a cacophony of bells, chimes, glockenspiels, carillons, cuckoos, and alarms. It sounds like a hundred clocks—from a wrist beeper to Big Ben—have simultaneously struck twelve. Followed by, "Da da da dum . . . Da da da dum." After which, Beethoven himself speaks, "What's that you say? What's that? I can't hear a thing." Watanabe wheels around in the direction of the voice. Across the room, atop its marble pedestal, the composer's head has come to life.

Then, from behind Watanabe, on another pedestal, the bust of Franz Liszt is animated and calling out, "I say, Ludwig, are you deaf?" Watanabe heads for the door but finds it locked. He crouches and edges around the room, looking as if he's trying to elude an attack from insane spirits. He fails. A riot of babbling sculpture assaults from every direction.

Tchaikovsky: "They're coming to take me away! Ha ha! They're coming to take me away!"

Mozart: "We're all mad. We've always been mad."

Bach: "Speak for yourself, Amadeus."

Beethoven: "What's that you say? What's that? I can't hear a thing."

Liszt: "I say, Ludwig, are you deaf?"

Chopin: "Listen, Lud, they're playing your song."

Wagner: "Your song has no words. Why no words?"

The music has segued into a crashing, extended "Ode to Joy" that concludes Beethoven's Ninth, chosen by Namiko because, she's now telling Rae, most Japanese know it by heart. "It's our national Christmas carol," she explains.

Watanabe looks terrified as the composers, now switching to Japanese, endlessly repeat their single line of daffy dialogue. The chorus is joined by Mendelssohn, Strauss, Stravinsky, and a gaggle of others, all mouthing inanities at a shifted pitch or altered tempo.

Mahler: *"Moshi, moshi, Watanabe-kun! Anata-no atama-no nakanidare-ka-ga iru. Demo sore-wa anata ja nai."*

"What's he saying?" Rae asks excitedly.

"'Hello, little Watanabe. There's someone in your head, but it's not you,'" Malcolm translates. He adds, "Stuart loves Pink Floyd, so he did a riff on one of their lyrics. He made it even scarier by calling out to 'Watanabe-kun' as if he were a young boy."

After being repeatedly addressed by his own name, and from every direction, Watanabe covers both ears and sinks slowly to the floor. Malcolm decides *le petit saboteur* is sufficiently frazzled, so he powers down the effects and unlocks the door. Watanabe stumbles to his feet, brushes off his rumpled blue suit, and staggers out of the room.

Wide-eyed, Rae looks over at you, pointing to your propeller continuously spinning from drafts of ventilation. "Masa, Gene, Kris, are you enjoying all the madness you concocted?"

You spread your palms, replying, "Actually, I must give all credit to the mushrooms Farnsworth thought he could poison me with."

Rae chimes in to explain to the others: "Yeah, Kris told me about it down in the passageway. Said some voices showed him a preview of what would unfold. We didn't have to dream up hardly anything ourselves."

"What voices?" Megumi asks.

"Shūgō-teki muishiki," Namiko informs her. "'Collective unconscious,' I think is what they call it in English."

"Uki-uki spooky Kabuki! That's the way we like it!" sings Megumi.

"No, ladies, it wasn't them," you inform. "We can thank our shroom and button friends."

"Perhaps you'll turn back here sometime," says Stuart jovially, "to watch it all over on your internal DVR."

You nod, saying, "Stuart, you may not believe this. But that's what I'm doing right now. At least part of me thinks so. Now if you'll excuse me . . ."

You return to your friend's next question, thinking how amazing it is that you can regulate this flashback. How when you're "outside Time," as the Storytellers term it, you can, seemingly at will, make it stand still, pause your internal VCR.

"So, Kris, when the game's all over and you've returned, does your scenario self mix with your normal, everyday self?"

"Candy, I always thought it doesn't, and it never did before, but now I'm not so sure."

"What do you mean?"

"You can't be in two different physical locations at once, right?"

"Of course."

"And I always thought the mind's the same—that you can never occupy two separate conscious states, twin personas, dual mindsets, whatever you want to call it, at the same time and stay healthy."

"Um, acute schizophrenia?"

"Exactly. But now I'm finding out I was wrong."

"Whew, this is a little hard to follow, Kris. Are you saying you're possessed or something?"

"Maybe, but not in a bad way. I'm learning that with these drugs, I'm able to relive special moments—as I'm sure I'm reliving, Time and again, this reunion with you."

"Wow! So you're saying that, right now, as we are living this, you often *relive* this?"

"Sure—past and present, imagine two-one. Heck, Candy-O, I might even write a novel someday and include this encounter just to fill in any missing blanks."

"Kris, I'm sorry, but now they're calling my flight. Gotta dash. Loved our talk."

"Bye, Candi-O. Until we meet again and again."

You tune back in to Stuart's call to Kobayashi. Again, everyone is impressed with his impersonation of Farnsworth. Megumi offers a summation for Rae. "This fib was too crazy." She giggles, rubbing her palms together, her face flushed with mischievous mirth. "Stuart was Fake Farnsworth again and told Kobayashi-san an ambulance was coming to take Masa to a hospital in Shirakawa. He said 'Ginza-san' may be difficult, so he needs Kobayashi-san to help him and the paramedics capture the madman, Masa Ginza!"

Megumi is now struck by an involuntary laugh attack and can no longer continue, so Namiko takes over. "Fake Farnsworth told Kobayashi-san that, on the chairman's orders, you guys—Stuart, Malcolm, Raemond—were *not* to be told beforehand."

Stuart laughs and points to the screen. "Oh, look! *Le grand saboteur* has completely fallen for it, so shall we return to our monkeyshines?"

Kobayashi is outside the armory door, knocking furiously. "He had to get dressed," Malcolm says. "Probably can't believe he's the first to arrive."

"Just doooo it, baby," Rae exhorts, flailing his arms at the screen. Finally, Kobayashi opens the door himself. As soon as he steps inside, Rae closes and locks it remotely. Kobayashi hears the clicking sound and turns around slowly, already looking panic-stricken.

Megumi plays another theme for the room: "Dum . . . de dum-dum . . . dum . . . de dum-dum dehhh!"

"Wow! Megumi!" Rae exclaims. "*Dragnet*'s more than eighty years old and, jeez, you nailed it." She gushes appreciatively.

The lights dim and a suspenseful, low-pitched hum ensues, followed by, "Boom-boom . . . boom-boom . . . boom-boom." That unmistakable heartbeat—the percussive opening to *Dark Side of the Moon* reverberates throughout the room. Kobayashi grabs his chest, and Rae observes that, since a guy like him doesn't listen to such music, he probably thinks it's his own heart pounding. "It's teleportation time!" Rae yells, throwing another switch. "See ya later, alligator!"

"After while, pedophile!" Megumi calls out. "F-bomb you!" she adds while shaking her fist.

"Megumi, it's 'crocodile,'" Rae corrects. "And 'F-bomb you!' Do you even know what you just said?" he asks.

"Oops? Not really, but kinda," she replies. "They print it on TikTok a lot when someone's angry. After that party in Tokyo, I never say the real word anymore."

The armory, now dazzlingly bright, fills with dry-ice fog. The heartbeat pounds on in full quadraphonic, rattling the collection of full-sized medieval statues standing along the walls. The holographic floor plan appears. A red beam traces a preset destination. The fog achieves zero visibility. The walls and ceiling noiselessly revolve 180 degrees as the lone table in the center is lowered and replaced by a holographic floor covering. The fog lifts. Everything has changed—everything, in just a few seconds. Just as the helicopter sounds and screams from the soundtrack recede and music begins, Kobayashi faints dead away.

But *le grand saboteur* eventually stirs and staggers to his feet, gaping at the transformed scene of swords, shields, heralds, and standing suits of armor, all housed in glass cabinets. He gapes, too, at the centermost spot in the room where the table should be but no longer is, then at a ceiling that has changed from cedar boards to white plaster.

"You've got a round-trip ticket, dude!" Rae shouts as he throws the switch, triggering the sequence that restores—in the time it takes for the vocals to begin—the original room. "Breathe (In the Air)," which Kobayashi-san attempts to do. But as he pants heavily, the gang can see that his face registers the look of a man who would be well advised to seek a cardiologist. Malcolm motions to Rae to unlock the door, and another blue-suited automaton staggers away in search of his sanity.

CHAPTER FIFTY-TWO

Returned. Again. This time for good? You sure hope so.

You greet everyone in your normal persona and ask if you'd kept them waiting.

"Not too long." You can see that Uncle Stuart is visibly relieved as he speaks. "But it took a great deal of effort to get you back this time," he says. "Then suddenly you were off again. Gave us a bit of a fright."

"Sorry about that," you tell him. "I've never replayed the past during a return. Vaguely recall catching up with an old friend."

"We heard bits and pieces," Malcolm says. "Perhaps you'll fill us in sometime."

"Well, not right now. That encounter is already receding." Then you ask, "So, team, don't keep me in suspense. How was it? How did we do?"

"Great. Everybody thinks so," Namiko says, gesturing toward the wall of playbacks. "You can see for yourself."

"Your game persona certainly thought so," adds Stuart. "Said he'd had the Time of his life."

"That reviewer get here in time?" you ask.

"He did," says Stuart, handing over a printout. "As we predicted, he found the puzzles a bit thorny."

You're dying of curiosity about some of the game elements. "Did I figure out Year of the Tiger?"

"Nope, you didn't pick up on it even when watching the clip," Malcolm answers. "The Christopher character had to prod you."

"Maybe that one's got to go," you tell them. "So how about the *X-Files* theme? Was worried about that one—it's almost forty years old now."

"You actually got it," replies Malcolm. "We were quite impressed. The cast members present at the time had not actually seen life-sized Lord Hanover speaking before, so Farnsworth's, Van Scoy's, and Christopher's stunned reactions were all quite genuine."

You skim the review, wincing at the negative parts, then swivel around to face Stuart, saying, "The reviewer is complaining that the Godiva story 'contained no clues, never went anywhere, seemed to have no connection, was just filler.' How come?"

"Our blunder," says Stuart. "We placed the story in the wrong broadcast and neglected to link Lady Godiva's age clue to anything in the game."

"No big deal," you tell him. "We'll fix it, going forward. How was Serena? Shame we're losing her."

Stuart sighs. "She was spectacular. But, alas, they come, they go . . . Ah, but that reminds me. Before you returned, when we were debriefing, you brought up a fascinating possibility, one we'd never considered—namely, what if our player becomes romantically attracted to a villain?"

You nod, saying, "Hmm, we do need to mull that one over. Hard to picture anyone going for our off-putting and condescending concierge, though. Maybe the chef, if our protagonist is gay. Let me give it some more thought. But what about Farnsworth? *Les saboteurs*?" You've been worried about them ever since you remembered yourself.

"James was splendid in his role," Stuart replies. "Later, we learned he was up to no good behind the scenes. Tonight, the saboteurs were all making nuisances of themselves—as always."

You're concerned. "They do any real damage?"

Stuart grimaces, saying, "The other you claimed that James fired a pistol at him in the lobby a few hours ago, but we're not sure if that really happened."

You shrug. "Well, this me has no memory of anything like that. So what good does it do to worry about it now?" Stuart nods understandingly.

The gang takes turns filling you in on all the sabotage the bad guys tried and the shenanigans the team pulled in response. They tell you that you were here a short while ago and at times seemed to be enjoying watching the lunacy unfold, but at others, your attention was elsewhere. So they're not sure how much of it you absorbed.

"Okay, back to *Manor House*. I bust any moves?" you ask sheepishly.

Rae tries putting you on. "Kris, you were dandy but randy."

"No, no, you behaved," Malcolm assures.

"Really?" you exclaim. "Well, I may not have been able to resist a sensuous Cynthia Rollinsby. Cast anyone yet?"

"Nope. Still auditioning, for both Roland and Cynthia," says Stuart, who then good-naturedly needles the director. "Malcolm here has turned down several who act superbly. But no one's been built well enough, in his view."

Rae can't resist. "Go figure."

You give Rae a smirk and wag a chastising finger before asking, "So how was the rest of the cast?"

"Excellent overall," replies Stuart. "Oh, but your arrival got off to a bit of a botched start. I think they had a collective case of opening-night jitters. They kept running backstage, confused about where they should go and what they should say and do next. As a result, they left you in limbo at several junctures."

Next, you inquire about the special effects, hoping to hear that everything worked okay. "The big outdoors effects, holographic projections inside, both flawlessly," says Stuart. "Alice in Wonderland and the Nobel Ceremony, just fabulous. Only a few minor glitches. You and I made a detailed list earlier. We didn't attempt the armory teleportation trick—in fact, you never got into that room. Or the music room. So we didn't animate the statues either." Then, arching an eyebrow, he adds, "On you, that is."

"Yeah, that was great," you tell him. "But those scenes are definitely starting to fade from memory now." Malcolm smiles and says they got the impression you had several consciousness leaks because at times you exhibited bizarre behavior. "Could be," you tell him. "I do have a faint memory of constantly hearing voices and seeing apparitions in there. Heads floating above, conversing with me."

"Maybe those memory drugs turned you into some kind of bicameral dude," Rae speculates. "You told me about the voices after we visited your place. Said they're straight out of olden times."

"Rae," you respond, "you really should reread the Old Testament and ancient Greek and Roman myths through a different lens. They're like a prehistoric *Time* magazine. Much of it actually happened. Back then, God spoke. People listened."

“God spoke? Really?” Rae looks incredulous.

“Well,” you say. “I don’t know exactly who was commanding, but primitive man sure thought so—and obeyed.”

Rae looks stymied. “How come you could hear them, but we can’t? How can I get them yakking in my brain?”

“I don’t know, Rae, it’s almost impossible to explain in simple terms. From what I’ve read, they seem to pop in whenever they feel like it and say stuff like, do this or do that, say this or say that, go here or go there. Plus a lot of don’t dos, don’t says, and don’t goes.”

Rae has another question. “Kris, you once told us that early man, while unconscious, had it *all* going on mentally—and in stereo.”

“Right!” you exclaim. “Vocal commands from the right hemisphere, submissive replies from the left, plus telepathy, psychokinesis, clairvoyance, the bicameral works! No wonder those Greek and Roman gods were so awesome.”

Stuart, who you know doesn’t hear voices but has read Carl Jung and Julian Jaynes extensively, weighs in. “Rae, when you were a tyke, did you ever watch that American sitcom *The Big Bang Theory*?”

“No, not back then,” he replies. “But the reruns are still on the satellite channels. Cool show.”

“Do you recall their theme song lyrics?” Stuart asks. “Something about math and science and history all starting with a big bang?”

“Sure, lots of catchy lyrics in that tune,” says Rae. “Love the group’s name too—Barenaked Ladies.”

“Shut your mouth up, Rae!” yells Megumi.

“Uncle,” you venture, “I think I get where you’re going with this.”

Stuart quickly replies, “Weighty concepts, nephew. I’m trying to use pop culture to do the heavy lifting here.” He turns back to Rae. “Math, science, history, Rae, that’s precisely why you, and almost everybody else, don’t hear the voices any longer.”

Rae signals he still doesn’t get it, by singing the opening lines of an old song about not knowing much about history, biology, or any subjects he took in school. The girls know the tune, so they happily join in. You found out a long time ago that this quartet will seize on any opportunity to break into song and dance.

You're laughing as you say, "Rae, what Stuart means is that about three thousand years ago, across the globe, nearly simultaneously in every culture, there was another bang—this one we'll call a 'little big bang.'"

Rae pauses his jive-step to say, "Okay, tell me all about the little big bang."

Stuart is happy to explain. "The little bang largely shut off bicameralism in most humans. All of a sudden, everybody kind of woke up, started talking to one another, and became conscious. We then knew who we were as individuals apart from the collective. We realized all of the thoughts in our head were now our own. No longer were we bots walking about in a fog."

"Bye-bye, dictating voices," you chime in. "We no longer had to obey them. But, sadly, bye-bye, telepathy as well—we could no longer project our thoughts to others or receive theirs."

Malcolm sums it up. "Stuart, you conjecture that acquiring math, science, history, written and spoken language literally means that even if God or anyone in the collective is still speaking to us, we're no longer able to hear them? That 'little big bang' somehow deafened our inner ear."

"Right, Uncle—But hey, gang," you call out, "enough of this for now—let's save the rest for the pub. We need to get back on track here."

"Well," says Malcolm, "the whole thing worked fab. By the way, Kris, Rae says you turned elsewhere when the two of you went to your cottage earlier tonight."

"That can happen, especially when one is turned to begin with," you explain. "But the new regimen obviously worked. How long was I inside my scenario mindset?"

"Nearly a week," says Malcolm, "plus the three days it took to reprogram your memories and get you into character."

"Terrific," you reply. "I mean, to my mind, I just got off work here. Right now, I don't remember a thing about my game. But, man oh man, do I ever feel spaced out."

You notice Uncle Stuart and Rae are squirming.

"Nobody was supposed to give me anything psychoactive in there. Sure hope nobody did," you singsong.

Says Stuart, "Kris, it's time to tell you. Somebody did—in prodigious amounts, we're afraid."

"Who?" you blurt. "Surely not our chef."

"No, not Stefan. *Les saboteurs* were behind it, but they were never on the set that we know of."

You rub your chin while gazing up at the ceiling. "So that leaves . . . jeez, I still can't believe James would actually try to physically harm me. Sure, he wants my job, doesn't like these new scenarios. But this is too radical."

"On the way back from your cottage," Rae breaks in, "you told me you'd seen Farnsworth and his buds, but they didn't see you. Said you overheard them discussing mushrooms they'd secretly substituted in your meals, some weird mescaline tea they'd brewed, and how they'd laced gelatins and chocolates with acid."

"No way!" you exclaim. "That sure sounds sinister. Kind of like those old Agatha Christie scenarios we used to put on. Really? I told you all that?"

Rae nods. "You said they'd even outfitted James with a pistol and ammunition."

"Unbelievable!" you exclaim.

"I'm afraid we've found that, once again," Stuart deadpans, "the butler did it."

"Very funny, Uncle. But, damn, still can't internalize this."

Malcolm is smiling. "You know, Kris, we've been analyzing everything. As you'll soon see, you exhibited a lot of erratic behavior in there—your pub antics, for example. Several times the others asked me backstage what's going on with Kris making these long speeches, jumping atop benches, acting crazy, like you were possessed or something."

You deliberate for a few moments, finally saying, "Well, Malcolm, I don't remember now but I suppose if you mix psychedelics with all those memory drugs, you'd have stirred up quite an unpredictable cocktail, don't you think?"

"Indeed, you would," he replies.

"Like maybe I'm an accidental psychic pioneer here."

The team nods in agreement. Maybe you are.

Rae is glowing. "I loved it! Never witnessed a return. Not to mention being locked in mortal combat with the nefarious James Gang." He turns to his female colleagues, rapidly pumping a fist. "Killer job, ladies! Just killer!"

You think enough's been covered for one night. You tell the gang you're going to crash for a few hours. You honestly can't remember when you last slept.

"Let's all get some down time," suggests Rae. "We need to rest up for tonight."

"What's on for tonight?" you inquire.

"The cast party of course!" he replies. "Everyone's dying to see you—they just don't know which one of you is gonna show!"

CHAPTER FIFTY-THREE

Eventually, the entire cast drops by—including Timothy Lovett, who, you soon discover, looks and acts a whole lot different in real life than the endearing Christopher Robin persona you'd created for him. Dressed in high-top sneakers, a Runaway Dogs rugby shirt, backward ball cap, and baggy pants, the kid greets you with a cheery, "So, 'Mister Masa Ginza a.k.a. Gene Guy,' do you now remember your real name?"

"I most assuredly do, Master Christo—excuse me, Timothy—" You start to say more, but the teen has already darted away, having spied none other than Miss Alice in Wonderland herself at the pub entrance.

Reggie, Barry, and Mildred rush forward, all smiles and exuding great enthusiasm. "Lovely scenario, Kris. You're such a pleasure to work with—in either mindset," gushes Mildred, squeezing your hand.

"Aw, mate, me and Reg much prefer the you in there," says Barry, slapping your back. "All the drinking, dancing, and carrying on, why I reckon—"

Reggie interrupts, sweeping his hand before the crowd. "Kris, m'lord, any chance we could round up some of this bunch after a bit for a rousing game of Three Families? Most of 'em have never played, and me and Lord Bruce here are sure they would take great pleasure."

"I haven't had a chance to review that part of the video," you tell them, "but it sure sounds like you two would enjoy another round."

Mildred looks at her husband in mock disapproval. "Oh, they would, enormously, Kris, trust me," she says. "When you look at the replay, you'll soon see for yourself."

"But now that they know how the game works, that it's fixed from the get-go, wouldn't it spoil it for them?" you ask her.

Barry interjects, "No, mate, quite the contrary, it would only make it better." Reggie shakes his head in vigorous agreement.

Next up is Savannah, who offers a wide smile. "Oh, Kris, we really did it! This is going to be huge. I had an awesome time in there." She pauses, seeming to collect her thoughts. "There was one thing, though. Late in act three, when I supposedly got back from The Village. I saw you from the top of the rotunda stairs, but instead of talking, it felt like you and I were exchanging thoughts, like reading each other's minds. It was the strangest thing. I think you wanted me to dance for you. Something like that."

"I've no recollection," you tell her sheepishly. "Do I need to apologize for something the other me said or did? God, I hope not."

Savannah laughs. "Not at all. Actually, it was highly amusing."

Your tone becomes serious. "So tell me, Savannah, did you happen to drink any pinkish tea or eat any gelatin squares that night?"

"Why, yes, I did," she quickly replies. "I was waiting in the whisky bar to do my next scene and was famished. So I scarfed down a bunch of those squares. Washed them down with the tea. Why—is there a problem, some danger?"

"You okay now?"

"I feel fine."

"Don't worry, then," you tell her. "It's something we're looking into. I'll let you know."

Someone from across the pub calls out to her. As she turns to walk away, she gives you her patented wink.

Turning back around, you find you're face-to-face with the hardest-working anchors in television. "Michael! Meredith! I just saw some of your newscasts. They were hilarious! You both were great."

"Thanks, Kris. We really enjoyed cutting those spots, broadcasting round the clock." Michael beams.

You turn to his female counterpart. "Meredith, I've just got to ask, where did you come up with '*eau de bowwow*'? Nobody here wrote that."

"Oh, I don't know, Kris. Just popped in, seemed the right thing to say at the moment."

"Well, that line, plus holding your nose while reciting it was a huge LOL. The best bit in the whole Crunch saga, IMO."

Says Michael, "We heard the latter installments didn't make it into production."

"No, they didn't, Michael. But Malcolm said it was only because they were pressed for time. Don't worry—I just saw them. Definitely will be included in the production version. Everybody loves a happy ending."

Speaking of Crunch, you next spot James and Jamie at the bar, so you rush over to congratulate them. "Hey! I just saw the clips. You two were fabulous. James, you cracked me up. Jamie, you scared me to death!"

"Oh, thank you, Kris," James says. "Those scenes were a bit difficult since Sis and I are so close in real life."

"But you both enjoyed it, right?"

"Immensely," replies Jamie, beaming while clutching her brother's arm.

"Well," you tell them, "Stuart, Malcolm, and I have big plans for you two, which we'll reveal very soon."

"Can't wait," replies Jamie. She turns to her brother, bares her teeth, and hisses, "Until then, I'll see you in court." James and you crack up.

Ah, you now see Thomas and Penelope, the lovebirds, heading your way. "Good evening, Mr. Robinson," greets Thomas buoyantly. "We are immensely honored to have been chosen for this production. The past six days were thoroughly enjoyable."

Penelope is clutching Thomas's arm with both hands as she looks up at him adoringly. She turns and says, "Oh my yes, it was a dream come true."

"I'm really glad to hear this," you tell them. "I was away when Malcolm cast you both. So tell me, are Thomas and Penelope your real names?"

They both smile and shake their heads no. "I'm Alexis, not Penelope, and it's so very nice to meet you at long last, my lord," she says, extending her hand, which you take in yours.

You then turn the hands so yours is on top, then kiss it. "Nice to meet me!" Alexis nearly collapses in laughter. You turn to your headwaiter, smiling warmly. "And you, sir, are?"

"Kris, the pleasure is all mine. I'm Penley, a.k.a. Thomas, at your service." The two of you exchange a normal handshake.

"Tell me," you ask, "did you two know each other before joining our family?"

"We did not," Alexis replies, her eyes aglow. "When I first read my character sketch, I thought, 'Sure hope I like him.'" She leans up and kisses Penley on his cheek. "Oh goodness, did I ever."

"Same with me," Penley affirms. "I loved my role at first read and her at first sight."

"But Penley," you remind him, "the script required that you keep your attraction to her under wraps until the very end."

"Yes! That was indeed an acute challenge for me," says Penley.

Alexis is giggling. "My part was easy. I was supposed to adore him from the start, and adore him from the start I did!" She gives Penley's arm another squeeze.

"So, let me guess," you venture, "you two are now a couple in real life, obviously. And it was all because of *Manor House*?"

"We are! And it was! And we'd also like to tell you we're officially engaged!" Alexis can barely contain herself as she shows you her ring.

"Love comes quickly—particularly when you're caught in the magical spell of *Manor House*," observes Penley.

"Well, congratulations to you both. Just don't tell me you're leaving—like Serena."

Now Alexis lightly kisses your cheek. "We're staying as long as you'll have us."

"This manor . . . this fantasy is," Penley pronounces, "our new home, our new life, which we are most eager to continue living."

And they're off. "Thank you again!" they call out in unison.

Across the pub, you spot Malcolm being roundly congratulated by a small gathering. Since those offering felicitations are neither cast nor i21 members, you figure it's about something else, not your production.

"Hey, Malcolm, what's up?" you call, approaching him. "You look ecstatic. Did you give yourself a fat raise when I was not me in there?"

He laughs. "Kris, I've landed a part in the next *Hissatsu Shigotonin* yearly special." He points up to the television. "They've just announced the cast on TV Asahi." You look up—of course, now that the game's over, the manor TVs have switched back to regular Japanese channels.

"Wow, Malcolm—you got on *Murder's My Job*. That's awesome. Are you on the assassin's squad or one of the villains who gets done in exactly seven minutes before the end of the episode?"

"Not sure," Malcolm replies. "I'm a Portuguese trader whose ship sunk and has washed ashore. I haven't read enough of the script to know if I'm with the good or the bad crowd. But they wouldn't have named me if it were only a bit part. So I'm chuffed."

"Right. And well you should be," you tell him. "Well, kudos—this is a wonderful opportunity for you."

"Indeed. Cheers," Malcolm says as he continues to receive congrats from a crowd of well-wishers.

You make a point to find Serena to offer congratulations on her upcoming marriage and express how much everyone's going to miss her. "You'll be almost impossible to replace," you tell her with the greatest sincerity.

Serena becomes misty eyed and pulls you into her arms in a prolonged embrace. "Oh, Kris, I can never thank you enough for the roles I've had here. And I can tell you this—your *Manor House* is going to be a smash. I just know it. I so loved being in the test run."

"Well, Serena, we loved having you," you tell her before turning away. For some reason, her scent, the warmth of her breath causes you to recall a conversation you had with Uncle Stuart one pub evening several seasons ago—long before she'd met her intended and gotten engaged.

"I say, nephew, have you ever given Serena any thought as someone you might like to court?" he'd asked whimsically.

"Uncle," you'd confessed, "she's the total package all right—beauty, brains, charm, talent, and sophistication. But somehow—no way to explain it, really—just not my type in that regard. And then, of course, the age difference."

"Verily, love's either quickly there or 'tisn't," observed wise old Uncle Stu. Then, with a Lord Hanoverian twinkle in his eye, he gestured across the pub to where Savannah was standing and chattering with Barry and others. "I was just speculating on whether gentlemen do in fact prefer blondes."

Nodding in Savannah's direction, you shrugged and told him, "No, not her either. I'm old enough to be her granddad."

In response, as Shakespeare, he sighed, "Ah yes, to woo or not to woo a workmate, that is the proposition. Better to not, methinks."

Yes, Uncle's always watching over, dispensing wise counsel, and usually in a witty entertaining fashion. You've come to realize that, in addition to being the uncle you never knew you had, and in addition to all the other roles Stuart plays in your life, he's also become, over time, your best friend. Indeed, you consider yourself the lucky one on whom true fortune has brightly shone.

Speaking of best friends, Uncle's lifelong close pal from England strides up smiling and offering profuse congratulations. His real name is Stephen Mark, and he moved to Japan to join your enterprise a few years after Uncle arrived. You think Stephen's a terrific fellow, and terrific in his multiple roles as Mark Stephen, your driver, a news correspondent, and Lord Dennis Rollinsby, the mad scientist who brought teleportation to the world! "Well, Lord Kris, did you enjoy our jiffy jaunt to Stockholm?" he asks, as Rollinsby, in greeting.

"Stephen! So glad you could make it. I saw the recording. The Nobel attraction really worked! For the first few moments, it looked like we'd actually been transported to the ceremony. But even knowing it was all CGI and holograms, it didn't matter—the scene in my movie was so spellbinding!"

Stephen smiles, adopting his chauffeur's Cockney accent and persona. "Well, m'lord, if you require further assistance to any destination, perhaps you should enlist the services of Sir Dennis Rollinsby, who I'm certain would be up to the task."

The gathering continues to swell, the celebratory hubbub to rise. Megumi rushes up with a small box. She's dying for you and her colleagues to meet her new pet.

She opens the box. "*Mina-san*, looky! Looky! It's my new pet parakeet, TooWimuBooLee-san!"

"Kawaii!" the girls squeal endlessly, crowding around her.

You bow formally to the bird. "*Hajimemashite* Twimbley-san, nice to meet you."

"What are you going to teach it to say?" you ask Megumi.

Namiko has a suggestion. "How about, 'Wow! Unbelievable! They've even got sushi bars in Japan.'"

Next comes Rae, just back from the local animal shelter, where he's adopted a young rottie mix.

"Kris, I'm sure you can already guess what I've named him," he says, as the puppy licks faces all around amid more shrieks of *kawaii* pouring forth from every direction.

It's an easy guess. "Can't wait to introduce Crunch II to Monty. By the way, Rae, did you remember to feed my pooch?"

Rae laughs. "Yes, I remembered. But your doggo didn't seem to miss you one single bit. I think he'd prefer to remain with Crunch and me."

"Ha!" you exclaim. "When I show up to take him home, we'll see where his true affections lie."

The incomparable Stefan a.k.a. Chef Noël Elle Léon appears, accompanied by waitstaff bearing platters of Japanese delicacies. You sample one and try to guess, "Wonton?"

The chef, still in character, doesn't miss a beat. "Not now," he replies with his usual dazzling smile.

You try a new wrinkle. "Noël Elle Léon, who's never odd—"

"Or even!" he calls triumphantly. "Kris Robinson, a nut—"

"For a jar of tuna!" you quickly respond.

You watch Megumi, with her parakeet now perched on her shoulder, move over to the hors d'oeuvres, obviously hoping her bird can find something tasty to peck. She holds her hands in prayer position, bows her head, and says to Stefan, "Mercy buckets garken. *Butadakimasu*!"

Stefan's expression turns to confusion. "'Mercy buckets'? Mademoiselle, it's *merci beaucoup, garçon*, I'll have you know. Besides, I thought Japanese always say *'Itadakimasu!'* for 'Let's eat!' That's all I ever hear down in Ni-Chome."

"They do," Rae informs him, "but Megu-chan here likes to fracture old expressions. Or invent new ones that translate in a cute, quirky way. Go ahead, Megumi-san—please enlighten our dear cast member."

Delighted to be summoned to center stage once again, Megumi steps forward and bellows so the entire room can hear: "*Butadakimasu mina-san!* Let's pig out, everyone!"

There's laughter from all corners, even a smattering of applause. Megumi takes a bow. It's hard to see, you muse, how this gathering could get any more *kawaii*. Somebody may have to call in the cute police to stem the outbreak. But what a lovely trio, you think. So lucky to have them—and your great cast and work colleagues. So lucky to have them all.

Conspicuous in his absence, though, is Farnsworth, of course. No way he'd show his face in here tonight, you're certain. He's probably back in his room fuming over having the wool completely pulled over and seeing all his dreams, schemes, and machinations blown to smithereens.

You continue to yak and *kampai* endlessly about the rousing success of the trial until, as usual, you're the last one standing.

CHAPTER FIFTY-FOUR

You're in high, high spirits over how well the game went and how enthusiastic the cast seems. Making your way home through the labyrinthian underground passages you know so well, you can hardly keep your eyes open—revelry, alcohol, lack of sleep.

You hear happy adolescent voices and turn in their direction. "Kris! Glad we found you," young Timothy hails. "We've heard all about your trippy apartment and hoped we could stop by and take a quick peek since we have to return to Tokyo early tomorrow."

"We shan't stay long, we promise," says Alicia. With a charming smile no one could resist, she adds, "Sorry to be a nuisance."

"Sure," you tell them. "But it'll take me several minutes to fire everything up so that you can get the full effect when you walk in."

"Sounds great," says Timothy. "Do you mind texting when you're ready for us?"

"Will do."

The two of you quickly pair phones. Watching them walk away hand in hand, you think what a cute teenage couple they make. You continue on into the large roundabout from which several passageways spike out. Yours is at two o'clock.

Then without warning: "I *knew* I'd find you here! *Do not* try to escape. You *will not*. You *cannot* this time!" Good God, it's Farnsworth, bellowing, and rushing toward you from a distant passageway. He draws closer, brandishing a very large revolver, his face contorted in a maniacal rage.

You raise both hands, imploring, "James, for God's sake, don't shoot me! Tell me what's happened."

"The president has just notified me that I'm to be di-di-discharged," he stammers. "*You did this*! Stop pretending otherwise." His eyes burn with fury.

"James, calm down, please, I beg of you." You try being disingenuous. "I've no idea what you're talking about. I haven't seen the president."

"*Stop lying*," he roars. "I was tricked into writing him a memo, and now I'm finished here. I *know* you were behind it! And now *you shall pay*!"

Trying with both hands to hold his weapon steady, Farnsworth starts shaking uncontrollably. He drops the pistol, which spins upon hitting the ground and discharges rapidly in all directions.

You make a mad dash through the roundabout toward the two o'clock passageway, lurching into it while dreading the gunfire that could resume at any second. Sprinting toward your door about fifty meters away, you hear more angry shouts. More gunshots. More putrid smoke. Zigging and zagging, heaving and shaking, you stagger up to your entrance and prop yourself against the door, somehow managing to press your index finger against the recognition pad.

The door unlocks, opens. You duck inside and fall to your knees, gasping for air, sweating profusely, eyes stinging. "Hey, door," you yell, "close!" It does. "Hey, door, lock!" It does.

You fall flat to the floor, panting and trembling violently. Your cell chimes—it's Stuart on video call. "Dear God, nephew, are you okay?" he cries out, his face registering great relief at seeing yours. "We heard the gunshots," he says. "The security cameras picked up some of it. Were you hit?"

It's hard to speak, but you lean forward, muttering, "Not hit. Where . . . is . . . James?"

"Gone," Stuart quickly replies. "Some people took him away."

"Police?"

"Didn't appear as such. No uniforms. All dressed in black. Namiko said they were the chairman's 'secret people.' But I've no idea what she meant."

"She say where they were taking him?"

"All she said was that she's sure we'll never see him again."

Your breathing has returned to near normal, so you can more readily speak. "So what about Kobayashi and Watanabe? Rae said the other me told him *les saboteurs* received guns from the yakuza and gave them to James. Are they still out there?"

Stuart answers in hushed tones, “Namiko said we’ll never see those two again either.” He pauses, then observes, “Nephew, you’ve had quite a time.”

“Indeed, dear Uncle, the Time of my life.”

Above, several Storytellers appear. One of them calls out, ***And that’s your story. We’ll be going now. Do enjoy your past, present, and future Times!***

EPILOGUE

Well, dear reader, you may be wondering about those Storytellers—now that I've completely returned to my authentic mindset. Regrettably, our connection broke entirely. Actually, I never knew anything about them firsthand until Rae disclosed how the other me had described them in detail. They sure sound like an ideal group to commiserate with.

I would have liked to talk over their role in my game—what was real, what wasn't. I would imagine that this would be hard to sort out because of all the variables at play—drugs I intended to take, drugs I never intended to take, the surrealistic milieu of the Manor House and the scenario itself. I love watching my movie, which the team has edited down to feature-length of just under two hours. I can see that if we work out the kinks and make the psychic journey safe, these extended scenarios could become breakthrough entertainment—especially when we get celebrities to play.

Oh, and yes, *Manor House* did get final approval. Sailed right through the i21 board meeting, thanks mainly to Rae's recording deal. In the meeting, the chairman grimly announced that Kobayashi-san and Watanabe-san had recently suffered nervous breakdowns, and thus, regrettably, he'd been forced to transfer them to another of his companies—some nondescript factory down in Kawasaki that he hopes will be less stressful on them. Then—big surprise!—*Kaicho* asked *me* to start looking around for their replacements! This means that, at long last, I can build my own marketing team. I'll tap Namiko to run it. She's ready.

But, if that weren't shocking enough, the president announced he'd fired James Farnsworth the day the test run concluded. Even called immigration and had his visa revoked. At *Shacho*'s request, the Japanese secret police whisked him off to Narita; our "butler" has already been deported. It will be tough, however, to find a replacement who can command the role as well as he did. That's now Malcolm's top priority.

Farnsworth, our president disclosed, had barged into his office earlier that day claiming that Stuart, Malcolm, and I had *all* gone mad, as evidenced by our turning the manor into a venue resembling an insane asylum. Farnsworth also had the audacity to hand over a lengthy memo detailing why he should be placed in charge.

Recounting this, *Shacho* shook his head and said that Farnsworth himself was so far gone he'd even claimed *Shacho* himself had left a voicemail ordering him to prepare this outrageous missive. "Imagine me," he said indignantly, "instructing someone not to go through proper channels."

The chairman grunted his strong disapproval of our ex-butler's ultimate corporate transgression. No mention was made of Farnsworth's meltdown and shooting spree. But knowing the chairman's total aversion to even a hint of scandal, I didn't have to ask about criminal charges. "Attempted Murder at Camelot!" would be the last headline *Kaicho* would ever want to see.

In response to all their disclosures, I told *Shacho* and *Kaicho* that I must issue a heartfelt apology for not being able to reconcile the warring factions in the company—I didn't achieve *wa* like I had in the game. They nodded slowly and silently, indicating that I should learn from this and strive to do better next time. I nodded solemnly in reply, indicating that I most assuredly would.

Once again, I was reminded that those two have but a passing fancy in anything we are actually producing at Camelot. Their abiding interest is in the scenarios we are living here, in our so-called real lives. We're all convinced they have some secret way of knowing, of actually *watching* everything behind the scenes—from further behind them. I state this based on what Reiko has recently reported to the team in strictest confidence.

The other night, she and Namiko drove the chairman's personal secretary and principal confidant down to one of those swanky dining clubs in Shirakawa. After plying her with drinks, Akiko-san became "very forthcoming." Among the beans she spilled was the revelation that *Kaicho* and *Shacho* had actually watched recordings of Farnsworth and the two sales-marketing guys plotting in the passageways on earlier occasions and decided things had gone too far. That was the real reason, Akiko-san told them, that Farnsworth got the ax. Not going through channels, while grievous, was just their ostensible reason. Then came an even bigger shock. Akiko-san revealed that *Kaicho* and *Shacho* have some "secret ninjas" they call upon for "special jobs" from time to time. In this instance, they had them slip into Farnsworth's quarters on several occasions and substitute blanks for the live ammunition, which means nobody around that night was ever in any mortal danger! The secretary said *Shacho* and *Kaicho* just wanted to see how far the butler and his cronies would go.

Oh, those two! We can never figure them out. Never know what they're really up to, why they nurture incessant palace intrigue and then step in only when matters truly get out of hand. But I think I already know. You see, as Megumi chanted, we're their spooky *Kabuki-za* cast, tragicomic characters they just love to watch. For any *henna gaikokujin* (strange alien) working for direct descendants of medieval shoguns, it goes with the terrain. In fact, that was the very first thing I told Uncle Stuart he'd have to get used to when he moved over here to start a new life.

End

ACKNOWLEDGMENTS

I must first and foremost credit my beloved wife of over three decades, Megumi, whose contribution to this endeavor could not possibly have been more significant: the story was originally her idea. One day, many years ago, she said to me, "You should write a manor mystery about an uncle you never knew existed who dies and leaves you a fortune." And thus, the central premise of this novel was spawned. Obviously, the book must be dedicated to her as well.

Before this work became a novel, it was a DVD adventure game I created in the late '90s. I credit Doug Jackson's compelling early drafts of Lord Hanover's correspondence and humorous news articles for the game, several of which were adapted for the novel.

While developing a screenplay adaptation, Kristin Johnson contributed several new scenes and character dialogue that were brought back into the novel. She was assisted by her intern Lauralee Leonhardt, who contributed scene ideas, along with recommendations for the neo-psych/alt-pop music cited in the story.

In between the time I started working on this story and now, I took twenty years off to help raise our daughter by parenting and working as a software developer. I'm deeply grateful to my then CEO, Cheryl Wachtel of Designing Success, Inc., who remains a dear friend and the best boss one could ever hope for.

I'm also grateful to my mentor in Japan, the late Anton Goodings, who as a board member of the Sano Educational Foundation provided support and encouragement for my team's efforts to develop the immersive game version, from which this novel was derived.

The story contains several excerpts from humorous news articles I wrote for *The Japan Times* and other publications in the 1980s. I remain indebted to the then managing editor, the late Gyo Hani, for his support of my quirky journalism under various aliases.

The Three Families game account in the novel was inspired by StarPower, a role-playing game I used to stage at California colleges and social agencies back in the 1970s.

I owe a debt of gratitude to Kelly Roberts and his i21 team, who created stunning graphics and videos for the game. And to Raymond Starr, who created an original score for the production. The scenes and music described in the novel were inspired by these works.

I want to also thank numerous individuals who critiqued this story and provided valuable feedback. They are: T. B. Murphy, Karen Harwood, Melanie Young, Gloria Schneller Vicks, Kate Donovan, Richard Arcus, and Harri Drake.

Finally, I'm most grateful for all the lucky stars I've long traveled under.

ABOUT THE AUTHOR

CHRIS MATHISON resided, relaxed, or did business in over forty countries during early adulthood. As such, he missed most of the '70s and all of the '80s and '90s in America.

Along with changing locales, Chris frequently changed careers. He worked as a college instructor, concert producer, discotheque designer, circus advance man, freelance journalist, real estate developer, computer programmer, and a few other odd jobs he says he can no longer recall. One highly memorable gig, however, was a brief stint as a feature writer for *Blue Swan* (the in-flight magazine of Aeroflot Soviet Airlines) at the height of the Cold War.

Looking back at those decades abroad, Chris so appreciated being profiled by Kosaku Shirota in Japan's leading newspaper, *Asahi Shimbun* (November 1987), as one of three foreigners who had made significant technical contributions to Japanese society.

He also recalls with great fondness his appearance as an invited speaker representing Apple's nascent voice-recognition technology at New Zealand's inaugural multimedia conference in 1994. Following Microsoft's Bill Gates's address, Chris greeted the audience with, "Hey, everybody here knows my predecessor. But nobody knows me. Yet our stories are really the same. Just delete six zeros."

Since returning to the States, Chris has authored database-intensive web applications, edited his wife's scientific papers, curated his late father's art, and coached his daughter's soccer teams. His prized possession is a trophy he received upon his retirement from coaching inscribed with WORLD'S OLDEST SOCCER COACH.